A PLUME BOOK

PASTORS' WIVES

MATT DINE

LISA TAKEUCHI CULLEN was a foreign correspondent and staff writer for *Time* magazine. CBS is currently shooting her drama pilot, *The Ordained*. Cullen grew up in Kobe, Japan, and lives in New Jersey with her husband and two daughters. Her first book, *Remember Me: A Lively Tour of the New American Way of Death*, was a Barnes & Noble Discover Great New Writers pick. *Pastors' Wives* is her first novel.

Praise for *Pastors' Wives*

"With a reporter's eye for detail and a writer's heart for the everyday truths we all face . . . a terrific first novel, fast-paced and fresh."
—Laura Zigman, author of *Animal Husbandry* and *Piece of Work*

"Lisa Takeuchi Cullen is such a beautiful writer that she somehow tricked me into reading a book about romance and religion."
—Joel Stein, *Time* magazine columnist and author of
Man Made: A Stupid Quest for Masculinity

Pastors' Wives

Lisa Takeuchi Cullen

A PLUME BOOK

PLUME

Published by the Penguin Group
Penguin Group (USA) Inc., 375 Hudson Street,
New York, New York 10014, USA

USA I Canada I UK I Ireland I Australia I New Zealand I India I South Africa I China
Penguin Books Ltd, Registered Offices: 80 Strand, London WC2R 0RL, England
For more information about the Penguin Group visit penguin.com

First published by Plume, a member of Penguin Group (USA) Inc., 2013

P REGISTERED TRADEMARK—MARCA REGISTRADA

LIBRARY OF CONGRESS CATALOGING-IN-PUBLICATION DATA

Cullen, Lisa Takeuchi.
  Pastors' Wives / Lisa Takeuchi Cullen.
    p. cm.
  ISBN 978-0-452-29882-8
1. Spouses of clergy—Fiction.   2. Career changes—Fiction.   3. Life change
events—Fiction.   4. Big churches—Fiction.   5. Georgia—Fiction.   6. Domestic fiction.
7. Pastoral fiction, American.   I. Title.
  PS3603.U5835P37   2013
  813'.6—dc23

                                2012037108

Printed in the United States of America
10   9   8   7   6   5   4   3   2   1

Set in Granjon
Designed by Eve L. Kirch

PUBLISHER'S NOTE

For my mother, Hiroe Takeuchi Reilly
(1943–2008)

and my father, Thomas Joseph Reilly
(1933–2009)

Chapter One

Ruthie

On the first day of my life as a pastor's wife, I decided to buy a *Star* magazine.

Not *People*. Not even *Us*. No: *Star*, trashy *Star*, with its cover promises of fabulous people in unfabulous situations, page after page of full-color schadenfreude. You know. Porn for housewives. If I gave it any weight at all, which certainly I did not at the time, I would have to call it a $3.99 act of defiance. A purchase to attest things had not changed, *I* had not changed. That Ruthie Matters still belonged to a population that consumed celebrity gossip without guilt or thoughts of spiritual consequence.

Still, I hesitated. I stood there in the airport newsstand, my hand hovering over Jennifer Aniston's chin. Funny thing about becoming a pastor's wife: You felt watched. Not by God, exactly. Just . . . watched.

With a start I realized I *was* being watched, by the cashier, an Indian woman with chipmunk cheeks packed tight with chewing gum, black eyes steady and suspicious. It took a moment to comprehend why. I almost laughed. So much for my new status as a moral pillar of society. If a shopkeeper could suspect me of filching a supermarket tabloid, then clearly I did not yet reek of saint-type values.

I withdrew my hand, and the cashier turned back to help the next customer.

Hands in my pockets, I wandered toward the back of the store, past the blister packs of Dramamine and leopard-print neck pillows and twelve varieties of trail mix. Finally I reached the books. Books sold in airports fascinate me for their schizophrenic jumble. Jackie Collins next to Malcolm Gladwell smooshed right up against Jane Austen. Anyplace else, the reading public could expect some distance between pie recipes and the vampire apocalypse.

And here, in a stand-alone display labeled INSPIRATIONAL, were the Greens.

The Greens. Aaron and Candace Green, of Greenleaf Church, coauthors of *Serve Your Marriage*. It was the latest in a blockbuster series by Pastor Aaron Green, its premise the application of Bible scripture to serving your country, your worship, yourself. Unless you're in the market, you probably don't pay attention to books like these. I never did, either. Once you do, though, you realize they're huge. Just last week I opened up the Sunday *New York Times* and saw that the book was number one in the self-help category.

Even among the other glossy titles by spiritual sorts, it seemed to me the cover of the Greens' book popped. Against a white background, Aaron stood behind Candace with his hands on her shoulders, a full head taller than his wife. He looked as silvery and dashing as ever, but then anyone with a TV set knew what he looked like. The George Clooney of the pulpit, they called him.

The surprise was Candace. I forgot my resolve not to touch

anything in the store and picked the book up for a closer look. Candace's face looked etched, her features exact, as if their creator had deliberated over every detail. Her hair was curled high and away from her face, tendrils spun like blue-black cotton candy, defiant of any notion of gravity. Her nose had one of those tiny squares at the tip, like its sculptor had completed it with a push. The inky plume of her lashes fanned out from around her beetle-green eyes. Her lips hinted, just hinted, at a smile. She wore a fitted black suit with a leaf-shaped emerald pin in the lapel. In bearing she resembled Jacqueline Onassis, as played by a thin Elizabeth Taylor.

The surprise was not her beauty, exactly. After all, I'd seen her once or twice, when the camera panned to a close-up during her husband's telecasts. The surprise was that the woman transcended a two-dimensional surface. That scant smile was like a sorcerer's wand: One flash and you performed as bidden. It scared me just a little.

"Think that could be us someday?"

Jerry had snuck up behind me. I saw that he'd already inhaled half his bag of peanut M&M's, his in-flight comfort food. I glanced over my shoulder at the shopkeeper. But Jerry projected goodness, just radiated it. I was pretty sure no one had ever suspected my husband of shoplifting so much as a loose gumball. Sure enough, all I saw of the shopkeeper was the long braid trailing like an oil slick down her back.

Jerry took the Greens' book from my hands and peered intently at the jacket.

I snorted. He glanced up. "What?"

"The thing about us," I said. "Becoming them."

We looked at the book cover together. "Yeah," he said finally. "You're probably more of a Tammy Faye."

I took the book back and whacked him with it.

"Hey!" he said. "It says *Serve Your Marriage*, not *Beat Your Husband*."

As he took my hand and led me out of the store, I found myself repeating this exchange in my head, sifting it for underlying intent. Was he joking? It sounds crazy, but I wasn't entirely sure. In our recent life together, I'd lost my grasp of his meaning, my ability to read between his lines. It's like when you're channel surfing and you stumble upon a Sandra Bullock movie and you're happily settling in only to realize it's dubbed in Spanish. On the surface, all was familiar. But at times like this I became aware I no longer felt fluent in our language.

As we lined up to board, I inspected Jerry from behind. He was even taller than I was, a discovery that had relieved more than attracted me when we first met. It's not that I minded shorter guys; it's that they minded me. He still let his wavy dark hair grow over his collar, a style he'd never bothered to change even when he worked on Wall Street. His cheeks were leaner, his jaw more often set. His eyes had taken on the cast of a hotel pool before a summer storm. But otherwise he looked like the Jerry I'd met years ago outside Professor Baker's office.

Except he wasn't. He had ceased to be the Jerry I knew that morning in April when we woke to the rain machine-gunning the windowpane and he turned his face to me and said, "I had the most incredible dream."

The dream. Some might say *that* was the day I first became a pastor's wife. When does a man become a man of God? Is it the day he joins a ministry, or the day he's called?

The word *incredible* caught me—Jerry wasn't given to hyperbole—but I grunted a sleepy "huh" and pursued it no more as I padded out to start the coffee. He didn't mention it again until later that evening, when he returned from work with Thai takeout.

A new place called Basil had just opened down the block in a store-front notorious for the brief life span of its inhabitants. We called it the Cursed Corner. I took a mouthful of shrimp pad Thai and promptly spat it out.

Jerry frowned, upset. "I said no cilantro. I *said*."

"Gah," I said, flailing for water. Cilantro tastes like stinkbugs smell. No need to argue; it's a fact. "Curse the Cursed Corner!"

Once he refilled my glass and sat down, he clicked off the TV and turned to me. "So about that dream I had," he said.

I put down the beef satay (more or less a Slim Jim dipped in peanut butter), tucked one leg under the other, and smiled at my sweetheart. His dream. What dream?

He hadn't even asked me about my day yet, and that was unlike him. Not that I had much to report. I was between jobs, which is to say I was between careers, which is to say I had no clue what to do with my life. Ever since I'd left my job as an assistant publicist at a book-publishing company, I'd spent the days online, reading up on graduate schools. Journalism at CUNY. Film at NYU. Creative writing at the New School. No sooner would I work up the enthusiasm to download an application than I would alight on another, sparklier option. It's so hard to choose a future.

Still, he always asked, and he always listened. And Jerry was exceptionally good at listening. He'd put down the prospectus in his hand and look in my eyes. He laughed in the right spots. He asked pertinent questions. If I grew vexed, as I admit I often did, Jerry stroked my forearm with his thumb, a sensation I liken to what a cat must feel when it's rubbed under its chin. It occurred to me only recently that as the middle child of five, I was wholly unaccustomed to anything resembling undivided attention. I never even knew until I met him that I had craved it all my life.

So I faced my husband that night to hear about this dream of his. For despite the casual wording, something in his tone indicated it mattered.

I had no idea how much.

Jerry took a deep breath. "It's not that I remember the dream so much," he said. "There was a kind of lightness. Like warm light. Like someone was hugging me."

I raised my hand. "That would be me. Your wife. I was cold."

He smiled. "It was . . . I don't know," he said. "This feeling of coming home." He was quiet for a moment, his eyes scanning my face like it held some sort of answer. "I think I was called."

"By who?" I asked, reaching for a rice chip.

Jerry blinked at me.

"*Whom*," I said through a mouthful of chip. "By *whom*."

The silence stretched.

"You know," he said. "By God."

If my marriage were a timeline—the kind they run in newspapers to mark the meaningful moments in a course of events—this conversation would get a boldfaced mention. Everything up till then was B.C., Before the Call. You might wonder at how dense I was. How I'd utterly failed to understand. But in my defense, B.C., this was not our language. Despite or maybe because of my Catholic upbringing, despite or maybe because of Jerry's theology degree and his ongoing exploration of faith, religion had heretofore existed in our marriage as an abstract. A topic of intellectual discussion. Words I would soon hear proclaimed at every turn—"I was called," "I was saved," "I accepted Jesus"—back then, B.C., this kind of talk was nothing short of alien.

Later I would think of the Tower of Babel. You know the story. These people gather from all over the world and decide to build a structure that will challenge God's glory. Of course, God doesn't like to be fronted like that, and in his fury he not only blows the tower to smithereens but smites the people with disparate tongues so they can no longer communicate. That was kind of what it was like for us. Like the marriage we'd built was a tower God recognized as temporal. In the moment, I did not see. Facing my husband on the couch, bad Thai food congealing on the coffee table, I did not see the pillars and stanchions crashing down around us, the ruins that promised to swallow our marriage whole if we did not find each other soon and hold fast.

Meantime, I had questions. No sooner did I spit one out than another crowded up. "What does that mean?" I spluttered. "How do you know? What did God say? Are you feeling warm? Could it be stress? Or that homeopathic crap you've been taking for your sinuses, that weed of Saint What's-his-face—"

Jerry took my face in both his hands. I loved those hands; I trusted those hands. Instinctively I nestled my cheek against his palm.

"I don't know what it means," he said. "I don't know how I know it was God—I just do. He didn't say anything. It was more of a feeling. And I'm not sick. I'm not hallucinating. I've never felt better in my life. In any case, I'm not doing anything about it yet. I just wanted you to know." And then he leaned forward and kissed me.

He just wanted me to know. It was one thing to know and another to understand. I pulled back to stare at my husband. And for the first time I wondered: Who *are* you?

* * *

It all happened so quickly. Months after Jerry's dream, on a Saturday morning in July, he called me over to his laptop.

"Hold up," I said, looking over his shoulder as I extracted the bagel clamped between my teeth. "They advertise church jobs *online*?"

Jerry laughed. "How else?"

"I don't know. Maybe a holy grapevine. A want ad from above." At least that's how it seemed to work in the Catholic church.

We looked at the listing together. It read:

SEEKING: Associate Pastor

Evangelical church (20,000 members and growing) in suburban Atlanta seeks gifted, motivated young pastor with finance and/ or business experience to assist in management of sizable endowment. Academic degree in theology accepted in lieu of pastoral experience. Pay commensurate . . .

In the weeks and months following Jerry's calling—though it still felt weird to call it that, and I avoided the word—we had discussed the implications. That maybe he would leave Wall Street. He had always said he would, sooner rather than later, and now he had somewhere to go. He had been called to serve. A church job made sense, as a start.

"The question is where," said Jerry. And I understood he wasn't referring to geographical location.

A Catholic is a Catholic is a Catholic. So I marveled at the way Protestants could flit from one denomination to another. Jerry had attended Presbyterian services growing up in a wealthy suburb of New York City, and over the years had sampled from a pupu platter of Protestantism: Episcopalian (too Catholic), Baptist (too emphatic), Charismatic (flat-out insane). He liked the inclusivity of the Unitarians, but not their loosey-goosey services; the work ethic of the

Lutherans, but not the pole up their backsides; the politics of the Methodists, but not their lousy worship music.

"You should start your own church," I joked, then immediately realized this had already occurred to Jerry.

"I need to learn the ropes first," he said.

What kind of man contemplates starting his own church? Who *are* you?

"Greenleaf Church, it's called," Jerry was saying, tapping the computer screen. "In a place called Magnolia, outside Atlanta. What do you think?"

What did I *think*? My *Wall Street Journal*–reading, NPR-listening, Yankees-loving husband was looking at a job opening at a Southern evangelical megachurch, and he wanted to know what I *thought*?

I said the only thing I could say with honesty. "I think they'll love you."

* * *

"Flight 4502 to Atlanta," called the gate agent.

Passengers surged forward. The family of four ahead of us was dressed in shorts and flip-flops, which I thought premature; ten-to-one the little girl in the sleeveless shift would throw a fit when the flight got chilly. The snowbirds to my right showed off the kind of bone-deep perma-tan that's a formal invitation for melanoma.

I caught myself. Judgy. That's what Candace Green would think I was: uncharitable and judgy. Just what she'd expect of a Northeastern liberal, not to mention a papist. No one needed to tell me that for a pastor's wife, there were certain behaviors that simply would not fly. But someone *did* need to tell me which. Was there a handbook? Some sort of guide?

We settled in our seats, a window and an aisle. The middle seat remained open, just as the nice ticket lady had promised. People did things like that for Jerry. He smiled and the world turned to goo. Jerry took the aisle seat to stretch out his long legs, and before takeoff he'd fallen asleep. This, too, was a gift, one I envied at least as much as his talent for public speaking and facility with names.

It was then I remembered, with disproportionate regret, that I had failed to purchase my *Star* magazine. I wanted to cry.

I looked out the window. There below was the New Jersey Turnpike, stretching like a concrete scar across the belly of my home state. As I always do during the ascent, I craned my neck to see if I could spot my hometown. It isn't far from the airport, but we were pulling south, not north, and in any case no landmark distinguished Hoogaboom from the air. Growing up, the compass I'd used to orient myself was the Manhattan skyline to the east, in particular the World Trade Center. So direct and unobstructed was our line of vision that my father saw the first of the twin towers struck while walking home from Mel's Bakery with a bag of doughnuts.

The horizon wasn't all that had changed in Hoogaboom, named in 1772 for a Dutch settler who could not have foreseen that his family name would one day be mocked by a late-night TV comedian as the dorkiest place name in America (over Hackensack and Ho-Ho-Kus—both, naturally, also in New Jersey). Two Catholic churches bookend Main Street still: Saint Ann's for the Irish, and Saint Adalbert's for the Polish. Our clapboard split-level home just off the main drag also housed the law office of my father, Frank Connelly. That central location and his social ubiquity meant he served many residents at one point or another, drawing up their wills or transferring their deeds. Old-timers called him Mayor, even though he'd handed off that thankless post years ago to Stew Ko-zlowski of Kozlowski Funeral Home.

When the Koreans began to arrive in the 1990s, the town trans-formed seemingly overnight, Caffrey's Drugs replaced by a bulgogi barbecue, Anka's Pickles now a Hello Kitty boutique. When long-time residents groused, my father played peacemaker. It was Dad who persuaded one of the first arrivals, Soong-sa Kim, to start the Korean Merchants' Association. I remember Mr. Kim and other men knocking on Dad's office door with Chivas and cigars to look at blueprints and discuss ordinances. Many of them retained him for counsel until one of their own opened up shop.

The signage issue crept up. Up through the late 1990s, the mer-chants advertised their wares in proud if sometimes odd English (KOREAN BURNED COW, read a sign in the window of a barbecue joint). But some newcomers argued against having to explain their services in English, as they expected to cater primarily to their countrymen. The new lawyer in town, Stanford Lee, got all hepped up over their First Amendment rights. Dad talked him down. He liked to tell his children that had he not gotten Lee to settle, this case had Supreme Court written all over it. It could have been the case of his career, he said. But that wasn't Frank Connelly's style.

"Never let your ego decide what's right," he told me.

That was unlikely. My ego had a hard time just showing up. As a child I distinguished myself in little, accomplished not much, and stood for nothing at all. I proved difficult to label, unlike my sib-lings. Tom, the oldest, was the smart one. Vivian, the second, was the beauty. After me came the twins, Paul, the comedian, and Mi-chael, the athlete. But me—I was just Ruthie. Toothy Ruthie when I grinned, and then Juithy Ruthie during my abominable orth-odontia years, when I both sprayed and lisped.

In college, I took the concept of liberal arts literally, giddily loading up on one bullshit course after another. Appalachian Anthropology. Symbolic Imagery in Animé. History of Hip-hop in the Harlem Renaissance. For one semester I rode the intercampus bus twice a week to the arts school to take classes in Tamenaibuga, an African friendship dance. I know.

Despite my lack of direction—or maybe because I could indulge it—I loved college. I felt for the first time independent and free and unique from my siblings. Even though all of us attended the same school, its teeming student body and scattered campuses meant I rarely ran into them. By the time I matriculated, Tom was in law school on a campus in a different city. Paul and Michael disappeared promptly into a fraternity and became known as "the Tau Sig twins."

In college the snippy rivalry that had characterized my first eighteen years with my sister mellowed into something resembling friendship. Vivian is eleven months older than I am, and we grew up squabbling over everything. Our shared bedroom, our shared Guess jeans, our one yellow Sony Discman. We looked somewhat alike and on occasion were mistaken for each other, an occasion that pleased only me. Vivian was beautiful. She had perfectly symmetrical features: a straight nose, puffy lips, and wide, lashy eyes. You could stare at a face like that and marvel at God's work. People did.

If you drew a charcoal sketch of Vivian's face and smudged it, you got me. As a teen, I spent many, many hours at my mother's vanity wondering how such tiny alterations in the features—slightly smaller eyes, barely rounder cheeks, a lower jaw just a tad askew—could create such a different effect. Boys did not fall speechless at the sight of me, as they did my sister. No one looked at me and praised creation.

Until Jerry.

In my senior year of college, I responded to an ad in the student newspaper for a part-time secretarial job at the political science institute, the one that lent the college a national reputation for its highly publicized polls around election time. At least, that's how I knew of Brandywine, a name I found weirdly inappropriate before learning it belonged to its deceased founder. The building was on the main campus, or rather off slightly to the north, set apart by an ancient grove of oak trees. A long, straight path led up to the brick structure, fronted by white columns and crowned with a white bell tower. The college brochure featured Brandywine on the cover; when dignitaries came to visit, politicians in particular, they spoke on its steps. In the fall, with the oak leaves turning, it looked like New England in the middle of New Jersey.

I got the job. I joined a rotating roster of students who assisted a political science professor named Stephen Baker, who wrote op-eds for the *New York Times* and had authored five books, all of them on presidential elections. Student groupies trailed him from lecture to lecture. When I reported my new post over Sunday dinner to Dad, he sat back in the dining-room chair and grinned. I felt proud. Though my parents never pressured me, I admit: I was anxious to find my thing. I didn't need to be the best. I just wanted to locate my place, to discover that one thing I did fairly well.

That thing, at first, was filing. Mostly I filed Professor Baker's notes, in manila folders in steel cabinets lining a long, cramped hallway on the institute's third floor. Baker's stuff kept spilling out of his offices, but given his value, Brandywine's president allowed it. Also I sorted his mail: speaking requests; readers; media. The professor responded to all, but always to journalists first. The first time I overheard him taking an interview by phone, I was awed by his effortless eloquence, the way he spoke in sentences and paragraphs. Later, when I took charge of his media appointments, I learned he kept in his head a ready arsenal of reusable sound bites.

One day I came in to work to find a young man sitting across from my desk, waiting for the professor's office hours to begin. I said hi and began opening mail. When I looked up, I found he was looking at me. He smiled.

I smiled back. I wasn't shy around boys, maybe because I never assumed a boy's interest in me that way, or maybe because I had three brothers. I looked down at the appointment book and read aloud: "Jeremiah Matters." I looked at him again. "That sounds biblical."

He laughed. "I go by Jerry," he said.

I studied him. "Poli sci, minor in . . . econ?"

Vivian had warned me freshman year against asking a person's major the second we met. Completely unoriginal, she said. So my own twist on this lame line was to guess. I swear I was right about eighty percent of the time.

Jerry laughed again. I liked to hear him laugh, to watch his long, still face ease open. More important, it meant he found me funny, and that was extremely attractive.

I sat up a little straighter and adjusted my sweatshirt. "Athletic XXL," the sweatshirt read across the front, though I was neither. Why had I worn it? It made me look like my sport was sumo.

"I'm taking Professor Baker's lecture, but I'm not officially at the college," he said. "I'm at the theology center."

I knew of it. It stood among a row of affiliated institutes, not unlike Brandywine, that took residence on a leafy lane hugging campus. I walked past it every Tuesday on my way to Sociology of Scrapbooking. (I know.)

"So," I said, "the biblical name fits. Either that or you were named after the bullfrog."

He laughed again. Three times now that I'd made this strange boy laugh. Only, now that I evaluated him, he wasn't a boy. I remembered then that the theology center's programs were graduate level.

Jerry leaned back, stretched his long legs, and cocked his head all at the same time. Like a cat. I liked that. He was comfortable in his body, not like the other male specimens I saw every day in the dining hall, all shuffling or preening or spastic.

"And you? No, no"—he held up his hands—"let me guess. Your name is Ruthie. And you're undecided."

My eyebrows lifted.

He pointed. Next to my head, taped to the wall, was a scheduling calendar of all the students who filed and answered phones for Professor Baker. Under Thursday, from two to six p.m., highlighted in pink, was my name.

"Okay, I guess I asked for that," I admitted. "But I'm a senior, I'll have you know. I had to declare a year ago." I said this last with resignation. Because he was right: I was undecided. In every way. "Communications," I volunteered. "Whatever the hell that means."

He tipped his head in apology for his assumption. Then he said, amicably and not ironically, "Without communication, humans would still be monkeys."

I relished the lob. "So the theology center acknowledges evolution, then?"

Before Jerry could respond, the door opened and Professor Baker beckoned, still cradling the phone against his ear.

I felt the moment and the man slip away. How many times had I begun promising conversations with young men at the college only for class to end or the intercampus bus to arrive, and I'd never seen them again? The college was so big, you could make and lose a friend a day. Besides, surely a guy this good-looking and this self-assured was merely making polite conversation.

I gave Jerry a quick smile and made myself look busy shuffling some envelopes. And when I looked up again, he was closing the professor's door behind him.

I realized I was sweating under my sweatshirt, and I took it off. Underneath I wore a tight T-shirt. I shot off to the ladies' down the hall to check my hair and face. Not tragic—not walking-dead tragic. I dabbed gloss on my lips and wished I had something to spritz in my ridiculous hair. There would come a day when I appreciated the rotini pasta that corkscrewed from my scalp. But there and then, I wished hard for sheets of silk I could ripple in his direction like a fishing lure.

By the time I scooted back into my chair, though, the office door was open and Jerry was gone. The professor was on another phone call. Or who knows; maybe he'd never gotten off the first one. Baker was an affable guy, but that was also his problem—he couldn't *not* take a call or a meeting or a lunch, even if he had other plans, like a call or a meeting or a lunch. Once I began making his press appointments, I'd learn his schedule book was basically a work of fiction.

My heart hurt. *Of course,* I thought as I walked home later. The oak trees around Brandywine had just begun to turn, the leaves paused between green and red, an intermission of color. *Of course.*

But as I reached my dorm, my cell phone buzzed. I didn't recognize the number.

"Hello," I said.

"It's Jeremiah," he said. "Like the bullfrog."

It took me a moment. Then it hit me: The scheduling sheet

outside the professor's office for his part-time assistants, the one Jerry had used to divine my name, had my phone number on it, too.

This time I grinned as I thought it: *Of course*.

* * *

"So what's it like?" Vivian asked.

"What's what like?" I said.

"What's it like when the guy you married decides to marry God?"

Vivian burrowed deep in the sofa, her feet up on Paul's shoulders. Paul sat on the floor in front of her while Michael reclined in Dad's orange Barcalounger, as far back as it could go. Tom stood near the old air conditioner in the window, banging it occasionally with his fist to keep the cool air pumping.

I faced my jury. I sat in a straight-backed kitchen chair I had pulled into my parents' living room. I had picked Tuesday night to gather my siblings, when Dad would head reliably out of earshot to Bob Reinhardt's poker night. Since Mom's illness, we had taken to holding family meetings without him. It was just easier that way.

Vivian's body lied. Her slouch, her loose legs, even her hair—the pose reminded me of a Ralph Lauren ad, the ones with the improbably gorgeous girls splayed artfully on some haystack. Viv looked the picture of relaxation, even, or especially, with the pregnant belly. But unlike the carefree eyes of the models in those magazine ads, hers told another story. And Vivian was furious.

I didn't have an answer. I'd rehearsed obsessively for a week, and I didn't have an answer to that one. I felt my hand groping for Jerry's, even though I knew he wasn't there.

He'd wanted to come. "It's me," he'd said. "We're going

because of me, and I ought to be the one to explain. I owe it to them."

I refused, with more vehemence than I'd known I felt. "They're *my* family. If you come, they'll pull their punches. They won't say what they really feel, and then they'll stew about it, and then come Christmas there'll be some confrontation. With shouting. And a flying ham."

There was another reason I wanted him to stay out of it: I needed to spin the story. I would emphasize the job, not the calling. The financial management, not the pastoral duties. The place to crash in balmy Georgia, not the five states' distance to New Jersey.

It did not go as planned.

I began as scripted: "Jerry's taking a job at a church—"

"I knew it!" said Vivian. She turned to the others. "I told you all it was a matter of time."

Tom stroked the air in front of him, a gesture that said to Viv: Settle. Then he faced me. "So, is that it? He heard his calling, or whatever?"

I looked around at them, stunned. "How did you—"

Tom shrugged. "We talked about it once. Last Thanksgiving, I think."

"Yeah, yeah," said Paul. "When we were throwing the football out back."

"We were talking about how useless our degrees were," said Michael. "And Paul asked Jerry if the master's in Godology helped him pick stocks."

I glared at Paul.

"What?" said Paul, palms up. "*Joke.* Anyway, he laughed."

"And then he said he thought he'd use his theology degree one day, maybe soon," said Michael. "And Paul said—"

" 'You gonna ditch the Street and go be a minister?' " Paul said. Michael nodded. "Then he got all quiet."

Vivian was stretching her neck and working her mouth. Next to Jerry, Viv was the person I knew best in the world, and I could read all her signals. I braced myself.

"What kind of church?" she demanded.

I shrugged. "Evangelical, I guess."

"You *guess*?"

"It's all so new."

"So what are you now—a pastor's wife?"

"By default. I suppose."

"And you'll do what—throw tea parties and lead Bible study?"

"I don't know yet. It's up to the Greens."

The boys had been watching the volley between their sisters, back and forth, back and forth. Like an umpire, Tom held up a hand.

"Whoa, whoa," he said. "The Greens? As in, Aaron Green?"

"The dude on TV?" said Michael.

"Hey, yeah," said Paul, kicking the Barcalounger. "We watched that one time at Tau Sig when we were too hungover to change the channel. Remember? Dude talked for, like, two hours straight, man. It was impressive."

"I just got that *Time* magazine with him on the cover," said Tom. "Him and Rick Warren and the pretty one with the teeth."

My brothers looked at me with . . . not admiration, but something close. As if proximity to fame suddenly made our venture worthwhile.

"So," said Viv, cutting their awed silence. "Are you converting?"

"What?" I said, startled. "Of course not." Suddenly, though, I wondered: Did becoming a pastor's wife automatically make you a member of that church? I tucked the problem away for later examination and continued, "But it's not like I'm a practicing Catholic anyway."

At that, Viv's eyes narrowed. The boys ducked and covered. Like me, they knew Viv's moods, and this one was going to rip.

What came out was something between a rumble and a hiss. "How can you say that," she said, "after what we just went through with Mom?"

There it was.

After a moment, Paul spoke up. "Aw, jeez, Viv," he said softly. "You don't gotta throw the Mom bomb, do ya?"

But it was too late. My ears filled with the wheeze of the balky air conditioner and my mother's voice.

* * *

"He's a keeper."

That was what my mother told me the first time I brought Jerry home.

We were in the kitchen, Mom washing the dishes wearing yellow rubber gloves, the secret to hands still marvelously supple after thirty years of housekeeping and gardening. I wiped. Mom had made her roast beef, which Dad called roast beast, and which I knew signified the importance of the event. She didn't whip out that dish just any old day. Since Rupert Benedict, my disastrous junior prom date, Jerry was the first boy I had ever introduced to my parents.

Come to think of it, Jerry was the first boy I could properly call my boyfriend. He courted me. Seriously: courted. He asked me on actual dates. He paid for dinners and movie tickets; he opened doors; occasionally he produced a single red rose. We spent hours and hours walking around campus, talking about everything and nothing. We held hands. I crept toward this idea of *we*, a pronoun I'd never before applied to a romantic unit, until it became easy, natural. That night at my parents' house, he brought Mom a cake from Mel's, because he remembered me mentioning she would beat down her own children for the bakery's chocolate seven-layer.

"Yep," I agreed, not bothering to hedge the happy. "He's a keeper."

The next time I brought him home was over Thanksgiving, when all my siblings would be around. I had already taken him to meet my sister, over lunch at a sidewalk café in Hoboken, from where Vivian commuted to her job in Manhattan as a sales assistant for an evening-wear designer. He'd met Paul and Michael, too, when we bumped into them while strolling hand in hand in the vicinity of Greek Row. (They followed us for a while, strolling hand in hand as well.) Within minutes of arriving at the Connellys', Jerry settled into the Giants game with the boys while Tom told him about a case before the Trenton judge for whom he clerked. Later, at the table, Jerry cried laughing at Paul and Michael's reenactment of me throwing up on my date at junior prom. I didn't even mind. My family loved my beloved. Was there a higher joy?

Religion raised a bit of a bump.

It wasn't until Christmas that I let slip Jerry was not a Catholic but a Protestant of indeterminate denomination. Maybe I was naive. Certainly I was naive. Still, I felt his earnest faith and spiritual studies would preclude much dissension from my parents. Though I could not tell them this, his faith far outshone my own.

"Well, Toothy," said Dad in his Voice of Authority, to indicate this settled the matter, "you can love a Protestant. But you can't marry one."

"Now, Frank," said Mom, putting a hand on his arm.

Edith talked to Frank. This was a typical resolution to family drama: Dad would bluster, and Mom would talk him down, usually to a result in favor of the children. "We could use some joy," I overheard her saying.

It was right around the time of her first cancer scare. "*Breast* cancer," she scoffed when she telephoned me with the news. "It's nothing. A little snip, a little chemo, and we're all done."

I was the first to marry of the five, in and of itself a first for me to be first at anything. Jerry consented to wed at Saint Ann's, and my parents overlooked the denial of a full Mass, being that Protestants could not receive our Communion. Dad walked me down the aisle, Mom wore a silk scarf wrapped around her head, and my siblings hogged the front pew. The three boys had shaved their heads in solidarity with Mom, and only her frantic begging had stopped me and Viv from doing the same.

The cancer was not nothing. It metastasized to a cluster of lymph nodes in Mom's right armpit, which the surgeon assured us he had successfully removed. When her white blood cell counts kept dropping, her oncologist switched chemo cocktails, then switched them again. For a time she seemed to recover, even spending a year taking only maintenance meds. That was a banner year for the Connellys of Hoogaboom, with the twins' college graduation, Viv's wedding and the prompt arrival of her own set of twins, and Tom's promotion to assistant district attorney in Trenton. Dad celebrated by renting a beachfront house for a week in Ocean City, where everyone gathered for a Fourth of July lobster bake, Mom lolling on a deck chair and beaming at her family as the fireworks splattered the sky.

Toward the end of the year she complained of pain in her right hip, and a scan showed the bone eaten through with cancer. From there the illness galloped from organ to organ, and within months Tom was signing her up for in-home hospice care.

We took shifts, the five of us, days at a time, whatever work or child-care duties we could get off, whenever we could drive over. As a nurse, Dad was useless. He trotted off in the morning to his law office out front, returning all jovial and expecting lunch. The grim faces of his children seemed to baffle him. He referred to the hospice workers as "Edith's maids," and kept alluding cheerfully to future events, chiding his wife that she'd better get her butt out of bed if she still wanted that Easter trip to Dublin.

"I'm going to kill him," Viv muttered. "I'm going to shove him into Mom's coffin and nail it shut."

I myself was an inadequate nurse. Left alone with my mother, I felt clumsy and inefficient, bumbling around the bedroom-turned-hospice straightening medical supplies and organizing get-well cards. Mostly, she slept. The morphine drip countered the unspeakable pain. One day, I glanced over in the middle of sorting Dad's sweaters to find Mom watching me.

"Come here," she said, patting the side of her bed.

"I just have to—"

"Oh, Ruthie. Put the stupid sweater down."

I put the stupid sweater down. I sat down next to my mother and began to cry.

"Why, honey?"

"Because," I said. "Because. I don't want you to go."

"Oh, baby." Her satin hand rested on mine. "You just need to remember—you are not alone."

I nodded, over and over, like the bobble-head doll of Derek

Jeter on the windowsill. Paul had secured it for her by shoving away ten-year-olds at a recent giveaway game. My mother adored the Yankee shortstop.

"Do you know what I mean?" she asked, in a voice so loving it summoned from me a fresh gush of tears. "You are not alone. You always have *Him*."

My mother's faith seemed a simple but abiding thing, a fact, as irrevocably a part of her as—I would have said *as a limb*, but now her actual limbs failed her and yet her faith remained unbroken, unbowed. My faith, in contrast, had gone missing. I don't know exactly when or how. But somewhere between Sunday school and late-night dorm debates on the origin of species, my doubts had overtaken blind belief. How could I tell her this?

As the morphine pulled her under again, I sat by my mother's side, careful not to touch the parts of her body that hurt. I watched her drug-calmed face. I thought about her words. *You are not alone. You always have Him.*

Even though I knew she meant God, I decided my mother also meant Jerry. If I could not believe in *Him*, I could believe in *him*.

* * *

Jerry was stroking my forearm with his thumb.

He had slid over into the middle seat. I kept my forehead on the window and stared at the clouds, stacked vertically like teetering towers of coins. In time I turned to bury my face in his shoulder, taking a breath to stave off a sob. But it rattled out anyway.

What's it like when the man you married decides to marry God? In the weeks since Viv had asked the question, I had pondered it over and over. If I were a woman who believed, I imagined my husband's betrothal to the church would work out like a happy three-way. For me, it was more complicated. But strangely, unexpectedly, it began to feel like a lifeline. A beginning. An escape from my trinity of loss—of my home, of my faith, of my mother.

When I felt it was safe, I lifted my head and looked at my husband. He handed me a cocktail napkin. I blew.

"I miss her," I said.

"I know," he said.

The plane began its descent. I reached for Jerry's hand. And told myself: You are not alone. You are not alone. You are not alone.

Chapter Two

Candace

Malfunction in the smoke machine.

Candace Green noticed this during the Friday morning run-through. The sanctuary's three thousand stadium seats stood empty, waiting. On stage, the worship team held their instruments in check as they listened to their leader. Beams cast the musicians in light, then in shadow, then in light again as below them dozens of staff bumped around checking sound and lighting. This being a Communion week, a squad of volunteers arranged tables in a horseshoe down before the stage, setting out wicker baskets for the cubed bread and neat stacks of plastic, shotglass-sized cups for the grape juice.

Candace stood in her usual spot, fifth row, aisle, stage left. The location allowed unobstructed visuals—not just hers but *of* her, by the roaming cameras. Television viewers loved to glimpse the senior pastor's wife, especially during Aaron's sermon.

The seat also allowed the staff access to Candace during the service. They materialized at regular intervals, whispering in her ear, relaying urgent issues and problems. She listened intently and decreed swiftly. King Solomon in a skirt suit.

The worship team broke into laughter. Hugh Dolly, their leader, must have made a joke about his wife's impending delivery, for he had his hands on Missy's Hindenburg of a belly. Some women viewed pregnancy as an invitation to an all-Mallomar diet. Speaking of elephants, Candace thought of another one in the room: Hugh had yet to tell Missy they were holding auditions today to replace her in the vocals lineup. Candace had no idea why he procrastinated. Missy couldn't very well expect the worship team to await her return from maternity leave, could she? Maternity leave. How a pastor's wife could insist on taking three months off, Candace simply did not know.

Candace set down the leather-bound King James Bible she almost always carried, and fished in her purse for an Imitrex and a water bottle. If she took it now, the migraine medication should kick in by audition time.

The smoke machine spewed again, this time so violently that the band startled. Her earpiece crackled. It would be the control room.

She answered without speaking, eyes closed to the excuses and apologies. When the babbling stopped, she said simply: "So you'll take care of it, then." And she hung up.

"Thing is gonna kill somebody."

Candace knew without opening her eyes that it was John Swain, the head elder. She nodded without expression. She was well aware of where John and the rest of the church founders stood on the smoke machines. Not to mention the telecasts, the electric guitars, and the Jumbotrons.

"How may I help you?" Lately, Candace had to work to melt

the frost from her voice when addressing the elders. The feeling was mutual.

"Actually, I wondered if *I* may help *you*."

At this, Candace turned to look at John. He had aged these past years. His long ponytail had dirtied to the color of motor oil when it puddles on a road. Wrinkles splintered his tanned face. Candace remembered with clarity their first meeting, at the abandoned theater on Palmtree Avenue that had been the church's first home, and that he looked the spitting image of Clint Eastwood in *Pale Rider*. Now he looked—well, she supposed he looked like Clint Eastwood did these days.

John continued. "I understand the new associate pastor arrives today," he said.

"Jeremiah Matters," said Candace. "And his wife, Ruthie. They fly in today and start next week."

"I wondered who would be showing them around."

"Why, Pastor Aaron will introduce Pastor Jerry, of course. And I suppose I'll get Ruthie acclimated."

"Doesn't Brother Aaron have to prepare for his interfaith conference?"

It irked Candace that John referred to Aaron with that prefix. It implied an equality not matched by reality. "Of course," she said. "But that's not till early November. Pastor Jerry is a big boy. I think he can manage on his own for a few hours. He'll have plenty to do meantime getting acquainted with our financials."

John nodded. "What I'm saying is I want to offer my help." He turned and faced Candace. "Ever since we restructured, I feel I haven't been serving as much as I'd like. I've been here the longest. I know us better than anyone. Maybe I can help acquaint Pastor Jerry."

Wrong. Past tense: Elder John *knew* us better than anyone—the Greenleaf that was, not the Greenleaf that is. But when she saw his face—plaintive for once and not combative—Candace's irritation ebbed. She knew what it took for him to ask anything of her. And it was not an unreasonable request. She could afford this olive branch.

She placed a hand on his arm. "Pastor Aaron will be glad of that," she said.

John looked relieved. "Fine, then. Shall I talk to him?"

She gazed at him for a moment before she smiled. "Let me take care of it."

* * *

"*What? Know ye not that your body is the temple of the Holy Ghost which is in you, which ye have of God, and ye are not your own?*"

Corinthians 6:19, thought Candace.

"Corinthians 6:19," said Lacey Borden.

Lacey spoke from the other end of the room, and yet Candace felt she whispered directly into her ear. Those Anchor LDP wireless microphones worked like magic. At twenty-four hundred dollars, they'd better. Candace lay flat on her yoga mat and relished the peace.

The yoga studio had been her idea. In fact, the entire wellness complex was her baby. Candace preached the gospel of health and self-maintenance. She'd devoted an entire chapter to it in her book. How ought a Christian woman keep up her marriage when she looked and felt like a dump truck?

Candace worked out every day but Sunday. She had sampled many of the gyms in the vicinity, and concluded none, but none, lived up to any self-respecting Christian woman's standards for modesty and sanitation. The last straw had been a coed step class at a Bally's where, during the final stretch, the ape in front of her bent forward and assaulted Candace's nostrils with a blast of sweaty testicles. She decided then and there: Never again would she set foot in a public gym.

The elders doubted the value of a church-based athletic compound, but then that was to be expected. These days, she could count on the elders for dissent.

She had appealed to Aaron. Every megachurch, from Second Baptist in Houston to Willow Creek in Chicago, offered congregants their own gym. Aaron cringed at the term *megachurch*—he refused to use it himself—but Candace viewed it as an honest assessment. A megachurch was a community, a city unto itself. And did not a city need a gym? Did not the Bible itself command us to care for our God-given bodies?

Aaron greenlighted the project, as she had known he would— so long as Candace raised half the funds on her own. She did so by appealing to female church members to make a separate donation in their weekly tithes. Wouldn't it be nice, she asked them in coffee circles and study groups, to work out among other Christians? To leave the kids at the Children's Center? To sweat to worship music instead of that awful Lady Gaga?

Candace collected the funds in three months. She personally would supervise the design and construction of the three-thousand-square-foot center, to be located on the Greenleaf campus, on the grassy knoll behind the church, overlooking the man-made pond. Every wall would be stenciled with inspirational Scripture. The sound system would play Avalon and Canaan's Crossing. There would be Peak Pilates machines and NordicTrack treadmills, to be wiped down after every use with nontoxic antibacterial solvent. Neat stacks of fluffy towels would wait outside the showers—showers with doors, not those flimsy curtains at all the other gyms that allowed a Christian woman no privacy. And—oh, crowning glory—a yoga studio.

When she presented the blueprints to the elders, they erupted.

"Yoga!" cried Elder Philippa. "Sister Candace, what are you turning us into?"

"What does yoga have to do with church?" asked Elder Pete. "It's heathen!"

"Actually," corrected Elder John, "yoga is a Hindu practice."

"There you go," huffed Elder James.

Elder John concurred. "Candace, with all due respect, it does sound off-message."

Candace looked around the boardroom at the dozen men and women seated at the table. The elders. Aaron liked to remind her that Greenleaf would not exist without them, that the elders were the seeds that had grown into their tree. It crossed her mind that once seeds sprouted, their hulls became fertilizer.

Aaron sat at the opposite end, trying to hide his smile behind his hand.

Candace raised her palms to the group. "Ladies, gentlemen," she said, in her sweetest, slowest voice. Like molasses in January, her father used to say. "I thought the same thing. Then I realized all the principles are the same as ours. Prayer. The focus on breathing. It's the answer to devotional exercise that the West has not invented. The Hindus *gave* us yoga. Christian yoga is a movement—"

"Greenleaf is not about following *movements*," sniffed Elder Simone.

Elder Simone. Of course she would oppose. The woman had

probably not broken a sweat intentionally in twenty years. Elder Simone was a burrito on legs.

Head tilted to one side, hands clasped at her heart, Candace coated them with her sugary plea. "Brothers and sisters," she said. "Our role as stewards of this church is not to follow. It is to lead." She leaned in for the kill. "And is not our introduction of yoga—*Christian* yoga—exactly in the spirit of interfaith friendship toward which Pastor Aaron labors?"

Twelve pairs of eyes slid toward the back of the room. Aaron shrugged and grinned. The elders glanced at each other and understood: fait accompli.

Of course, Candace had known that going in. More and more lately, she regarded the elders as a figurehead group. She ran decisions by them out of courtesy, but even that had become burdensome and disagreeable.

The opinion of the church family, on the other hand, mattered greatly to her. The faithful were the soul of any church. Without sheep, wherefore the shepherd?

Sometimes she felt she alone among the Greenleaf leadership understood that churchgoers were fickle. Long gone were the days of occupying the same pew from cradle to grave. The values that once tied people to their church—family, tradition, societal obligation—*poof!* had disappeared. In one of the surveys of Greenleaf members she commissioned regularly from a professional polling company, six in ten confessed they had sampled a different church in the past six months. Six in ten! In the past half year! This was Georgia, after all. In Magnolia alone, one could tour a different Christian church every week from New Year's to Christmas. The minute they found something better, the faithful were no longer—faithful, at least, to Greenleaf.

Thus, yoga. Even in the meeting with the elders, Candace could barely bring herself to say the word, so absurd did she find the practice. Yoga. How could you call it exercise when you spent half the class aspiring toward a corpse?

The truth was, Elder Simone had hit a nerve. Candace did indeed follow church trends assiduously. She had read an interview with Lacey Borden about Christian yoga in *Just Between Us*, the magazine for pastors' wives. Plus she had learned through the wives' grapevine that All Souls in nearby Decatur was shopping for incense and tea-tree oil.

No, Greenleaf was not about trends. Greenleaf was about spreading the Gospel. But trends got butts in the seats. No trends, no butts, no Gospel.

She attended the inaugural yoga class to set an example, fully prepared to die of boredom. So she was amazed to find she loved it. She loved the peace. The quiet. Lacey's plinking voice, like the lower register of an acoustic guitar, reminding her to meditate on Scripture. She loved opening her eyes to revel in the perfect space she had created, sunlight pouring through the floor-to-ceiling windows and pooling like melted butter on the bamboo floors. Looking around at the blissful faces of her fellow faithful, women she knew bore the ceaseless responsibilities of children and home, she loved knowing she'd brought them this quiet communion with God.

Lacey continued. "That's right. Open yourself up. We'll do the final breathing to the Jesus Prayer."

Inhale. "Jesus Christ."

Exhale. "Son of God."

Inhale. "Have mercy on me . . ."

Exhale. ". . . a sinner."

"Now bring your hands together in prayer," murmured Lacey.
"Let go and let God."

"Let go and let God," said the class, bowing.

"Be still and know that I am God," said Lacey.

Psalm 46:10, thought Candace.

"Psalm 46:10," said Lacey.

* * *

"I got a new one," Aaron was saying as Candace slipped into his
office. With Aaron were Rabbi Joshua Bernstein and Imam Amin
Chaudry, his two closest compatriots in his interfaith ministry.
They convened every Friday in one of their places of worship, lately
in preparation for a global conference on religious conflict, to be
held in London later this fall.

"So a third-grade teacher asks the children to bring something
in for show-and-tell about their religion," Aaron said. He sat forward in his chair, propping his elbows on his widely spaced knees,
like he couldn't wait to hear his own punch line. "One boy stands up
and says, 'I am a Muslim, and this is a prayer mat.' Another child
says, 'I am a Jew, and this is a menorah.' And another child stands
up and says, 'I am a Southern Baptist, and this—is a casserole.'"

Imam Chaudry guffawed. Rabbi Bernstein chuckled and shook
his head.

Candace smiled to herself. Aaron looked especially handsome
today, if she did say so, in the tea-green tie she'd selected from the
Neiman Marcus Web site. Candace preferred shopping in person,
fondling textiles and drinking in colors, holding objects up to the
light. Once she deemed a store suited to her tastes and standards,

she became its best customer, ordering favored items in a rainbow of multiples. Just as restaurateurs kept watch for influential reviewers, so shopkeepers and sales managers in the area lay in wait for an appearance by Candace Green. Her own consumption aside, her stamp of approval guaranteed a rush of business from the hordes of women who copied her every choice. She was the Oprah of Magnolia.

That was the problem. Wherever she went, someone recognized her and stopped her to chat. They assumed Aaron's gregarious nature applied to her, too, though in truth she was anything but. While Aaron loved nothing more than to plunge into a sea of admirers, Candace was far too busy assessing the person and the situation, evaluating and judging and calculating the outcome, to enjoy small talk. Their son Anthony likened her brain to the Terminator's. She could see his point.

And so she smiled. And somehow, all her life, that seemed to be enough. People read what they wanted into her face—benevolence, grace, agreement, understanding—and came away feeling a connection. Beauty paired with position bought that kind of goodwill.

Her true smile she reserved for her sons and her grandbabies. And, of course, for her beloved, her husband. Her Aaron.

"What do you think, hon?" Aaron called from the other end of the room, as the men stood up to leave. "Can I use that in a sermon?"

"I don't know," said Candace. "Casseroles are sacrosanct around here."

Aaron shrugged as he walked over for a kiss. "Whatever you say," he said.

She smiled. His entourage of advisers and aides grew as

Greenleaf's operations did, but everyone who worked for him knew the only opinion that truly mattered to Aaron Green was his wife's.

As Aaron saw the men out, Candace picked up his phone to go through his messages. God love the man, but he was hopeless with technology, unable to remember even the sequence of buttons to access his voice mail. Then again, why bother, with Candace around? Her mother once chided her for making life too easy for Aaron, and that fostering such reliance would come to haunt them both. Candace had scoffed. This was her *role*, she explained, as if her mother, herself a pastor's wife, would not know, would not understand. This was her *job*.

A message from the mayor's office with an update about today's event. One from the youth minister with a change to the children's service. And another one from Juan Diaz, of the *Atlanta Journal-Constitution*.

The reporter had called every day for a week, requesting face time with Aaron. Candace put off returning the call, thinking it a good introductory task for Ruthie Matters, who according to her résumé had experience in publicity. Divine timing, too, what with Candace having to fire the last publicist for getting too chummy with that *Time* magazine writer and divulging Aaron's income in that cover article.

Not that Aaron's million-dollar salary shamed Candace. He deserved every penny and more, considering he personally drew in much of the church's annual tithing revenue. Plenty of CEOs who did far less earned far more. Besides, she felt the salary covered her services, as it went without saying that her de facto role as chief operating officer went officially uncompensated.

What bothered her was that Joel Osteen, of Lakewood Church, noted in the same article that he declined his own $220,000 salary and lived solely off the income from his books. "I have been blessed with more riches than I could ever need," he told the magazine. "Church money belongs to the church."

Sanctimonious ninny.

"In case I didn't mention it before," Juan Diaz was saying at the end of his message, "the focus of my article is Pastor Green's interfaith work and how 9/11 changed him."

Candace lifted an eyebrow. Hmm. Mr. Diaz had done a little research. Many reporters called with a vague desire to write about megachurches, and Aaron Green was reputed among journalists to be a friendly source. His jokey charm, his active intellect, his marquee smile—his was the face of evangelism the secular world wanted to see. But lately, Candace tried to restrict media access to those who wanted to talk about Aaron's interfaith work. It was his most important cause, after all.

Like clergy throughout America, Aaron had indeed been changed by 9/11. Candace well remembered that terrible morning when John Swain called to tell Aaron to turn on the TV. Her small irritation at the head elder's disturbance of their tranquil morning routine turned to horror as they watched those familiar buildings fall. When she turned to speak to Aaron, she saw that her husband was weeping.

He left that day, got in his Escalade, and just drove away. She was beside herself with worry, even though she knew from past episodes that he had gone to fast and pray. On the third day he returned, gray and weary but with a dim light returned to his eyes. That light brightened over the months as he formulated his plan.

In January the following year, Aaron Green invited religious leaders from around the region to Greenleaf for a secret meeting. Rabbi Joshua Bernstein, from the largest synagogue in Atlanta, came. So did Imam Amin Chaudry, representing the surprisingly large Muslim population scattered throughout the state. It took much cajoling, but Chuck Lawdly, the outspoken leader of the Southern Baptists, showed up, as did leaders of most of the other Christian denominations. There they formed a pact: They would support one another, avoid recrimination and blame. Aaron presented a calendar of events to build interfaith trust and understanding.

The pact was soon tested. A radio talk-show host based in Florida, a noted right-wing firebrand, tried to incite a boycott of all merchants with Arab-sounding names. The Friends in Faith, as they now called themselves, mobilized. They spoke out from their pulpits against the boycott. Aaron, Rabbi Bernstein, and Imam Chaudry wrote a joint op-ed in the *Atlanta Journal-Constitution*.

That was when the national media tuned in. It began with a warm profile in the *New York Times* of the blooming friendship between the pastor, the rabbi, and the imam, leading with a color photo on the front page of the three of them sitting cross-legged on a rug in the imam's mosque, laughing uproariously. In the blitz that followed, the three appeared together on the *Today Show*, then *Larry King Live*, then *The View*.

Until then, Candace had been wary of Aaron's ministry. She worried it distracted him from his sworn mission, to share the word of Jesus Christ. She fretted about unwanted attention from zealots and bigots. She wasn't the only concerned party; Aaron's new cause alarmed many church members, who cornered her to vent their fears and suspicions.

But it came down to this: She believed in him.

It was not for her to question Aaron's calling. It was for her to make it happen. This was what she signed up for when she married

Aaron and became a pastor's wife. This was God's role for her. This was *her* calling. Aaron was placed on earth to spread the Good News. And Candace was put here to make damned sure the people heard.

There was more. Wired as it was for business, Candace's brain could not help but recognize in Aaron's interfaith ministry that rare and precious thing: a brand. Rick and Kay Warren had global AIDS. Joel and Victoria Osteen urged self-improvement.

Aaron and Candace Green would preach peace among the warring religions.

* * *

"You've got the ribbon-cutting with the mayor in an hour," Candace told Aaron. She squinted at her watch. The Cartier sported a face so tiny she could barely tell the time, but because Aaron had given it to her she wore it anyway. "I've got to get to auditions for the worship team."

"Took your migraine meds?"

Candace tapped her temple. "You know it. Six-fifteen for dinner. Pasta primavera from Bella's."

"It's a date." Aaron leaned down for a kiss. "To the mayor's, Tosh."

An Asian man dressed in head-to-toe black materialized behind him and followed them silently down the corridor. As they left the inner sanctum and entered the lobby, Tosh caught Candace's eye and nodded. Then he walked with Aaron toward the parking lot, his eyes sweeping the perimeter all the while.

Candace had fought for the bodyguard.

When she first suggested it to Aaron, over a candlelit dinner of pork medallions with balsamic honey glaze delivered from Baldacci's, it curdled into one of their rare arguments.

"A bodyguard? For a pastor?" he asked, incredulous. Then he laughed. "Come *on*, Candace. Who do you think I am—the President of the United States?"

She prickled. Aaron's habitual self-effacement endeared him to most, but to Candace, it sometimes smacked of willful blindness. For in her mind, the senior pastor of a major, influential church was indeed similar to the leader of a small country. After all, in the community of pastors' wives, wasn't Candace known as a First Lady? To be quite frank, she felt the moniker apt, considering her public responsibilities, her role in diplomacy, and the demands upon her time and person.

One can tell a lot about a couple by the way they fight. Aaron joked; Candace bristled. Aaron held forth; Candace reasoned. Aaron scowled; Candace stood firm. Never did she raise her voice. Never did she give way to passion and unreason. Over the years she had honed her ability to clear her mind of murky recrimination and focus on the issue at hand. She never, ever lost.

She began with the irrefutable. "You're taking on dangerous work," she said, her voice unfreighted with emotion. "And these are dangerous times."

Aaron shrugged, but he didn't disagree. "No one wants to kill me," he said.

"Yet," she said.

He wiped his mouth with the linen napkin and chuckled. "This is Georgia, my love. Not Afghanistan."

Her voice chilled a few degrees. "After 9/11," she said, "I am surprised any American believes he is safe, even on our own soil."

Aaron wadded up his napkin and leaned his elbow on the table. His eyes twinkled in the candlelight. "Darling. Terrorists are not targeting Magnolia."

"It's not the terrorists I'm afraid of," she said. "At least, not the foreign ones." She tapped the side of her glass with her nail. "Some people would believe that a Christian pastor fraternizing with imams and rabbis is reason enough for a hit."

"A hit?" Aaron said. "A *hit*? Really, Candace." He pushed away from the table and stood up. "A pastor has to be approachable. Our church family has to feel they can come to me for anything. I've worked hard for that—too hard. What'll they think if suddenly I'm walking around trailed by some—some goon?"

He really could be so blind. In truth, with church membership in the tens of thousands and TV viewership in the millions, its senior pastor had not been approachable for years.

Folding her napkin with the precision of origami, she, too, stood to deliver the last word. "Whatever they think, they surely will value the safety and security of their pastor above all else."

That night, she prayed on it.

In Bible studies and women's groups, Candace was often asked how she prayed. People believed that accepting Christ into their hearts invited them into a 24-7 conversation with Him. Candace disagreed. Yes, God heard all. But the nonstop babble coursing through one's head was not prayer. Constant requests for mundane assistance were not prayer. One did not ask Jesus to help pick between the Scott and the Charmin. One did not shake Him down for today's Mega Millions numbers.

No. As in anything worth doing, ritual mattered in prayer. In this, she felt the Catholics had it right. They believed ritual in itself was a form of prayer. That was the point of all their bells and smells.

Evangelicals, what with their creative services and rejection of a central hierarchy, thumbed their noses at public ritual. But it had always seemed to Candace that a private audience with God deserved careful consideration.

First, the form. Candace trusted absolutely in the pursuit of good form, even in private acts. A kneeling posture was best, back ruler-straight, hands tightly clasped, head sufficiently bowed.

Second, wording. One did not amble into prayer as one would a chat with a neighbor over the garden fence. That was one thing about the British; they understood decorum. They wouldn't dream of addressing the Queen with a "Hey, whassup," now, would they? One should begin prayer by giving thanks for all of one's many blessings. For every creature able to pray is blessed.

Third and most important, content. One must pray not for goals or success—it went without saying one never prayed for material goods—but for the tools to attain those things. Only a fool believes God grants wishes.

Of course, this was not what Candace said. When people asked her what she thought about prayer—or politics or Bible passages or the worship team's wardrobe—what they were really asking was what Aaron thought. She had learned over the years to toe the company line, beginning her responses with "Pastor Aaron feels . . ." It was easier that way.

In private, however, she hewed to her own set of rules. So on this night, Candace asked the Lord to help her keep her husband safe. Kneeling in a demure silk nightgown on the embroidered stepstool by her bed, head bent and back erect, Candace gave thanks and whispered her prayer.

"Give me the wisdom and the facility to know how I may protect my beloved from harm," she prayed. "Show me the way."

The next morning, well into a manicure at her favorite nail salon, Candace realized with displeasure that the only reading material within reach was a *Glamour* magazine. Even worse, it was the issue featuring the most eligible bachelor in America.

Candace had good reason to despise this publication and its bubble-headed annual feature: Her own son Timothy had been selected as one of those very bachelors some years back. It was the handiwork of another of Greenleaf's former publicists, who had persuaded her and Aaron that promoting the handsome, single associate pastor would bring national exposure for the church. Ha. The article exposed him, all right—to very much the wrong woman, whom he married three months later. Candace fired the publicist, and never opened *Glamour* magazine again.

Until now. In her peripheral vision, she noticed a vaguely familiar customer eyeing her as if for conversation. The best way to fend off small talk was to appear busy and engrossed, and lacking any other option she reached for the magazine.

It flipped open to the bachelor article. The page featured a photo of a tanned, muscular Asian man. Despite herself, Candace leaned in to read the blurb under his photo. It said Tosh Takai was one of Hollywood's highest-paid stuntmen specializing in the martial arts.

And—there it was—he had recently found Jesus. In a quote to the magazine: "I hope to leave Hollywood and find work serving a church someday soon." Bingo.

"Thank you, Lord," Candace whispered.

The manicurist glanced up.

Candace gave her a smile. "God is good," she said. "A little rounder on the tip."

In short order she located Tosh through a fan Web site

dedicated to stunt actors, which mentioned his Hollywood talent agency. Candace sent him a ticket to Atlanta, and picked him up herself at the airport. Once at Greenleaf, Tosh introduced himself to Aaron as a new supplicant seeking a way to serve. Tosh suggested security. Just as Candace had coached him.

That night, Aaron arrived home with a bouquet of three calla lilies, flowers Candace favored for their elegant simplicity and powerful stems.

"Darling," he said, "I still think you're silly to worry about me. But it's my great blessing that you do. So I've done it. I've hired a bodyguard."

Candace held the flowers to her heart and lowered her eyes. "Thank you, my love," she said, "for indulging me."

Within a month, she promoted Tosh to head of security with a budget to hire a five-person team. She greenlighted a security command post to rival a bank's. Three months later, cameras kept watch over every corner of Greenleaf, from the Children's Center to the remotest corner of the parking lot. Tosh preferred to man Aaron himself, a silent and black-clad ninja. The perfect goon was an invisible one. Few church members even noticed.

* * *

It had been three years since their twenty-eight-million-dollar campus first opened, but Candace still thrilled every time she stepped into the lobby of Greenleaf Church. Oh, it was like no church her Lutheran parents would recognize—no pews, no steeples, not even an altar. It far more resembled a concert hall. She'd heard the complex likened to a mall. But to Candace it served as testament: If you build it, the faithful will come.

She peered at her watch. She'd have a minute before the auditions to see her special someone.

"Hi, Candace." Jeannie Holbrush, a British expat and longtime church member, manned the entrance to the Children's Center. She always said the same thing: "Popping in for a snog?"

Candace, playing her role in the routine, nodded and winked.

Jeannie buzzed her in past the electronic fingerprint scanners. "I think we've got you on file," Jeannie said, as usual.

Candace made her way under a hanging planetary system and through a corridor designed with curved walls to look like a tunnel. The tunnel was dark, illuminated only by thousands of sparkly LED stars. Visitors emerged on the other end right into the open arms of a larger-than-life wax statue of Jesus. It felt every time like traveling through the universe into the Son of God's waiting embrace. The kids loved it. So did she.

In entering the Children's Center, Candace felt she could deposit her grown-up self, the to-do lists and the contact sheets, at the other end of that tunnel. Children did not ask for reserved parking spots or advice on dealing with a wayward spouse or for their original compositions to be performed during service. Children did not complain about the ply of the toilet paper in the restrooms or the ergonomics of the sanctuary seating. Children did not care that she was Candace Green, the senior pastor's wife.

She passed the mechanical rocking chairs of the brightly lit nursery, the sing-along for the preschoolers, until her searching eyes landed on a certain head with crazy sticking-up tufts of brown hair. Natalie Hernandez, one of the aides, caught her eye, and Candace put her finger to her lips. She snuck up behind her grandson, crouched down, and whispered, "Boo."

Jordan turned around, brown eyes wide behind plastic-rimmed

spectacles, a rubber dinosaur in his hand, and began talking in the way that he did, as if they'd been carrying on a conversation for hours. "So Mamie," he said. He pronounced it *may-mee*, and while not the proper French for "grandmother" that Candace had intended, she admitted *mah-mee* would confuse strangers. "Did you know, I read on the Internet, dinosaurs got extinct sixty-one million years ago?"

Oh, dear. What was her grandson, all of five, doing reading on the Internet? Didn't Ginger monitor him at all?

Jordan continued with hardly a breath. "And I told Miss Adaleen at Sunday school and she said that can't be true because Adam and Eve were the first ones on earth and dinosaurs are made up and if that's true then I would be sad because then that means Stevie Stegosaurus is a lie."

Natalie, the aide, overheard Jordan, and Candace could tell she was listening for her response. Nose-to-nose with her grandson, Candace assumed a thoughtful face. She made it a rule never to talk down to children, and certainly not to her Jordan.

"Well," she said, "God created all. The earth, people, animals. Stars. Moons. If there were dinosaurs, you can bet He created them."

"She says if it's not in the Bible, then it isn't true."

Candace simmered at this Miss Adaleen. What a simplistic thing to teach a child. As if they would not question. As if children's brains were not *wired* for questioning.

"The Bible doesn't say 'Mamie loves Jordan,'" she said. "The Bible doesn't say 'Jordan loves Bubble Trouble ice cream.' But those things are true, aren't they? The Bible would have to have a hundred million billion pages to hold every truth in the whole wide world."

Jordan's eyes were fixed on his Mamie's. "So dinosaurs are true?"

Candace shrugged. "All I know is we saw their bones in the museum, you and I, and those looked pretty real to me."

Jordan lowered his voice to a whisper. "Should I tell Miss Adaleen?"

Candace gazed at him a moment before she smiled. "Let me take care of it."

* * *

"There she is."

Hugh Dolly, the music minister, waved from the front of the darkened sanctuary.

Candace made her way down the aisle toward him. Thank the good Lord for Hugh. At least she wouldn't have to suffer the auditions alone.

Hugh was one of her first hires and among her most important allies at Greenleaf. She'd found him and his wife, Missy, performing at a pastors' convention in Nashville, where they had a thriving career as singer-songwriters. Their duet, called "And He Led Me to You," left everyone in the room teary-eyed. Gifted though they were, the recording industry was an unpredictable one, and they leaped at Candace's offer of a six-figure salary, car, and rent-free home. Hugh directed the twelve-member worship team and arranged the music. Missy sang backup and would again, presumably, when she returned from maternity leave in three months.

For now, though, they needed a replacement. "So who do we have?" she asked as she settled in beside him.

Hugh handed Candace a folder with head shots and résumés. "The usual suspects," he said, making a Ferris wheel of his eyeballs.

Besides the music ministry, Hugh led Greenleaf's reparative therapy group for ex-gays, called Happy! Not Gay! The therapy drew on the research of a Christian psychologist who found that homosexual attraction can decrease through abstinence or a meaningful heterosexual relationship. It modeled itself on Alcoholics Anonymous and involved twelve steps, support groups, and sponsors. Hugh, who himself had been treated by the psychologist, presented himself as Exhibit A—a former homosexual now happily married to a woman and living a life in Christ. "Can he get a refund?" Candace's son Anthony once joked. "Because I don't think it worked." Gay, straight, reformed—Candace honestly didn't care. Hugh provided her with refreshingly honest commentary on their sometimes suffocating world. He voiced her thoughts.

Candace flipped through the photos in her lap. She sighed. The usual suspects, indeed. There was Louise McCoy, the wife of Elder Pete, duller than an old nickel. Mary Flanagan, who wore sunset-colored caftans and belted with gospel affectation unbefitting a middle-aged white woman from Louisiana. Tanya Danziger, who fancied herself Mariah Carey's sister. As Hugh put it, "her much older, much fatter sister."

The music ministry had been borne of a vision. When Aaron and Candace joined Greenleaf twenty-five years ago, the few dozen members sang from musty hymnals inherited from a defunct Methodist church. But Aaron heard something different—not old saws wheezed out on organs and mouthed dutifully, but something exciting, something awesome. A band. With guitars and drums and professional singers.

"Our music could be a draw," he told the elders in a council meeting. "Why can't worship music be great? Why can't it make us so happy we dance in the aisles?"

The elders cheered. Back then, they stood in thrall of their charismatic new pastor, and they responded to his every suggestion with enthusiasm. After all, they had called him themselves.

They were a sorry lot. John Swain was an accused swindler, a financial planner acquitted on a technicality of fleecing clients in Maryland. He had found Jesus, relocated to Magnolia, and begun anew a life of service to Christ. The others had similarly straggled in from out of state, exiled or running from failed careers and ruined marriages, their faith battered but still somehow flickering. John and Pete and a few of the others met at a local Methodist church, where they discovered their common disenfranchisement over pound cake in the church basement, their shared longing for something more, something *else*. When John happened upon an abandoned theater in downtown Magnolia, he and the others knew they had found their spiritual home.

Now all they needed was a pastor.

Late one night twenty-five years ago, as a hurricane cleared its throat outside, the twelve elders gathered at the theater to pray. They knelt in a circle on the stage. They joined hands.

"Heavenly Father," said John, "we beseech you. Send us a son—"

"Or a daughter," muttered Simone.

"—to lead us," John continued. "If you hear us, call him. Tell him we await. If you hear us, send him a sign."

At that moment, a thousand miles away in Wilkes-Barre, Pennsylvania, Aaron Green awoke from a dead sleep.

Candace woke, too. Aaron usually slept like a baby—an expression she disliked, considering how their two babies slept, or didn't, and how her husband managed to snore through their midnight squalls. In those days, she felt his work as a Lutheran minister robbed her of his time, robbed her of assistance with two boys in diapers, robbed them all of the creature comforts they might afford on an even remotely reasonable income. In those days, she regarded his job with red resentment.

Aaron jerked upright, like that little girl in that horrible movie about the exorcism. His back quaked and he panted. When he turned to look at her, she could see the whites framing his irises.

She waited, unsettled but too fatigued for alarm. "What is it?" she asked.

"I don't know," he said, touching his face and looking at the sweat on his fingers. "I don't know."

The next night it happened again. And the following night, again.

"It's a sign," he told her over his morning coffee the next day.

Standing at the stove, Candace stirred Aaron's oatmeal in the pot with one hand while holding Timothy on her hip with the other. Anthony sat in his high chair spooning cereal into his hair, but Aaron didn't appear to notice.

After she was sure it would not come out a bark, she spoke. "A sign of what, dear? That you need to rest? That you need a physical? Remember what Dr. Sedavich told us the last time about coronary symptoms—"

"I didn't have three heart attacks on three consecutive nights at the same exact time," snapped Aaron. "Twelve-oh-one. I woke up each night at twelve-oh-one exact." He pushed up from the table then.

That was the first time he went away to pray. But she did not know that. All she knew was that he got in their rickety-rackety church Oldsmobile and vanished.

The seventy-two hours that followed tested Candace. Church members called and called, needing this, needing that. She handled them as best she could while the babies cried. She mentioned nothing of their missing pastor. At night she sat alone in the darkened den and shook.

After two days, she called the police. An officer was at the house when, on the third day, he returned. In her fury, Candace barely recognized him.

The Aaron who had left was an overworked, underinspired pastor ministering to an aging congregation in a traditional church at whose every stricture he chafed. The Aaron who returned was a shining vessel of God.

Returning home from his prayer retreat, Aaron had stopped at a gas station and bumped into a friend from seminary who had joined the evangelical movement. The classmate had in his hands a newsletter, which he showed to Aaron. A want ad for a pastor. A new church in Georgia. A bunch of recovering Lutherans and Methodists and Unitarians in an old theater. Calling themselves Greenleaf.

"You could answer," his friend said, pressing the newsletter into his hand. "Aaron Green of Greenleaf. Maybe it was written. Maybe it's a sign."

Candace did not know this yet. All she knew was that her husband, gone MIA, now stood on the threshold of their home, which was not their home at all but an annex of the church, a falling-down two-bedroom with mold in the wallpaper and their name in block-letter stickers on the mailbox, barely obscuring the block-letter name of the previous inhabitants. He stood soaked through with rain, his eyes alight with hope, but also with humility. As the police officer inside packed up his things, Aaron made an announcement to his wife.

"I need to begin again."

Candace clenched and unclenched her teeth. The officer held out some paperwork for her to sign, but she ignored him. She saw only her husband, the man to whom she'd pledged her life, the father of her children, the man who'd disappeared without a word for three days, returned to tell her the past few excruciating years had been nothing but a false start, asking for—no, demanding—a do-over.

Candace said, "Give me a day to pack."

A week later, Candace stood beside Aaron on a street lined with palm trees, in front of an abandoned theater, staring at an old-fashioned marquee with missing letters. It read:

WELCOM PASTR GREEN TO GR NL AF
WE CALD YOU CAM

* * *

"Abide with me; fast falls the eventide.
The darkness deepens; Lord with me abide.
When other helpers fail and comforts flee,
Help of the helpless, O—"

Candace nudged Hugh.
"Thank you," he called.

"—abide with me . . ."

"Thank you!"

Louise McCoy's voice trailed off, like a bagpipe leaking air. She squinted through rimless glasses into the seats. For a moment her eyes locked on Candace and narrowed in contempt. Or so it seemed to Candace.

"Thank you, Louise," Hugh called. "We'll be in touch."

Louise pivoted on her granny heels and plodded off the stage.

"Maybe next time, she'll pick a song written sometime in the last hundred years," said Hugh. "I guess we can be thankful it wasn't Gregorian chant."

Louise and her husband, Elder Pete, were forever trying to drag Greenleaf back to the times of Luther. They complained endlessly about the services, how the drum set hurt their ears and the smoke machines stung their eyes. Given their dissatisfaction, Candace wondered sometimes why they still clung to the church. Like rust. They clung like rust.

Candace touched her fingers to her temples. *Please, Imitrex. Do your job.*

"May I begin?"

Mary Flanagan wafted center stage, her eggplant-colored dress billowing around her eggplant-shaped body. Candace sighed and nodded.

Hugh raised his arm, and Tony, at the synthesizer, began the opening chords to what sounded like a spiritual. Hugh's elbow dug into Candace's arm as the zaftig white woman on stage began to sway.

> *"Oh, I woke up dis mornin wid mah mind*
> *An' it was stayed, stayed on Jay-sus . . ."*

Hugh's eyes bugged. Candace's mouth formed an O, which she covered with her hand. Mary Flanagan, of the Shreveport Flanagans, heiress to a sugar fortune, her skin the color of Splenda, her great-granddaddy a proud slave owner, was performing her very best approximation of a nineteenth-century Negro.

"Cain't hate yo neighbor wid yo mind
If you keep it stayed on Jay-sus . . ."

Candace smacked Hugh in the arm.

"Thank you!" said Hugh, jarred out of his horror. "Next!"

Tanya Danziger tottered on stage looking like a cocktail sausage balanced on toothpick legs. It appeared Tanya had invested in some hair extensions for the occasion. Hugh hissed, "Now she looks like Mariah Carey's older, fatter *brother*—in drag."

Candace closed her eyes and braced for some high C's in the key of D.

She had only herself to blame, thought Candace as Tanya wobbled off the stage and the parade of wannabes followed. It was thanks to Candace that the worship team excelled, and that so many aspired to its ranks. She was the one who'd secured the funding to pay for the professional musicians, the top-of-the-line instruments, the rehearsal studio. She was the one who'd convinced Aaron (not that it took much) to allot them more and more time during services. And she was the one who'd met with the record producer last month to score a contract for its first album. She'd even christened the band: Evergreen. Gave it kind of a hip vibe, if she did say so.

Hugh was tapping her arm. Candace opened her eyes.

"Giovanna Disantana," he said.

Disantana. She knew the name. Must be the daughter of Diandra, who had crispy skin and dressed like a flamingo and seemed to materialize wherever Candace most longed for privacy, on Bible retreats or at the lingerie store. But this daughter of hers looked nothing like her tropical cocktail of a mother. Giovanna stood at center stage with her back straight and her hands folded, her dark hair tied back in a loose ponytail. She wore a patterned sundress that reached to mid-calf, and a cap-sleeved sweater buttoned at the collar.

"Call the exterminator," said Hugh. "We have a church mouse."

He raised his arm. Tony opened with the chords of a song from *Godspell*. Giovanna looked calmly straight toward the judges.

"On the willows there . . ."

Hugh and Candace glanced at each other, their eyebrows aloft. How had Diandra Disantana, who had the voice of a donkey, produced a daughter with the voice of an angel?

"Who knew?" Hugh whispered.

Giovanna launched into the refrain, her voice soaring into its sweet spot.

"Sing us one of the songs of Zion . . ."

Candace sat back, steepled her fingers, and smiled.

* * *

At ten past six, Candace surveyed the scene.

She had set two places at the glass café table. The antique hydrangea and rose hips she'd arranged as a centerpiece in a ruby-red cracked-glass vase. She thought the persimmons at the base a creative touch. The sunset-colored linens she'd folded eloquently to evoke pinecones. She always double-plated, using an accent color for a base plate to echo the table's theme (today, burgundy). Three ice cubes for his glass, ginger ale on the counter.

The Greens never dined in their dining room. Aaron disliked its formality—"I don't want to feel like a guest in my own home," he said—so Candace had created this space, in a tiled nook overlooking the lake. Nothing pleased her so much as seeing Aaron's face ease when he sat down here to a beautiful meal.

The meal itself she had picked up from Bella's, Bella herself stepping out of the kitchen to offer up the wrapped containers. Aaron enjoyed fine food in fine surroundings, but restaurant dining meant visits from other patrons and another hour of wearing his public face. So Candace had devised this elegant solution.

With the pasta primavera, roasted garlic head, and fresh baguette warming in the oven, the tricolor salad dressed and tossed, Candace stepped to the powder room to freshen up. Never, not even as a teenager, did she waste a lot of time with mirrors. Plain people called beauty a blessing. *Judge not according to the appearance*, it said in John 7:24, but people did. Candace thought of her looks less as a gift and more as a tool. It loaned her great advantage in a world where she had been born to little.

She had not wasted it. It got her out, didn't it? To be precise, it got her Aaron, and he got her out, got her to Magnolia and to Paradise Estates. Their very own gated Eden.

"Honey, I'm home."

The Candace in the mirror lit up, and for a moment she was again the twenty-year-old daughter of a mirthless minister, the girl who had spotted her father's handsome young successor across a church basement in Wilkes-Barre. Here she was, half a lifetime later, and her heart still beat faster at the sound of his voice.

This man, she thought. This good man. This man of God. She would do anything for him. Anything.

Chapter Three

Ginger

In the dream, he dies quickly and without pain.

Timothy is driving home from work when suddenly he sees a mama possum in the road trailed by her bitty babies. He swerves to avoid the waddling balls of fur and the car launches into the swamp. His head smacks against the wheel and it's lights out before the car sinks into the murk. The policeman who comes to tell her the news hails Timothy Green a hero to roadside rodents. Ginger stands bravely at his graveside while everyone praises his selfless sacrifice. The widow's composure stands in marked contrast to the burbling mess that is her mother-in-law.

Ginger woke up with a smile.

It's not that she wanted her husband to die, she told herself as she tiptoed to the kitchen to warm some milk. Her toes curled on the tile. Timothy liked to keep the air blasting through the night. He said it helped him sleep, that she of all people should know he needed his rest. She'd forgotten that in his absence she could turn the thermostat back up.

The milk in the pan frothed, and Ginger poured it into a mug. She stopped for a moment, caught by the Greenleaf symbol emblazoned on its ceramic side. Even her cupboard couldn't escape the family brand.

She took the mug to an oversize armchair in the family room, the one by the bay window, where she read her Bible in her few daily moments of quiet. It sat there now on a small side table, her comfort, her respite. The leather-bound King James was from her mother, Ceecee, a wedding gift, a choice for once appropriate and appreciated. Though Ginger protected it with a pink plastic Bible cover she'd found in the Greenleaf bookstore, in these six years its binding had broken and its pages thinned to onionskin.

She settled onto the couch and opened the book. Ah. There. The book of Psalms. They were like old friends, the Psalms, each with specific counsel to mirror her needs—some for wisdom; some for thanksgiving; some for lament. Tonight she sought forgiveness for dreaming her husband dead.

Psalm 32. She read aloud, softly. *"Blessed is he whose transgression is forgiven, whose sin is covered."* Her finger scrolled down a few lines to her favorite part. *"Thou art my hiding place; thou shalt preserve me from trouble; thou shalt compass me about with songs of deliverance."*

Ginger leaned her head back and closed her eyes. *Thou shalt preserve me.* The words rolled around her mind like marbles, cool and with reassuring heft. *Thou shalt compass me about. Songs of deliverance.*

No, she did not want her husband dead. In her desolate moments, when charity deserted her, she blamed her predicament on her father, or rather the lack of him. She knew the lasting pain of growing up without one, and that was enough to keep her from wishing such a fate on anybody, let alone her own children.

Plus, she loved Timothy. Through it all, she loved him. Ginger Green was a good wife, a good Christian wife. She would never—*could* never—wish her husband dead.

But she did dream it. With regularity. She did fantasize, if only in her subconscious dreamscape, of a blissful, blameless escape.

If she allowed herself to flesh it out in her waking moments, the fantasy would continue like this:

Timothy would die, quickly and without pain, in some way by which no one could possibly find her at fault. There would be a funeral, small and simple. Aaron, her father-in-law, would hand her a check with many zeros. "Go on," he'd say. "Take it. Start anew." And Candace, once she'd controlled her wild bawling, would take both Ginger's hands. "You were a good wife to my Timothy," she'd blubber, "and you're a good mother to his children." Afterward Ginger would pack Jordan, Talitha, and their things into a car—any car but the church Prius—and drive into the sunset.

She would be free. Free of Greenleaf. Free of Candace. Free of this life. Free of a husband who was never home, never available, never hers or the children's alone. Free of pretending to be this perfect woman, this saint, this pastor's wife.

Eyes still closed, Ginger shook her head and asked herself how it had come to this. How had she come to think her husband's life a fair price for her freedom?

Deep down, she knew the answer. Widowhood was the easy way out. Escape without the recrimination and stain of that other exit, the exit she decided in this very moment she was heading for: divorce.

"Mommy?"

Ginger opened her eyes. Jordan had fumbled into the family

room. Without his glasses, she knew, she would be a blur. His coarse brown hair tufted up like a crazy person's.

She patted her lap. He shuffled over and curled up against her. Upon his fifth birthday he'd suddenly spurted, and his legs dangled off the armrests. "Couldn't sleep?"

"I had a bad dream," he said. He sniffed her collarbone, a weird little habit from infancy that somehow always calmed him. "Did you have a bad dream, too?"

Ginger stroked her boy's paintbrush hair. "Yes," she said. "Mommy had a bad dream."

* * *

3 family-size bags of pretzels
10-pack Bounty
2 cases Juicy Juice (NOT Capri Sun—too sugary!)
Bakery order, 50 cupcakes, under "Green"

Ginger pondered Candace's neat, tiny penmanship, etched on a sheet of ivory notepaper crowned with her initials—*CFG*—in forest green. She imagined her mother-in-law sitting at the antique secretary desk in her home study, back perfectly straight, child-sized hands holding her favorite Cross pen, making out the list. After she finished, Candace probably surveyed the list and added that Capri Sun note. Even a Costco shopping list was a teaching opportunity.

"What a sweetie," someone said, and Ginger looked up. A middle-aged woman whose bosom strained her Atlanta Braves T-shirt cooed at Talitha, who grinned obligingly from the child seat in the shopping cart. The woman looked at Ginger. "God bless her."

Ginger inhaled. This, she knew, was an opening. She could respond with, "God bless *you*." And then—"Have I seen you at church?"

The woman would tell her the name of her church. If it wasn't Greenleaf or Timothy's offshoot, Newleaf—or if she didn't belong anywhere in particular—Ginger could take the opportunity to invite the stranger for a service or a tour. That's what a true evangelist would do: Remain ever on the lookout for new souls to save. More important, that's what a good pastor's wife would do.

Instead, Ginger froze. The woman chucked Tali's chin once again, touched her hand to her heart in a gesture that said, "I can't bear the cuteness," and wandered off toward the electronics aisle.

Another failure.

Tali made a smacking noise. "Hungry," she said.

Ginger dug around in the diaper bag and came up with only a two-pack of soup saltines. "Oh, noodles," she muttered, as she remembered the Ziploc bag of animal crackers sitting on the kitchen counter. The thought of an almost-two-year-old's hunger tantrum in the middle of Costco kick-started Ginger into action. She handed Tali the saltines, looked at the list again, and gunned the cart toward the bakery section.

As she always did on errands to the warehouse store, Ginger marveled at the massive quantities of stuff. Jugs packed with a thousand tablets of aspirin. Vats of ketchup. One-hundred-count packs of frozen chicken wings. Every Christian she knew shopped here, and now she wondered if it was because they knew something she didn't: Maybe they were preparing for End Times. With a one-ton sack of nachos and a hundred miles of toilet paper, who couldn't ride out the Apocalypse?

"Cupcakes under Green?" she asked the man behind the bakery counter.

He disappeared for a moment and returned with a large, flat box. "Fifty, right?"

Ginger shook her head in disbelief. What two-year-old knew fifty people? But then, it wasn't Tali's party—not really.

The baker appeared puzzled. Then she remembered his question. "No, I mean, yes, that's us."

The cupcakes were iced to appear as one enormous cake. A bunch of animated produce pranced on the icing, characters Ginger recognized from *VeggieTales*. Candace disapproved of secular television for her grandchildren, but she allowed DVDs of that Christian children's show.

"Look, baby," said Ginger, as the man held up the cake. "It says, 'Happy Birthday Talitha.'"

Tali's eyes widened with glee. She reached for the cake. "Hungry?"

"No, that's not for now," said Ginger, motioning for the man to place the box in the cart.

Tali's eyes filled and her fists balled. "Hungry!"

Lord help me, thought Ginger.

The baker took pity. "Here you go, sweetheart," he said, handing the baby a sugar doughnut. Tali grabbed it and jammed half into her mouth. Ginger threw the man a grateful look as she turned the cart and pushed as swiftly as she could toward the cashier. On the way she passed another mother dragging a shrieking toddler by the wrist. There but for the grace of God, she thought.

In the parking lot, she wedged the cupcakes into the undersized trunk of the Greenleaf Prius. A few years ago, Aaron Green read a book about America's reliance on fossil fuels and how it affected foreign policy and interfaith relations. He promptly ordered the senior staff to return the Cadillac Escalades leased for them by the church, and replaced them with Toyota Priuses, the most fuel-efficient car on the market, each car a sage green with a little gold leaf stenciled on its side. The move prompted such a run on Priuses by the congregation that the local dealers had six-month-long waiting lists. As churchgoers gazed at her car with longing, Ginger wished she could tell them she'd trade it in a heartbeat for a beat-up Chrysler minivan.

Only after she'd buckled a sticky-faced Tali into her car seat did Ginger realize she'd forgotten the Bounty. And the juice boxes. And the pretzels.

In the six years since she'd been saved, she had never cursed. The four-letter words that once rolled off her tongue now resided in an unmarked tomb of memories, along with the unlovely bones of her former life. But if ever there was a time to slip off the wagon, it was now.

Instead, standing next to Tali's open car door, Ginger did the next best thing. She stamped her feet, punched the air, and scrunched her face. She blurted: "Shrek! Marketing! Fluffernutter!"

She opened her eyes to Tali staring at her. "You didn't hear that," Ginger told her.

Ginger thought hard. Probably she had five minutes before the cupcakes would start melting, locked up in the car in this Georgia heat. The clock was ticking.

She snatched Tali out of her car seat. She ran back into Costco, stuffing the baby into another shopping cart and careening through the store toward sundries. When she emerged again, heaving like a racehorse, sweat spitting from her face, Ginger checked her watch. Fourteen minutes. The lines. Slow cashier.

"Oh, mother of turtles—the cupcakes!"

She held Tali as she opened the car trunk and held her breath. Together they peeked inside.

* * *

"This doesn't look like *VeggieTales*, Mamie," said Jordan. "It looks like a cauliflower mugging a porcupine. In a hurricane."

Candace gave her grandson a look, as if wondering at the mysteries of a five-year-old imagination. Then she leaned closer to look at the cake.

Jordan stood next to his grandmother and read the iced inscription aloud. "Herpy Brndoh Tolitba."

Ginger held her breath.

"Hmph," said Candace, frowning. "Costco. I knew I should've gone with the Cupcake Café."

Ginger exhaled.

Someone called from the front door. Candace reached for Tali. "Come on, birthday princess," she said. "Let's go greet your guests."

Ginger had spent the past hour decorating Candace's house in yellow ribbons and pink balloons. Candace's florist had arrived early with bouquets of daffodils and tea roses. The humidity ruled out use of the deck, which was a shame, as Ginger loved to lean out over the lake and pretend she was at sea. But Candace's guests would prefer their gourmet canapés in crisp air-conditioning.

Ginger looked toward the front of the house at the faces she vaguely recognized streaming into her daughter's second birthday party, and felt the old anxiety well up. If only Timothy were here. He worked magic with crowds, diving in, hand extended, eyes engaged. He was his father's son. Jordan, on the other hand, suffered his mother's shyness, while Talitha was just about ready to run for office.

Still, Ginger was grateful. Candace knew how to throw a party, while she—well, she could just about manage dinner for four. Every child deserved a birthday celebration, and Candace would know how to do it right. Ginger had zero experience with these things. Growing up, the most Ceecee could ever swing for her was a sundae at Friendly's. Candace had proper candles and party hats and a growing mountain of festively wrapped gifts. There was talk of a face-painting clown.

No, this was best. Just look at Tali's shining face. The toddler preened in her grandmother's arms, the new tea-rose taffeta dress Candace had procured from Lili Gaufrette poufed out adorably around her diapered rump. And look at Candace. Mamie, as she had decreed the children would call her, as if Magnolia were a suburb of Paris. However much her mother-in-law terrorized her, Ginger softened whenever she saw Candace with the grandchildren. With Tali's chubby arm slung casually around her neck as together they greeted guests, Candace looked like she could float with pride and joy.

Besides, a birthday at home would mean a guest list of three: Ginger, Jordan, and Tali.

Timothy was abroad again, on another mission. Besides planting Newleaf, Timothy had founded and led Faith Corps, an organization helping people in strife. There were many Christian aid groups, of course, but his didn't just send money. He required volunteers to venture to the torn lands, carrying gauze bandages and mosquito nets and Bibles. It meant frequent and often spontaneous trips to Somalia. Indonesia. Chile. Iraq. And now, today, on his daughter's second birthday—Haiti, devastated by an awful earthquake.

She closed her eyes and remembered their conversation the night before he left.

"Fifty thousand dead, Gin," Timothy had reminded her, as he stuffed a duffel with protein bars, iodine, and soap. "And that's just the government figures. So far."

Ginger sat on their bed and hugged her knees. "It's just Tali," she said miserably. "Her birthday and all."

Timothy was counting the bandages. "She won't even notice I'm not there," he said.

"I will," Ginger mumbled.

"Hm?"

"Nothing. Don't forget the antibacterial socks your mom got you. She'll ask."

Timothy moved on to counting small electronic gadgets. Faith Corps had recently partnered with a company that created audio Bibles, aimed not just at the iPod crowd but also at illiterate people around the globe. The tiny MP3 players were called FlashBibles and came with earbuds. Charlton Heston narrated the English version.

"She'll be two," he said through a pen clamped in his teeth. "She'll have, what, sixteen more birthdays under my roof. At least."

Ginger didn't trust herself to respond. Instead she watched him move around the room on his knees, jotting down inventory on his BlackBerry, eyes squinting in concentration. He pushed a hand through his coarse brown hair, and it tufted up like a crazy person's. The resemblance between father and son should have made her smile.

Finally he looked up at her. A twitch in his right cheek betrayed his irritation. "Honey, don't give me that face," he said.

Still on his knees, he hobbled over to the bed. He placed his hands on her bare feet. They felt as warm and dry as a towel after a soaking rain. She closed her eyes. How long had it been since she'd felt his skin on hers?

"This is my work," he said, in that voice like a breeze through the reeds. She opened her eyes and gazed into the face of the only man she'd ever loved. "It's *His* work." Timothy's voice picked up excitement. "Think of all the people suffering over there. Think of the help we can bring. Think of the souls we can save. Man, are we *blessed*."

He let go of her feet, sprang up and into the bathroom. With the hem of her T-shirt she wiped away her tears.

* * *

The clown couldn't make it. In his place, he was sending his colleague, billed as a children's storyteller.

Candace tapped her cell phone against the kitchen counter. Her mouth formed a thin, straight line. Ginger edged away.

"You'd think a Christian business would keep its word," Candace said softly. "A storyteller. What in heaven's name is that?"

Ginger didn't answer. She'd learned the hard way that when Candace spoke in her presence, she should not presume to respond. When Candace asked what appeared for all intents and purposes to be a question that no one but Ginger was around to answer, the question was usually rhetorical.

Her mother-in-law had disliked Ginger on sight, but then a lot of women did. "Nobody respects a redhead," Ceecee told her from before she could remember. "The boys want to screw you and the girls want to kill you." That didn't bother Ceecee at all. When her natural copper tones faded, Ginger's mother gleefully spiked her own head with Manic Panic Vampire Red. As for her daughter, Ceecee named her without apparent irony. "Say it loud, say it proud," she always said. "I'm red till I'm dead."

But it wasn't just that. When women met Ginger, they saw in this order: hair the color of a Miami sunrise; Julia Roberts smile; boobs. That was where the head-to-toe sweep-over stopped cold. If the women could bring themselves to continue, they noted a hand-span waist and Barbie-doll legs, which of course did not help. But the Barbarella D cups were usually all they needed to conclude that she was not a woman to trust.

With Candace, the evaluation had been more subtle, if just as swift and fatal. When Timothy first introduced Ginger to his parents, two days after they had met and a few weeks before he proposed, his mother eyed his son's date while wearing a smile Ginger mistook as welcoming. She later realized Candace presented the same beatific smile to many people on many diverse occasions, and like that famous painting in France from that Tom Hanks movie, her smile conveyed what the viewer wanted to see.

The day they met, the Miami sky was that shade of springtime blue so sharp it stung her eyes. Ginger had selected a short, form-fitting shift with a tulip print, paired with flat gold sandals and a light summer cardigan. An outfit for a lunch date with a new man at an outdoor café: cute but with the promise of sex.

When Timothy showed up, he pulled from behind his back a bouquet of gerbera daisies—and his parents. Aaron Green, *the* Aaron Green, beamed at her, then was immediately ambushed by a well-wisher at the next table.

"And this," announced Timothy, "is my mother, Candace."

Ginger kept a photograph in her head of that first glimpse of Candace Green. Candace stood at the side of the round table, her blue-black hair curled away from her valentine-shaped face. She wore a short-sleeved silk sweater the color of the ocean with a matching cardigan tossed over her shoulders like a cape, a white knee-length skirt, and white open-toed pumps. Her green eyes looked deep into Ginger's.

Once she became a mother, there were a few things Ginger would come to understand about Candace. One was that look. Candace did not look at Ginger the way many women did, with envy and competition, assessing the threat level to their man. Upon that first meeting, Candace looked at the younger woman as a mama fox would a snake intent on swallowing her young. She may as well have bared her teeth.

Candace spoke like a librarian, hushed and refined. "I understand you met at the magazine event," she said.

Timothy was in Miami to attend a party toasting *Glamour* magazine's Hottest Bachelors issue. Ginger, having recently quit her former career, had picked up a gig tending the party's open bar. She didn't even know the nature of the festivities when she put on her uniform. This being Miami, the uniform consisted of a black bikini top and low-slung jeans.

"Make sure you do that thing a lot," said the event manager, a greasy-haired guy named Donnie, demonstrating. "You know that thing, where you shucka-shucka the cocktail shaker over your shoulder."

Ginger nodded. So long as it didn't involve a pole, she thought.

The party and its honored guests attracted the usual horde of barely dressed Miami husband hunters. As the party got louder,

Ginger tried without making it too obvious to ignore the women's shrieked orders in favor of the men. Even at an open bar, guys could be counted on to tip generously and place simple orders that didn't necessitate curaçao and crushed mint leaves. As her tip purse bulged, Ginger congratulated herself on good business strategy. Now that she was on her own, she could sure use the money.

"Could I get a soda?"

Ginger considered ignoring the call—sodas weren't exactly a big tip generator—but the guy caught her glancing at him. Plus he accompanied his order with a nice smile, his eyes on hers and not on her breasts.

She filled a glass with ice and club soda, and motioned at the tray of lemon and lime wedges. The man shook his head. He took the glass and extended a few singles, which she waved away.

He kept his elbows on the bar. The party had peaked an hour ago, and some of the honorees were leaving, many with drunken vixens on their arms.

She began to wipe some glasses, warily eyeing the man. He looked amused but tired. He appeared to be around her age, in his early twenties, with tanned skin, not Miami bronze but the walnut brown of someone who spent a lot of time outdoors. His hair was tousled and in need of a cut. His eyes were a spectacular aquamarine, and when he smiled the skin crinkled at their edges.

Ginger was not one to initiate conversation with a man. Plus, Donnie had warned them against fraternizing with party guests, and that suited Ginger just fine. But something about him told her it would be all right.

"You look like you're glad it's over," she said, raising her voice a little to be heard.

He laughed. "I am—whew," he said, pretending to wipe his

brow. "I felt like an open buffet at a bulimia convention." Then immediately he frowned. "I'm sorry. That was in poor taste."

She grinned and shook her head. "I don't throw up my food."

"Well, then," he said, looking around. "Care to join me in finding some?"

Some people say they find Jesus at church. Others cite the birth of a child, the loss of a job, the peaks and troughs of human experience unattributable to fate alone. Ginger found God when this good man looked in her eyes late the night they met and told her that he loved her. Twisted up in Timothy's hotel sheets, her body and history laid bare before him, Ginger did not choose faith. Faith chose her.

* * *

"There's my Talisaurus."

Tali squealed as she ran from Ginger's side to the kitchen entrance. Anthony, Timothy's brother, scooped her up. "Uncle Anty!" she cried.

"No, *I'm* the Auntie," said Sophie. Ginger couldn't see her sister-in-law behind Anthony's bulk, but who else did she know with a French accent? Sophie squeezed in past her husband carrying an armful of gorgeously wrapped presents.

Candace clapped her hands. Her mouth broke free of its bleak horizon into a sunrise of genuine delight. "You made it! But I thought you weren't back till next week."

"And miss our baby girl's second birthday?" said Anthony. Tali pulled at his nose, and he obliged by honking. She cackled. "Team cut us loose early."

"And my season got scaled back," said Sophie, sighing. "We lost a major sponsor."

"I saw it in the papers," said Candace to Sophie, laying a commiserating hand on her flower-stem arm. Archly, to Anthony: "I may not read the sports pages, but I do read the arts."

"Ginger, this is for the kids," said Sophie. She leaned in to air-kiss Ginger, and only after they pulled apart did Ginger realize—*voilà*—she was left holding the pile of gifts. "Three for Tali, and one for Jordan. So he does not feel left out." Sophie plucked a small box off the top, one wrapped in especially exquisite paper the color of new grass and bound with a few twists of twine. She turned to Candace. "And this one is for you."

"*Moi?*" Candace placed a hand on her chest. "Whatever for?"

"For being so *magnifique*," said Sophie, squeezing Candace's shoulders. Standing side by side, tiny shoulder to tiny shoulder, they looked like they could be fairy sisters.

Candace opened the parcel. Inside was a glass teapot along with a satchel of marijuana. No, no, it would be tea, of course. Loose tea. She cradled it in her hands and held it up to the light.

"I found a boutique on tour and thought of you," said Sophie.

"You thought of me," Candace marveled. "Unlike your husband, who never even remembers to call."

Anthony laughed as he turned toward the party, still carrying Tali. "Where's the cake?" he said. "I was promised cake."

That was Anthony, thought Ginger—shrugging off disapproval and thereby dismissing it, smiling and wiping away another's frown. If her husband was a comet hurtling across the night sky, his brother was the moon: dependable, functional, universally beloved. While both brothers' drivers' licenses recorded their heights at six feet, Timothy weighed at least forty pounds less, his body all copper wire and iron rods. Yes, Anthony had pursued the career in sports. But Ginger knew it was Timothy who'd dazzled coaches on the soccer fields of their youth, a rocket engine of speed and determination. Baseball suited Anthony, who was built for power and lots of sitting around. He shifted Tali so her foot rested atop his bubble butt.

Sophie tucked her arm through Candace's. "Come, *Maman*," she said. "We better make sure he does not hoover the whole thing." They trooped out into the crowd of guests, leaving Ginger standing alone in the kitchen, holding a pyramid of presents.

Mom, thought Ginger. She calls her Mom.

When it came to her sister-in-law, Ginger could not help but think of Martha and Mary, the sisters of Lazarus. Jesus stopped at their house on his journey, as Luke told it, and while Martha ran around cooking and cleaning to make him comfortable, her little sister, Mary, just sat at his feet and lapped up his every word. When Martha complained, Jesus told her this:

> *"Martha, Martha, thou art careful and troubled about many things: But one thing is needful: and Mary hath chosen that good part, which shall not be taken away from her."*

The pattern established itself a few years ago, shortly after Anthony and Sophie married, on a family trip to Hawaii paid for by Aaron and Candace. The cross-country flight and the puddle-jumper to the Big Island battered Ginger, who was heavily pregnant with Talitha. She flew alone with Jordan, who threw up on both flights. Timothy planned to meet them there on his way back from a Faith Corps mission to tsunami victims in Thailand.

By the time she arrived by taxi at the rented condo on the Kailua coast, the others had already settled in. Sophie was entertaining them by reenacting an embarrassing spill one of the male dancers had taken in the ballet, one that resulted in his tights splitting on stage. They were laughing so hard it took a while before they noticed Ginger in the doorway hauling a passed-out Jordan and kicking along their luggage.

Sophie looked radiant. She wore a sarong wrapped around her ballerina body and a matching red hibiscus behind her ear. Her dark-chocolate hair, usually constrained in a tidy bun or ponytail, rippled to the vicinity of her waist, if she had one.

Ginger retreated to their room, gathered together their vomit-caked clothes, and went to find the laundry. There she found a basket with everyone else's dirty travel clothes, so she washed those, too.

And that pretty much summed up the week for Ginger. The others sampled five kinds of Kona coffee; she swept up the grounds. They snorkeled in the clear blue grotto; she made sand castles with Jordan. They took a midnight helicopter tour of a live volcano; she watched TV as her son slept.

The one thing she didn't do was cook. Cooking for a crowd took a degree of confidence that Ginger most certainly lacked. She left that to Candace, who assembled macadamia-encrusted ahi and sliced mango salad one night, barbecued skewers of pork and fresh pineapple another.

One afternoon, Candace came in, tired from playing with Jordan in the surf. "Roast the chicken, will you?" she called to Ginger as she headed toward the master suite for a nap.

Ginger opened the fridge. There indeed was a whole chicken, maybe a twelve-pounder, just sitting and staring at her like the pimply white face of a teenager.

She stared back. And asked of it, "How?"

In Ginger's experience, chicken came in pieces, barbecued or fried. So she supposed you began by cutting the thing up. In the drawer she found some paring knives, a bread knife, and a cleaver. She touched her finger to the blades, blunted from years of use by who knows how many other vacationers. These could barely cut butter. Here goes nothing, she thought.

An hour later, Ginger stood in the kitchen, both hands over her head, wielding the cleaver. Chicken carcass littered the counter. Poultry blood pooled. Bits of fat speckled the tile backsplash.

"Oh. My."

Candace stood in the kitchen doorway, looking fresh as an orchid, skin dewy from a shower, eyes wide with—what? Shock? Bafflement? Disgust?

Before Ginger could speak, Candace swept in. She cranked the oven to four hundred and pulled a large baking dish out of a cabinet. She washed and wiped dry the chicken pieces, dashed them with sea salt and pepper, then threw them into the baking dish. She smashed some garlic cloves with the blunt end of one of the clean paring knives, peeled them, and tossed them into a bowl along with a handful of fresh pineapple sage. She drizzled in olive oil, then rubbed the mixture over the chicken limbs. When all the pieces were coated, she shoved it all into the oven and slammed the door shut with her hip.

The whole ballet took less than ten minutes. Ginger watched without saying a word. Then she turned around and went to shower off the poultry particles.

It was a year before she screwed up the courage to tell Timothy her version of the week—the humiliation of going to Hawaii so she could be the family maid. But he just laughed.

"Gin," he said fondly, tucking her hair back from her face. "No one asked you to do all that stuff."

Which, once she thought about it, was pretty much what Jesus told Martha.

While Ginger hustled to Costco and picked up dry-cleaning for her in-laws, Sophie flitted in when she pleased and soaked up their love and affection. But—and this was what stung—who had Ginger to blame but herself? Timothy was right. No one had asked her to play the dutiful daughter-in-law. She had taken on that role on her own.

Mary hath chosen the good part. And Martha hath chosen the laundry.

* * *

The storyteller arrived at the same time as Jeremiah and Ruthie Matters.

Ginger observed as Candace assessed and then handled the situation. First, Candace welcomed the new associate pastor and his wife with signature grace into her home. She asked Jordan to fetch Poppy, and the boy skittered off obediently, presently pulling Aaron by the hand to take in the new guests. Only then did Candace turn to the sour-looking woman dressed in a jumble of rags that Ginger could only hope was a costume.

"The storyteller, I presume," Candace said. "Come with me."

Ginger watched, fascinated, until Aaron stepped into her line of vision.

"And this is Ginger, my other daughter-in-law," he said, his hand on her arm.

Ginger smiled automatically. The couple smiled back. She heard the young pastor liked to go by Jerry. Ruthie, the wife, was as tall as she was.

"Ginger, Ginger, Ginger," Ruthie mumbled.

Jerry was grinning. "You'll have to excuse my wife," he said. "She has a hard time with names."

"And a house full of people to meet," said Ruthie, looking with some despair toward the living room. She turned back to Ginger. "Is it rude to ask for business cards at a birthday party, do you think?"

Ginger didn't even try for a witty response. She was never much the talker anyway, but lately her company consisted for the most part of two children under six, and she'd learned the banter muscle weakens without regular exercise. Candace told her the new couple was from New York. No way she could keep up with New York repartee.

Aaron took Jerry by the arm to lead him into the fray. Jerry glanced back at Ruthie. Their eyes met. His asked: You okay? Hers answered: Go, I'm fine.

That. That wordless communication between partners, the silent signals of caring, the checking in during strange situations. *That* was what Ginger craved.

She watched Ruthie watch Jerry. She recognized that small smile, that look among pastors' wives, a wistful pride as her beloved left her side to attend to God's work.

Alone with Ruthie, Ginger recalled Timothy's advice on meeting strangers: When in doubt, ask questions. "How was your move?"

"You mean how *is* our move," said Ruthie, making a face. "We just got in last night. I woke up this morning drowning in boxes. It's death by bubble wrap."

"I could help, if you want," said Ginger shyly. "I'm on Golden. Candace said you're on Luck, which is around the corner."

"Well, that *is* golden luck," said Ruthie, looking pleased. "This place—Paradise Estates. The name's so apt. The lake, the lawns. It truly is paradise."

"Once you dig out from the bubble wrap," said Ginger, surprising herself. That wasn't half-bad.

Ruthie laughed. "Oh, before you think us horribly uncouth," she said, "we failed to bring a birthday gift. But I promise I'll make it up, once I locate the closest Toys "R" Us."

"Just make sure it's not anything made in China," said Ginger. She was on a roll. "Candace is the leading expert on arsenic in toys."

Together they looked toward the living room, where Candace hovered around the storyteller, herding the children and telling guests where to sit and stand.

"Protective grandma, huh?" Ruthie smiled, and Ginger thought she looked a little wistful again.

They moved closer, toward the edge of the ring of children sitting on the floor. The storyteller held her arms up for silence. The children, trained in Sunday school, complied.

"Once upon a time," the woman began in an overly theatrical voice, "there was a man named Noah."

"I know Noah!" cried a boy Ginger knew from the neighborhood. "And the ark!"

The storyteller broke character. Slowly she turned to the boy. "What's your name?"

"Taylor."

"Taylor. Are you going to tell the story?"

Ginger heard Ruthie give a little gasp.

"No," said Taylor, shrinking back.

"Right. Where was I? Noah. One day, God came to him and said"—and now the woman assumed a deep, booming voice—

"'Noah, you must build a great ship. A flood is coming. You must select two of every animal, a male and a female, and put them on your ship.'"

"Is the ship the same as an ark?" Ruthie whispered to Ginger.

The storyteller glared in their direction. Ruthie gripped Ginger's arm in mock terror. Ginger pursed her lips to stop from giggling.

"You!" Both Ruthie and Ginger jumped, but the storyteller was pointing at Jordan, sitting nearby.

"Me?" Jordan whispered.

"You," she said. "Be the elephant."

Jordan looked back at his mother. He would sooner die.

The storyteller continued to point, like Moses on the hill. "Be. The. Elephant."

"Be. The. Grown-up," Ruthie hissed. "Can't she see he's terrified?"

Tali jumped up. "I do!" she shouted. "I do ollie-font!" She waved an arm in front of her face and trumpeted.

The storyteller appeared to weigh the crime against a suitable punishment. Finally she rolled her eyes and moved on. "You!" she said, pointing to a cowering little girl. "Be the goat."

When all the children in the room had been bullied into emitting an animal sound, the storyteller continued. "All the people made fun of Noah and his giant ark." She raised her voice to a simper, acting out the role of the clueless civilian. "'Ooo, look at Noah and his big, dumb boat!'"

The children tittered nervously, but gulped back their giggles when the storyteller resumed her stern visage.

"Then the rains began. Noah herded the animals on deck. The people cried for Noah to help them. Go on," she barked at the children. "Beg. Beg me for a spot on the ark!"

Ruthie and Ginger inhaled.

"Please," said Taylor, torn between obedience and stone-cold fear. "Please let me get on."

The storyteller smirked at Taylor. "No!" she shouted. "Never!"

Taylor began to cry.

The storyteller's eyes narrowed at the little boy and her face turned an alarming shade of purple.

"She's gonna blow!" Ruthie whispered.

At that moment, Candace stepped directly in front of the woman, so close that the storyteller's nose poked into the back of Candace's hair. Ginger twisted her neck around to see. Yep. Her mother-in-law's spike heels dug squarely into the storyteller's toes.

"Now watch this," Ginger said to Ruthie.

Candace faced the children, her face aglow with reassuring kindness. She clapped twice. "Time for cake!" she announced.

They bounced to their feet. As they scattered, Candace caught Taylor by the shoulder and bent down to his eye level. "You," she told him solemnly, "are quite the actor. I'm going to tell your mother I want you to try out for the Christmas pageant this year." She wiped a tear from his cheek. He beamed.

When the children cleared out, Candace turned to the story-teller. She rotated on her heels, slowly, twisting, driving spikes into toes. Crucifixion by stiletto.

Finally, Candace faced the storyteller, their noses a few inches apart. She gathered the entertainer's hands in her own. All color had seeped from the woman's face. Ginger almost pitied her.

"Are you familiar," said Candace, in a voice Ginger and Ruthie had to strain to hear, "with Matthew 18?"

The woman shook her head.

Candace nodded and closed her eyes as if to summon the verse.

"Take heed that ye despise not one of these little ones; for I say unto you, that in heaven their angels do always behold the face of my Father which is in heaven."

With her eyes still closed, she held the storyteller's hands a moment longer. When she opened them, they glinted like Kryptonite.

The storyteller's voice shook. "Amen?"

Candace tipped her head toward the door. The woman bolted.

"She'll never work again," said Ginger.

Ruthie gaped. They watched as Candace smoothed her blouse, touched her hair, and arranged her face in a smile. Then she turned to the children clamoring for cake.

"Wow," Ruthie said. "I think I'm in love."

"Good luck with that," said Ginger.

Chapter Four

Ruthie

I n the many years during which I'd spent a portion of Sunday with my butt on a wooden pew, I had come to accept three facts about church.

1. Of the 168 hours that comprise a week, the one spent there was definitely, without question, absolutely by far the longest.
2. The pulpit was no place for original thought.
3. There's no such thing as a good hymn. There just isn't.

Most of the pews I had occupied resided in a church of the Catholic persuasion, but I'd done some time in Protestant services, too, accompanying Jerry on what I called his Great Church Search. I'd sat in a Baptist church and a Presbyterian church and a Unitarian church. My brother Paul loves to repeat this story: Once, by mistake, I attended Christmas Eve Mass at Saint John the Divine cathedral in upper Manhattan, which I assumed to be Catholic and not Episcopal. Cut me a break here. Cathedral equals Catholic, does it not?

My error came to light during the processional, when I realized a few members of the clergy looked possibly female.

There were some differences between Catholic and Protestant proceedings, of course. The order of events. The style of the sermons. The gender of the person at the pulpit. And I had some notion of the fundamental disagreements that had caused the denominations to split off in the first place.

But what threw me were the little things. For instance, the phrasing of recited prayer. It just felt, I don't know, *wrong* when the words were arranged even a little differently. Like walking into your favorite supermarket after a store renovation. Following the Lord's Prayer at a Methodist service, I blurted out, "For the kingdom, the power . . . ," causing the old lady in front of me to turn around. Who knew?

In the end, though, here's what I concluded: Aside from a few tweaks in the script, all church services tell the same story. Same set. Same camera angle. Same score. Similar actors in similar costumes. Even the female ministers look kind of mannish. You have to admit.

So to say I was unprepared for my first Sunday experience at Greenleaf Church is not an understatement so much as a profound revelation.

Jerry and I woke early that Sunday in September, our first Sunday in Magnolia. We maneuvered around the moving boxes and sheets of bubble wrap toward the kitchen, where Jerry had set up the coffeemaker the previous night with grounds we'd bought on a late-night run to the 7-Eleven. Chock Full O' Nuts. Not exactly Zabar's fresh-ground Colombian, but as a caffeine delivery system, it would do.

My forward-thinking husband—formerly known as my anally retentive husband, which isn't as gracious, and I was striving for gracious these days—had already located the boxes that held our churchgoing wardrobes. Or, to be more precise, our work clothes. Neither of our religious traditions made much of a distinction between suits worn on Sunday and Monday.

"You look nice, honey," I said, as we paused on our way out the door.

He did. My husband looked handsome in his light wool summer suit, a gray so dark it read black. He had dampened his longish hair and combed it neatly back, or as neatly as the waves would allow. His cheeks were shorn pink. He had selected a seaweed-green tie with a pindot pattern. Clever touch, I thought, scanning my own black A-line dress and regretting the lack of green anywhere. Somewhere in these boxes that held our lives was a feathery silk scarf the color of leaves in springtime, a thoughtful accent that would have said I cared enough to note the church's signature color. Damn.

Sensing my uncertainty, Jerry put his hand on the door I had just opened and closed it again. He circled one arm around my waist and drew me in close, touching his forehead to mine. His two eyes soon merged in my vision, as I knew mine did in his. Mr. and Mrs. Cyclops.

"Thank you," he said.

"For what?"

"For coming on this journey with me."

With that, he planted on me a sweet, brief kiss. Then we opened the door to our new world.

There was so much to get used to. The wet heat that blasted me when I stepped outside. The little green Prius with the strange, blade-free key. The house, so new and unmarred it looked like a facade on a Hollywood set.

As the car rolled silently down Luck Lane, I spotted other families getting into cars identical to our own parked in driveways identical to our own. Ginger told me Greenleaf had bought up a number of properties in Paradise Estates to be occupied by senior church officers. Good thing the place is gated, I thought. What with all the residents at service, every burglar in town would know that Sunday is payday.

"Good morning, Mr. Matters, Mrs. Matters," called the guard in the security booth as he pushed a button to open the gate.

"Good morning, Horatio," said Jerry, waving. When had my husband managed to learn the guard's name?

A winding road lined with palm trees took us out to a main thoroughfare called Prospect Street. We passed a strip mall with a Kroger supermarket, a Ford dealership, and a seafood restaurant called Uncle Jack's Out Fishin'. No building stood taller than two stories; nothing obscured the cloudless sky. Nothing, that is, until we came to a stoplight, and a billboard cast a shadow on my arm.

I smushed my cheek against the window to check it out. It was one of those high-tech billboards with the digital screen, its message changing every few seconds. As I watched, letters curled onto the screen in a languorous cursive:

Believe

Then:

Belong

Then:

Be Loved

Then:

Greenleaf Church
All are welcome
Turn left here.

I looked left. And there it was.

"Greenleaf," I breathed. I looked closer. "Or is that a mall?"

Maybe it's the Jersey girl talking, but the church looked like a Macy's or maybe a Nordstrom, the anchor store in an upscale suburban shopping center. Nothing on its blank concrete face indicated religious affiliation—no cross or crucifix or dangling cherubim. In fact, the only apparent signage was a single green neon leaf, high above the main entrance. Like it had floated down and alighted there from some electronic heaven.

Jerry chuckled but didn't answer. When the light changed, we joined a crush of cars bottlenecked at an entrance to the church parking area. I craned my neck toward a uniformed worker directing traffic. "Is that a cop?"

"Guess so," said Jerry, distracted, focused on the proximity of bumpers. Sure enough, three squad cars manned each entrance to Greenleaf, with uniformed officers sweating in the sun to organize churchgoers.

"Funny," I said.

"Hm?"

"Guess I wouldn't have thought church traffic a police matter."

When an officer noticed our green Prius with the gold leaf emblem, he waved it around the logjam toward the side of the church: employee parking. I clung to Jerry's hand as together we joined the church members swarming toward the main entrance.

Difference number one between Greenleaf and other churches I've known: Everyone here was smiling. Back where I came up, at Saint Ann's in Hoogaboom, parishioners assumed a dour demeanor as they trod into Sunday service, befitting the sobriety of the event. Religion is no laughing matter, their faces said. The people of

Greenleaf had apparently missed this memo. The young family with the toddler in shorts and strap-on leather shoes. The teens in jeans. The bald guy with a Bible in his hand. The handsome retired couple in matching pastel polo shirts. They beamed at each other, at other worshippers, at us. Everyone. Was. Smiling.

We stepped through the sliding glass doors into the lobby of the church. I sniffed the air. It smelled not unlike the lobby of a hotel in Manhattan where I'd once met Vivian for drinks. Like new suits and Christmas. Then, as if two fingers had hooked into my nostrils and given them a yank, the smell of coffee invaded and obliterated all else. I spied the source: a smoothie bar and café, its line snaking in a neatly squashed M. Next to it was the bookstore, a cozy Barnes & Noble–type shop with cherrywood shelves and stripy sofas. At its entrance stood a life-size cardboard cutout of Aaron and Candace Green, the same image from their latest book cover.

A bank of screens caught my eye. People lined up at each of them, and by the stoop of their heads I knew the machines must be ATMs. Of a sort. A sign above read, TITHING CENTER; a smaller sign below read, ONE-TOUCH GIVING! ASK US ABOUT AUTOMATIC BANK DE-DUCTIONS.

"Okay, I get your point," Jerry said to me.

"Right?" Mall.

Jerry's hand guided my elbow through the padded double doors. My eyes blinked in the swallowing darkness. We entered what looked like a theater. Like Madison Square Garden, in fact, where I'd taken Jerry on his thirtieth birthday to see a Bruce Spring-steen concert. Nothing about the space identified it as a place of worship. Instead of pews, there were cushioned stadium seats. There was no altar I could see on the wide, spotlighted stage, where a band was setting up. As on the exterior, no crucifix or even a cross.

Jerry led us down a sloping aisle and toward the stage. At one point I looked back over my shoulder and saw there were not one but two balconies. Though it was dark, I could tell by the rippling of the shadows that both were teeming with people.

"Here we are," said Jerry. And I turned and came face-to-face with Candace Green.

Or should I say chest-to-face. Somehow I hadn't realized at Talitha's party just how tiny she was. She's one of those small people who carry themselves like giants. Like Napoleon. Or Tom Cruise. The opposite of me.

Instinctively, I hunched. But when I looked into her face, she was smiling that same smile from the book jacket. Her smile exposed no teeth and did not quite reach her eyes. Upon inspection it no more than curled the corners of her lips. So I can't explain its effect, but somehow it unclenched my heart.

Candace tucked a book under her arm and faced Jerry, squeezing his forearms with her hands. It was something between a handshake and a hug—a physical greeting for someone who was no longer a stranger, not yet a friend. "Great tie," she said.

I thought again of my green scarf. Damn, damn, damn.

"Here," she said, untucking her book and placing it in my hands. "In case you didn't bring yours." It felt warm and alive. I looked down and realized it was a leather-bound Bible, King James Version, its cover worn soft as a puppy's belly.

Candace waved us into her row, pointing to seats that had placards on them reading RESERVED. We had yet to sit when the lights dimmed. The crowd hushed. But instead of taking their seats, they bustled to their feet. Drumsticks clacked together, and a voice on stage called out: "One, two, three, four!"

Light and sound exploded as the band burst into song. The

tidal wave of chords rocked me back on my heels. As I blinked to take it in, a white cloud blasted from a machine not twenty feet from us. It scared the bejesus out of me.

Holy Moses. Smoke machines.

When the cloud cleared, I made out an acoustic guitar, two electric guitars, bass, drums, synthesizer, flute, fiddle, and four singers who sang in four-part harmony:

"I lift my heart in sweet surrender . . ."

Difference number two: This church could *rock*.

The acoustic guitar player jammed directly in front of me, looking simultaneously buttoned-up and glam in fitted pants and a shirt of shiny purple material. I could swear he wore guyliner. Like the other band members, he bounced on the balls of his feet, eyes burning, singing full throttle as if he meant every word.

"I lift my life in your majesty . . ."

All around me, people danced. A bespectacled man waved his arms high in the air, temporarily blocking my view. A man with his left arm in a sling rocked back and forth. In the aisle a woman wearing what appeared to be a bedsheet stamped her feet to her own imagined beat.

"I lift my heart . . ."

I heard a familiar voice singing the words, and I turned in surprise to Jerry. I'd never known him to listen to Christian rock. How did he know the words?

Following Jerry's eyes, I saw that behind the band on the white back wall were the lyrics, projected presumably from a hidden control room. Only they weren't just thrown up there like a slide show: The lyrics appeared on the screen line by line in a vibrant, pulsating font, exploding as each line concluded. This was no PowerPoint. This was script choreography.

The song ended, and I made to sit down.

"One, two, three, four!"

Another song. As that one ended, the purple-shirted man, who seemed to be the band leader, nodded at the drummer, who launched into yet another. I recognized none of the tunes, though at times I caught lyrics familiar from hymns of church services past. *Glory to God in the highest . . . make thee to shine like the sun . . . you are my shepherd, I shall never be in need.*

Set to electric guitar and pounding drums, though, the hymnal verse was transformed into a different language. Likewise, the sounds of rock were altered by the accompanying words. It was like the marriage of rock music and biblical verse created a whole new category of sound, at once base and ethereal.

I turned to share this profundity with Jerry and found a big black circle of glass staring right at me. I yelped.

Jerry looked to see. "TV," he said.

A cameraman lurked at the end of our row, his equipment aimed squarely not at me after all but at Candace Green.

Jerry nudged me and pointed skyward.

Above our heads hung a Jumbotron. On the screen was a close-up of Candace, her Liz Taylor eyes fixed on the stage, that ever-present smile making her appear both engaged and deep in thought.

Difference number three: Sunday service was televised.

The crowd fell silent, or as near to silent as three thousand people could. It was rather more like a collective intake of breath. All eyes held on the stage as it fell to black.

Then, a single beam of white light in its center.

Then, in that spotlight, a lone man.

A man dressed in a silvery suit, its sheen perfectly matching his hair. Arms outstretched, smile wide, eyes sweeping.

"Friends in Christ," boomed an unseen announcer. "Pastor Aaron Green!"

For a moment I felt like I had as a child when I played in the surf on the Jersey shore, only to be ambushed by an unexpected wave. The roar of sound—the clapping and the stomping and hollering—washed over me, swooped me off my feet, and knocked me sidelong. I struggled to find my footing, to tell up from down, air from sea, as Greenleaf greeted its leader.

Pastor Aaron stood still and looked out at the masses for what seemed a long, long time. Then, into the diminishing roar, he said a word I didn't expect.

"Fear," said Pastor Aaron.

With that word, he began his sermon. With that word, he hushed the masses. And with that word, I identified what had left me queasy all morning.

My old nemesis: fear.

"Fear," said Pastor Aaron again. His voice was low and mellifluous, almost conversational. A trick of the top-flight audio system, surely, but it felt for all the world like he spoke directly to me. "Fear is all around us. In our hearts. In our homes. In our lives."

"Mmm-hmmm," I heard from close behind me.

"When Jesus walks on water in Matthew 14," Pastor Aaron

continued, "Peter cries out in fear. Jesus says: Fear not! It is I. Do not be afraid."

More murmurs, more grunted assent.

The pastor's voice deepened in timbre like a timpani tapped at its center. "When Abraham takes his family to the Promised Land, he is afraid. God says: Fear not, for I am your shield and your reward will be great."

A man nearby shouted, "Hear ye!"

Pastor Aaron nodded as if he had heard. "When the Jews stand at the Red Sea and see Pharaoh's chariots on the horizon, they are afraid. Moses says: Fear not—and see the salvation of the Lord."

Shouts of "Yes!" "Tell it!"

Now the pastor took a step forward and lowered his voice. "When the angel comes to Mary and says she will bear a child, she is afraid. The angel says: Fear not, for God favors you."

Then, as the people shouted, Pastor Aaron stepped closer still. He continued, "Fear not. The Lord is with you. He has bled for you. With Him by our side, nothing shall we fear. I fear not."

The people reached for him now, beseeching. The pastor kept walking right to the edge of the stage, toward them, toward us. Toward me.

"Say it with me," he commanded. "I fear not."

"I fear not," said the people.

"I fear not!" Pastor Aaron repeated.

"I fear not!" "I fear not!" "I fear not!"

The declaration shot around the sanctuary. A heavyset woman sank to her knees in the aisle. Another woman's bony shoulders shrugged up and down as she sobbed in her seat. A teen in a Pong T-shirt jumped up with his fist in the air.

I turned in time to see Jerry smiling in a way he had not in many months, a smile that cracked open his face so beams of light poured out. My husband said the words.

"I fear not."

Me, I hugged Candace's Bible and held my breath.

I fear not.

Suddenly everything was too much: the smoke, the shouting, the people, the message. I turned to Jerry for support when I realized someone else was watching. Candace. We stared at each other, me through a blur of tears, Candace through her inscrutable smile.

* * *

"So," said a voice. "How'd I do?"

My eyes were still adjusting to the lights. Service had ended, and worshippers made their orderly way toward the exits.

"How'd you do?" I heard Jerry say, sounding amused. "Are you serious?"

Pastor Aaron joined Jerry and Candace. His hair looked a little damp from the heat of the spotlights, but otherwise he looked like his book jackets. Hollywood handsome. Airbrushed.

Candace laughed. "I'll critique him later," she said, and winked. "It won't do to get complacent."

"What did *you* think?"

I realized Pastor Aaron had addressed me. He, Jerry, and Candace turned my way, smiling, waiting. I creaked to my feet, straightening out my skirt to buy time. I had absolutely no idea what to say. No priest or pastor had ever approached me after a sermon for my independent evaluation.

Candace stepped in to fill my increasingly awkward silence.

"I think," she said, her eyes on mine, "the new pastor's wife is still taking it all in."

I nodded weakly and handed her back her Bible.

A man in jeans and a ponytail greeted Aaron and held out a hand to Jerry. I recognized him as the head elder, though I had no hope of pulling out his name. An official-looking woman hurried up to Candace, clutching an iPad the way her boss held her Bible. Relieved to have lost their attention, I sat down again.

I needed to think.

Pastor Aaron's sermon had triggered a memory of a Gospel reading, a fragment flickering at the edge of my recall, words I'd heard intoned from any number of pulpits by any number of holy men.

The Lord is my light and salvation. There it was; that was it. *The Lord is my light and salvation. Whom shall I fear?*

Whom shall I fear? Right. Whom—and what—shall I *not* fear?

I feared small insects and large rodents. I feared nearly empty subway platforms. I feared losing my teeth. I feared people with un-usually light-colored eyes. I feared the prospect of introducing two people and forgetting both their names. I feared the ire of my sister. I feared sleeping alone. I feared living a life of regret.

It was ordinary to fear, I told myself. Everyone had fears. Once I'd read a book about phobias for Psych 101, and I'd been astonished by their number and diversity. Genuphobia: fear of knees. Dextro-phobia: fear of objects on the right side of your body.

Mind you, none of my fears rose to the level of crippling psycho-sis. Frets, my mother used to call them, in a soothing tone, as she tucked me back into bed after a nightmare. *You're having a fret. Go back to sleep, everyone; Ruthie's just having one of her frets.*

My father believed therapy was "for wackadoos," or I might have begun addressing some of my fears at an early age in a professional fashion. The remedy my parents prescribed in its place was faith.

As I saw it, this was the central message, the main purpose, of religion: to banish fear. Fear of loneliness (eremophobia). Fear of people (anthropophobia). Fear of death (thanatophobia). All were addressed in church, where believers could in essence punt their fears to the purview of a higher power.

Yea, though I walk through the valley of the shadow of death, I will fear no evil.

Father O'Riley spoke those words to my mother two weeks before she died. He visited near daily then, the old friend who'd baptized all five of her children. I was on bedside duty, though in those last days there were few moments when some or all of my siblings weren't present. At the time of Father O's visit, Viv had dashed home to relieve her babysitter until her husband got off work. Tom was on his way up from court in Trenton, and Michael and Paul from their trainee jobs at a Newark insurance company. Dad was busy-making in his office out front, no doubt waiting to catch Father O with a scotch and the Yankees score on his way out.

Mom lay pressed against her pillow, her hair bled of color and pasted to her skull, her eyes darting and wild. Sometimes she woke like that, looking at us and the hospice nurses as if we were unpredictable strangers. I worried her oddness would chase off the priest, but Father O sat in his usual seat, the good leather chair by the bed, wrapping my mother in his kindly gaze. His presence seemed to calm her, for her eyes grew still, her breath more regular.

Mom made a croaking sound. I reached for a drinking appara-

tus supplied by the hospice, a miniature watering can of a size suitable for a garden gnome, and put it to her lips. The water freed her
tongue.

"Father," she said.

"Yes, my child," Father O answered, taking her hand and leaning in close.

The exchange, one I'd heard a million times between these
two, never failed to strike me as off. Edith Connelly and Seamus
O'Riley were the same age. They'd practically grown up together.

She stared at her priest in silence as she worked up the energy
to speak. The panic had left her eyes, and now they conveyed urgency. After long moments, she spoke.

"What," she said, each word a labor. "Comes. Next?"

Perched on a stool on the far side of my mother's bed, poised with
the gnomish watering can at the ready, I held my breath. For once I
knew instantly what Mom meant. She hovered on the precipice of the
great unknown, and she wanted to know—

What. Comes. Next?

My mother was afraid.

In the sinking quiet I watched my mother watch her priest.
The window was closed to seal out the late spring balm, and the air
felt dry and almost cold. Outside the sun was setting, and orange
rays stained the room. A cricket began to rasp its evening song.
Down the street, children shouted in play.

Finally, when I could bear it no longer, I looked at Father
O'Riley and saw that he was weeping.

At first I was so surprised I could hardly register the sight. A
man of the cloth, dressed in black and collared in white, a *priest*, for
Christ's sake. Crying.

Then I felt a swell of anger so powerful it blinded me momentarily. Here was my mother on her deathbed, seeking solace—not solace, *answers*—from the one earthly creature licensed to provide them. And all he could do was cry?

"I don't know, Edith," said Father O softly. "I don't know."

I wanted to hit him.

It was then he opened his Bible and read Psalm 23. "*Yea, though I walk through the valley of the shadow of death, I will fear no evil; for thou art with me; thy rod and thy staff they comfort me.*"

I saw that my mother had closed her eyes.

Maybe they did. Maybe the rod and the staff did comfort her. They sure as hell did not comfort me.

* * *

"So," said Ginger. "What did you think?"

I continued to break down a cardboard moving box. As promised, Ginger came by after church to help me unpack. She brought Jordan and Talitha, whose eyes widened with glee at the mess. This house was a playground of packing materials.

It is important not to barf out an answer, I reminded myself. Just because Ginger is friendly doesn't mean she's your friend yet. She's your husband's boss's daughter-in-law.

Ginger read into my prolonged silence. She laughed. "That overwhelming, huh?"

I ripped open a new box, this one packed with kitchen utensils. "That's the word for it," I agreed, pulling out a colander. "Overwhelming." I realized something. "Where do you sit? I didn't see you guys anywhere."

"We weren't there," said Ginger. "Didn't Candace mention?

Timothy planted a few years ago. Newleaf. That's where we attend service."

"Planted?"

"That's what they call starting a new branch of an existing church," said Ginger. "You know? Like taking a sapling from a tree."

"Oh," I said. "Like that god—what's his name—who sprang from Zeus's thigh."

Ginger looked mystified. Note to self: Avoid references to polytheistic mythology with new Christian friends. I tried again. "Or how MTV gave birth to VH1."

Ginger laughed. She had a light, pretty laugh that flushed the sadness from her face. "Gosh, I miss music videos. Sometimes I sneak a peek on YouTube. Did you ever see that baby dancing to Beyoncé?"

"Only about four hundred times." I grabbed a whisk to use as a microphone and mimicked a toddler bouncing up and down. *"If you want it, then you shoulda put a ring on it . . ."*

Talitha emerged from a box, intrigued. I handed her a ladle. Together we began to bop. *"All the single ladies, all the single ladies . . ."*

Ginger collapsed on the floor, laughing.

Jordan appeared in the doorway, alarmed by his mother's behavior.

I caught his eye and shrugged. "Women," I said.

He kept staring. Man, that's a serious kid.

"Hey," I said. "You wanna help me roll your sister in bubble wrap?"

"Bubba wrap! Bubba wrap!" Tali chanted.

Jordan gave no appearance of comprehension until, at last, a smile cracked his little mask.

Ginger gasped to catch her breath, leaning against a box and watching as Jordan and I proceeded to roll her daughter in sheets of bubble wrap. Only Tali's head poked out, a pink-cheeked caterpillar in a plastic chrysalis.

"Are you and Jerry . . . ?"

I looked over my shoulder at Ginger. Just then, Tali tipped over and fell. Cocooned in bubble wrap, she made a *fthwap* as she hit the ground.

Ginger flew across the room, laughing anew, and began to free her daughter. Her eyes warm, she asked me again. "Are you and Jerry . . . trying?"

Fact is, I knew what she meant the first time. Any married woman of childbearing age gets used to the question. Even living in a city like New York, where no one's supposed to assume any such thing.

I just hadn't figured out how to answer.

Don't barf, I said to myself. Don't barf your problems. I tried for honest but vague. "We aren't *not* trying," I said.

The truth was I'd stopped taking birth control pills not long after we married. Jerry and I weren't exactly abstaining. My gynecologist detected no hostility in my reproductive parts. I was breathing hard on thirty, but, my God, women gave birth well into their forties these days. Still I had not conceived.

Ginger patted my arm. "It'll happen," she said. When I didn't respond, she cocked her head to answer a question I had not asked. "When God wills it."

* * *

If I found Sunday service at Greenleaf overwhelming, Monday knocked me for a loop.

In my experience, church was a lonely place during the week. Sure, there was typically a daily morning Mass: brief, sparse, attended exclusively by very old people. Outside of that duty or perhaps a midweek confessional, priests stayed cloistered in their rectory, a building set apart from the church. Saint Ann's in Hoogaboom was for that very reason a refuge of sorts on weekdays. Despite my growing alienation from the church, I had ascended those steps a number of times over the past year to sit inside alone. Not to pray. To breathe. Just to breathe.

When I arrived with Jerry at Greenleaf at nine a.m. on Monday, a queue at the café already awaited lattes and smoothies. The bookstore appeared to have an author reading going on, with people picking their way among rows of folding chairs. Parents streamed in and out of the childcare center, dropping off their little ones.

"There you are," said a helium-high voice.

A weed of a woman rustled up, clutching an iPad the way secretaries used to hold clipboards. Everything about her seemed to blend into one color: hair, skin, clothing, iPad case, all a sort of watery French's Mustard hue. Even her rimless glasses seemed selected to fade into her monochromatic scheme. She bustled in a manner that translated universally as, *I'm on official business.*

"Alice," said Jerry, with a smile.

Alice looked pleased and a little surprised, as if she wasn't used to people remembering her name. "We've been waiting for you," the woman said. She nodded at me. "Nice to see you again."

Had we met? I racked my brain and vaguely recalled an assistant trailing Candace at the service yesterday. But like the North Star, Candace tended to dim the presence of everyone around her. And if you lacked color to begin with, well, I mean, come on.

We followed Alice to a set of double doors so heavily padded they resembled mattresses propped upright. Soundproofing? Bullet-proofing? Alice placed the tip of her right index finger on a glowing red panel. It beeped. A fingerprint scanner. The doors swung open.

We stepped inside to what looked like airport security. "All bags, purses, cell phones, laptops," droned a security guard. A green leaf was embroidered on her uniform vest above her heart. Jerry was already snapping off his belt and popping it onto the tray.

I shoved my purse into the next one. "Shoes, too?" I asked.

The guard stared, shaking her Hydra head of braids ever so slightly. "No shoes," she said. She did not add, "dummy." But I heard it anyway.

"Why was that a stupid question?" I mumbled. "You do it in airports. What's wrong with that question?"

Jerry didn't hear me. He had already caught up to Alice, waiting on the other side of security. She led us through another set of double doors, and we emerged into a cubicle farm. Row after row of beige-walled pens lined the windowless, low-ceilinged space. Warm lighting and green houseplants softened the *Dilbert* vibe. Everyone seemed to be on the phone. As we walked past, I heard snippets of conversation: "Yes, sir, we surely do take credit cards. Visa?"

"What are they selling?" I whispered to Jerry.

"They're taking donations."

Oh.

Alice walked in short, quick steps. Like a hamster on a mission. Come to think of it, she was kind of hamster colored.

I hurried to keep up. Beyond the cubicles, we turned a corner to a long corridor of offices with polished wooden doors. Executive offices. I saw Alice stop at an open door down the corridor and then escort Jerry inside.

When I caught up, a tad out of breath, I saw the gold nameplate on the door: CANDACE GREEN. Jerry and Alice stood inside at a desk, talking presumably to Candace, though I couldn't see her eensy frame around their bodies.

Unnoticed, I stole the moment to look around. The plate-glass windows looked out on the Greenleaf campus. A well-tended gum tree stood in the corner, and a blown-glass vase on a side table held three calla lilies so perfect I doubted they were real. On second thought, Candace didn't seem the fake-flower type.

But she was apparently the fake-art type. The ornately framed oil painting on the wall closest to me looked just like a priceless classic I'd studied in Art Appreciation. The Virgin Mary gazed down upon her infant son, nestled in the crook of her arms. It's hard to describe, that look, but I knew I'd seen it before, in Vivian's eyes as she nursed her twins, in my mother's as she listened to one of our dinner-table stories. An expression unique to mothers watching their children when they think no one notices. It's not the love-struck look you'd expect but is instead almost resigned. A look of surrender. I will wake in the dark of night at your first cry. I will give you the very cloth off my back. I will deliver you from evil. Blessed is the fruit of my womb.

"That's my favorite," said Candace. The two of us were alone. Jerry and Alice stood in the hall, jabbing at Alice's iPad screen.

Together we admired the painting. "Something about the way she looks at her child; it just gets you"—Candace tapped her heart—"right here."

I shook my head in wonder. "It's an amazing reproduction. It looks just like a—"

"Raphael?" said Candace with a smile. "That's because it is.

Oh, it's not ours," she said, scanning my face. "Not in our permanent collection. It's on loan from the Vatican."

"But why?" I blurted. "How?"

Candace stared at me a moment before she answered. It could have been my imagination, but I sensed in those nanoseconds of silence a judgment of my intellect. "As you know," Candace began.

I winced. People who said *as you know* usually meant *as you should know but obviously don't.*

Candace continued: "Interfaith harmony is Pastor Aaron's ministry. We had an audience with the Pope earlier this year to further that cause. In appreciation, the Vatican added Greenleaf Church to its U.S. tour of some of its artwork. Now," she said, glancing at her watch, an exquisite piece of craftwork that fit her porcelain wrist perfectly, "someone is waiting for you."

* * *

During my stint as Professor Baker's press coordinator, I learned to categorize journalists' demands by medium. Newspaper reporters typically needed just fifteen minutes of the professor's time, rapid-firing their questions over the telephone as they banged toward a deadline. An hour for radio, whose producers preferred to show up in person with their recording equipment, the better to capture his nasal, smarty-pants voice. TV took longest of all: half a day to ride in the chauffeured Town Car, get made up, wait in the green room, sit on a set, comment on the topic of the day, then get chauffeured back. Half a day for maybe three minutes of airtime.

Before working for Professor Baker, I assumed experts like him got paid to yap on TV. I was surprised to learn all that time and effort earned him not one penny. "I think of it as free advertising for my books," the professor once told me. "Every time I appear on the *Today Show*, my Amazon ranking goes up tenfold. *I* should be paying *them*."

After I graduated, the professor helped me land my first real job, as an assistant publicist at Glendale Publishing in New York, where during my job interview I was told I would court editors and reporters over expense-account lunches at Michael's and Nobu Fifty Seven. Sounds fun, right? Glamorous, even? Sure, if you like your miso black cod with a side of snake.

My first lunch with a journalist was my worst. Avi Goldberg was a book reviewer for Quill, a Web site that covered the publishing world. Since its launch in 2004, the site had gained a lot of influence among booksellers and librarians, who relied on its tart—in my view, sour—reviews to inform their choices. My boss, Louisa Lee, worked hard to cultivate a relationship with its editors and reviewers, plying them with early galleys and fancy meals.

On the morning of her quarterly lunch with Avi, Louisa came down with swine flu. "You've got to go for me," she wheezed into the phone. "Hang on." She retched. When she came back on the line, she was gasping. "Just talk about the list. When in doubt, tell him I'll get back to him. Don't make me look bad."

Nugget of wisdom: If your boss tells you not to make her look bad, it means she expects you to make her look bad. I did not disappoint.

Avi Goldberg was already seated when I arrived at Aquavit, a restaurant Louisa had selected because Avi liked Chef Marcus Samuelsson's Swedish meatballs. He had already ordered. "I'm on deadline today," he said, as if this were a socially acceptable greeting. "Tell me what you got."

I launched into a recitation of the spring list. About a dozen authors in, Avi looked up from his cleaned plate. He mopped his mouth with his napkin, then held up a hand.

"You're young," he said, "so I'm going to give you a note. I have degrees from Vassar and Yale. I'm capable of reading a catalogue on my own. Next time you get a pitch meeting, try pitching." He put down his napkin and pushed back his chair. "Tell Louisa to call me." Then he left.

Humiliated as I was—and believe me, my horror rendered me mute for the rest of the day—I took the note. I never again met a journalist without zealous preparation. I read their previous reviews, double-reading the ones on our authors. I noted their preferred genres, their favorite writers, their partiality toward Swedish meatballs or sushi. For small talk, I checked their Facebook profiles and Twitter feeds for their recent travels and the names of their children. At night and on weekends I plowed through our authors' manuscripts so I could discuss them with knowledge and opinion. In my last evaluation, I'm proud to report Louisa singled out my pitching skills for praise.

So imagine my confusion and panic when Candace informed me, as we strolled toward the lobby, that Greenleaf was between publicists, and how pleased she was to see a background in that line of work on my résumé (I had no recollection of sending one), and that she intended to put it to use immediately by having me meet on Greenleaf's behalf with a reporter from the *Atlanta Journal-Constitution*.

"Uh . . . okay," I said, trying to sound game. "What am I supposed to—what does he want?"

"What everyone wants," said Candace. "Pastor Aaron. Ah, there he is."

The reporter was waiting in the café. He stood up. The first thing I noticed about him was that he was young, maybe about my age. We clocked in about the same height, too, so that when he put out his hand, we looked straight in each other's eyes. His were a toffee brown, like his skin. Vertical creases marked his cheeks where dimples would be, like parentheses around his em dash of a mouth. Where dimples would be if he was smiling. He was not.

"Juan Diaz, meet Ruthie Matters, our new press officer," said Candace. "I leave you in good hands." And with that, she swept away.

I stared after Candace as she glided toward the inner sanctum. *Press officer?* Did my church duties really come with a real-world title?

I turned back to the reporter and tried not to hyperventilate. I realized with defeat that I'd already forgotten his name. José. No, Juan. It was Juan.

"Shall we sit?" I asked, before I noted a half-finished coffee on the table. He must have already waited awhile.

"Ruthie—it's Ruthie, right? No offense, but I'm on deadline."

Fantastic. Déjà vu all over again. Only this time, I didn't have a list to recite. Scratch that. I didn't even know what I was selling.

Get a grip, I told myself. You're a seasoned professional now. You're the saleswoman; he's the customer. Make the pitch.

I sat up straighter. My mother always said confidence begins with good posture. "Well, then, let's get started. How can I help you?"

Juan didn't bother masking his annoyance now. "Really? She didn't fill you in?" Then he crossed his arms and expelled a sigh. The drawn-out sigh of the long-suffering reporter.

It was the sigh that got to me. You know what? This dude was out of line. Who did he think he was, anyway—Bob Woodward in a Mario Lopez suit?

"Look," I snapped. "It's my first day here. No one's explained anything. I don't know who you are or what you want. Yet I'm the one you got. So if you plan on getting what you came for, you better start by telling me what the hell it is."

Juan stared. And then he smiled. His lips spread across his face until they bared most of his Mentos-white teeth. I was right: dimples.

"You said 'hell.'"

"Ah, hell," I said. Then—what else could I do?—I smiled back.

"It's just I never heard one of you people curse," he said.

"One of who people?"

"Church people. Greenleaf people."

So that's what I was now, to the outside world. A church person. A Greenleaf person.

"Okay," he said. "Let's start over."

"That would be peachy."

"I'm Juan Diaz of the *Atlanta Journal-Constitution*."

Juan Diaz, Juan Diaz, Juan Diaz. It always helped to write it down. I pulled out the small notebook I kept in my purse, the one I used to scribble down to-do lists and the other crib sheets of the chronically forgetful. The page I opened to began with *Socks*. I scratched it out and wrote his name. "Ruthie Matters. Of—Greenleaf Church."

"I'd like to write a profile of Pastor Green, on his interfaith work."

"Okay," I said, writing. "So far, so good."

"I'll need interviews."

"Can't see why not."

"More than interviews. I want access to the pastor over the next month or so, leading up to the interfaith conference in London. Follow him around. Really get inside."

At this, I raised my head. My public-relations antennae twitched. Little as I knew about Greenleaf culture, I guessed all-access passes weren't easy to come by. "How far inside?"

"Well, for one thing, I'd like to get behind those doors." Juan nodded toward the padded double doors on the other end of the lobby. As we watched, a staff member hurried up, pressed his finger on the scanner, and the doors whooshed open and then shut. The inner sanctum.

I looked back at Juan. "That's probably a tall order."

"Well, then," said Juan, leaning forward with a smile, "I'm placing my order now. With you."

It occurred to me that all the adjectives people used to describe good reporters—pushy, aggressive, tenacious—were actually pretty unflattering. That made sense. The words captured an ambivalence toward the press that I too often felt. Louisa, my old boss at Glendale, summed it up nicely: "We need 'em, but we still hate 'em."

I didn't hate Juan. In fact, I kind of liked him. Of all the people I'd met here so far in this strange new world, he was the most familiar. If Greenleaf was Mars, Juan Diaz was an interloper from Earth. Like me.

"I'll see what I can do," I promised.

* * *

"Are these all your olives?" I called to a clerk at Kroger as he hustled by down the aisle. I adore big, bright supermarkets, the likes of which you don't find in Manhattan, starved as the island is for square footage. But in my years of patching together the grocery list at Fairway and Zabar's, I had grown accustomed to a selection of international cheeses, artisanal breads, and gourmet coffees. And olives. Fresh olives curing in tubs, ready to scoop—the fat green manzanilla, the bruise-purple kalamata, and my favorite, the salty, firm picholine.

But after ten minutes of scouring the Kroger deli section, all I could find was a single brand of canned and pitted black olives. The clerk turned around with a look of such befuddlement that I just waved him off with a muttered "Never mind." I didn't have all day. Jerry had texted earlier that he'd make it home for dinner by seven, and I wanted to make the most of our time.

In the week since we'd arrived in Magnolia, Jerry had all but disappeared into his new job. At least in the beginning, much of his role at Greenleaf Church seemed to involve spending time with Aaron, tagging along on public duties, watching and learning, offering opinions when asked. At this he excelled.

I was glad. Their budding relationship touched me, all the more because I knew Aaron filled Jerry's ideal of a father figure. Lord knows his own father didn't. Maybe that's par for the course when your dad is the kind of person who names buildings after himself. I tried sometimes to put myself in the two-thousand-dollar wingtips of Ernest H. Matters, who managed the retirement funds of thousands through the brokerage firm that bore his name. How would the day-to-day concerns of a small child figure, I wondered, in a mind consumed with the caretaking of billions of dollars?

Evidently, not at all. Jerry's father had left the raising of his only child to his wife. Who in turn left it to a series of Caribbean nannies. I knew that my husband had gone into the family business not because his father expected him to, but in hopes that it would bring them closer together. That it would give them something to talk about. Jerry once told me that the longest conversation he'd ever had with his father was about the future of mortgage-backed securities. It broke my heart.

Given his upbringing, it amazed me no end that Jerry turned out so normal. At least, normal in the sense that he wanted the same things ordinary people did. Love. Family. Work he cared about. And he'd finally found that last.

Which is why I felt a wee bit Grinchy pointing out that his job did not seem to match its original description. Jerry's official role at Greenleaf—the reason he was hired over two hundred other applicants—was to manage the church's money. His responsibility at Greenleaf, as he had explained to me in Wall Street–speak, was to "corral the disparate holdings into one cohesive portfolio that would then yield stable dividends"—a steady river of income for church activities. He was to be assisted in this by Elder John Swain, who Jerry said also had a financial background and who was intimate with the church bookkeeping.

But just as I found myself with a job I didn't expect, so, too, did Jerry—as Aaron's right-hand man. Maybe this is how all churches operate. They're like black holes of volunteerism. Not that he complained. In fact, he seemed thrilled to spend so much time with the senior pastor. But all those ribbon cuttings and elder councils meant less time for his real job.

So Jerry had begun working at night. Every evening, he hauled home stacks of papers—Bloomberg printouts, stock prospectuses, portfolio analyses. After scarfing down dinner, he'd kiss me and head to a room I'd planned to outfit for guests but had reluctantly ceded as his office. After a couple of hours of skimming reality shows about fat camps and psycho brides, I would wander by.

"Bedtime," I'd yawn, stretching and posing in my best Bettie Page. Which was meant to be funny because I dressed for bed in his old shirts, not the corsets and gartered hose of a burlesque star.

"Be there in a sec," he'd say, not looking up from his reading. At which point I'd shuffle off down the hall. And by the time he did finally lift the duvet and crawl in, I'd be asleep or pretending.

So it went lately in the Matters household. He needs time to settle in, I told myself. We both do. Heck, I hadn't even managed to free all our furniture from bubble wrap, let alone locate enough of our pots and pans to prepare a home-cooked meal.

In the absence of a dining table, I decided to spread a picnic out on the wooden floor with my cobbled-together smorgasbord of deli-type items: cubed orange cheddar, day-old Italian bread, and (sigh) the canned olives. I was uncorking the wine when he told me about London.

"Aaron's got that interfaith conference there in November," Jerry said, his jaw grinding on the processed salami. "I get to tag along."

"Jealous," I said.

"I asked."

"And?"

"Candace isn't going. And if she's not, none of the wives are."

"That's all I am now—one of the wives?"

"Yep. You're my plus-one."

"Well, I'll be perfectly fine minus one, thank you."

The phone rang. Jerry picked up. "Viv," he said. "Are the kids ready for a visit to the land of Krispy Kreme?" He listened, then laughed. "Okay, we'll stop practicing CPR for now."

I took the phone out onto the deck. The house wasn't lakeside like Candace's, but from the deck I could glimpse the water, still as a bowl of lime Jell-O.

I heard a knock on the window. I looked back inside to see Jerry blow me a kiss, then take his plate upstairs to his office. So much for our picnic.

"Hey," I said.

"Hey?" said Viv. "Just hey? Don't you people have some special greeting? 'God bless you,' or 'Gesundheit,' or—"

"Second time this week I was referred to as 'you people,'" I said.

"That's what happens when you go over to the Dark Side. You become the Other."

"How're the kids? Hubby? Baby bump?"

"Kids are fine, Jason's fine, bump is fine," said Viv. "It's Dad."

My insides dropped. "What about Dad?"

"He's met someone."

My gut righted itself. I snorted. "No, seriously."

"Remember Soong-sa Kim? Of the Hoogaboom Korean Merchants' Association?"

"Dad's *gay?*"

"Idiot. I can still call you idiot, can't I? They won't hex me?"

"Greenleaf is not a coven. Tell me."

"Mr. Kim died earlier this year. It's his widow. Dad helped settle his estate. He and Mrs. Kim got—friendly."

I groped around for something to sit on, but we had yet to buy deck furniture. I flopped against the railing instead. My father, my grieving widower of a father, the man whose beloved wife of thirty-seven years had just died—was *dating?*

I heard a blip on the line. "Listen, I think that's Tom," said Viv.

"We're all in an uproar here. You can imagine. Anyway. Just wanted to, you know, keep you updated. Talk soon."

I held the phone in my hand and looked out toward the man-made lake. The sun was setting in the distance. A swan—honestly, a *swan*—paddled slowly on the water.

Here I was, in Paradise. And there they all were, in New Jersey. And the only place I wanted to be was home.

CHAPTER FIVE

Candace

"Did you hear about the Lasseters?"

Candace looked up. Hugh Dolly leaned into her office. By the look on his face, he had come into some delicious gossip.

Removing her glasses and rubbing the bridge of her nose, Candace waved him in. Ordinarily she brooked no interruptions while she wrote, and in any case few dared just pop in without an appointment. Only Aaron and Hugh. The music minister was her favorite, and he knew it.

Hugh sallied in and plopped onto her couch, its white Balinese silk a serene palette for his peacock-blue shirt. He crossed his legs at the knees and feigned distress. "Oh, Pastor Bob," he sighed. "We hardly knew ye."

"Don't be coy," said Candace. "Out with it."

Hugh leaped forward to the edge of his seat. "He's opening a sex ministry on the Internet."

"A . . . what?"

He waved his arm. "A ministry. For sex addicts."

Candace's hand fluttered up and landed on her chest. "What about—"

"Jo? She's going to run a co-ministry. For the spouses of sex addicts."

"My word." Then, "How did you—"

Hugh put a finger to his lips. "I have my sources."

Candace shook her head. "Poor, poor Jo."

Hugh's evil grin dropped away and his voice gentled. "Have you spoken lately?"

Candace shook her head. Jo Lasseter had once been her closest friend. They met during a pastors' convention in Dallas, at a luncheon for the wives. Seated together, they fell into conversation like marathoners chugging water, both women parched for friendship. For such a public role, being a pastor's wife can be the loneliest job in the world. No member of a congregation wants to befriend the bedmate of their spiritual leader, lest news of their base humanity filter back to him and handicap their shot at heaven. Many pastors' wives homeschool their children, adding another layer of isolation. As for the pastor himself, well, his wife will always play second fiddle to his calling.

Candace well remembered Jo's bashful pride when she described her husband's work. Bob Lasseter had launched an evangelical church in Tampa, attracting young and old alike with his passionate sermons about family values. Within ten years he'd built its membership to close to ten thousand. Of late he had made national headlines by exhorting married congregants to quit Facebook, which he called a gateway to adultery for connecting users with old flames (dozens of Facebook campaigns mocking him had followed). His charisma and popularity were such that the local Republican machine was courting him for a potential run for office. Jo confided that Bob was considering the offer.

Of course, that left Jo largely alone to manage their household and five daughters, beauties and high achievers all. And Jo did, with aplomb. She had an effortless grace about her that Candace admired, a way of selecting just the right *wabi-sabi* ceramic bowl to set off her autumn table, of overseeing all her daughters' schedules so that Mandy's cleats were always clean and Janna completed her Kumon on time. At Jo's invitation, Candace once traveled to Tampa to attend Lori Lasseter's NCAA finals tennis match. Bob managed to make the last set, but spent it under the bleachers on his cell phone. Jo only smiled and shrugged.

The week Bob Lasseter announced his candidacy for Congress, a filthy Web site trafficking in lurid videos of political candidates found him in its crosshairs (no doubt aided by an industrious operative from the opposition party). Video caught Bob entering a Motel 6 with not one, not two, but *three* hookers in tow. Naturally, the liberal media roared to the scene, gleefully playing snippets of Bob's sermon about the evils of Facebook adultery. Dozens more street-corner hussies—an astonishing number, actually—popped up for their moment in the spotlight to claim the patronage of one Bob Lasseter, senior pastor of Shadowbrook Church.

Candace didn't wait for Jo to call. She drove to Tampa herself and picked her up, along with the youngest two children, who still lived at home. Then she drove them back to Magnolia to hide out within the gated confines of Paradise Estates. No reporter could penetrate its walls, let alone the shield of Candace's wrath.

Not surprisingly, Bob withdrew from his political run. As he nursed his wounds, the council of elders at Shadowbrook convened.

Backed by the congregation, the elders fired Pastor Bob. The news knocked the wind out of Jo. "Fired him from the church he founded," she wept. "From the church whose cornerstone he laid with his own bare hands!" Candace said nothing.

When Bob appeared on the Greens' doorstep, his hat literally in his hands, Jo threw herself into his arms. Candace watched, silent. She helped Jo pack, helped her children into their father's car. Jo clasped her long and hard before she got in.

"He's changed," Jo said.

Candace did not respond.

"With God's help, we'll make it through," Jo said.

Candace still said nothing.

"He's the father of my children."

Candace only nodded. She waved as the Lasseters pulled away. Then she walked to her bedroom, closed the door, and experienced what in retrospect she would recognize as her first full-blown spiritual crisis.

You cleave to your spouse. She remembered this from her wedding vows. *Cleave.* The word sounded so raw, so animalistic. *Cleave.* Two shall be one flesh. Yet it was not what liberals might call an equitable union. Ephesians 5:23 called the husband the *head of the wife*.

But the verse continued: *Husbands, love your wives, even as Christ also loved the church and gave himself for it . . . so ought men to love their wives as their own bodies. He that loveth his wife loveth himself.*

And did not the Bible exhort again and again against infidelity? Proverbs 5:15, for goodness' sake:

Drink waters out of thine own cistern, and running waters out of thine own well.

*Let thy fountains be dispersed abroad and rivers of waters in the
streets.*
Let them be only thine own, and not strangers' with thee.
Let thy fountain be blessed: and rejoice with the wife of thy youth.
*Let her be as the loving hind and the pleasant roe; let her breasts
satisfy thee at all times; and be thou ravished always with her love.*
*And why wilt thou, my son, be ravished with a strange woman,
and embrace the bosom of a stranger?*
*For the ways of man are before the eyes of the Lord, and he
pondereth all his goings.*
*His own iniquities shall take the wicked himself, and he shall be
holden with the cords of his sins.*
*He shall die without instruction; and in the greatness of his folly he
shall go astray.*

Serving her husband was the duty of the Christian wife. Yet the
deal required quid pro quo, as they say in the law. He shall treat her
as he would himself: with love and with respect. When a husband
breaks that covenant, how ought a wife respond? If, God forfend,
Aaron should commit such a betrayal, ought she to sever her flesh
from his?

Smacking into this conundrum, Candace felt again the searing
loneliness of the pastor's wife. For this would be exactly the kind of
question a Christian woman might put to her pastor. But when said
Christian woman was *married* to her pastor . . . well. The second
choice, to query her Bible group, was equally unacceptable. It would
not do for congregants to suspect the pastor's wife suffered marital
doubts.

So instead she prayed on it. She studied the Bible, read Ephesians and the Proverbs and John, Matthew and Mark and Luke.

And one morning, as she slid Aaron's egg-white omelet onto an oven-warmed plate, she heard Him answer.

At first she thought her husband had spoken. She looked over at Aaron, sitting at the café table, skimming the front page of the *Wall Street Journal* and sipping the orange juice Candace had squeezed for him by hand. He turned to look at her and smiled, content as a just-fed cat. He had not said a word.

Never let him go, was what she heard.

As soon as the words formed in her head, she understood. She had been asking the wrong question: What should a woman do when her husband strays? Surely the answer was to make sure he never strayed in the first place. That meant keeping him satisfied, in every way a woman can.

Later that day, Candace sat down at her antique secretary table, pulled out a sheet of ivory paper, and began to write her book on marriage.

She finished it in just over four months. It was published under the aegis of Aaron's Serve Your Faith series, the better to ride and build the brand. *Serve Your Marriage* (the publisher talked her out of *Serve Your Husband*) hit best-seller lists immediately, establishing Candace as a leading if somewhat controversial thinker on the life and mind of a modern Christian woman. Her advocacy of a return to traditional wifely values earned her the adoration of conservatives and the mockery of feminists.

It also doomed her friendship with Jo. Nowhere in its pages did Candace refer to the Lasseters or even hint at their situation. But Jo guessed the book's genesis.

"You *judged* me," Jo said over the phone, her voice shredded with tears. "I thought I was your best friend. Little did I know I was just *material*."

Despite many efforts to contact her, Candace never heard from Jo again. It wounded her.

Candace's second book would be more introspective. As Hugh left her office after a sympathetic squeeze of her shoulders, she turned back to the ivory writing paper on her desk. She wrote in longhand, using a gold Cross pen, the one Aaron gave her on their twenty-fifth anniversary. She paused, then wrote:

What is my purpose?

* * *

By the time Candace arrived, the conference room hummed with conversation. The elders clustered in small groups, their faces customarily dour. Alice, her secretary, bustled around the table calling up today's agenda on the elders' iPads. As part of Greenleaf's green initiative, Aaron had decreed a paper-free policy for all church meetings, presenting each senior staff member with the pricey gadgets instead. But the elders refused to learn how to use them.

Over in a corner, Ruthie Matters spoke to that reporter, Juan Diaz. Overruling Candace's wariness, Aaron had decided to allow Diaz to tail him for the past weeks. The article was timed to coincide with the Global Interfaith Conference in London. Candace had assigned Ruthie to monitor the reporter to make sure he didn't veer off course.

At the other end of the room, Hugh was introducing Elder John to Giovanna Disantana. The girl, who went by Gee, had in the short time since winning the audition risen from Evergreen's replacement backup singer to featured star. A prominent role on the worship team meant a higher profile around the church, and for Gee that meant letting Hugh lead her around from Bible group to elder council as he made her introductions.

Gee maintained a demure look, not like so many young women these days who dressed like whores in training. The only thing loose about Gee's appearance was her hair, which drifted softly around her shoulders. She kept what seemed to be a good figure covered up in a long-sleeved blouse buttoned to the neck and a denim skirt that stopped below her knees. Downright dowdy, honestly, but for one thing: her confidence. Candace recognized in Gee the self-assuredness of one who feels chosen to deliver a unique gift. Pride may be a deadly sin, but Candace found little fault with awareness of one's God-given talent.

Hugh guided Gee over to Aaron and Jerry. Perhaps because her nerves still jangled from memories of Bob and Jo Lasseter, Candace leaned in to watch as this young woman paid her respects to her husband.

Gee looked straight at Aaron and smiled, in a natural, girlish manner. Candace relaxed a little. She knew when women were hitting on Aaron, and Lord knows hundreds did. She could read their subtlest physical cues, from the upturned faces and the widened eyes to the mirroring of his stances. Gee exhibited only respect.

Not that Candace had any cause for real worry. Aaron had never, not once, indicated the slightest romantic interest in a woman other than her. Unlike many wives, she didn't have to wonder, either. During their courtship, Aaron had taken her to a movie whose plot had long since escaped her but involved, she recalled, an adulterous affair. Afterward, over coffee and pie, he looked her square in the eyes and said, "I would never betray you like that." Right there in a booth at Andy's River Road Diner. On their third or fourth date. She was stunned silent by his declaration. "I just wanted you to know," Aaron said, as he tucked back into his cherry pie.

Candace smiled, remembering. She was about to turn away

when she noticed something. Gee shifted her focus from Aaron to Jerry, and *wham*—her demeanor changed. Away fell the girl. Up swelled the woman. Gee's eyes locked onto Jerry's. She grasped his hand in both of hers. She pushed her chest out and tucked her chin in.

Jerry had his back to Candace, so it was impossible to tell his reaction. But he didn't move away. Aaron had turned to discuss something with Hugh. Now Gee clutched both Jerry's hands in hers, eyes closed. Praying?

Candace slid a few steps to her left for a better view. Yes. Jerry, too, had his eyes shut, his mouth moving in what could only be shared prayer.

Candace glanced over to the far corner to see if Ruthie, too, was watching. Of course, by now the new pastor's wife was probably getting used to strangers grabbing her husband's hands for impromptu spiritual communion. And anyway, Gee was no stranger; Ruthie knew that her husband was working with the worship team in the run-up to the Christmas pageant. Indeed, Ruthie remained engrossed in discussion with the reporter.

When Candace turned back to Jerry and Gee, she saw that the prayer session had ended. Jerry said something to Gee, and she tossed her hair and laughed, an almost comically exaggerated gesture. With the meeting about to start, Hugh took Gee's elbow and all but dragged her out.

Candace was going to have to keep an eye on that.

Aaron leaned his head in close to Jerry's, then the two of them threw their heads back in simultaneous guffaws. This heartened Candace. In the month since the Matterses' arrival, the two men had grown close. Aaron brought Jerry along to management meetings and public appearances. Jerry had even begun to resemble

Aaron, it seemed to her—not so much in physical appearance but in comportment and speech.

Yes, it was a good thing for Aaron to cultivate a worthy protégé. Even if it could not be his own son.

Anthony, of course, had chosen another path. His baseball career appeared stalled in the minor leagues, but then Candace always knew he lacked the drive to succeed as a professional athlete. His happy-go-lucky personality was better suited to coaching children, which was exactly what he intended to turn to as soon as his current contract expired. Sophie's career as a ballerina would also likely end soon, and she, too, spoke of teaching, of opening a studio in Magnolia. Candace couldn't wait for them to settle down full-time in the home she and Aaron had waiting for them in Paradise Estates. It was about time they provided her with more grandchildren.

As for Timothy, she'd once had high hopes. It wasn't that he'd disappointed her—not really. He had, after all, followed his father into pastoral work, at least of a sort. Aside from their calling, however, Timothy and Aaron had little in common. Timothy was brash, excitable, passionate, adventurous. He was ambitious, all right, but his ambitions didn't include plodding his way up the ladder in his father's shadow. His plans were grander, even revolutionary. As young as a teen he'd talked of reinventing evangelism through technology, a goal he pursued through his global Christian aid group.

Candace was proud of Timothy. Oh, how she loved those green-blue eyes when they sparked with excitement over a new mission clear around the world. She wished he spent more time at Newleaf, the church he had planted in an abandoned arcade with funds from Greenleaf. If he had married a woman with more organizational wherewithal, perhaps, Candace wouldn't worry so much. A take-charge pastor's wife who could run a church in her husband's absence. But Candace wouldn't trust Ginger to run so much as a bake sale.

Which was why Candace had decided to audit Newleaf. She dispatched Tosh Takai and his team to sift through its finances, personnel, and operations. Though she had Aaron's blessing, she wouldn't tell Timothy about it just yet. She had no appetite for raised voices, and Timothy's temper could flare sky high. No, she would just tiptoe in, check to make sure things were running properly, then tiptoe right back out. No one would be the wiser. No one but her.

* * *

"A green fair?" said Elder John.

Candace fixed her gaze on Ruthie Matters. The young woman looked fetching today in a smart black pantsuit. Candace flattered herself that just as Jerry had begun to resemble Aaron, so Ruthie was modeling her. It took a week or two, but the new pastor's wife now met the standards of the Greenleaf team, at least in appearance. Of course, there was little to be done about that hair. From Ruthie's head sprang brown curls straight out of the Old Testament, which combined with her name led more than one church member to wonder hopefully if she was a Jew. For an evangelical Christian, no brass ring outshone the prospect of converting one of the Chosen People.

Ruthie stood at the conference table, looking around at the seated elders and senior church staff. This was the first time she had spoken up at a staff meeting, let alone presented an idea. Spots of excitement stained her cheeks. She was no public speaker, this one, but her enthusiasm made up for her stammering presentation.

"Pastor Aaron's last sermon mentioned Creation Care, which, to be honest, I'd never heard of," said Ruthie. "I guess I never thought about Christians and environmental stuff together, but, you know, why not? So I thought that we could, like, push the message of taking care of the earth. Because I notice that people around here throw their trash out car windows and don't recycle and stuff. No offense."

Interesting.

In the hiring of Jeremiah Matters, Greenleaf had skipped the customary couple's interview because of the urgency of their need for his financial expertise. In lieu of a face-to-face evaluation of Jerry's wife, Candace had made do with a dossier compiled by Tosh and his team—résumé, photographs, debts, criminal background check. Thus she learned of Ruthie's religion.

The Roman Catholicism failed to faze Candace. Greenleaf was nothing if not a refuge camp for other denominations. Few Christians were *born* born again. In his interfaith speeches, Aaron liked to quote a Buddhist saying: "There are many paths to the top of the mountain, but the view is always the same." Even if that were so, the path mattered to Candace, and the right path was Christian.

A Catholic is not a Christian. One who confines her relationship with Jesus to an hour every Sunday is not a Christian. A Christian does not delegate her conversations with God to a celibate man wearing black.

It did not bother Candace that Ruthie had been raised Catholic, so long as she was open to another path. Following her husband into pastoral life indicated as much. But Candace suspected that Ruthie was not your typical seeker. Candace's radar alerted her whenever a stranger wandered into Greenleaf seeking a place of worship, a new denomination, the One True God. What she sensed instead in Ruthie was a dry hollow where faith ought to burn.

The path mattered to Candace. Still, the journey mattered

more. If Ruthie had renounced faith altogether—if she stood at the base of the mountain and declined to climb, no matter the path—Candace needed to know. This little presentation of Ruthie's displayed a level of engagement heretofore not in evidence. It pleased Candace enormously.

"Creation Care Day," said Aaron. "I like it. We could do it next spring."

"Invite local merchants to display their earth-friendly products," said Jerry.

"A farmers market with local produce," said Ruthie.

"A petting zoo for the kids," Alice piped up, then immediately blushed. She rarely spoke in meetings.

"We tie it all back to the message," said Aaron. "All things are God's creation, and we are the caretakers."

"It'll make good press," said Ruthie, elbowing Juan, the reporter, who stood against the wall taking notes. He shrugged and nodded.

The elders traded glances. Here it comes, thought Candace.

Elder Simone hoisted a lumpen brow. She cleared her throat. "I don't know," she said. "Sounds like Woodstock."

Aaron grinned at Simone. "You were there?"

Simone's face soured still more. "Probably attract a whole lotta hippies."

"You're right," Aaron said, rubbing his chin. "A whole lotta hippies. *Young* hippies. Hugh, could Evergreen perform?"

Hugh tapped his iPad. "All you need to give me is a date."

"Craig." Aaron turned to the youth minister. "Could you fire up your recruitment team?"

"Lock and load," said Craig. "We'll wear tie-dyes and infiltrate the crowd."

Aaron sat back and looked delighted. "Looks like we have our-selves a festival. Great idea, Ruthie."

Ruthie flushed and grinned.

Simone lunged, a needle jabbing at balloons. "Have you forgotten? We vote on it."

For the first time this meeting, Candace spoke up. She made it a rule never to waste words in a public setting. The better to make the few she spoke count.

"Actually," she said, her voice fluttering in on butterfly wings.

All heads turned toward her.

"The new bylaws state," she continued, "that the planning of church events now requires no vote."

"What?" gasped Simone. The other elders looked at each other in bafflement.

Candace smiled. "We voted on it."

"I remember no such vote," Simone huffed.

"It was during the midyear elder council, for which you were each given the amended bylaws a month prior."

Now the elders looked guilty. Those tomes of legalese still sat unread, gathering dust on their nightstands, Candace could be sure. In fact, she had counted on it.

As the group rose to disperse, Candace overheard Elder Philippa grumbling to Elder Pete: "What else did we agree to?"

Elder John caught Candace's eye, his face like a tombstone.

Candace smiled.

CHAPTER SIX

Ginger

1 cup pecans in a Ziploc baggie
Wooden spoons
1 teaspoon vinegar
Bowl
3 egg whites
Scotch tape
Pinch of salt
Bible
1 cup sugar

"Check, check, and—check," said Jordan. He surveyed the ingredients arrayed on the kitchen table. "This is gonna taste weird."

Tali grabbed the Bible and pretended to take a bite. "Yummy," she said.

Ginger gently dislodged the cover from her toddler's teeth. "We don't eat the Bible, silly," she said. Then, frowning, she picked up the recipe again. "I don't think."

Candace had left the recipe in Ginger's mailbox this morning with a note. "Please test this for our Christmas fund-raiser cookbook, as per our discussion," it said. As per our discussion. Who talks like that? To family? Ginger felt an uncomfortable mix of gratitude and resentment at the task. Years after they'd planted Newleaf, Candace still called upon Ginger to perform duties for what Timothy called the mother ship. Her mother-in-law took it upon herself to share projects that would benefit both churches. The implication being that Ginger was incapable of organizing such projects on her own.

Of course, Candace was right. Ginger would never have thought of a cookbook titled *Reasons for the Seasons*, with recipes related to every Christian holiday. And they weren't just recipes; each was designed as a Bible lesson to be shared with children. Collecting these recipes turned out to be a cinch; many Greenleaf parents home-schooled their young, which made them home-project experts, which in turn supplied Candace with an arsenal of tried-and-true recipes. There were eighteen for Christmas cookies alone. Even so, Candace wanted each and every one tested by someone else before inclusion in the cookbook. "We all remember Mrs. Durkin's exploding fruit-cake, God rest her soul," she told the roomful of volunteers. Ginger had not put her hand up, and yet the recipe had appeared in the mailbox.

Jordan peered at the recipe. "Res-urr-ec-tion Cookies," he read slowly.

"Very good, honey," Ginger said, only a little surprised. He could sound out words even she had trouble with. His teacher, Mrs. Replinger, said he had the best reading comprehension of any kinder-gartener she'd ever seen. Upon hearing that news, Candace promptly ordered the entire Frog and Toad series for him, which he insisted on reading to himself at bedtime, alone. Ginger could hardly refuse. But she missed stretching out with him on his big-boy bed and marveling at illustrations of dragons and knights.

"What does it mean?"

"Well," said Ginger, considering. "You know how Jesus rose from the dead at Easter time?"

"Easter!" shouted Tali. "Bunny!"

"Right," said Ginger, hoisting the toddler on her hip to put some distance between her fingers and the sugar. "That's resurrection."

Jordan thought. "Were there cookies in the cave?"

"No, honey," Ginger laughed, then frowned. "I don't think."

"So what are we making, exactly?"

"Let's find out." As per the instructions—see, she could talk like office folk, too—she placed the baggie of pecans on the table. Ginger picked up a wooden spoon and handed Jordan and Tali two more.

"Ready?" They surrounded the nuts. "Now, hit! Hit the baggie!"

Together the three of them raised their wooden spoons and smacked and pounded the nuts to smithereens.

"Phew," said Jordan, wiping his brow.

"Pew," said Tali, copying.

"Okay," said Ginger, opening her Bible. "It says I should now read John 19.

"Then Pilate therefore took Jesus, and scourged him.
And the soldiers plaited a crown of thorns, and put it on his head,
and they put on him a purple robe,
And said, Hail, King of the Jews! and they smote him with their
hands.

" 'Smote' means beat," she said, before Jordan could ask.

"What does that have to do with nuts?"

"I guess we're sort of acting out what happened to Jesus."

Jordan looked horrified. "So the nuts are Jesus? Did we just . . . *beat* Him?"

"It's just pretend," said Ginger. Candace could have warned her, she thought. She of all people knew how sensitive Jordan was.

Well, in for a penny, in for a pound, as her mother-in-law would say. It meant they better go whole hog. "Now," said Ginger, reaching for the vinegar bottle and twisting off its cap. "Smell this."

She put the bottle under Jordan's nose. He recoiled. "Blegh!"

"My turn, my turn!" said Tali, grabbing the bottle and inhaling dramatically. Her mouth twitched. Her eyes watered. She began to wail.

Ginger laughed, gathering her in for a hug. "I know," she said. "Stinky, right?"

"Why did you make us do that?" Jordan whined.

"Well," said Ginger, reading from the recipe, "when Jesus was on the cross, he was thirsty. But instead of giving him water, the mean soldiers gave him vinegar to drink."

"He had to drink that stuff?" Jordan's voice wobbled.

In response, Ginger read:

"Jesus knowing that all things were now accomplished, that the scripture might be fulfilled, saith, I thirst.
Now there was set a vessel full of vinegar: and they filled a sponge with vinegar, and put it upon hyssop, and put it to his mouth."

Ginger scanned ahead but stopped reading aloud. For the passage continued,

*When Jesus therefore had received the vinegar, he said, It is finished;
and he bowed his head, and gave up the ghost.*

It was the saddest part of the whole Bible. *It is finished.* Jesus's
last utterance always made her cry. She knew it might make Jordan
positively howl.

He looked like he might anyway. "This is a terrible recipe."

I think so, too, Ginger wanted to say. Instead she put on some
cheer and said, "Mamie wants us to try it out, so we'll just keep going. Okay? Right. What's next?" She handed Jordan the recipe.
Maybe if he read it himself, he'd feel more in control.

"'Put vinegar in the mixing bowl and add egg whites,'" read
Jordan. "'Eggs represent life, and Jesus gave us his life. John 10:10.'"

Ginger opened the Bible to John 10 for Jordan to read, while she
cracked and separated the eggs. She loved the King James Version,
loved the ancient language and the unfamiliar words, as she knew
her father-in-law had in selecting it as Greenleaf's official Bible. But it
wasn't exactly kid friendly. Still, Jordan tried.

*"The thief cometh not, but for to steal, and to kill, and to destroy:
I am come that they might have life, and that they might have it
more abundantly."*

He struggled a bit on a couple of the words, but no more than
she did extracting the slippery yolk from the whites.

"Good!" Ginger exclaimed. "What's next?"

Having him read the instructions worked. Jordan seemed on
firm ground again, picking up the salt shaker and sprinkling a bit
into his hand. "Taste this, Tali," he said to his sister, who dipped a
finger into his palm and licked. She made a face.

"It not sweet," she complained.

"No, it's salt. 'Salt represents the salty tears of the people who loved Jesus,'" he read from the recipe. He added a pinch to the bowl of egg whites and vinegar.

"This cookie yucky," said Tali.

"Wait!" said Jordan. "Here comes the good part. 'Add one cup sugar. It's sweet, like how Jesus loves us.'"

Ginger revved up the handheld mixer and beat the concoction on high speed. Stiff white peaks formed in the mess, just like the recipe promised. She found this wondrous. So did the children. Jordan read on. "'The color white represents the purity of those who have been cleansed of sin.'"

When the egg whites were folded, Jordan brought over the Ziploc bag of smote nuts and shook them into the bowl. They each took spoons and plopped little mounds of the mixture onto a baking sheet. "'These represent the tomb where Jesus's body was laid,'" read Jordan. They worked on in solemn silence.

With the bowl emptied and the baking sheet in the oven, Ginger gave each child a piece of Scotch tape. "Now we tape shut the oven door, just like Jesus's tomb was sealed."

"Like this?" said Tali, placing the tape over her mouth.

"Just like that," said Ginger.

Ginger flicked on the oven light. They knelt in front of the door to watch. Bored, Tali wandered off. From the other room they soon heard the *plink, plink* of her toy xylophone. But Jordan and Ginger remained, their eyes fixed on the contents of the oven, all but holding their breaths. As the recipe instructed, they read from Matthew 27 about Jesus's entry into the tomb.

"Look!" said Jordan. Inside, one mound, then another puffed

up, like a bullfrog filling its throat, then quickly turned golden brown.

"Now we break the seal," said Ginger. Carefully she peeled off the tape, opened the oven door, and slid the cookies out.

Lured by the smell, Tali came scampering back. After the cookies had cooled, Ginger placed one in each hand. They were as light as cotton puffs.

"On the count of three," said Ginger. "One, two—"

They took a bite. Jordan's eyes popped. "It's empty!" The inside of his cookie was indeed hollow. "Just like the tomb!"

Ginger and Jordan stared at each other, united in awe. The miracle of Resurrection. Behind them, Tali stuffed one, then two, then five cookies into her mouth.

* * *

Having rescued enough of the cookies from Tali to pack a plastic container, Ginger drove the package over to Newleaf. Its parking lot stood mostly empty on a weekday morning, unlike Greenleaf's. The usual suspects populated the staff section. She recognized the cars' owners by their bumper stickers. The van with the rainbow peace symbol on the rear windshield belonged to Rain, a twenty-three-year-old who handled travel arrangements for Faith Corps. The two-tone Miata with the fish decal was owned by Milton, a computer whiz kid who lived most of the week on the deflated couch in the IT room until an accumulation of laundry necessitated a drive to his parents' beachfront mansion on Wilmington Island.

Timothy liked to surround himself with young people, and likewise they flocked to him. Groupies would just flutter around his flame, if he let them. But he didn't. He demanded they work. Donor solicitation, accounting, sponsor management, recruitment. Not to mention the overseas missions. Faith Corps required so much labor, the less dedicated among them soon drifted away. The ones who remained, though, were the hard-core believers, kids who'd gladly donate their boundless energy to the cause.

Of course, that left Newleaf less a budding church than an operation center for Faith Corps. For Greenleaf, the idea behind church planting was to grow the network, expand the community. That's what Aaron had tasked Timothy with when he okayed it. Ginger knew that Aaron and the Greenleaf elders were at odds about the choice of leadership. It was the rare instance—the only one she knew of, actually—on which Candace and the elders agreed. Timothy was too young, they argued. He was immature. Brash. Impulsive. He wasn't ready to helm a church.

Aaron persisted. But it was Timothy himself who convinced the elder council.

"To a lot of people, Greenleaf can seem like a closed club," he said, making his case, pacing Greenleaf's conference room floor like a caged leopard. Even from the back of the room, Ginger could see the flash in his eyes. "The young. The disenfranchised. Folks who don't own a single piece of clothing in pastel."

At this, Elder John cracked a smile. The head elder must be pushing sixty and he still dressed like a down-and-out rocker.

"History is full of examples where the church got too big for its people," Timothy continued. He spoke directly now to Elder John. "Back when you were in that cruddy old theater downtown. The one you first called Dad to. Did you ever think you'd be sitting here at a table made of"—he knocked it twice—"Brazilian teak?"

Ginger thought she saw Candace flinch. She knew her mother-in-law had selected the table herself; Timothy's dig came at her expense. But Candace represented only one vote. The elders held all the others, and Timothy knew to play to the majority.

Elder John grinned broadly, and the other elders were nodding, gratified to be acknowledged, glad of a chance to show their discomfort with Greenleaf's material splendor.

"Who'll lead the services?" asked Elder Simone. Ginger could swear the elder batted her eyelashes at Timothy. He had a particular effect on older ladies.

"I will," said Timothy. "I've led youth services at Greenleaf for three years now. I'm all degreed up. I'm ready."

"Have you located a site?" asked Elder Pete, who, despite his sour tone, looked as charmed as Simone. "Too close and it eats into our membership."

"I have," said Timothy. "What used to be an arcade, like for games. It's fifteen miles north, near Granger College. Just far enough that folks around there might not want to drive all the way down to Magnolia in Sunday traffic. And you know how lazy college kids are."

The elders chuckled. Aaron, standing near Ginger, just about reeked of pride. That's my son, he was thinking; Ginger was sure of it. A chip off the old block.

Timothy was wrapping up. "I don't need much," he said. "A place where people can gather and hear the Word. I'll run Faith Corps from there. And the bonus—you get me out of your hair." He looked straight at his father then. But Aaron didn't appear to notice the barb.

Elder John got up and clapped Timothy on the shoulder. "We'll miss you, son."

True to his word, Timothy's concept of Newleaf did not in fact require much. With Greenleaf seed money, he bought the arcade, which in addition to being abandoned had suffered a fire a few years back. He and a corps of volunteers gutted the building, ripping out rotted carpet and cracked toilets. They raided Greenleaf's storage for folding chairs and tables, lighting fixtures, and kitchen equipment. A large chunk of seed money went toward technology, toward the audio system and the computers and the high-speed Wi-Fi.

True to his word, Timothy led a once-a-week Sunday service there. Word spread about a new, young pastor with Green Day hair and a scorched-earth delivery. College kids filled the seats, but other neighbors came to check it out, too—young couples with pierced noses and onesied infants, artists with gray hair to their waists. Some musician pals of Timothy's formed a worship team, though they preferred to call themselves a band, and indeed their music sounded a lot more like rock than the gospel pop favored by Evergreen, and they'd probably shoot each other in the head before they dressed like their counterparts at Greenleaf, in color-coordinated outfits.

True to his word, Timothy made Newleaf the new headquarters of his overseas Christian missionary project. Except for on Sunday, Faith Corps volunteers and staffers had the run of the place, brewing cheap coffee in the kitchen and sprawling around the makeshift sanctuary—the whole place was really one big room—with their laptops and cell phones. Except for when he was traveling on Faith Corps missions, Timothy spent almost all of his waking hours there.

Which meant that finally, Timothy, true to his word, got out of Greenleaf's hair.

Timothy hadn't lied. He hadn't hoodwinked anyone. In fact, he did exactly what he said he would do. He seeded a church, and he attracted a whole new membership to it.

But even Ginger could see that it could be so much more. Renovations had halted after its initial, rudimentary fix-up. It went without saying that it had none of the facilities and services of its parent church: no childcare, no fitness facility, no café. No place to mingle. Of course, those were luxuries. But Newleaf even lacked basics like Bible study groups and Sunday school. When Ginger inquired, Timothy just shrugged and said he'd get to it, when he had the time. He never did.

Candace dropped in on occasion, visits Ginger would learn about only later from Candace herself, in the form of a criticism—or many. "They were all out of toilet tissue in the ladies'," Candace would say. "The lightbulb was blown out in the northeast corner." "I noticed trash in the hallway, by the back exit." "Someone really must ask that Rain girl to wear deodorant."

By "someone," Candace of course meant Ginger. "The upkeep of a church is the purview of the pastor's wife," she'd say, time and again. Ginger knew her mother-in-law was right. But she had a house of her own to keep, and two small children to raise. What was she supposed to do? Even if she felt up to the upkeep of the church, she couldn't imagine how to go about it. Would she just march in, mop and bucket in hand, and start ordering people around? Wouldn't they just laugh at her? Moreover, wouldn't Timothy look at her like she'd started speaking Chinese?

So once a week, Ginger would drive up to Newleaf with some sort of offering. Cookies, lately, ever since she'd become one of Candace's test bakers. Sweet iced tea, sometimes. Paper towels, Dixie cups, and other supplies donated by Candace from the Greenleaf supply closet.

Timothy was on the phone when they arrived. "Daddy!" Tali shrieked, hurtling across the floor toward him. He snatched her up with one arm and, still talking, tickled her until she collapsed on the ground.

Jordan stayed glued to Ginger's side. The rasta-haired types made him nervous. "What's wrong with their hair?" he'd once asked. "It looks like furry worms." Ginger wanted to tell him dreadlocks were a way for rich white kids to feel at one with the have-nots, but she couldn't think of a charitable way to say so.

"Fore!"

Ginger turned just in time to get walloped with a Hacky Sack smack between the eyes. She lost her footing, backed up over the tangled vines of laptop cords, and fell in a heap. The container in her hands flew open, and Resurrection cookies scattered all over the dirty carpeting.

"Mommy!" shouted Jordan. He picked up the Hacky Sack and spun around, ferocious. "Who threw this!"

A volunteer with a fuzzy beard and a Spin Doctors T-shirt raised his hand. "Here, kid. Toss it here."

Instead, Jordan marched up to him. "You hurt my mom! You should not play ball inside!"

Lifting herself up on her elbows, Ginger marveled at the sight. Her boy, her wee little boy, shirt untucked and shoelace untied, defending his mother's honor.

"Okay, sport. Okay." Timothy stepped in front of his furious son, still cradling his phone against his shoulder. He turned to the oafish volunteer. "You know how many people are suffering in Uganda while you play your stupid game?" The young man hung his head. "Go make yourself useful. Or get out."

Timothy put his hand on Jordan's shoulder. "Good man," he said. Jordan's face lit. It wasn't often he had his dad's attention, let alone his praise.

Ginger saw a shape before her face, and saw that her husband was extending a hand to help her up. "You okay? I'm sorry about this mess here. We're just gearing up for Africa and the shipment hasn't come in—" He was looking at her but she wasn't sure he spoke to her, what with the phone still at his ear.

Suddenly it seemed Ginger could hear every sound in the building. The tinny whine of the fluorescent lights. The grating chatter of the volunteers. A rat scuttling along the overhead pipes. Suddenly the place and the people ceased to intimidate her. Suddenly she felt angry. Why was *this* more worthy? Why should she and her children come second to *this*?

Ginger got up on her own. She stood eye-to-eye with her husband. "I want you to come home," she said.

Timothy halted midsentence, as if he wasn't sure he'd heard her right. "What?"

"I want you to come home," she repeated, raising her voice. A pigtailed young woman lying nearby on the carpet looked up from her laptop.

"Is everything okay?"

"Yes. No. I—we just want to see you."

"I'm working," he said, surprised.

"Then what time are you done?"

"I don't—"

"How about six? Then you can bathe the kids and eat dinner with me."

Timothy blinked at her. Then he said, "Okay."

Now it was Ginger's turn to be surprised. "Okay?"

"Okay." He touched her cheek before he turned away to resume his call.

* * *

True to his word, Timothy was home by six. So she asked him again the next day. He complied. And again, a few days later.

After a few weeks of this, Ginger felt emboldened enough to ask him to take a Saturday off. Pastors don't know from weekends, Candace liked to say. That was one thing at Greenleaf, which held six two-hour services between Friday and Sunday, each to packed houses of three thousand. Newleaf only held one.

"What for?" Timothy asked.

To spend time with your family, Ginger almost said. "To go to the aquarium."

The children were already in bed. Ginger would not have asked in front of them, knowing their squeals of anticipation might very well be punctured by disappointment.

But Timothy said, "Okay."

So off they went. Though they lived only an hour from a world-class aquarium, Ginger had never been. She had volunteered too late to act as chaperone when Jordan had a class trip there, and anyway the terror of minding twenty kindergarteners would have tarnished the wonder. As they waited in line for admission, Ginger bounced up and down on the balls of her feet.

"What?" she asked Timothy, who was looking at her strangely. She wiped at her nose. "Something on my face?"

He shook his head. "You look like them," he said, pointing at Jordan and Tali. They, too, were bouncing on the balls of their feet.

"This is my first time," she confessed.

"I know," he said. "I'm sorry we haven't—"

"My first time in an aquarium," she said. "Ever."

She felt some pressure on her shoulder and realized her husband had put his arm around her. "This was a good idea," he said. Long after he took his arm away, she could feel its warmth.

At home they bathed and tucked in the children, delirious with exhaustion, recounting their experiences from one exhibit to the next. Jordan had spent nearly twenty minutes at the otter habitat, cheering on the startlingly clever creatures, a male and a female, as they liberated a frozen fish from a rubber chew toy. Ginger would never forget standing before a vast tank as a whale—a whale!—glided past. Aside from Tali getting her head stuck in between the guardrails at the gift shop, it had been a perfect day.

At least it had for Ginger and the children. In a tunnel of glass winding under an oceanic tank, Ginger had watched her husband. Timothy carried Tali on his shoulders, gripping her tubby calves as she reached up toward the shark gliding just overhead. Silver light rippled across his face. What was he feeling? Was he happy? Bored? Thinking about his next mission overseas? She found it impossible to tell.

When had this happened? When had she stopped knowing her husband?

That night, Ginger and Timothy retired early, too. There was nothing different about their routine. They brushed their teeth; Ginger got in bed with a book, while Timothy clicked through the sports channels. Eventually Ginger turned off her light, and then Timothy put away the remote. He lay on his side, as always, away from her.

Only this time, in the dark, she reached out and placed a hand on his back.

There followed a few seconds, a few horrible seconds when she thought he might reject her. But then he reached behind to touch her leg. He turned, and soon they were kissing, pulling off their T-shirts and boxers, twisting limbs around limbs. His mouth rediscovered all her swells and hollows. The warmth of his hands on her thigh made her gasp. Her memory had not lied. They said nothing. Afterward, after toweling off in the bathroom and crawling back into bed, after she heard his breathing slow to sleep, only then did she cry.

CHAPTER SEVEN

Ruthie

Once a week, on Monday, Candace took me to lunch. "Off-site," she would say, meaning we'd go someplace off the Greenleaf campus, preferably out of town altogether. That was because in town we never failed to bump into someone who knew or knew of Candace, and that someone inevitably crashed our table. Nothing dissuaded them from leaving, including Candace's murderous smile, a smile I'd come to regard as something of a Rorschach test. In the face of the senior pastor's wife, people saw what they wanted to see.

My own view of Candace had evolved since that day we met, when I watched her simultaneously rescue her granddaughter's birthday party and tear the offending party performer a new one. She appeared to me then as an avenging superhero in a cotton-candy coiffure. I knew now she was so much more.

Candace Green, in my humble opinion, was a NASA-level genius who discreetly ran Greenleaf from behind her velvet smile. She was the Wizard of Oz. I watched as she stood at Aaron's elbow and greeted church members, feeding him name after name plucked from her brain. I listened in as she negotiated a recording contract for the worship team in the dispassionate dialect of a lawyer. I saw her edit GreenleafChurch.com, shaping the rambling or inane entries of church members into spiritual advisories perfect in their brevity and tone. I heard her school the Bible teachers on chapter and verse, correcting them on even the hoary bits in the Old Testament.

Who cared that she had hired me without my knowledge or permission? When you have a chance to learn at the elbow of Oz, I don't care—you take it.

This day she drove us to nearby Peach Orchard, a boulevard known for craft shops displaying local artists' work. I'd been meaning to get here with Jerry—it was exactly the kind of place we used to love to roam on lazy Sundays, or rather the kind of place *I* loved to roam while Jerry tagged along and speculated aloud on creative uses for bronze gongs and blown-glass elephants. But here, there was no such thing as a lazy Sunday.

A cold winter front had pushed in from the north, driving us into the Bistro Pêche and toward a table near its tiny hearth. A waiter soon appeared with glorious steaming bowls of butternut squash soup, a swirl of sour cream and a sprinkle of diced chives at its center.

Candace seemed distracted this day. From the beginning, she had set a pleasant and professional tone for our lunches, making it a forum for questions about church matters and light gossip about members. Today she said little until the waiter glided out of earshot.

"You know you can come to me about anything, don't you, Ruthie?"

I halted, my mouth hanging open to receive my spoon, halfway from bowl to lips. How odd. What did that have to do with the price of milk? Reluctantly, I lowered the spoon.

"Of course," I said. In my sudden discomfort I added, "But you don't mean *anything*." You'd think I'd learn. My joking usually fell flat with her. Still I persisted. "You don't want to hear about a hangnail or a rash or the thing I couldn't get on last Sunday's crossword puzzle. Like, do you know the scientific name for 'bedbug'?"

I babble when I'm nervous. A trait I'm certain Candace has noted. "Ah," she said. She closed her eyes briefly, and it seemed to me that under cover of her lids, she rolled them.

"You know I put the church first," she continued. "After God and family, of course."

I saw my chance at the soup and took it. Sweet and spicy, with a hint of—what—cumin? I *had* to come back with Jerry. We'd find the time.

"Those are the priorities of a pastor's wife. God, family, church. Never forget that."

I refrained from adding, "Then soup." Something told me this was not the time to crack wise.

She leaned across the table now. "How are things with Jerry?"

I glugged my mouthful of soup. Hot. Very hot. Her laser-green eyes didn't blink. I bought some time by swabbing my lips with a napkin.

"I . . . we—they're fine. I think." I swigged some ice water. Better. "Why?"

She didn't answer that. Instead, she asked, "Are you and Jerry thinking about children?"

Also, when I'm nervous? I giggle.

"Is that funny?" Her tone stayed mild, her eyes keen.

"No," I said. "Yes. I mean, no, it's not funny, like ha-ha funny.

It's funny, like strange funny, how around here that's considered public information."

That last bit came out sharper than I'd expected. But after I said it, I realized I'd meant it just that way. I felt a prick of resentment. Why was this any of her business? Why was this anybody's business but our own?

"Pardon me for prying," she said. Ever the lady.

"It's okay," I said, although it wasn't. "I guess all I want to say about that is we aren't *not* thinking about children. Again, though—why? Does it bear on our work?"

"No, of course not," she said. "Aaron and I are delighted with you and Jerry. The two of you make a wonderful addition to the Greenleaf team, and we hope you'll stay with us a very long time."

Praise is nice. In any context, praise is nice. All bosses should learn this. But it begged the question: If not that, then what?

She took a little sip of her soup. "Did you read my book?"

"Yes," I lied. Well, not totally lied. Let's just say I skimmed it carefully. It was about marriage and the sanctity of the wife's role and frankly it kind of read like a homemaker's manual from 1953. Also, there was a chapter about sex. I refused to read about my own boss's sex life. Just the thought of her and Aaron—*ew*—

"So you know, then, the one thing I think every marriage needs to hold it together."

Oh, God. Was it sex? Was she going to say sex?

"Prayer," she said.

I exhaled.

"Prayer is the glue," she continued. "Together. Every day, no matter what."

She leaned forward, all conspiratorial like. "Do you know, Aaron and I have prayed together every night of our marriage. And let me tell you, there were days when, oh, boy, that was the last thing I wanted to do. I was pooped from the kids, I was mad at Aaron for being away, the church people were driving me crazy. Trust me, I did *not* want to kneel and hold my husband's hands and pretend everything was going to be all right."

She leaned back in her chair then and looked around the room, in thought. "But then, you know what? Afterward, I would know everything *was* going to be all right. That's the magic of prayer. And when you do it together every day, it's like—like reminding yourselves about that string holding your hearts together, and tightening it just a little bit."

Candace fixed her gaze back on mine for a response. But I had nothing to say. She may as well have suggested Jerry and I incorporate goat's milk into our daily diets. Not that goat's milk in and of itself was so bizarre. But it was alien to *us*. As was the idea of a daily shared prayer.

Maybe that was the problem. A doubt surfaced: What if this was what Jerry wanted? Someone to pray with. A nightly prayer with his wife.

Candace was dabbing her lips with her napkin and nodding. "Yes, prayer keeps a marriage strong," she said. "That, and sex."

Oh, dear God.

"A satisfied man won't stray," she continued. "More so than any other job, yours is to keep Jerry happy."

Okay, that was it. I let my spoon handle clunk against the side of the bowl. Was this conversation really happening? I looked around to see if anyone else was catching this. But the retired couple nearest us were murmuring contentedly over their croque-monsieurs, and the waiter was listing the specials to a table of attentive ladies. I realized I was angry. Keeping Jerry happy was *my* job? My *job*?

Settle, I told myself. You don't want to be picking a fight. Not with this lady. In a measured voice I replied, "And what about him? Is his job to keep *me* happy?"

She sipped her ginger ale and moved her gaze to the window. Outside, a stiff wind whistled past, pushing a puff of leaves. Candace pulled her wrap tighter around herself.

"Of course," she said.

* * *

By the time Candace and I returned from our lunch, Juan Diaz was waiting for me in the lobby of Greenleaf Church, walking in circles in front of the tithing center like a large, impatient dog.

"Shoot," I said, snapping my fingers. "I forgot about him. Thanks again for lunch."

Candace placed a hand on my arm. "Remember what I said." Which part? I wondered, before she continued, "You can talk to me about anything." Her tiny hand gave my arm a tiny squeeze and then she turned to go, walking right past Juan without even a nod.

"She still hates me," said Juan, squinting after Candace as she disappeared through the padded doors.

I didn't bother assuring him he was wrong. Juan had managed to persuade Aaron. His article was timed to coincide with the Interfaith Conference in London. For a newspaper like Juan's, a profile of a local pastor would provide a hook to an international news event; for Greenleaf, a front-page feature in the hometown paper would drum up more local interest in Aaron's work. Win-win.

At least that's how Juan pitched it to the Greens. Candace remained skeptical of Juan's motives, and of the promised outcome.

"Don't trust a reporter as far as you can throw him," she told me. "All this garbage about the First Amendment and the Fourth Estate. What he wants is his own name on page one. Nothing more, nothing less." She relented, on the condition that I monitor his every move. "When he's on Greenleaf business, never, ever let him out of your sight."

Which was why I'd come to spend so much time lately with Juan Diaz. To be honest, I didn't mind. I didn't mind at all. We talked easily and comfortably about—well, everything I didn't talk about with my Greenleaf colleagues.

"Hear about Israel?" he asked as we walked to his car, a used Honda that looked and smelled like he slept in it. He admitted he did, sometimes, when he pulled all-nighters at the paper. Closer than his apartment, and more comfortable than the newsroom floor. I liked his car.

"Nope. What happened?"

As I cleared newspapers and Arby's wrappers off the passenger's seat, Juan stood outside the driver's side, hunched over his iPod. He was big on deejaying the soundtrack to his life, and lately to correcting my poor—or, more accurately, nonexistent—taste in music. When he asked, I told him I couldn't actually name a favorite band and that I had trouble even identifying them, seeing as most bands these days had names that sounded like sentence fragments. "What're you, eighty?" he had asked, less in sarcasm, I think, than astonishment. Now, every time we drove somewhere, he programmed his gadget with my musical education.

"They're not letting aid into Gaza," he said, plugging his iPod into the car stereo. "They might be giants."

"Who might be giants?"

"They Might Be Giants. The band. Please tell me you've heard of them."

I seesawed my hand: vaguely? He shook his head. I was hopeless.

The plight of the Palestinians was one of our current hot topics. Let me make it clear—it's not like I lie awake fretting over world events. But in every other place I'd worked, news was the number one watercooler topic. When I casually mentioned the Middle Eastern unrest that dominated headlines to Candace, however, she warned me that Israel was a sacred cow best not debated within Greenleaf walls.

In contrast, I found Juan willing and eager to talk about what was going on in the rest of the world. The upcoming World Cup. The serial murders of prostitutes in Oregon. That new movie with the robots versus the mutant androids.

We didn't just talk. When I complained I couldn't find a good selection of fish in our landlocked county, he drove me an hour to a giant indoor farmers market in Decatur for the most splendid fish counter I've ever seen. He seemed to get a kick out of showing me new things, of watching me wander around that market ogling the bright-gilled whole snapper and slippery smelt, of bringing me a book on megachurch economics, of pointing out local landmarks.

If we were colleagues, I'd call him my work husband. Which was the issue. We weren't colleagues. We were *like* colleagues, at least for this past month, as I tracked him as he tracked my boss. But that wouldn't last forever. Once his article published, I'd have no reason to see him so regularly again. This thought depressed me. I stared moodily out the window as he steered the car onto the highway.

"Hey," said Juan after a while. "You okay there?"

He sensed my grump. Some part of me was gratified. Maybe more; maybe flattered. His dimple twitched, but he was not smiling.

There were moments like these, when we sat so close I felt his body heat and smelled his antiperspirant, when his eyes traveled my face and seemed to pause—maybe, I couldn't be sure—on my lips. Moments I understood why other women looked at him like he was a big, fat steak.

I turned away quickly so he wouldn't see me redden. "I just realized your deadline's coming up."

"Don't say the *D*-word," he said, thumping a fist to his chest like it gave him heartburn.

We passed a green highway sign saying Atlanta exits approached. I checked the clock on the dashboard. We were in good time for a panel discussion about the history of Christianity, to be led by Aaron at Temple Beth-Israel, Rabbi Bernstein's synagogue.

"Why am I going with you again?" I said. "You know everyone by now. Can't you cover these events on your own?"

"Candace sicced you on me. Remember? Not like I asked you to be white on rice."

I raised my fist to slug him. He laughed.

"Fine," I said. "If that's how you feel, maybe next time Elder John can escort you instead."

He shot a look at me. "Why him?"

"I saw you guys talking in the parking lot the other day. Seemed pretty friendly."

"Me and Skeletor? Yeah, we're like this." He held up two fingers, intertwined. "I think he's trying to save me, to be honest with you."

"You're beyond saving."

"That's what I said. And what about you?"

"What about me?"

"When's it your turn to lay your burdens down by the river? Isn't it time you got born again?"

My smile faded.

"Sore spot?"

"Little bit."

* * *

After the panel, Juan headed to his newsroom, hoping to use comments by Rabbi Bernstein about the Israeli-Palestinian standoff to pitch a last-minute news item. I caught a ride back to Greenleaf with Tosh and Aaron. Candace had talked Aaron out of making Tosh ferry him around in the requisite staff Prius, and into bankrolling a hulking black SUV with tinted windows and reinforced steel doors. Much as I liked my little Prius, I had to admit it felt like a matchbox next to this ride. I stretched out my legs in the backseat, which I had to myself. Aaron always rode shotgun. Candace told me he hated to look chauffeured.

From the back, I eavesdropped as Aaron rehearsed this week's sermon. He would give the first of these at the Friday service, considered by the staff to be a run-through for the five weekend services that would follow. Each lasted almost two hours, and gathered about three thousand worshippers. Aaron led every one. The megachurch pastor is an endurance athlete. I don't know if people realize that.

This week's sermon was about intimacy. I knew this from the Web site, where the church announced each sermon topic weeks ahead to give members time to think and pray on it. This, too, was new to me, that church could be a spiritual seminar for which to come prepared.

In the front seat, Aaron mumbled his way through printed notes. I caught snatches—"the gift of closeness" . . . "what makes us human" . . . "God is love."

My mind drifted to my car ride with Juan. Recalling the way he looked at me, I realized with horror that the memory made my insides flutter. I was like a tweener learning her harmless crush on the cute new boy might in fact be reciprocated. Only I was no tweener. I was married. To someone else. Someone I loved.

So Candace's lunchtime talking points weren't out of line after all. Turned out she was right: I did need reminding that my mind ought to be on my husband and his happiness. *Our* happiness.

The sun dimmed as we pulled up to Greenleaf, its lights blazing. Tosh and Aaron headed toward the inner sanctum. I went to look for Jerry. He had mentioned ending the day with a Bible study.

The education wing was brightly lit but empty. I liked this section of the church. Scenes from the Bible were painted on the plaster walls of the corridor in an artistic style I could only describe as Sunday comic strip. Jesus walking on water toward a boat full of flabbergasted disciples; Mary and Joseph leaning over a manger; Adam and Eve in a cartoonish Garden of Eden. The church held Sunday school in the classrooms here, and I thought it spoke to the character of the kids that no one had yet graffitied in speech bubbles.

During the weekdays, this corridor was usually elbow-to-elbow with people attending job-interview workshops or addiction counseling or one of the many teen clubs. Most of these were open to the public. In fact, Candace had just received word of a soon-to-air *ABC News* interview in which the President of the United States would mention Greenleaf as a model for "faith-based" community services. Publicizing this PR gold was the topic that occupied the rest of our lunch, once the marriage counseling part concluded.

She wasn't the only one analyzing me today. *When's it your turn?* Juan had asked. *When's it your turn to lay your burdens down by the river?*

He'd meant it lightly, I was sure. Still, Juan had managed to jab an open wound. Because the more time Jerry and I spent here, the more I became aware of the widening divide between our faiths.

I chose to trace it back to the day of his calling, but in truth, our thoughts never had converged on this matter. Jerry knew when he married me that I harbored serious doubts, certainly about Catholicism, but also about God. And I knew back then, too, that even as he continued to seek the right house of worship, his core belief in a Holy Father never wavered.

We talked about it back then, back when we'd lie in the Sheep Meadow for hours playing with each other's hands, back when we'd meander around Central Park with no destination or deadline. I remember one day in particular, when there was some sort of walk-athon through the park raising money for a debilitating disorder. MS, I think. We watched participants streaming by, some in wheelchairs, wearing green event T-shirts, hooting and cheering.

"Like with my mom," I remember saying. It was during what turned out to be a lull in her illness, a remission that would end all too soon. "And how people always say they're praying for her. What Great-Aunt Cin said, about how whatever happens, it's God's will." I turned to him. "Is that kind of what you think, too? That it's God's will?"

"I do," he said. He took my hand as we watched a boy on crutches pass. "Do you?"

"I don't think I do," I said slowly. "I guess ascribing the mysteries of the universe to some great overseer in the sky just feels . . . I don't know. Wrong."

"Ah," he said. "And to me, that's exactly what feels right."

"Is it okay?"

"Is what okay?"

I searched his eyes. "That I don't believe the same thing as you?"

He leaned toward me and touched his forehead to mine. "Let's agree to disagree."

This truce still held, as far as I knew. Yet I sensed he drifted further from me in his convictions, and I from him in mine.

Greenleaf was like fertile soil for Jerry's faith, allowing it to take root and sprout and blossom. It did not do the same for me. Jerry never pressured me one way or the other. Upon reflection—everyone else was analyzing me, why shouldn't I join in?—he must have sensed recent events affected my readiness. For the past few years he'd listened to me rant with disgust at the Catholic church for covering up the crimes of abusive priests. But had I not wrestled already with doubt, the grotesque arrogance of the Vatican might have propelled me into the open arms of my husband's church. Had I not struggled already with basic belief, the allure of Greenleaf might have reeled me right in.

Instead I found myself losing my religion, and religion losing me.

I thought about pretending. I did. I thought about embracing the faith of my husband and those around me and ignoring the lack of my own. What would be the harm, really? Especially if it would—what was it Candace had said?—tighten the string holding together our hearts.

Already I suspected Jerry withheld from me the daily journey of his faith. He would make mention of attending a Bible study, but only in a recitation of his schedule, as he had that morning, not to share any spiritual discovery. Sometimes he would begin to muse aloud about some bit of Gospel wisdom, but then catch himself and shake his head as he remembered to whom he spoke. Aside from the pinch of feeling left out, I also felt bad that I wasn't that person for him: a wife who spoke the language. I bet Aaron talked Scripture with Candace. Jerry deserved that, too.

As if on cue, I heard Jerry laugh. The familiar sound, surprisingly light for a man of his height, came from a classroom around the corner. Trailing my hand along the comic-strip mural, I approached.

Inside, a dozen or so worshippers milled. They stood around one who held open what looked like a schedule book, probably planning their next meeting. I didn't see Jerry. Then I heard his laugh again.

He sat on a folding chair with his head bent over what even I could tell was a Bible, using his finger to underline a passage. A woman sat beside him, her head bent so close it almost looked like she'd laid it on his shoulder. Then she looked up at him. I recognized Giovanna Disantana.

Her long hair was pulled off her face in a loose bun, framing her lit-from-within skin. Her style always struck me as fundamentalist Mormon, as in the ankle-length dress and fuzzy cardigan she wore that day. Her eyes shone with an intensity that made me uncomfortable. The intensity of the devout, I supposed.

I must have made a noise, because Jerry raised his head. Gee looked up, too, and gave me a wave before turning to talk to the woman next to her. The other Bible students glanced over, saw I was not accompanied by Candace, and went back to their business. Jerry clapped his hands on his thighs and got up.

"See you next week, Pastor Jerry," a woman with frowsy hair called. "Don't forget—"

"I know, I know," said Jerry, laughing. "John 4:8."

They all cracked up. It was Greek to me.

Still chuckling, Jerry put his hand on my shoulder. "I'm starving. Did you eat?"

How long? I wondered as we walked out into the night. How long could two people sustain a marriage when one believes what the other does not? I could love a man of God. I could, and I did. But as I edged toward the side of the infidels, could a man of God love me?

CHAPTER EIGHT

Candace

Meg Sinderell lived in a carefully distressed mansion on a former cotton plantation in the rural outskirts of Magnolia. The plantation's many acres had been converted into a luxury development "retaining the antebellum charm of our storied history," according to the management company's brochure. When the homes first came on the market, Candace drove by to take a peek. The plaque at the entrance proclaiming EST. 2004 made her smile. The price tags for the homes made her laugh out loud.

As the current copresident of the Greenleaf Women's Committee, Meg was hosting its biannual luncheon for new members. Turnover at Greenleaf week by week could equal the entire congregations of ordinary churches, so the committee asked that a new member attend services for at least a half year before admission. Even then, the invitation was a coveted get. Candace heard tell of grown women squealing with delight upon arrival of the card, which by her own decree came on heavy stationery embossed on the envelope with a tiny metallic green leaf.

The card was not just any card, of course. It signaled an invitation not just to a meal but to Magnolia's most prestigious inner circle. The Women's Committee met for tea weekly at an officer's home, each a grand display of new money. The agenda consisted typically of a wide range of church concerns, from the high (changes to the core syllabus of Sunday school) to the low (the sodium content of the café's carrot smoothies). These the officers and members dispatched with haste, efficiency, and relative equanimity. For what they really wanted to get to was the gossip.

By nature, Candace had little taste for gossip. As it says in Proverbs 18:

> *A fool's mouth is his destruction, and his lips are the snare of his soul. The words of a talebearer are as wounds, and they go down into the innermost parts of the belly.*

While she took no personal enjoyment in the dissemination of other people's misfortunes, she conceded that knowledge was her most valued commodity. In that regard, the committee teas were a helpful source of intelligence on her flock. The tea was how she learned the reason Athena Kalifinakis had stopped attending service, for example. "Foreclosure," whispered Yasmina Dauhaj, Athena's closest friend.

"Did you hear about Dot's son?" said Leonora Thibodeaux, setting down her English Breakfast. "Addiction. Oxy. After knee surgery for, you remember, that soccer thing."

"Can you imagine?" said Debbie Frieholdt.

"Being treated now at a clinic in Milwaukee. Same one where Gina Carlos went. You remember."

"Where's Priscilla Weir these days?"

"You haven't heard? Her husband."

"Ran off with a *man*."

Candace heard about church members' job losses and affairs and arrests. She learned whose child was rejected by which university and whose husband saw a hypnotist to cure his erectile dysfunction. Thrilled by their chance to rub up against the senior pastor's wife, committee members eagerly betrayed the juiciest confidences of their most intimate friends.

If the women talked of themselves, it was usually to brag by complaining. But Candace gleaned plenty by what they didn't say.

"Marco and I, we just got back from Pont du Gard," said Shawna Jimenez, showing off her tanned arms. "The jet lag is killing me." But Candace noted the anxiety in her eyes and the fast-fading smile. Pont du Gard was driving distance from Monaco. Maybe Marco was gambling again.

"Olivia placed first in vault, second overall," said Lizbeth Ruffalo. "All these away meets—oof. Eats up all your time." Time she could be spending with her son, Tyson, institutionalized after a suicide attempt last fall.

Even so, Candace did not judge them. Not really. Magnolia was no Eden, free of sin and pain. That she knew. Finding Jesus did not necessarily mean finding peace. The teas were a safe place for these women to unload their burdens, their fears, their jealousies.

But knowing the tribulations of the flock did help guide in their care. For while Candace never gossiped for the sake of gossiping, she systematically analyzed the data for her husband. When she noted an increase in tales of financial distress, for instance, she passed this assessment along to Aaron, who then incorporated relevant messages into his sermons. This contributed to a sense among church members that they were known, that the senior pastor spoke directly to their troubles.

Candace didn't have to attend a tea to know money was on a lot of people's minds these days. Even Meg Sinderell, with her winding driveway and her uniformed help, was serving cold sandwiches instead of hot roasts. Meg's husband, Walter, worked for the Atlanta office of a French trading concern that Candace had read lost a billion dollars this year in the market turmoil. His bonus would reflect that.

Looking around at the women, Candace could not identify a single one who had grown up rich. New money, every last one of them. There was old money in these parts, to be sure, but they tended to stick to traditional houses of worship, the ones attended by their grandpappies before them. Greenleaf attracted transplants and local strivers.

Candace could relate. She wasn't of old money, though she knew from it. Back in Wilkes-Barre, the summer homes of the old Pennsylvania coal barons loomed like kings atop the hills. As the prettiest girl in the county, she had dated some of their sons. She could have had her pick. Even a Mayflower family would not have said no to the breathtaking daughter of a respected pastor.

Instead she had chosen Aaron.

Truth to tell, there'd been many a day, a week, a year, when she regretted her choice. Not of him. Not exactly. But of the lifestyle that came with being a pastor's wife. The paltry pay. The horrid housing. The social calendar of Sunday school and choir practice. Looking back, even she found it remarkable that her love for Aaron never wavered.

"You're how I know," he told her once, the day they arrived at

Greenleaf, the day they began their new life. "That I'm on a special mission. That I've been chosen. I know because God sent me you."

Candace excused herself from Meg Sinderell's parlor and stepped outside. Candace was usually the featured speaker at the new-member luncheons, but today she had invited two guests to stand beside her: Tova Bernstein, wife of the rabbi, and Kristin Chaudry, wife of the imam. The three would together make a fund-raising plea for the Harmony Center, an institute their husbands were building in downtown Atlanta, dedicated to interfaith studies and understanding.

Candace also regarded this as an opportunity to set an example for the ladies of Greenleaf, to influence behavior through modeling. Observant Jews and Muslims tended not to congregate in this particular suburb, choosing to live near their own houses of worship, closer to the city. Love her flock though she did, Candace knew ignorance bred prejudice, and plenty of uninformed opinions shaped church members' views. The women of Greenleaf spent little time with Jews and probably knew not a single Muslim. They simply weren't aware how much they had in common with women of other faiths.

Tova Bernstein pulled up the driveway in a Toyota minivan with five car seats. She and the rabbi had six children, the oldest, Shoshanah, finally big enough to ride in the front. Today Tova drove alone. She hopped out of the car, brushing crumbs off her ankle-length black skirt and smoothing her long brown hair into a black beret. She waved at Candace and hurried across the parking lot. Tova's beret caught a glint of sun, and Candace saw it was rimmed with sequins.

"Jonah threw up this morning and I had to leave poor Sho to clean up," she called. "I couldn't get out of there fast enough."

"Tell me about it," said Kristin Chaudry, who pulled up right behind. Imam Chaudry's parents had emigrated from Pakistan, but he himself was Atlanta born and bred, as was his high school sweetheart, a blue-eyed white girl from a nice Baptist family. She converted before they married, and Candace gathered that Kristin could by now recite prayers in nearly flawless Arabic. From under her neatly wound head scarf peeked a tendril of auburn hair. The Chaudrys had three children. The youngest, Azala, had Asperger's.

"I'm so glad you could come," said Candace.

"Are you kidding me?" said Kristin. "I've had the sitter booked for a month."

"A lunch with women who won't ask me why the rabbi can't personally preside over their seder?" said Tova. "And who won't wave their diamonds in my face and tell me the rabbi's wife should really drive something better than a Toyota? You had me at hello."

"Ugh," said Kristin, gripping Tova's arm in sympathy. "We just announced the renovation plans for the exterior of the mosque, and you should just hear the complaints."

Yes, they had much in common. Candace led them into the house, making the introductions.

* * *

The bottle stood atop Candace's desk in her Greenleaf office. The purple label read, JESUS WINE. Candace picked the bottle up and turned it over. The script on the back continued, *"And He turned water to wine. —*John 2."

She handed it to Ruthie. "What do they want?"

"To run an ad in *Christianity Today* with Pastor Aaron's endorsement."

"That's ridiculous," she said. "Pastor Aaron hasn't had a drink since 1988. Next."

Ruthie placed a papier-mâché sculpture on her desk. It looked like a toilet lid in the vague shape of a seashell.

Candace stared at it. "What is it?" she asked.

"An urn," said Ruthie uncertainly. She unclasped it, and the seashell yawned open. "I think you place your ashes here."

"Not *my* ashes," said Candace. She gave the thing a poke. "Why is it made out of paper?"

"So it'll dissolve at sea," said Ruthie.

Together they stared at the death clam, and together they shuddered at the thought.

"And they're sending it to us because . . . ?"

"The lady who called said their market research shows evangelical Christians don't yet embrace cremation. They want Pastor Aaron to sermonize on it. Oh, she said to make sure to mention the environmental superiority of cremation to whole-body burial. Looks like she did a little research on us."

"Not enough," said Candace. "Cremation pumps mercury into the air. And he certainly won't approve of flushing Grandma out to sea on a toilet-paper raft. Next."

Ruthie shuffled the letters. "This one's from a group called Life Donors. They want us to endorse Christian kidney donations." In a robotic monotone, Ruthie read from the letter. " 'We are God-loving Christians who want to call to other God-loving Christians to donate their organs.' "

"And what will they do with those organs?" Candace asked, narrowing her eyes. "Are they nonprofit?"

Ruthie scanned the papers. "Incorporated."

"Unbelievable. Organ harvesters, exploiting the goodwill of

Christians to fulfill market demand. How *do* they find us?" Candace rubbed her temples and reached for an Imitrex.

Ruthie handed her a glass of water. "Why don't we take a break?" she said, getting up. "I'll get back to these folks and we can do the rest later."

Candace swallowed her migraine pill and swiveled around to look out her picture window at the autumn sky.

What is my purpose?

Candace had taken to asking herself this question daily, hourly, on every breath. *What is my purpose? Why am I here? How shall I serve?*

It was not that she considered her duties superficial or meaningless. It was earnest work: the evaluation of requests, the consideration of demands on Aaron's time and name. Candace was the keeper of the Greenleaf brand. She would have it no other way. And with Aaron departing next week for his Interfaith Conference in London, she could spare little time pondering the Big Questions. She had staff to manage, projects to oversee, troubles to shoot. . . .

Is this it? Is this my purpose?

She gazed out at the clouds and asked aloud, "What do You want me to do?"

"Candace?"

She swiveled again. Tosh Takai, her head of security, stood in the open doorway carrying a laptop. Perhaps he'd heard; probably he'd heard. She didn't much care. Tosh was the soul of discretion.

She waved him in. He closed the door behind him.

"All set for London?" she asked. He nodded as he took a seat across from her. "What's security like at the conference?"

"Heavy," he said. "Police, ID checks, metal detectors at the convention center."

"Protestors?"

"Expected. Anti-Islam, anti-Israel, antiwar . . . you name it, they'll be there."

"Personal security?"

"Pastor Aaron insists on traveling with Imam Chaudry and Rabbi Bernstein. We've rented a limo with reinforced doors and bulletproof windows. I've vetted a local driver; I'll ride shotgun."

"Specific threats?"

He shook his head. "We're coordinating with Scotland Yard and MI5 on international plots, but they're unlikely to focus specifically on us. As for the usual suspects around here, we doubt they'll have the means to travel."

"Good," she said. "Good. Take care of him. You know I count on you."

"Thank you, Candace," said Tosh. But he did not get up. "There's something else. It's about the Newleaf audit."

Candace nodded. She had asked Tosh to vet all current employees of Newleaf, particularly senior staff. Candace happened upon a recent article in *Fortune* magazine emphasizing the inadequacy of conducting background checks only upon hire. A study found that one in ten current employees showed some sort of recent offense, everything from DUI to attempted rape.

"What did you find?" asked Candace. "Let me guess—the music minister. Always seemed a little shifty to me."

Tosh didn't smile, but then, he rarely did. He spoke carefully. "When you told me to vet everyone, I assumed you meant family, too," he said. "Forgive me if I overstepped."

Candace grew still. "What did you find on my son?"

Tosh placed his laptop on the desk and turned it toward her.

"It's not Timothy," he said. "It's Ginger."

CHAPTER NINE

Ginger

Not until she stood at the baggage terminal at the Minneapolis airport did Ginger fully accept that she was spending an entire weekend away from her children.

As she listened to the luggage conveyor to groan to life, she closed her eyes and stood still. Breathe in, breathe out. The chatter and clatter of arriving travelers bothered her not one bit. No one talked at her. No one pulled her hand. No one demanded Goldfish crackers or someplace to lie down or pee pee in a potty really, really now.

At Door 6, where she had been instructed to wait, Ginger saw another woman, maybe in her forties, dressed in pressed chinos and a sweater set with a pumpkin pattern that she remembered seeing in the Talbots catalogue. She recognized not just the uniform but the solicitous expression of a pastor's wife. Sure enough, the woman caught Ginger's eye.

"Hi," she said. "Are you going to the retreat?"

Ginger nodded. The woman waved in greeting. "I'm Cindy. First Baptist in Dubuque."

"Ginger. Newleaf in Magnolia."

"Georgia!" Cindy exclaimed. "Now why aren't we having our retreat *there*?"

Outside, snow blew sideways across the pick-up lanes, dragnetting the already jammed-up cars. Ginger shook her head. "Imagine how *I* feel," she told Cindy. "My first vacation in years, and I had to pack long underwear."

Cindy laughed. Ginger congratulated herself, though really she had Ruthie to thank. Ever since they became friends, Ginger got to flex her conversational muscles almost daily. Having someone to talk to—someone clever and witty, who made her feel that way, too—did wonders for her self-esteem. So much so that she'd agreed to represent Greenleaf at this retreat for pastors' wives, an annual event she'd avoided strenuously in previous years. The prospect of a weekend with a hundred strangers no longer made her want to hang herself.

Timothy had agreed to stay home with the children. Tali had giggled maniacally upon news of a Daddy Weekend. Jordan had grilled her about the date, time, and absolute certainty of her return. It would be the first time she had ever left her husband alone with her children overnight. But he betrayed no anxiety. "Go," said Timothy. "Have fun."

Fun was not the word she would use, though the Web site made it sound more like a girlfriends' getaway than a prayer retreat. A spa night. Hot-tub chats. Manicure and massage. True, they'd be administering these treats to each other as exercises in bonding, but still. Ginger looked at her disastrous nails. She'd have to skip the manicure. Why advertise her nervous habits?

"I think that's us," said Cindy. A van pulled up outside the sliding doors. Two other women joined them as they batted away the snow and made their way toward the vehicle.

On the hour-long ride to a suburban Hilton, Ginger half-listened to the women chitchat as she gazed outside. At a red light she watched as a minivan skidded to a halt beside them, its driver a mom who whipped around in her seat to break up a battle between three small children in the back. By the time the woman turned back to the wheel, Ginger could practically see her temple throbbing. Been there, she thought.

The hotel wasn't fancy but aspired to something beyond ordinary, judging by the massive chandelier in the lobby. Light jazz tinkled from the bar. Ginger looked longingly at the men and women in business suits, ties loosened, top buttons undone, joking and laughing as they knocked back amber drinks on ice. She hadn't had a drop since she'd met Timothy. She didn't miss the alcohol. She did miss her place at the party.

"You got a roommate?" A petite and very pretty black woman stood before Ginger. "I signed up late and my husband, he won't pay for a single."

"My roommate dropped out," said Ginger. Ruthie had decided to stay in Magnolia at the last minute. Something about minding the fort while Jerry traveled to London, plus she needed to assist that reporter on his deadline. She pointed to the printed name tag that came with her sign-in packet. "Ginger. Like the spice."

The woman was writing her name on a blank tag. "K-A-Y-C-E-E." She pinned it on her shirt. "Rhymes with spacey. Lazy. Head-casey. Slow-pacey. Believe me, I heard 'em all."

Ginger wrinkled her nose in sympathy. "I got nicknames bad, too, growing up."

"Oh," said Kaycee. "That's just what my husband calls me."

"Ladies," said a stout woman wearing a hot pink T-shirt that said SPIRITS CONNECT!, the title of this year's retreat. "We're going to start with an opening prayer."

They joined the women entering a spacious, carpeted room, the kind hotels call a ballroom to attract mid-budget weddings. Indeed, it looked like they'd stumbled into just such an event. White table-cloths covered the round tables, adorned with cheap but cheerful centerpieces of carnations and daisies. Only this was a wedding with an all-female guest list.

Ginger and Kaycee joined a table at the back. The women already seated there made introductions, identifying themselves by church and location. No one spelled out their denominations, but Ginger had learned from Candace how to tell by the name of the church and the hairstyles. The intricate weave from Mount Zion: Baptist. Shellacked bouffant from New Directions: evangelical megachurch. No-fuss bob from Holy Spirit: Lutheran.

A titter rippled across the room as a tall, white-haired woman swept through. The word *statuesque* popped into Ginger's mind, though she wasn't exactly sure it meant what she thought it meant. "Is that Lorraine Lawson?" a woman asked. Another woman at the table nodded. They all stared after her in awe.

Kaycee leaned toward Ginger. "Am I supposed to know who that is?"

Ginger opened her sign-in packet and pulled out a glossy color flier to show Kaycee. It featured a photo of Lorraine Lawson standing on a cliff, leaning into the wind, like a picture in one of Jordan's library books, a figurehead on a ship headed for the New World.

Lorraine Lawson had founded Spirit Sisters, an international network of pastors' wives. The wife of a prominent Lutheran preacher in Minneapolis, Lorraine was herself an ordained minister and traveled the world to sermonize, mainly to women. Ginger once overheard Candace calling her "that she-man from up north," and seeing her in person, she supposed Lorraine did sport a square jaw and swimmer's shoulders. Candace denounced these retreats for their "touchy-feely, New Agey mumbo jumbo." But Ginger suspected her mother-in-law refused to attend because she resented ceding the spotlight to a woman of equal stature.

"Sisters in Christ," said Lorraine Lawson from the podium.

She spoke gently, leaning into the microphone. Her voice registered so low as to seem impossible for a human female. Like a didgeridoo, Ginger thought—the Australian instrument she and Timothy once heard played by a dreadlocked white man on a Miami street corner. A call of the wild.

"Welcome to the weekend that will salve your wounds. Welcome to sisterhood. Welcome to the love and warmth and acceptance of Christ. *Welcome home.*"

A strange thing happened. Ginger's body responded to the sound of Lorraine Lawson's voice. It washed over her and through her like a soaking rain, like a deluge that overwhelmed and bust open the dams that held back her every emotion. The other women in the room reacted the same way. Some surged to their feet to shout. Others gasped forth their tears.

For all the natter endured by a pastor's wife, no one spoke *to* them like this. No one saw through their smiles to their pain. No one welcomed them home.

"We are here for a reason," Lorraine continued, her voice calm and unaltered, as if she did not notice the put-together women before her transforming into a sea of heaving breasts. "We have gathered here for a purpose. We have not come by accident. We are here because we need help."

Ginger felt the vise that had clamped her heart for six years snap. She tried to breathe but instead gulped a loud sob. Embarrassed, she looked over at Kaycee. But her new roommate looked about to faint herself.

Lorraine leaned forward. "You need help," she said. It was not a polite thing to hear from a stranger, not an encouraging thing at all. And yet her voice offered only kindness, bottomless kindness. She said it again. "You . . . need . . . help."

Lorraine stretched her palms toward the crowd. "There is no shame in this. In fact, let's wipe out all the shame right from the get-go. All together now. I . . . need . . . help."

"I . . . need . . . help," the room of women howled.

"We need help because we carry a great burden," said Lorraine. "We are married to men of God. And yes, this is important work, to support and sustain the messengers of God's word. But listen to me, sisters."

At this, Lorraine leaned forward. So did Ginger.

"*We matter, too.*"

Ginger's head knocked back as if she'd been sucker punched.

She heard a wail. It sounded like it came from across the room, but when she looked for its source, she saw it was Kaycee. The ballroom erupted with the emotions of women lifted, for a time, of their loads.

"This is what we'll discover this weekend," soothed Lorraine. "You will learn your worth. You will know your value. And you will go home to your husbands and children and congregations refreshed and reborn. You will begin anew."

Through her tears, Ginger nodded emphatically. As though Lorraine spoke to her alone and required some sort of response.

"This," said Lorraine, "is your balm of Gilead."

* * *

"Do you love your husband?"

Kaycee whispered the question into the dark. Ginger lay a few feet from her in her own double bed, making snow angels. It felt so odd to stretch out all alone on clean, starchy-scratchy sheets. Her own bed at home smelled of Timothy's sweat and her coconut foot lotion. Ginger never slept alone; in his frequent absence, and usually even in his presence, she awoke with one or both of her children tucked into the crevices of her body.

They had been talking for hours. Or, rather, Kaycee had been talking and Ginger had been offering increasingly softer murmurs of acknowledgment.

Ginger squinted at the digital clock on the nightstand between them: 12:09 a.m. After Lorraine's speech and the group prayer, they grabbed sandwiches and milk from the snack table and headed up to their room. A standard-issue chain hotel room, but Kaycee squealed like they'd found themselves in the Ritz-Carlton. At some point after their toilettes Ginger flicked off the bedside lamp, but still Kaycee continued to talk.

"Mmm," said Ginger sleepily, though in truth she lay with her eyes wide open. She knew Kaycee would soon fill the silence.

"I do," sighed Kaycee. "I love him like he's the sun and the moon and all the stars in heaven. I love him almost more than I love Jesus."

So that's why you can't leave him, thought Ginger.

Kaycee had all the markings of an emotionally battered woman: the eroded self-confidence, the needy eyes, the delusional denial. Ginger marked her the moment they met. And in the cool darkness of their shared hotel room, Kaycee unpacked her sorry tale.

She'd had it rough, no doubt about that. After dropping out of high school her sophomore year, Kaycee began using. She soon slipped into prostitution to pay for the heroin. Kaycee celebrated her twentieth birthday with a score, and passed out on the steps of a boarded-up building on the frayed fringes of Memphis.

She woke up in heaven. Or so she thought: All she saw and felt and tasted was warmth. When her senses focused, Kaycee saw she lay swaddled in blankets on a sofa in a dim room. A serious man spoon-fed her soup. "Homemade chicken broth," she said, sighing at the memory. "I never tasted anything so good."

The man was named Devonn Washington. The boarded-up building was his, the site of his new church, a church to save the neighborhood's damned souls. "You'll be my first," Devonn told Kaycee. She swooned.

Devonn nursed Kaycee off her habit. To keep her from slipping, he leashed her. "That's right," Kaycee said proudly. "A real dog leash." He clipped one end on her belt loop and held the other, thus keeping her always in his sight. The shame she felt initially, say at the Home Depot while they picked up paintbrushes and lumber, faded as her love grew. He did this for her. He did this for *her*.

Together they fixed up the storefront church and created a cozy living quarters above it. Together they solicited new members, Kaycee handing out fliers on street corners as Devonn charmed passersby (the leash came off when it appeared to scare away would-be worshippers). The makeshift pews began to fill.

Devonn preached self-reliance. "Go out there and equip yourselves," he thundered from the pulpit, as the room rang with *mmm-hmm* and *you tell it*. "God gave you will. God gave you brains. God gave you purpose. Now go out there and use it."

Kaycee took him at his word. She found a Bible course online for women. After a few months she stumbled upon an Internet pastor-training course. She told Devonn of her discovery and her dream.

"I want to be a pastor," she said.

He laughed. Then he cut off their Wi-Fi.

"The thing is," Kaycee whispered to Ginger in the dark, "I think I woulda made a good pastor. I been through a lot. And I know I got a lot to learn. But I think I got something to say. And I keep hearing God telling me it's not enough to be saved. I got to save in return."

Ginger reached out and took Kaycee's hand. They lay like that, staring into the black, hands clasped across the divide, hanging on.

* * *

The small conference room divided into clumps of six women each. Ginger and Kaycee sat in a circle alongside a plain-faced mother-daughter duo from Indiana and two longtime friends, both missionaries in Europe. Their team leader, Ann Downer, worked very hard to defy her own name.

A cross, cut out of cardboard and painted white, stood propped on the chair next to Ann. Someone—probably Ann—had gone Martha Stewart on the cross, scalloping the edges and glue-gunning it all over with white tissue flowers. Why a cross needed decorating, Ginger did not know. It was like those pink handguns she'd seen on the news. You just can't make a murder weapon cute.

"This exercise is called Cross Your Heart," chirped Ann.

The women smiled politely. Earlier this morning, perhaps to

make up for their outburst of untrammeled emotions last night, the wives took care to exhibit their professionalism. The buffet breakfast in the ballroom buzzed with friendly introductions and ladylike laughter. Every time Ginger filled her mouth with scrambled eggs, another manicured stranger would tap her on the shoulder with a greeting.

Kaycee seemed a different person, too. She blossomed under the charm assault of the other wives, her smile shedding its hesitance. Her social awkwardness just made her all the more adorable. When Lorraine Lawson herself approached their table for a quick hello, Kaycee inexplicably dropped into a curtsy.

After breakfast, Lorraine recited a prayer. One of the volunteers played synthesizer, and they sang half a dozen hymns. Kaycee's voice grew louder with each song, till she was throwing her head back and belting out riffs like a contestant on *American Idol*. When the music ended, the women around them clapped for Kaycee, who squeaked with delight.

"I have a special treat for you this morning," Lorraine said, as the women took their seats.

Over the sound system, a Muzak version of the old church saw "On Eagle's Wings" began. A woman with long graying hair strode up beside the podium and took a seat at an easel. A camera had been set up beside her to project her blank canvas onto a large screen at the front of the hushed room.

As they watched, the canvas began to fill with a pastel rendering of a river. A few strokes of green chalk and suddenly the scene transformed into a forest. The women sighed in recognition. Another few strokes of blue, and again the scene changed, this time into an ocean. The women burst into applause.

"What does this tell us?" asked Lorraine, who watched from her podium. "It tells us we cannot trust our eyes. We cannot always trust our senses. We don't know what we think we know. All we can trust is God."

Ahhh, said the room.

Next, Lorraine introduced Pastor Lionel. It was strange to see a man in the room, like a timid fox amid a vociferous chicken coop, and he didn't exactly look overjoyed, either. "I come for penance," Pastor Lionel began, and the room was riveted. A year ago, he led a nondenominational congregation of nine hundred in Dallas, his wife and three children by his side. But driven by demons of inadequacy and boredom, he said, "I sinned." He began an affair with a church member, a young divorcée whom he was counseling through depression. He was caught. The church fired him, his wife divorced him, even his lover left him.

"Lawd," whispered Kaycee.

"My message is that Jesus heals and Jesus forgives," he said. "I'm not asking for your absolution, for me or for your husbands. Not that your husbands are doing what I did. What I mean is, I'm not asking you to overlook our errors. But I'm hoping my story will help you understand that even a good man, even a godly man, can sin. Even a pastor is human."

He paused and blew into a tissue. Many of the women in the room dabbed their eyes, too. "Every day I begin with the first words of Psalm 130," he said. "*Out of the depths have I cried unto thee, O Lord.*"

After lunch, Ginger and Kaycee pored over the day's sessions together. Ginger was slightly scandalized by the offerings: "How to Treat Your Husband's Porn Addiction." "Sex and the Pastor: Satisfying a Godly Man." "Rekindle the Romance: 10 Bedroom Tricks!"

"Sex, sex, sex," she heard another wife say as she read the agenda. "This reads like the cover of *Cosmo*."

She and Kaycee chose the least salacious sounding of the offerings, which was how they found themselves in this room, smiling at a woman who had made a craft project out of a cross. Ann Downer explained the exercise. "We're here to bond," she said, locking eyes with each of the women. "And to bond, we're going to have to share."

Uh-oh, thought Ginger, feeling her stomach turn. Sharing was not her strong suit.

Ann handed out lavender-colored notepads. "Write down a sin," she said. "And I don't mean forgetting to say grace at dinner last night." The mother-daughter duo tittered. "I mean something that has shamed you, that you've carried around as Jesus carried this cross."

Ginger had a sudden image of Jesus dragging a BeDazzled cross through the streets of Jerusalem.

"You'll pin it on this cross. At the end of the weekend, we'll go outside and burn the whole thing. It'll set you free of your sins!"

Kaycee was already scribbling on her notepad. The two missionary friends looked at each other, shared encouraging smiles, and began to write. The mother and daughter from Indiana turned their backs to each other for privacy.

"Don't tell me you have no sins," Ann said. Ginger realized Ann meant her. Her tone was teasing, and the other women looked up with smiles.

"I have so many, I'm having trouble picking," Ginger said. The women giggled. Her insides churned again. She bent her head and pretended to write.

Soon Ann clapped her hands. "Okay, ladies! Time to fess up."

The women looked at each other, alarmed. "We have to . . . tell?" said one of the two missionary friends, the taller one.

"Of course!" Ann said. She folded her hands under her chin and looked around eagerly.

"What is this, Truth or Dare?" whispered Kaycee apprehensively.

The taller missionary woman stood up. "Well. Okay. I guess I can go. I'm Sandy," she said, pulling at her cotton blouse so that the rest could see her name tag. "I'm with Faith Church in Barcelona." Unlike many of the wives here, Sandy looked ill-acquainted with a makeup kit or a curling wand. And yet Ginger thought her beautiful. Both she and her friend wore bright scarves around their necks in that effortlessly sophisticated European manner. Style must just rub off on you over there.

"About a year ago," Sandy began, and then she stopped. With a blink her face slammed shut. She stared at them but appeared not to see.

Sandy's friend stood up and embraced her. The other woman was neater, more compact. Tina, her name tag said. Tina held Sandy and whispered in her ear for what seemed a long time. When she pulled away, Sandy's face ran with tears.

"About a year ago," she began again, "I lost a child."

Ginger's hand flew to her heart. Every mother's worst nightmare.

"Miscarriage. Second trimester." Sandy rubbed her belly, as if she could still feel the bump. "Used to be I thought about him all the time. Every day, every hour. But lately—no. We're so busy with the mission and our other children. My sin is that sometimes I go for an entire day without thinking of him. And once recently I caught myself telling someone I had two children, not three. I always included him before."

The women sat, silent, in shared sorrow.

"The Lord has him now," said Ann. "May we pray with you?" They took each other's hands and bent their heads.

Sandy's missionary friend, Tina, stood up next. "My sin is I hate to evangelize," she confessed. "Here we are, in France, the most beautiful country, filled with all these—elegant people," she said. "I should *want* to bring them the Gospel. I should strive *every day* to share His love." She hung her head. "But I'm afraid. I can't bear the rejection. The way they just turn away, like they've got a million better places to go. Or that look they give me. Disgust. Pity. So I tell my husband I just can't learn the language."

Tina pinned her note to the cross. "*Je regrette*," she said, in what sounded to Ginger like a flawless accent.

The younger of the mother-daughter duo stood up. She smoothed her denim skirt over plump thighs. Her sweet, plain face looked mournful. "Sometimes, I hate my congregation," she said.

"Oh, now, Melissa," said her mother.

Ann held her hands up. "Hut tut tut," she scolded. "Swallow that thought, Judy. This is a judgment-free zone."

Judy obeyed, clamping her mouth shut.

Her daughter continued, her face grave. "They just sit there and, and—*complain*," said Melissa. She threw her voice up an octave. "'The sermon's too long.' 'The sermon's too short.' 'The Christmas tree's too gaudy.' 'The pastor's suit looks cheap.' 'He should drive an American car.' 'The *last* pastor's wife played organ.' 'This ziti tastes like dung.'"

The women nodded in sympathy and tried to look solemn. Sandy's lips twitched. Tina snickered. Even Ann smirked.

"Just last week, we had our annual Washing of the Feet,"

continued Melissa, worked up now. "The old ladies march in and take off their shoes and plop their gnarly feet in the buckets. I start to wash and I realize *they haven't taken off their stockings*."

Kaycee shrieked. Sandy and Tina collapsed on each other, nodding and cackling. They understood.

"They wanted their feet washed—in their knee-highs! 'Oh, no, dear, I can't take those off,'" Melissa mimicked in a flutey, old-lady voice. "'The *last* pastor's wife didn't mind. Watch my bunion!'"

By now even Judy's shoulders heaved up and down. They laughed so long and hard that the other groups turned to stare.

Finally, Judy stood up, wiping tears of laughter from her furrowed cheeks. "My sin is one of omission," she said. "It's just that I've been so busy. The children, the grandchildren, the church, Sunday school, hospital ministry, bake sales . . . I've been married to my husband for almost fifty years, and I don't know if he knows I still love him."

Melissa got up and hugged her mom. Tina reached over and squeezed the older woman's hand.

"That's one you can fix," said Ann kindly.

Kaycee took her turn. "I don't even know where to begin," she said. But she didn't look afraid. An hour ago, these women were strangers. Now they had the intimacy of shared experience. "I guess I should just say that I done a lot of really horrible things in my life, things you ladies can't imagine being part of. You think you sinned? I was a sinner of the worst kind. Mary Magdalene's got nothing on me. Now if you put Mary in a ghetto with a crack-whore mom and a stepdad who beat her, then we're getting somewhere."

Judy, who sat next to Kaycee, reached over and patted her arm.

"But my worst sin of all was I didn't know Jesus."

Ann beamed. "Another one we can fix."

As Kaycee pinned her lavender note on the cross, Ann turned to Ginger. "And now for our last confession."

Ginger waited for a wave of courage to overtake the nausea of fear. She looked around at the women, each of whom looked back with warmth. After what Kaycee had said, nothing she could reveal would shock this group. And anyway, what did it matter? This was a judgment-free zone.

Ginger inhaled deeply. She unfolded her lavender notepaper. Then she bent at the waist and threw up.

* * *

Ginger opened her eyes. She sat next to Kaycee in the hot tub, a tiled indoor Jacuzzi next to the pool. Kaycee had not left her side since the exercise, which she now called Cross Your Heart and Puke Your Guts. Sandy and Tina, the missionary ladies, had helped her clean up in the restroom. Melissa and Judy, the mother-daughter duo, fussed over her at dinner, fetching her saltines and ginger ale, making everyone at the table hoot with more stories of awful congregants.

Later in the evening, all the wives were urged to relax with one of three activities: a mani-pedi, a facial, or the hot tub. Kaycee lobbied for the first until Ginger informed her of the mutual participation. "After today, no way am I touching some lady's feet," said Kaycee, shuddering. They opted for the whirlpool.

All around them bobbed pastors' wives in swimsuits, most, including Ginger, in what Ruthie called momsuits: chaste swimwear equipped with high necklines and thigh-covering skirts. Ginger's even came with a built-in minimizer bra, designed to squash her breasts. Ruthie would look around and declare this a photo shoot for a cheesecake calendar—from the twenties. Suddenly, Ginger missed her friend.

"Where you going?" Kaycee demanded.

"Back to the room," said Ginger. "You stay. I just want to lie down."

Kaycee raised a concerned eyebrow. As Ginger toweled off she overheard her telling the other women in the tub, "Threw up this afternoon. Tossed her eggs right up all over my good shoes."

Wrapped in a hotel robe, Ginger waited by the elevator. Out of the corner of her eye she noticed something purple. There, on the wall beside the entrance to the ballroom, half a dozen crosses were pinned up. One of them was painted white and covered with tissue flowers and, now, folded lavender notes.

She walked over and saw the notes had multiplied, practically covering up Ann's decorative efforts. Then she noticed the lavender notepad tacked underneath, next to a sign inviting anyone to pin up their sins.

Ginger reached for the paper.

"Cross Your Heart," rumbled a voice.

Ginger startled. Lorraine Lawson stood beside her, looking amused as she surveyed the crosses.

"I always thought confessing your sins was a waste of time," said Lorraine. "I grew up next door to a Catholic girl. She'd go to confession once a month. Told me she said the same thing every time: 'I took the Lord's name in vain, I talked back to my mother, blah, blah.'" Lorraine chuckled. She turned to Ginger. "Us Christians, we talk to God all the time, not once a month in a booth through a man with a collar. So really there's no need for confession."

Ginger withdrew her hand from the lavender notepaper.

"That's not to say it's unworthy to reconcile your sins," said Lorraine, cocking her head. She studied Ginger. "What stops you, sister?"

"I don't know," whispered Ginger.

Lorraine laid a hand on Ginger's arm. Her fingers were long and unadorned, like twigs. Man hands, Candace would say.

"Everyone sins," Lorraine said. "Everyone. That person you idolize and whose judgment you fear? She, too, has sinned."

Ginger blushed with guilt. Could Lorraine read her thoughts?

"Church is a hospital for sinners, not a sanctuary for saints," said Lorraine.

"Is that from the Bible?" Ginger asked.

"No," said Lorraine. "Erma Bombeck."

* * *

Ginger opened the door to her room and was greeted with an outcry.

"There she is!" exclaimed Tina.

"Oh, thank the Lord," said Sandy.

Kaycee shoved them aside. "Where you been?" she shouted. "I been calling all over, so worried, you weren't here, didn't know where you got to—" She yanked Ginger into a bear hug. Over Kaycee's shoulder, Ginger saw Judy and Melissa, both dressed in pajamas and robes, sitting on her bed.

"Give her some air, honey," said Sandy, tugging Kaycee back.

"Poor Ginger," said Tina, seeing Ginger's confusion. She began to laugh. "You had no idea."

Kaycee smiled, too, as she wiped tears from her face. "Girl, you can't just disappear like that, not when you been sick and acting so weird all day. I got so worried I called in the troops." She gestured to the women.

"I'm sorry," said Ginger.

"Where were you at, anyway?"

"I was talking to Lorraine Lawson."

The women murmured and nodded. "Any words of wisdom to share?" asked Judy. They arranged themselves on the beds and waited. Ginger remained standing.

"Yes," said Ginger. "Actually, what I want to share is my confession. I didn't get to go today because . . . well, you were there."

"My shoes were there, that's for sure," said Kaycee.

"Enough about your shoes already," said Melissa.

Ginger took a deep breath. "Until six years ago, I was someone else. I was a—I took my clothes off for money. First I stripped. Then the guy I lived with talked me into posing for a Web site. So I did some photos and video and before I know it, we're getting a million, two million hits. The money starts pouring in. Five thousand, ten thousand dollars a month. They wanted more and more. I drank to get through the day."

Ginger paused. Someone—maybe it was Tina—asked softly, "What happened?"

In her mind she could remember clearly, though back then her mind was anything but clear. She remembered staggering out of the shoot, wiped out from exhaustion and five shots of Absolut. She remembered weaving through the parking lot toward her shitty little Nissan. And there, as she fumbled for her keys, she remembered . . . looking up . . . to see, reflected on her windshield . . . a flaming cross:

S
I
R E P E N T Y O U
N
E
R

It was a neon sign advertising a nearby church, one she'd seen a hundred times but rarely registered.

"I quit the next day," said Ginger.

"What about the boyfriend?" Kaycee asked.

"Threw me out and kept all the money."

Judy growled.

"And your husband?" said Melissa.

"Met him a couple months later," said Ginger. "My second sign."

"And he forgave your sins, just like Jesus," said Kaycee.

"After I told him, he never mentioned it again."

"That's love," sighed Sandy.

"That's survival," said Ginger. "His family doesn't know about my past. If they did, they'd kick me right to the curb, faster than my no-good ex."

"Oh, I can't believe that," said Tina. "Candace Green seems so *good*."

Noodles. Here she thought she'd been flying under the radar, but they knew of her affiliation all along.

"She is good," agreed Ginger, and she believed it. Candace Green was a good Christian woman, her beliefs and values and faith utterly impregnable.

Maybe this was why Candace withheld her love from Ginger. Maybe it was because she sensed Ginger withheld the truth.

No. She could not chance it. While there dangled the possibility that the truth would set Ginger free, there remained the reality that the lie—the happy homemaker, the innocent pastor's wife—kept her family whole. She would not rob her children of Greenleaf, of Paradise Estates, of their grandmother's fierce, protective love. She had nothing to offer in their place.

"Oh, and one last confession," said Ginger. "I'm pregnant."

CHAPTER TEN

Ruthie

"Ready?" I called to Jerry as he bumped down the stairs with a carry-on suitcase for London. I picked up the Prius key and waited by the door.

This was it. I could no longer ignore the strangeness between us. On the surface, nothing had changed. With our shared workplace, we probably saw more of each other than ever before. But our lives were like two guitar strings, thrumming along in parallel but never intertwining. And so it had come to this: the Relationship Talk.

Confrontations and me, we don't mix. The very prospect of sitting my husband down for a Serious Discussion About Us made my armpits clammy. Putting it off till after the London trip tempted me, but I knew the week's separation would only heighten my sense of isolation. Distance makes the heart grow distant.

Nevertheless I procrastinated until the day of his departure. In my defense, no moment previous to said date presented itself as opportune. We'd have the forty-minute ride in the car to the airport, I figured—about as opportune as I'd get.

Jerry looked at me with surprise, then regret. "Oh, honey," he said. "I've got a ride."

A car honked outside. I opened the front door. Sure enough, a black SUV waited at the curb. Tosh Takai had the wheel, with Aaron in the passenger seat.

The back door opened.

"Gee," I said.

"What?" said Jerry.

"Giovanna," I said. "Disantana."

"Hi, Jerry," she called, heading toward us. "Mrs. Matters."

"What am I, your mom?" I muttered to Jerry. But when I looked up at him, he didn't seem to have heard.

Gee took the handle of Jerry's Samsonite from his hand, like a very cute porter. "All set?" she said, smiling brightly.

"All set," Jerry said, and turned to me for our good-bye. But something in my face must have stopped him. He said to Gee, "Can you give us a sec?"

"Oh, sure," she said. She took a step back, then stopped and continued to wait. Was this girl kidding? Could a woman have a private good-bye with her husband before he crossed an ocean for a week? So much for our big talk. I'd be lucky to get a solid kiss.

"Why's she here?" I mumbled, so she wouldn't hear.

"She's going to London," Jerry mumbled back.

This was news. "I thought you said no chicks allowed."

"She's performing or something. Just found out myself."

I didn't like this. I didn't like this one bit.

"Anyway," he said, leaning in close, "you gonna be okay? You seem a little, I don't know—"

The SUV revved its engine. "We're running late," called Aaron.

"I'm okay," I said to Jerry. "We'll talk when you get back."

Jerry looked unconvinced. I drummed up a smile.

"Really," I said. "Ta-ta. Cheerio. God save the queen."

Jerry leaned down for a kiss. At the last second, I turned my face. I couldn't tell you why. Here I was, longing—aching—for a moment of connection with my husband before he left me for a week, and I didn't even let him kiss me. Call it one of the millions of inexplicable moves we make in marriage. Or just call it stupid.

As the SUV pulled away, I looked down to find myself stroking my own forearm with my thumb. The specific and effective way Jerry used to comfort me. When had this become my habit—and not his?

* * *

"Ruthie? That you?"

"Of course it's me," I said to my sister. "Who else calls you from this area code?"

"Can't see the caller ID," she said. "The twins wrapped the phone in Bendaroos."

I slipped on my flip-flops and padded out to the porch. Hearing my sister's voice uncoiled me. This had become our daily ritual. Usually it was Viv. Once a week or so, Tom. The twins—my brothers Paul and Michael, not Viv's toddler set—graced me occasionally with a hollered greeting from a bar, three or four sheets to the wind.

These calls tethered me. They reminded me someone out there knew the real me, remembered who I was and always would be. That's what siblings are: a reality check. Try to become someone you're not—affect an accent, or start quoting the temperature in Celsius instead of Fahrenheit—and they're the ones who smack you upside the head. Siblings are like potters; they try you by fire, glaze you with taunts, finish you with well-aimed jibes. If you emerge from that kiln without cracking, you can survive the world.

That's not to say my move to Churchlandia had no effect. The loose camaraderie I'd always shared with Tom had stiffened into businesslike phone calls. The twins hadn't punked me in ages. As for Vivian, our still-daily conversations grew more and more one-sided. She told me how the hospital tech had vowed not to reveal the gender of the baby in her belly, as requested, then proudly showed her the ultrasound screen featuring a white shadow in the shape of a penis. I knew all about Dina and Donnie toppling a pyramid of mangos at Whole Foods and the ensuing melee as they hid from Viv's wrath and then fell asleep under a bushel of organic bananas. She told me of the neighbor who drove drunk over her bed of impatiens and the preschool teacher's maddening use of *irregardless*.

She talked. I listened.

It's not that she didn't ask, at least at first. All of them did. They queried me about Greenleaf, if not enthusiastically then with genuine curiosity. Paul wanted to know if Aaron's hair was real or plugs. Michael wondered how much the church grossed in weekly tithes. Tom asked for Aaron's position on a ruling in Texas allowing public schools to teach creationism. Early on, Vivian began every conversation with the same question, one I felt sure our mother would have asked in her stead: "How are you fitting in?"

They asked. I didn't answer.

In college, I briefly dated a boy my family didn't like. *Dated* is too strong a word. We met at a local pub playing drunken darts, and by the time the bartender kicked us out, we were making out like fools. Someone saw us and told my sister, who informed me with the thundering righteousness of Moses that he was already spoken for—by no less than a member of Viv's sorority.

My brothers, when she told them, couldn't care less about the besmirching of Kappa Kappa Gamma. They instead rose up against the nerve of this feckless boy in two-timing on their sister (never mind that I was the one he was two-timing with), and my stupidity for sticking it out. They at least had the sense to keep the news from our parents, who surely would have called a Family Conference.

I didn't care. Or maybe I did care, and the drama only heightened my madness. Drama! Over me! In retrospect, the boy was *so* not worth the trouble—in retrospect, are they ever?—yet instead of walking away from a bad situation, I walked away from the disapproval. I stopped returning my siblings' calls. Needless to say, I stayed far away from Viv's sorority house, where everyone and their mothers knew the sordid tale. I holed up with my worthless obsession in his shabby off-campus apartment, eating ramen noodles naked and adoring the gap between his two front teeth.

My own behavior startled me for many reasons, not least because I had always been motivated by a need to please. I sought approval the way a bee seeks pollen—purposefully and programmatically. I hated to let anyone down, especially the people I loved best. When I parsed this later, I wondered if maybe that was why I had drawn away. So deeply did my family's disapproval wound me, so harshly did it contradict my desire for this boy, that I could survive only by plugging my ears.

I still saw my family, of course. There was no disowning or even a confrontation. That's not the Irish-Catholic way. But the raucous teasing and good-natured jibes that constituted our relationship chilled to the point of formality. Maybe other families showed their love with Hallmark expressions. Mine planted a whoopee cushion. This, too, took me years to recognize. The absence of my family's jokey affirmation left a hole no romance could fill.

He dumped me, of course. Dumped me to return to his sorority queen. There was probably a lot of shrieking recrimination in the house on Greek Row where my sister lived. I don't know. She didn't tell me. I do know she moved out the following month and quit attending the many functions—the socials and rushes and pinnings that used to dominate her calendar. "It got boring," was all she ever said. And once, with ferocity: "Girls are morons."

In a way, Greenleaf was my new gap-toothed boy. My family didn't approve. I knew that. They harbored deep, intractable suspicions about non-Catholic Christianity, the Greens, megachurches, the South. Jerry's embrace of it all rendered him suspect as well.

They believed I went along for love. That, they could stomach. I could not tell them otherwise. I could not tell them about my admiration for Candace, the wonder of Sunday service, my pride in our work. To do so would betray their confidence that I was still Ruthie, their Ruthie. And I would not risk once again creating a family-sized hole in my life.

So when they asked me about our life in Magnolia, I simply did not answer.

"How's it going?" asked Viv, now on speakerphone as she attempted to pry Bendaroos from the panel of her phone.

"Oh, you know," I said. Usually, I left it at that, but today I added, "Jerry just left for London."

"Oh, yeah?" she said, still distracted. "Big fan of the crumpets?"

"What's that supposed to mean?"

"Whoa. Nothing. Touchy about the baked goods."

She would be, too, with a tasty treat like Gee around. I shook it off. "How's Dad?"

Lately, this was conversation topic numero uno among the Connelly clan. The romance between our father and Mrs. Kim—whose first name was Joon-ja but who went by June—had advanced with alarming swiftness. Vivian had the latest, and it was a doozy.

"They're moving in together."

"Wow."

"I know," she said. "They only just met!"

"Not really," I said. "If you think about it, they've known each other for twenty years."

"Whose side are you on?"

"I didn't think there were sides."

"That's because you're not here," she said.

"Ouch."

She ignored me. "We've all tried to talk to him. He's decided we're trying to sabotage his, and I quote, 'last chance at happiness.' Like he's going to kick it tomorrow, and like none of us, his kids or grandkids—like we mean nothing. It's getting to the point where I think he's going to cut us out of his life."

"He hasn't mentioned any of this to me."

Viv's voice brightened. "That's it," she said. "*You* talk to him."

"Me?"

"He hasn't labeled you the enemy yet. And you and Dad have always had your thing."

It was true. Since we were little, I'd played the role of Dad's audience, listening to his stories and providing the laugh track to his comedy routines. In return he took me along on errands that ended in ice cream and later took to mailing me newspaper clippings of articles he thought I might find funny or weird. The others accused him of favoritism and me of sucking up, but in truth we just enjoyed each other's company. His calls to me had lessened in frequency as his romance took flight. When we spoke, I was careful to remain neutral.

"You could come up. How about this week?" Vivian was asking. She was off speakerphone. The battle was won: Vivian 1, Bendaroos 0.

"I don't know, Viv," I said. "It's pretty crazy with Jerry gone."

"Just for a day. Just for a conversation. One-on-one. It's important."

Somewhere in the house, my cell phone buzzed.

"Listen, I should go," I said. "I'll look into a flight home this week. In the meantime, go easy on Dad." Then I said something I heard Candace Green say twelve times a day but that had never before crossed my own lips. "Let me take care of it."

* * *

"Martini, up. Gordon's. Not dirty but with as many olives as you can jam in there without alerting the manager."

T.J. Reilly's wasn't busy on a Sunday night. I ran my hands along the bar, an ancient slab of mahogany with initials carved in hearts by idle Swiss Army knives. Must've been bought and imported. Magnolia was the kind of place where business establishments boasted of being founded in 1998, and this piece of wood had clearly held up the pints for at least fifty years. Still, you had to love the attention to detail. Jerry would. He missed his musty pubs in our old Manhattan neighborhood.

As the bartender assembled my drink, I watched with the breathless attention of a child before a magician. The man had a mustache that drooped at its edges; he'd tucked his red tie neatly into the front of his apron. If Jerry were here, he'd mutter under his breath, "Hello, Central Casting."

Then, as I did all things these days, I surveyed the scene through Candace Green's eyes. She'd say it was plebian, yes. Base, probably.

And the drink? It hadn't yet come up, but I'd bet my boots she didn't touch anything stronger than ginger ale.

Should the disapproval of my boss and mentor have given me pause? Maybe. Certainly. But it was too late. Already I was lost in the vision of that glass before me, the improbable architecture of the upside-down pyramid on a stem. The evening light rendered the liquid inside a deep-sea green. Half a dozen fat olives bumped lazily at its conical base. Jagged shards of ice floated at the surface. An oily sheen revealed the mist of vermouth. The beauty of the thing crumpled me with desire.

Quickly I glanced right and then left. I hadn't taken such a thorough leave of my senses that I would forget to check for people I knew. Church people. The coast was clear. I scooped my hair back with one hand and leaned down, skimming the liquid with my lip. Then I slurped.

What—you wanted manners? Raise the glass with pinkie extended and sip like a lady? And risk spilling a drop of my first cocktail since I arrived in Georgia? You're out of your mind.

God. Was there anything better than the first sip of a martini? Anything at all?

Juan laughed.

"*What*," I snarled.

Juan Diaz sat on the next barstool, one elbow on the bar, watching me. "You just keep surprising me, is all," he said.

I blew air out my nostrils and rolled my eyes toward the pub's pressed-tin ceiling. Affectations that said, What-*ever*. But to be honest I felt flattered. Surprising a reporter? That's no small thing.

"Why am I here?" I asked.

Juan looked pensive. "Probably it had to do with a meeting of sperm and egg," he said. "But I guess that's the *how*. As to the *why*, you'd best consult your bosses. They seem to have all the answers."

I made to punch him, and he leaned back, laughing.

"You know what I mean," I said. "Why did you call me?"

He shrugged, still smiling, and turned away to sip his own dark brew. "Maybe I thought you'd be lonely," he said.

He may as well have splashed the martini in my face. Because he was right.

For the first time in my life, I was lonely.

I hadn't recognized the symptoms. The vague sadness. The lingering in busy places. The overconsumption of infomercials. You have to understand: Lonely was a luxury in a household of seven. Lonely was a weakness indulged in by spinsters and royalty. Lonely was a condition we heard about but suspected didn't really exist, like chronic fatigue or restless leg syndrome. Lonely was *alien*.

Even after I married, I never felt terribly alone. Eight million lonely people live in New York City, but at least we have each other. Besides, I wasn't alone. I had Jerry. He wasn't stapled to my side, of course, but I knew he thought of me throughout the day, and that was the next best thing. He'd wonder what I ate for lunch. He'd call to ask how a meeting went. He'd read something funny and store it away to tell me later.

In Magnolia, we shared a workplace, which you'd think would mean I'd see him all the time. I did, but always in passing, and always in the presence of others. I preferred the phone calls.

It wasn't like I was sitting around mooning at his photograph, you understand. I was busy, too. I had friends. Every few days I'd drop by Ginger's, and we'd gab over tea while little Talitha banged on pots and pans. I thought Ginger might be the sweetest person I'd ever met, and I knew she found me smart and funny. But our conversations felt somehow superficial. Like we were holding back our true selves.

I spent the most time with Candace. I couldn't call her a friend, exactly, and of course there's a limit to what you can discuss with your boss. But I enjoyed her company, and I would venture to say she quite enjoyed mine.

And then there was Juan. I saw him less and less these days, now that he was completing his reporting on Greenleaf. He'd scored an unusually long lead time on the article because he'd pitched it so far ahead of the news peg, which was this London conference. His editors had green-lighted it under the condition he keep up the police blotters and community bulletins. He was a general assignment reporter, after all, and a rookie at that; the profile on Aaron would be his first big enterprise piece.

I missed him. I missed the stink of his car. I missed my musical introduction to Foster the People and Death Cab for Cutie. I missed debating health care policy and Hollywood morality and what was to be done with Brazil nuts after you licked off the salt.

I turned to him with a too-chummy grin. "How far along are you, anyway?"

"Twelve weeks," he said in a girly voice. He patted his stomach. "Am I showing?"

I missed the dumb banter. "Mazel tov," I said.

"It's done," he said in his normal voice, taking a sip of his brew. "Written. I was gonna proof it tonight. Then all I have to do is hit 'send.'"

It was done. It was written. It was over.

Whatever "it" was. My friendship. My flirtation. My maybe. It was probably a good thing. No, it was definitely a good thing.

"Well," I said. I elbowed him. "It's been real." I knew I was slur-ring, and I didn't care.

One thing we didn't do was touch. We weren't stupid. Once in a while we bumped shoulders, on purpose, to make a point or show agreement. One time, after he asked me a particularly nosy question about the Greens' sex life, I flicked him on the forehead, hard. An-other time, he gripped my upper arm as we made our way through a church crowd.

His left forearm brushed against my right on the bar, and this time, he left it there. I looked down at our joined elbows. The hairs on his arm tickled. He had a mole I'd never noticed before on his wrist, a perfectly round one that bumped out a little like a wart. I wanted to touch it.

I understood now. He had asked me here to this bar to say good-bye, to mark an end to our collegial relationship. But it was also an invitation.

I'd be lying if I said this offended my ladylike sensibilities, or even came as a surprise. I'd be lying if I said I never fantasized about starting over with Juan, or someone like him. Someone whose favorite authors and fast-food preferences and top-five dream travel destinations matched my own. Someone who would not only get a *South Park* reference but would one-up me with follow-up dialogue.

Someone who wasn't a pastor.

I'd also be lying if I claimed I read *Playboy* just for the articles. Let's face it: Juan was hot. In truth he was much more my type than the man I'd married. I realized this one day as they stood shoulder-to-shoulder at Greenleaf listening to Aaron: Jerry, tall and cool and neatly pressed; Juan, disheveled and muscular and a little bit sweaty. Women admired and respected Pastor Jerry. But they'd have to be amphibians not to get a little warm around Juan.

And here was this man, this charming and desirable man, this man who found me charming and desirable, too, bumping his arm against mine on a bar.

Believers accuse nonbelievers of malicious obduracy, of gleefully denying the existence of God. They're wrong. I envied Christians their certainty. I *coveted* their certainty. I wished for nothing more than to reach a fork in the road and pick one path over the other without hesitation, just because the Bible told me so.

As choices go, this was not, on its surface, a big one. I could slide my hand just an inch to the right and touch a man's wrist. But where that would lead, even I, in all my inexperience and lack of biblical guidance—even I could guess at the trouble.

"Great working with you," I said, feigning a formality I did not feel. "Best of luck with your article. I hope you got everything you wanted."

When I glanced up at him, I saw his eyes fixed on the space between our hands. "Not everything," he said.

There it was. That fork in the road. His breath smelled of warm beer and toast.

I picked my hand up off the bar and stood up. A little unsteadily, but I managed. He stood, too. I started toward the door and stumbled. He caught my arm.

Too close. Way too close.

"I should drive you home," he said.

I straightened myself. "That won't be nesheshary." Damn it.

Juan did drive me home, in my car. We said little during the short trip. I remember asking him how he'd get back to his own car. He said he'd already called a cab. When we got to the house, he saw me to the door.

"Well," I said.

We stood awkwardly apart. How do work marriages end? A hug in front of my house—in view of all my neighbors, who were also church colleagues—seemed wildly inappropriate. Plus it would mean touching him in a way I wasn't sure I wanted to remember.

I stuck out my hand.

He smiled with half his mouth, forming one, just one, dimple. But he took it.

"Good-bye, Ruthie Matters," he said.

"Good-bye, Juan Diaz."

The cab pulled up, and he was gone.

* * *

The martini buzz had pooled into a thumping headache. I poked around the bathroom cabinets for some Tylenol, then remembered a bottle of it in my bag. Which I must have left in the Prius. Padding out in my flip-flops, I groped under the passenger's seat and came up with a bag. Juan's bag.

Juan carried an over-the-shoulder messenger bag similar to mine. We'd commented on it one day as we drove to a Greenleaf event, about how convenient they were and how much crap they could carry. I remembered because after I used the word *crap*, he told me he liked me.

"I like you," he'd said, with a big grin on his face that defused any misconstrual. The way you'd say it, if you were the type to say this sort of thing, to an acquaintance after you discovered a mutual passion for, say, collecting rare comic books. What I mean is that there was nothing between those lines. At least, that's how I took it then. Now I found myself rewinding it and all our other times together, sifting through words and deeds for their hidden meaning.

I had Juan's bag. He must have grabbed the wrong one by mistake after he drove me home. Which meant he had mine. Which meant I would see him again.

My first reaction was relief. I would see him again. His last memory wouldn't be of me as a sloppy drunk. I could say a proper goodbye. Or not. Maybe our friendship could be salvaged. Surely he'd want that, too.

I would take his bag inside and call him. Luckily I'd kept my cell phone in the pocket of my jacket. How long before he dropped off my list of recent calls?

Dialing while walking requires a modicum of coordination, especially after a mammoth martini. As I tried to kick off my flip-flops, I tripped and fell. Juan's bag dropped to the floor. Out skidded its contents: two reporter's notebooks, pens, some bills, and a manila folder labeled GREENLEAF.

Sitting on the floor in the darkening foyer, I groped around me to gather up Juan's things. A document slid out of the folder. It was a printout of his story, the one he meant to proofread tonight. It was formatted for the newsroom, but I could still make it out.

I don't remember how long I sat there in the receding light, reading and then rereading Juan's article. I don't remember getting up or going outside. But I do remember feeling that, for once, the right choice seemed obvious.

I needed to find Candace.

CHAPTER ELEVEN

Candace

There was a chance he didn't know.

This was what Candace, or any mother, really, would prefer to believe about her son. That Timothy did not know his wife was a whore. That her sweet son had unknowingly married a harlot who performed unspeakable acts for broadcast on the Internet. That there was trickery. Even entrapment. There was a chance.

It was unlikely, she conceded. In fact it would be just like her Timothy to rescue a fallen woman. God love him, the boy did suffer a savior complex.

She would ask him. Eventually. In good time. First, there was the business at hand.

Keeping her eyes on the road, Candace reached into her purse on the passenger's seat and groped for a blister pack of Imitrex. Her fingers located the sharp-edged square, only to find the plastic casing empty. And with the mother of all migraines coming on. *Lord help me.*

If Timothy knew, that meant he and Ginger colluded to keep

this secret. Some secrets were best left buried, people said. Those people were fools. Truth will out. Knowledge is divine. Eve ate the apple.

Still, this apple had the effect of those mushrooms in *Alice in Wonderland*, a story she'd read recently to Jordan. One bite altered reality. In this case, her knowledge of Ginger's past called into question everything she had ever believed about her daughter-in-law, and even about her son.

Had Ginger and Timothy really meet at the *Glamour* magazine event for desirable bachelors? Or did her pastor son frequent those sinful establishments where people like Ginger plied their trade? Had he *paid* her? An image popped into her head: of marshmallow-white breasts held so the pink nipples pointed straight up, of an arched back, of glossy lips yawning open. Of pubic hair the color of a penny. Of Ginger. Unmistakably Ginger.

Candace shimmied her head like a wet dog, as if she could shake off the picture of her daughter-in-law's private parts like so many drops of water. But memory didn't work like that. Not hers, anyway. Especially not hers. Once viewed, forever recalled.

Back in her office, she had stared at the video clip just a few seconds before pushing the laptop away. She had not looked at Tosh when she asked if there were others.

"Dozens," he said quietly. "All confined to one Web site. Miami-Xtreme.com. She's not the only girl featured, but she's among the most popular."

"Are you sure it's her?"

"She went by 'Flame.' But I made some calls. It's her. It's Ginger."

Candace cradled her head in her hands. "Why didn't we know?"

"It's a pay-for-content site. You wouldn't know unless you went looking."

Candace massaged her temples. "When did she . . . has she stopped?"

Tosh came around the desk and tapped on the laptop's keyboard. "I hacked into the page source to find the time stamp embedded in the code," he said. Up popped a screen of gobbledygook. He pointed to a series of numbers. "The last is dated six years ago. It looks like, yes, she stopped. Right around the time she met Timothy."

Sweet Jesus, that image. It burned. "If she's stopped, why are they still up?"

"I would guess she doesn't own the rights. Few porn . . . few adult models do."

Porn. There. The word slapped her across the cheek. She felt its sting, then its metallic aftertaste.

Her daughter-in-law was a porn star.

"Is there anything else?" she asked dully. "Posters? Centerfolds?"

"Not that I could find," said Tosh. "She didn't need it. The Web site alone gets a million hits a month."

A million pairs of eyeballs staring at her daughter-in-law fornicating with a man who was not her husband. Candace closed her eyes. Inhale, exhale. There would be time, she told herself. There would be time to process. To pray. To beseech Jesus for an explanation. Right now, the situation required action.

Inhale, exhale. She opened her eyes.

"Who knows?"

"No one here. That I know of."

"Get me everything," she snapped. "Family background, as far back as it goes. Every trailer park she's ever called home. Every john she's ever hustled. Every drug she's taken, every cigarette she's smoked, every disease she's carried. I want to know everything."

Tosh looked at her, his eyes reading her face. "I'll take care of all this when I return from London. It's not going anywhere. Let me handle this for you. Please."

Next to Hugh Dolly and now Ruthie Matters, Tosh Takai was the staff member Candace spent the most time with, and she trusted him perhaps the most. His foremost concern was her and her husband's safety. He knew his job. What's more, he was right: This wasn't going anywhere. The results she sought required an exact attack, a surgical strike, which in turn required preparation.

What is my purpose?

No. She could not wait. The thought of perverts around the world leering at the mother of her grandbabies made her want to scratch off her own skin. Every day, every minute the images remained out there was another that besmirched the family name.

"It's Tuesday," she said. "You leave for London on Saturday. I'll clear your schedule till then. That'll have to be enough time to come up with what I need."

She pulled on her headset and tapped a button. "Alice," she said. "Book me a flight to Miami. For Saturday."

Tosh looked alarmed. "It's not safe. I can't let you do that alone."

"I won't be."

* * *

The map was one reason Candace had chosen the Atlanta law firm of Grubman, Grubman, Roth, Sing & Feeley to represent Greenleaf affairs. A French sculptor of some renown had fashioned a map of the world out of steel, designed to occupy an entire wall of the reception area in the firm's Atlanta headquarters. Here and there on the map twinkled tiny blue lights. One in Paris. One in New York. Another in Los Angeles, another in Tokyo. Grubman, Grubman had outposts all over the globe. The map was marketing, she knew, and the firm's international presence affected her church not a whit. Nevertheless it boosted Candace's confidence.

The Miami office of the firm resided in a glass Rubik's cube of a building in the city's central business district. Its basement parking garage was surprisingly full, for a Saturday. The devil and his lawyer take no holidays, as Candace's father used to say. She pulled her rented PT Cruiser in between a cherry Porsche Boxster and a silver Jaguar convertible.

A young man awaited her on the fourth floor. He wore a suit so flawlessly pressed that he reminded her of the two-dimensional paper dolls she had recently bought for Talitha. He ushered her to a conference room with wraparound views of the ocean. A glass pitcher of ice water beaded with condensation at the center of the oblong table. The young man poured her a glass, but she went to the window and stood there, eyes on the horizon.

"Mrs. Green." A man with the body shape of a teapot waddled in, followed by two younger associates carrying armloads of files. "Gunther Weingarten. We spoke on the phone." He thrust out his hand for a terse shake, then turned to arrange his notes on the table. Back at the Atlanta headquarters, the partners would have spent half an hour charming her earrings off, then another thirty minutes boasting of all their recent accomplishments. A billable hour of kissing her rear end. This lawyer didn't even bother to introduce his cohorts. Candace liked his style.

"You're prepared," she said. It was not a question.

"Given the amount of time we had," he said.

The glass door opened. Escorted by the same paper-suited young man, her opponent entered. Darren Wu. Thirty-two, Tulane grad, engineering major, according to the dossier compiled by Tosh and his team. Owner of three downtown nightclubs, a beachfront penthouse appraised at $1.9 million, and Miami-Xtreme.com.

Darren Wu wore his hair slicked back and his cheeks freshly razored. His open-necked white shirt exposed an almost tasteful gold chain. His skin glowed with the copper sheen of a tanning salon, like many of the young people in this city. But then it was hard to tell what constituted natural coloring with these Asians.

His attorney, who recalled Casper the Friendly Ghost next to his Coppertone client, traded brisk greetings with Gunther, while this Darren Wu sat down and grinned at Candace.

"Hey, you're a church lady," he said. "I've seen you on TV."

She took a seat and said nothing. She imagined what he saw: a petite, older white woman, a grandmother, really, in beauty-parlor hair and a tailored suit. She presented her sweet, sweet smile. Disarm the enemy. The tactic always served her well.

Darren rocked back in his chair, drumming his fingers on the table. "Can we get started? I gotta get back to work," he said with a wink.

The devil and his lawyer, thought Candace.

His lawyer opened his notebook. "We understand you are interested in one of my client's properties."

Properties. Like her daughter-in-law was a two-bedroom condo.

"That's right," said Gunther. "The rights to one of your models' portfolios."

Darren was still grinning like this was all a big joke and rocking back and forth in his chair. Back and forth, back and forth. A nervous habit, surely, but as annoying as all get-out. "Which one?"

"Ginger Abrelly," said Gunther. "Flame." He slid a document across the table to Darren and his attorney.

As the two men scanned the paper, Candace thought about fencing. She had recently helped Jordan assemble a school project on the sport. This being kindergarten, the other children picked ordinary endeavors like baseball and swimming. Not her Jordan. In the library they selected a large book with colored photographs, and together they pored over the positions and the rules. As a professed Francophile, Candace predictably fell in love with the terminology. But also she grew fascinated by the game itself, the elegant attack, the polite violence. Fencing was a sport she'd played all her life. She just hadn't known it.

She watched as the document jolted Darren Wu out of his laidback amusement and back to his businessman's mien. Good. Now they could talk. She angled her gold Cross pen so its point aimed across the table, right at him, like a miniature saber.

En garde.

Both leaned forward for a rapid exchange. *Attaque.*

"You her mother?"

"An interested party."

"She's our only redhead."

"Not true. Amber, Jenny G, Tawny—" *Contre-temps.*

"She's one of our top earners."

"*She* doesn't earn anything."

"We bought her rights, fair and square."

"And now we're buying them back."

"She's worth more."

"We know exactly how much she's worth. Our offer is more than compensatory for a few six-year-old videos. Besides, you don't have a release." *Avantage*.

Uncertainty flicked across Darren Wu's face. He raised his chin at his attorney, who looked back, a pale blank.

"That predates my representation," the lawyer hissed.

Gunther slid a document across the table, this one a photocopy.

"My investigator found she never signed one," Candace continued smoothly. "That her rights were sold without permission by an ex-boyfriend. That signature, there? Forged. Here's her real one."

Once again Gunther produced a paper. The two men on the other side of the table looked from one document to the other.

Gunther cleared his throat. "I think you'll agree this is an infringement of copyright and privacy, giving the injured party grounds to sue for irreparable damage to reputation. Not to mention the pain and suffering."

"Lawsuits are expensive," tried Darren. *Challenge*. "You're telling me Flame—Ginger—has that kind of cash?"

"Oh, she'll be funded," said Candace. "We have resources you can't imagine."

"Trials can get nasty."

Candace folded her hands. "I would quite enjoy taking this to court, actually. A pornographer illegally displaying and profiting from naked pictures of a pastor's wife. I wonder how a judge and jury would rule?"

At this, a frat-boy smirk couldn't help but escape Darren. "Did you say pastor's wife?" he said. "That's hot."

For the first time since they had begun their conversation, Candace dropped her smile. She knew the effect of this slight shift in facial muscles, not so much from any mirror but from other people's reactions. Like a warm shower turned without warning to ice.

"I rather think they'd grant us damages. Big damages. Enough to shut you down."

The tittering stopped. *Battement.*

"But you know how juries are," she added, lifting her shoulders in a tiny shrug. "They want justice. Financial restitution just doesn't compare to the orange jumpsuit."

"Right," Darren scoffed. He wouldn't fold so easily. "Like you'd risk your churchy reputation with a front-page trial."

Candace regarded the man before her. Enough. "Maybe you'd prefer it if we went after your other properties. Your nightclub on Ocean Drive, the one with the crystal waterfall? At least twelve code violations, according to my investigator. The other one on Northwest—I understand it employs a high number of undocumented workers in some not-very-nice conditions. You're awaiting a line of credit from Southeast Providence. We know the board. A word from me, and your application goes in the shredder. Every development, every hire, every deal big and small—I can and will find a way to obstruct."

Darren Wu paled under his bronze lacquer.

Coup de pointe.

"Are you threatening me?"

"I'm reasoning with you," she said. "The other option is to sign right there."

She pointed her gold pen once again at Darren Wu.

His attorney leaned toward him in hushed conference.

Darren hesitated. He nodded. He took her pen. Then he signed.

As Gunther retrieved the papers, Candace held her hand out for her pen. Darren released it to her, then rocked back in his chair one last time, the sneer gone, arms folded, eyes hard. He, too, did not like to lose.

"I don't get it," he said. "Awful lot of trouble for one girl. You say she's not your kid. So what do you care?"

Candace met his gaze. Of course you don't get it, she thought. Men like you. Discarding a woman's dignity like a hamburger wrapper. Looking at someone's wife and mother and seeing only breasts and a rump. Paying a woman to sell her soul. What Jesus would have made of you.

What Jesus would have made of me. *Judging and condemning the wife of my son.*

"I care," she said to Darren Wu. And she realized she did.

Neither broke their gaze as Gunther recited the conditions. "You will pull all images of Ginger Abrelly off the site, effective immediately. You will remove all mention of her from your archives. You will confiscate all marketing materials containing her image or nom de plume. We will review the site tonight at twenty-four-hundred hours and monitor it regularly thereafter."

Candace stood up. "Oh," she said to Darren Wu. "I'm not a church lady." She smiled one final time. "I'm *the* church lady."

Salut.

*   *   *

Though her day trip to Miami taxed her beyond belief, Candace got up at dawn on Sunday morning for church. She believed if she were abducted by aliens and plopped on some foreign moonscape, she'd still wake up early the morning of the seventh day and prepare for church. Not easy to deprogram a pastor's wife. Besides, today's services would require her presence even more than usual, what with Aaron away in London. Only after the day's many duties were completed did she return to Paradise Estates, park her car in her own driveway, walk over to Timothy and Ginger's house, and let herself in.

Ginger's house was a mess. Pajamas sprawled across the foyer floor. Candace recognized Jordan's, in Spider-Man red and blue, and the grass-green wisp of Talitha's Tinkerbell nightie. Shoes kicked every which way. A Stride Rite slip-on balanced, improbably, on the banister.

In the kitchen, green and yellow ceramic bowls encrusted with cereal were piled one atop another in the sink. A frying pan with bits of scrambled egg rested on the counter, surrounded by used sippy cups. An empty pot moldered in the coffeemaker. She turned the machine off.

Candace did not spend much time in her son's house. For one thing, she did not like to visit when he wasn't there, and for another, he was never there. Oh, she popped by often enough to pick up or drop off the grandkids, but come to think of it she never stepped far beyond the foyer.

And Ginger never invited her in.

It wasn't because of the housekeeping. In fact, Candace had to admit the house was usually immaculate—insofar as a house occupied by two small children and Timothy can be. This mess, thought Candace, as she walked around scooping dish towels from the floor and tossing out an apple core, was the handiwork of her son, on whom adulthood had not magically conferred the skill of picking up. A weekend with Ginger away and Timothy at the helm had resulted in what looked like an FBI drug search. No house was Timothy-proof.

Ginger never invited her mother-in-law into her home because she was afraid to *let her in*.

Candace stepped into the family room. The houses in Paradise Estates came in three styles, and Candace had selected one with open architecture for her son and his bride. It lacked a dining room because, well, one look at Ginger and you knew she'd never entertain. Candace had insisted on nubby berber carpeting throughout the house, lest the grandchildren she expected would soon populate it tumble and bump their little noggins. Bucket lights instead of a hanging chandelier in the great hall, side stairs instead of a grand staircase. She hadn't asked Ginger what she preferred.

Looking around, though, Candace saw that her daughter-in-law had managed to make the house her own, and she found herself impressed by Ginger's simple yet comfortable taste. The entire house seemed given over to the children, which meant the decorative touches had to be indestructible. In her own house, Candace displayed locally blown glass objets d'art along a divider between the foyer and the family room. Ginger had lined the same divider with whimsical Lego designs of giraffes and robots. Where Candace exhibited cut flowers on a marble ledge in the foyer, Ginger had installed a boot bench hand-painted with the letters of the alphabet. The plates in the kitchen were a rainbow of cheery Fiestaware.

Here in the family room, Candace saw that Ginger had reserved one small corner for herself: a reading nook, or so it seemed, dominated by a chair so overstuffed it looked like a doubled-over down mattress. It sat in an alcove looking out on the yard. Perhaps her daughter-in-law sat here and watched the children at play outside.

Then Candace saw what lay open on the small stand next to the chair: a Bible. Despite its tacky pink casing, she recognized instantly the text-heavy pages, thin to the point of transparency, a yellow ribbon bookmarking a page like a tendril of hair across a girl's shoulder.

She had forgotten Ginger was a Christian.

Since learning of her daughter-in-law's past, Candace had struggled with fury and blame, and, yes, she must own up: hate. How dare this Jezebel trespass on their lives? How dare she sully the family name with her revolting history? And how had she, Candace Green, ignored her own gut and failed until now to root out this terrible lie? But then again, must she do *everything*?

Candace felt suddenly awash with fatigue. She let her knees bend and her rear perch on Ginger's chair. At least, she'd intended to perch. The chair enveloped her in a hug and she gave in to its softness, but not before flailing to reach for the Bible.

Ah. Ginger had been reading the Psalms.

Candace flipped to a passage in the book of Luke she had been aching to read since she learned of her daughter-in-law's past. Using the ribbon bookmark to guide her weary eyes, she read, and read again.

When she finished she let the chair enfold her and closed her eyes. Outside she heard the muffled peace of dusk. Paradise Estates was her home, her family's and her church officers' base camp; she herself had selected it. But she admitted that even the sounds of a gated development seemed somehow artificial, the birdcalls and children's voices piped in.

The children. Soon her son and grandchildren would arrive home from the airport, where they had gone to pick up Ginger.

Now was not the time. Now was not the time to confront her daughter-in-law with the calamity of her past. She got up and walked out of Timothy and Ginger's house, down the lane and toward her own home.

A figure awaited, pacing, outside her door. Ruthie. With one hand she twirled those silly curls round and round her index finger, an irritating habit Candace had already twice pointed out. In the other hand, Ruthie held a manila folder. Her posture, her expression—everything about her projected anxiety.

Candace's mind raced. Aaron. London. She hurried up her driveway. "My goodness, what is it?" she asked sharply.

Ruthie looked at her as if at a stranger. Candace got close enough for a whiff. "Have you been . . . drinking?"

Ruthie snapped to, embarrassed. "No. I mean, yes. But not—I mean, I'm fine. That's not what I—"

"Goodness gracious, calm down."

"It's just—" Ruthie thrust forward the folder in her hands. "You said. You said I could come to you."

Candace stared at her a moment. Then she took the folder, opened it, and read.

When she was finished, she looked up. "He gave this to you?"

Ruthie held up a black messenger bag. "He left this."

"In your house?"

Ruthie coughed. "In my car. I can explain—"

Candace waved the offer aside. Priorities. "When is this running?"

"He said he was proofing it tonight. So maybe . . ." They said it together:

"Tomorrow."

"Right." Candace stepped to her car. "Get in."

CHAPTER TWELVE

Ginger

She had it all planned out.

The house, she knew, would be a federal disaster zone, and it was. Her husband was a one-man cyclone, and the children had inherited his inability to aim a dirty sock at a hamper. Ginger had what she considered a healthy hatred of mess. As a child she'd peeped into a trailer home near her own, owned by a lady whose hoard of Dr Pepper cans, plastic flowerpots, and back issues of *People* magazine reached floor to ceiling. That image never left her mind. She sometimes wondered how something like that happened, how it all began. A small collection of pizza boxes, probably. A pile of dirty socks that had missed its intended hamper.

As Timothy hauled the kids off to bed, Ginger dumped all the dishes into the sink. She'd wash and clear later. For now she fished a menu out of the drawer and dialed up Panda Express. "General Tso's chicken," she ordered. "Garlic fried string beans. Char siu pork. Chicken lo mein." Chinese food gave her reflux, but Timothy could live on the stuff. Whatever he wanted tonight.

Then they'd sit down, for once, across a table from one another, instead of before the television. She liked the idea of candles but she didn't want to scare him. No. Candles would look forced.

She poured the sweet iced tea and set out the fork for herself; he would use the chopsticks that came with the delivery. She decided: When the food arrived, as they began to eat, that was when she would tell him.

"Guess what," she said, practicing. No. "I've got some news." There. Better.

And he'd smile.

She smiled thinking of his smile.

From upstairs she heard the children squealing in terror as Timothy roared like a lion. No, it would be a dinosaur, of course, for Jordan's sake. Ginger wasn't sure if scientists had ever documented that dinosaurs actually roared. She'd have to ask Jordan tomorrow.

"There is a balm—"

She crooned a phrase from the hymn, the only verse she knew.

"There is a balm in Gilead
To make the wounded whole,
There is a balm in Gilead
To heal the sin-sick soul."

As promised by Lorraine Lawson, the weekend had been her balm of Gilead. She was a woman reborn. This was the beginning of a new Ginger, of a Ginger who embraced who she was and what she wanted. And what she wanted more than anything right now was a few minutes alone with the Psalms.

Still smiling, she collapsed into her reading chair and reached for her Bible.

On its open face lay a small note. She opened it. It read:

Let's talk. Candace

Her mother-in-law—here. In her house. In her chair. In her Bible.

She remembered this feeling. She felt . . . exposed.

And here was the ribbon bookmark not on Psalm 130, where she was quite certain she'd left it, but on Luke 7, laid horizontally as if to underscore its point.

She read. And as she did, her world fell down.

And one of the Pharisees desired him that he would eat with him. And he went into the Pharisee's house, and sat down to meat. And, behold, a woman in the city, which was a sinner, when she knew that Jesus sat at meat in the Pharisee's house, brought an alabaster box of ointment.

And stood at his feet behind him weeping, and began to wash his feet with tears, and did wipe them with the hairs of her head, and kissed his feet, and anointed them with the ointment.

Now when the Pharisee which had bidden him saw it, he spake within himself, saying, This man, if he were a prophet, would have known who and what manner of woman this is that toucheth him: for she is a sinner.

And Jesus answering said unto him, Simon, I have somewhat to say unto thee. And he saith, Master, say on.

There was a certain creditor which had two debtors: the one owned five hundred pence, and the other fifty. And when they had nothing to pay, he frankly forgave them both. Tell me therefore, which of them will love him most?

Simon answered and said, I suppose that he, to whom he forgave most. And he said unto him, Thou hast rightly judged.

And he turned to the woman, and said unto Simon, Seest thou this woman? I entered into thine house, thou gavest me no water for my feet: but she hath washed my feet with tears, and wiped them with the hairs of her head.

Thou gavest me no kiss: but this woman since the time I came in hath not ceased to kiss my feet.

My head with oil thou didst not anoint: but this woman hath anointed my feet with ointment.

Wherefore I say unto thee, Her sins, which are many, are forgiven: for she loved much: but to whom little is forgiven, the same loveth little.

And he said unto her, Thy sins are forgiven.

And they that sat at meat with him began to say within themselves, Who is this that forgiveth sins also?

And he said to the woman, Thy faith hath saved thee; go in peace.

It was the story of Mary Magdalene.

Candace knew.

* * *

"She knows," said Ginger.

"Mm?" said Timothy, nose in his BlackBerry even as he descended the stairs, skipping around a lump of laundry.

Ginger stood in the kitchen, Candace's note in her hands, glued, frozen, stuck. "Timothy," she said, her voice conveying enough urgency that her husband looked up. "She knows. Your mother knows."

Comprehension stilled him. But only for an instant. "Okay," he said.

"Okay?"

"Gin. It was a long time ago."

"I don't think she'll see it that way."

"I'll talk to her. I should have done it ages ago."

"She wants to talk to me." She held out the note to her husband. He scanned it, nodded, and—unbelievably—he chuckled.

"That's Mom for you," he said. He assumed an ominous tone. "*'Let's talk.'*"

"This is funny?"

He sighed. The BlackBerry in his hand vibrated, and—unbelievably—he checked it. She wanted to grab that thing and hurl it clear across the room.

"Oh, man," he said, shaking his head as he read the message. "Typhoon in Indonesia. Call going out to aid groups. I gotta book a flight."

"No," she said.

He looked up.

"No," she said, balling her fists. "No! You can't go. You can not go right now. You can not leave me to deal with this—with *her*—by myself!"

Never before had Ginger raised her voice to Timothy, or even to the children in his presence. Her chest heaved, and her heart thundered against her ribs. When she could focus, she saw that her husband stared at her in surprise.

"What is the deal?" he said, his voice what's-the-weather-today calm. "So you did some stuff before we met. You're my wife. You're a Green. Her daughter-in-law. It's not like anything's changed."

The realization crushed her. "You don't understand."

He sighed at her tears.

"I need you," she said, and she hated how she sounded. Desperate. Pathetic. A fool. "I need you here for this."

Timothy leaned against the doorframe. In this light he looked decades older, a young man who'd seen too much. How small this must seem, how trivial. He was a man for whom the drama of the home front would never bear weight against tragedies of a global scale.

"Come on, Gin," he said. "Just talk to her, like she said. You'll be fine. Really. Don't worry so much."

She closed her eyes, for she knew in his mind he was already gone.

The doorbell rang. Ginger tensed, until she remembered: delivery.

"That's your dinner," she said, heading up the stairs.

"Don't you want any?"

"No."

"Sure? You said you didn't eat all day—"

She stopped on the stairs but did not turn around. "I'll be fine. Really," she said. "Don't worry so much."

* * *

She did not tell Timothy.

Ginger did not tell Timothy about their third child, growing peacefully—as far as she knew, anyway—snug inside her womb.

In the morning she dressed the children and fixed the family breakfast. She loaded the kids into the car and drove Jordan to school, then returned home with Tali. Silently she helped Timothy finish packing, then helped haul his luggage out when his ride to the air-port appeared.

He scooped up Tali for a smooch. Then he leaned toward Ginger.

She turned her cheek. She could not bear one more second of his exasperation, one more of his worn-through sighs. She watched his sandaled feet turn and head toward the car.

When she had cleared the dishes and wiped the counter, when she had picked up the pajamas, when she had set Tali up with three opened canisters of Play-Doh on the kitchen table, then, only then, did she think.

It was a mistake; she could see that now. It was a mistake to have kept her past from Timothy's family. Better to have owned up from the get-go and let judgment fall. But had she done so, no way would she be here in Paradise Estates, or allowed into Candace's protective fold. No way her children would have known the manna of their grandmother's love.

What was better—living an ugly truth or a comfortable lie?

Without Candace and Aaron's assent, would Timothy even have married her? Maybe, out of anger or pride. Back then, he fan-cied himself her prince in shining armor. But it might not have lasted. Independence aside, he respected his father and adored his mother. Their endless disapproval would have worn him down. He would have blamed her. They would have fought.

What would her life have been had she not become a pastor's wife? More bartending in skimpy costumes, probably, at least for a while. Not stripping, no porn—not that, never again. Maybe col-lege. Maybe a real job in a real office, one day. Maybe a man with a wonderfully dull career whose only calling was loving her.

"Buhd," said Tali, holding out a lump of banana-colored dough.

Ginger took the clay from her and with a few twists created a little bird. "How's that?"

Tali clapped her hands. "Twee. Twee."

Ginger reviewed her options. She could face Candace. She could go to her, as the note instructed, and as seconded by Timothy. She could lay bare her past and profess her shame. She could beg forgiveness.

Or she could run.

One thing she knew: She would not survive a showdown with Candace Green. Powerful people had tried to best the senior pastor's wife and had come away bloodied. Ginger could only imagine the weapons Candace would have readied for a head-on confrontation with her. The things, the terrible things her mother-in-law would say. The judging eyes and that cold, cold smile.

Worst of all, she had no defense, no excuse for her sins. She'd just have to sit there and take it. She deserved it. The shame, like a tidal wave of bile. The humiliation, the disgust. It had taken hour upon countless hour of prayer to bury those feelings. To bury that self. Confronting Candace meant digging up all those nasty old bones and giving them life again.

And what would follow? Not forgiveness; Ginger was sure of that. Candace didn't do forgiveness, no matter how many Bible studies she led on the topic. No. More like months of silence. Years of mistreatment. Disdain. Oh, Lord. The disdain.

But all this was a distraction.

The prospect of confronting her mother-in-law flushed her guts clear out; it was true. This, though, was not Ginger's true reckoning.

The true reckoning was with God and herself.

All her fussing and fretting about Candace hid the real issue: Ginger had never reconciled her own past. This new life had transpired so easily, so *magically*, that her sins seemed to sweep themselves into some dark hole. As if her years of wrongful living belonged to someone else, or perhaps had never happened at all.

```
        S
        I
R E P E N T Y O U
        N
        E
        R
```

Repent You Sinner. Sinner Repent You. The neon cross that had glowed on the windshield of her battered car and across her battered life. But she never had, had she? She never had repented. Repealed, yes. Retrenched, yes. Reborn, even. But repented—never.

Even given the express opportunity at the pastors' wives weekend, Ginger had been unable to confess her sins. So distanced did she feel from her wrongs that she couldn't even bring herself to write a vague admission on a piece of lavender paper and tack it to a frilly white cross.

Lorraine Lawson had seen this. The wise woman had witnessed something, felt something, maybe even envisaged the outline of a burden too great searing into Ginger's shoulder. Lorraine had seen the cross Ginger humped across Jerusalem, and advised her to put it down.

Now, for the first time, Ginger understood. She must repent.

But how?

Her cell phone buzzed.

"Tel-phone," shrieked Tali, grabbing for it. "I do, I do."

The panel read: KAYCEE. Before leaving the retreat, the group of friends from the Cross Your Heart exercise exchanged phone numbers, vowing to stay in touch. Ginger hadn't expected to hear from any of them so soon.

Ginger batted Tali's hand away and picked up.

"Ginge," said Kaycee. "Oh, Lord." Her friend was crying. "It's Devonn. My husband. I need help."

Chapter Thirteen

Ruthie

In all my life as a scaredy-cat, I have never felt so close to dying of fear as I did during the forty-seven minutes between Magnolia and Atlanta as a passenger in Candace's Toyota Prius.

I'd made this drive before, most recently in Juan's car, when I accompanied him to cover a panel discussion at Rabbi Bernstein's synagogue in Atlanta. It's fifty miles of highways and city roads, and Google told us it would take an hour and ten minutes, which it did, on the nose. Of course, Juan did not drive as Candace did that night, which is to say he drove like a normal person, not a NASCAR pro stunt double in a Hollywood chase scene straight from hell.

I was too busy concentrating on not dying to query Candace as to our destination. Once we arrived, there remained no need. I climbed out of the car on legs of gummy worms to stand before the headquarters of the *Atlanta Journal-Constitution*.

During my junior year at Hoogaboom High, my English teacher, Mr. Poore, arranged for us a field trip to the *Star-Ledger*, a newspaper in Newark. While the other students shuffled their feet in boredom and tried to steal Post-its, I gawked at the vast, cluttered newsroom, busy yet surprisingly quiet. The reporters and editors typed and phoned and conversed with such—such *purpose*. I remember thinking that when I grew up, I, too, would know purpose. I, too, would know what the hell I was supposed to be doing from moment to given moment.

I ogled the *AJC* lobby with a combination of that old awe and some residual knee knocking from our automotive dance with death. Meanwhile, Candace procured guest passes for us. I followed her as she sped through security and on to the elevator.

Finally, a moment. "Candace," I said, "what are we going to—"

The doors opened onto a newsroom, about the size of the *Star-Ledger*'s, just as cluttered, but louder. Deadline hour, must be.

Then I saw him. There, standing in a sea of desks, was Juan. He was on the phone and gesticulating dramatically. He scratched his scalp. Even from this distance, he looked tired. Fluorescent lights never flatter.

I felt a hand at my back and a small push. "Go," she said. "I'll just be a moment." At that she took a sharp left and headed off, sure as sugar. That was Candace. Purpose. She had purpose. Never a moment's hesitation.

Me, I'm all about hesitation. I turned back toward the elevator, whose closed metal doors offered some semblance of a mirror. I looked frightful, of course, strung out from the ride and—oh, nuts—flip-flops on my feet. Classy. No chance of a quick touch-up. All my stuff was in my bag. Which was with Juan. And his, with me.

I did have a purpose here. I straightened my shoulders the way I'd seen Candace do a hundred times, like she was carrying the weight of the world but adjusting the burden. Then I set off through the maze of desks.

When I reached his desk, he was sitting down, leaning way back in his chair, still on the phone.

"Hi," I said.

Juan looked up at me. Have you ever watched a soap opera with the sound turned off? Try it sometime; the actors' facial expressions are so exaggerated that you can tell exactly what's going on without any words. That's what watching Juan Diaz was like for the next few seconds: first, annoyance at the interruption; then, frowning confusion, as he tried to reconcile a familiar face in the wrong context; then, recognition, and right after that, shock. He so very nearly fell out of his chair.

I didn't laugh. I couldn't. We were past that now.

He slammed down the telephone without saying good-bye. "Ruthie! What the—what are you—"

Now, a new expression: guilt. Unmistakably, guilt. Like I was the wronged wife catching him with the other woman. Strange, isn't it? Considering.

I held out his bag. "You left it," I said. "In my car. Which means you must have mine."

He stared, first at the bag I proffered, then at the one by his feet. Sure enough, a ponytail holder I'd affixed to my strap identified its rightful owner. Slowly he handed the bag over and took his from my hand. I watched his expression stiffen in concern.

"Did you—" He opened his bag. He rooted around it, and pulled out his story.

There was so much I wanted to say. And maybe, just maybe, if I hadn't spent the past hour as a supporting character in *Too Fast, Too Furious: Pastors' Wives Gone Rogue*, I could have formulated the right words: You lied. And, How could you? How could you do this—to me?

By the look on Juan's face, I suspect my eyes conveyed those accusations plainly enough. His did not try for an explanation or a denial. They responded: I'm sorry. I'm so sorry.

Those sorry eyes then drifted over my shoulder. He looked baffled anew.

I followed his gaze.

Candace emerged from a corner office on the far end of the floor. An impressively coiffed woman of about the same age stepped after her. They shared one last laugh together. They gripped each other's forearms in that half hug, half handshake of powerful women, and the updo slipped back into her office.

"Who's that?" I asked.

"Catherine Oppelheimer," said Juan. "The publisher."

Then Candace looked across the newsroom at us. In my head, the clatter and chatter of the other reporters fell away into dead calm, an outer-space silence. She looked at Juan. And then, she smiled.

"Oh," he breathed. "Shit."

* * *

Candace inched the Prius back out of its spot, checking behind and to the sides for oncoming traffic, though the parking garage was empty. We rolled into a darkened downtown. The bat out of hell who hurtled us there from Magnolia earlier that night folded her wings and transformed back into a cautious lady driver, hands on the wheel at ten and two o'clock.

I twisted in my seat to look at her. Smooth, straight lines composed the profile of her face, like a draftsman's sketch of a building. I could stand it no longer.

"What happened in there?"

Candace paused at a stop sign, counted five Mississippis, then slid forward again. "The publisher and I discussed the article," she said. "After I informed her of my concerns, Cathy decided to hold it for further review."

Which meant it was as good as dead.

"I want to thank you," she continued. "Lord knows the consequences had those lies been published."

"How do you—"

"Know Cathy? Oh, we go way back. Museum boards, charities, that sort of thing." She paused to adjust the heat. The night had acquired a chill. "And Greenleaf is a loyal advertiser."

"Oh," I said. "I see."

Candace glanced at me. "Do you?" she said. "You understand, that's not why they held the story. Even in this economy, the loss of a single advertiser won't bring a newspaper like that one down." She looked thoughtful. "On the other hand, a lawsuit could do some damage."

There it was. Up till now, we had not discussed the veracity of the article. I did not know enough First Amendment law to say if it constituted slander. But I could not dispute that the piece Juan had written was a classic takedown.

MEGACHURCH MISSING MILLIONS

Questions Raised About Greenleaf Funds
Intended for Interfaith Center
By Juan Diaz

(MAGNOLIA) The 3,000-seat sanctuary was packed for a recent Sunday service at Greenleaf Church, a hugely popular evangelical megachurch in this affluent Atlanta suburb. The crowd went wild as its senior pastor, Aaron Green, took the stage.

Green, nationally known for his televised sermons and series of best-selling books, has lately gained international status for working toward understanding among religions. He is a featured panelist at the Global Interfaith Conference to be held in London this week, along with two Atlanta religious leaders—Rabbi Joshua Bernstein of Beth Aaron Congregation and Imam Amin Chaudry of Mosque of Central Georgia.

Along with Bernstein and Chaudry, Green has urged his congregants to give to a fund dedicated to their interfaith efforts, in particular a building slated for development in downtown Atlanta that will host various religious and secular gatherings intended, according to the Greenleaf Web site, to "build fellowship between all races, creeds and faiths."

A counter on the Web site shows that the fund for the building, dubbed Harmony Center, took in almost $2.3 million over the past three years toward a goal of $3 million.

Yet today, the fund stands nearly empty. According to financial documents revealed by a senior-level church insider, it held just $11.53.

When reached by phone at Hartsfield-Jackson Atlanta International Airport en route to the London conference, Pastor Green said he knew nothing of the discrepancy, and that he would look into the matter upon his return.

That was the coup de grâce, the killer scoop: evidence of possible fraud. Quoting "senior church officials" and "longtime members," the piece continued with a ferocious attack on Greenleaf's financial management, or mismanagement. Millions of dollars languished in a plain-vanilla account at First Mutual of Georgia, the piece alleged, tapped at whim by the senior pastor and his wife for increasingly superficial projects. It criticized everything from church expansion to Aaron's designer suits, and told of a pervasive dissatisfaction among worshippers with the direction of the church.

Damning as the article was, if I were perfectly honest—which I had no intention of being with Candace just then—I had not presumed its untruth. Much of Greenleaf and its operations remained a mystery to me. I'd aided and abetted Candace's assassination of the article not because I thought it was a lie, but because as a trained publicist I couldn't very well stand by and say nothing as a piece blasting my organization went to press.

And, if I were perfectly honest—which I had no intention of being with myself just then—I had acted in part out of mortification and hurt at my betrayal by Juan Diaz.

That's not to say I didn't care to know whether or not my husband and I were working for a couple of Scripture-quoting thieves. For that was the crux of it. If Aaron rarely ordered a sandwich without Candace's approval, then it stood to reason that any skimming of church funds would be masterminded by the woman driving this car.

I longed to talk to Jerry. It was his job, after all, to manage Greenleaf's finances. If there was fraud, he would know. Wouldn't he? The article never quoted Jerry, never even mentioned him. Unless he was one of the anonymous sources. But no, that made no sense. He spent most of our time here Velcroed to Aaron. No way he'd talk to Juan undercover. Did that mean, though, that Jerry was too close to the Greens to see the truth?

I tried not to hyperventilate. Here I was, *me*, with my full-blown allergy to confrontation, about to confront my boss with an alleged crime. Steady, I thought. Steady now. I thought back to my father's advice. In law, Dad said, mild questions always yielded far more useful answers than an attack—even, maybe especially, when the client was guilty. Just get the client talking, he said, then sit back and listen.

I assumed what I hoped was an innocuous tone. "What about those documents? The ones the article said were from an insider?"

When Candace opened her mouth again, out came a different voice, this one utterly devoid of syrup and measured drawl. This voice was hard—hard as the coal mined in the northern town where I knew she was born.

"Anyone can gin up dummy forms," she said. "That's exactly what I mean. None of this adds up. Embezzlement is a federal crime. Why didn't this so-called insider go to the FBI? Because the FBI would see right through this, of course. Even without my interference, there's no way in heaven the newspaper's lawyers would have allowed the publication of such an allegation based on so little evidence. Cathy told me that reporter—I can't bring myself to say his name—that he isn't even on their investigative team. My take is he's just a rookie trying to win some front-page glory. But he didn't act alone. No. Someone inside is trying to set us up. The question is who, and why."

As she spoke, I watched Candace's face. It burned with such righteous ferocity that my own doubts subsided. It read anger, not guilt. It occurred to me that this was the real Candace. Watching her reminded me of the movie *The Matrix*, her mask and its reassuring illusion of grace falling away to reveal streaming columns of green code, the beauty and terror of a brilliant mind at work. Though she had never spoken this way before to me, I suspected this was how her mind worked all the time, spinning forward, analyzing, assessing the situation and its possible outcomes. She dropped the mask now only because the stakes were so high. Doing so, though, she exposed a vulnerable flank, a part of her that didn't know how everything would turn out. And like the civilians in that movie, I immediately wished for the comfort of fantasy. I wanted to believe I worked for a woman who had all things under control. I wanted the old Candace back.

"He never let on?" she asked me, her eyes both wary and weary. "Juan Diaz—ugh, there, I said his name."

She wasn't accusing me, exactly. Still, I gave it careful thought. *Had* he let on? As his designated gatekeeper, shouldn't I have had a clue? Or had I been too close to Juan to see the truth?

With regret I shook my head. "But that's common when a reporter's got a scoop. He waits till the last moment, when he's got all his ducks in a row. Then he'll ask the subject for comment. A dirty trick, but common."

He'd known already, I realized. He'd known when he invited me out for a good-bye drink that his article aimed to maim my employers. He would have kissed me, if I'd let him, knowing that a few hours later he would hit "send." A purse of the lips, a push of a finger, and *boom* would have gone my marriage and my career.

"And is it common for a reporter to deceive his sources as to the intent of his piece?"

Could he be that evil? "It's possible he didn't set out with the intention of exposing us," I said slowly. Just as he didn't set out to fall in like with me.

Candace nodded. We sank into silence as we each chewed on our thoughts. She avoided the highway this time, choosing instead to pass through a gentrifying section of the city lined with cheerily painted clapboard row houses and condominiums fashioned out of old brick factories. We stopped at a traffic signal. One of the homes already displayed Christmas lights. It cast an intermittent glow across Candace's face. Red, black. Red, black.

I had to ask. "What happens now?"

It struck me that Candace did not yet know her next move. "One thing for sure," she said finally. "Not a word of this to anyone. Not even to Jerry."

Jerry. My God. Much as I longed to hash all this out with him, I wondered now how I would—if I could—have told him. How would I have explained the bar, the bag—Juan? I didn't do anything wrong, I reminded myself. In fact, I'm like the hero here. I did something right.

Then why did I feel so guilty?

"Who else knows?" Candace asked.

For a panicked moment I thought she meant about Juan and me. But, of course, she remained focused on the article. "Pastor Aaron?" I said. "Juan did call him for comment."

"Odds are he doesn't even remember," mused Candace. "Aaron's mind was on a single track toward that conference. He must have been running through the airport when that reporter called." She shook her head in disgust at Juan's methods. "I'm sure Aaron thought it was just a weird question and forgot all about it in ten seconds. I doubt he thought to mention it to anyone, even Tosh."

"Will you tell him? Pastor Aaron, I mean. About tonight."

Suddenly, she looked exhausted. I remembered then that she had traveled to Miami and back the day before on some church errand. This day she had raced around the Greenleaf campus troubleshooting before, during, and after services, only to find herself battling a mysterious antagonist for her husband's reputation by night. Here the moon hung high and still she could not rest. Without this woman, a megachurch would fall.

The light turned green, but Candace didn't move.

Finally, she spoke. "Pastor Aaron," she said, "is on a mission from God. I'll tell him after I sort it all out."

"What do you want me to do?"

In a blink, her mask returned. Queen Mona Lisa. She sat up and pressed the accelerator, eyes back on the road.

"Don't do a thing," she said. "Let me take care of it."

CHAPTER FOURTEEN

Candace

Like any cash-based business, a church is a prime ground for theft.

As long as organized religion has existed, so has its need for donations. Call it what you will—tithes, collections, the poor box— it compelled worshippers to dig into their linty pockets and pinch out some coins for the offering. Candace had read in the *Wall Street Journal* that giving to places of worship topped one hundred billion dollars a year in America, one-third of all charitable donations. She was surprised it wasn't more. Greenleaf's annual tithes alone topped eighteen million.

Just before the London trip, Jerry approached her and Aaron, saying he had questions about discrepancies in the books. He asked if he could bring this up at the next meeting of the board of elders, as he was required to do in the bylaws, which he had recently finished reading.

Candace winced. She must have overlooked that clause when

she updated the bylaws to exclude the elders from most church decision making. How frustrating.

"When's the next elder council?" asked Aaron.

"Not until after your return from London," Candace said.

"Good," said Aaron. "We'll deal with it after the conference, then."

Candace noted a slight frown on Jerry's brow, but it did not remain. "Okay," he said. "But I wouldn't like to delay too long. I'm sure there are explanations, but I need to hear them before I can proceed."

He means the Serve Your Faith series, Candace thought, with more annoyance than worry. She and Aaron had declared early on that they would divvy up the profits from their best-selling books among Greenleaf's various charitable efforts. But she had delayed completing the voluminous paperwork for the last two books, including hers, accounting for the earned profits but not yet the donation. Ugh. How could she have been so careless? Now her own procrastination would come to light, and before the hostile board of elders, no less. That would be a two-Imitrex meeting.

A migraine. That's all Jerry's concern had foretold for her. And then she'd read that reporter's article.

It was difficult for her to describe exactly what she had felt as she stood in her driveway, Ruthie fidgeting nearby, reading the printed-out draft of the story. Difficult to measure her rage as she read this fusillade of attacks on the church and on Aaron. Her fury as she read quote after accusatory quote from anonymous church "insiders."

Buried deep in the piece she'd found a bit more on the reporter's supposed subject, the one Juan Diaz had stated all along as his cover: Greenleaf's interfaith efforts. That would presumably come long after the jump, buried in the final column inches, well within the paper's guts. Aaron's life's work squeezed between ads for Mary Mac's holiday brunch menu and Towson's Ford Dealership.

The day following their visit to the offices of the *Atlanta Journal-Constitution*—which had in turn been the day following Candace's flight to Miami to rescue her daughter-in-law's reputation—Candace let herself into her office and sank into her chair. She allowed herself a moment to decompress. A moment to prepare for the next battle. She spun in her office chair and gazed out the window at the relentless sky.

What is my purpose?

She spun back and faced her computer. Entering a twelve-digit alphanumeric password she'd committed to memory, she called up the Greenleaf account on the Web site of First Mutual of Georgia. There they were, the special projects funds. She clicked the account in question.

HARMONY CENTER INTERFAITH $2,334,983

She sat back in her chair, stumped. While she admitted to something less than her trademark vigilance when it came to monitoring the other specials, as they called the funds earmarked for specific projects, she did check regularly upon the Harmony fund, if only because Aaron asked. And the fund today held more or less as much as she expected—not $11.53, as claimed in the article.

What was Juan Diaz talking about?

* * *

One thing Candace appreciated about First Mutual of Georgia was its lobby. The local branches of the national banks looked to her like

Talitha's pop-up books: colorful cardboard creations that folded out with the flick of a wrist, and thus could just as easily flatten to nonexistence again. In contrast, First Mutual's headquarters, right here in Magnolia, retained its Grecian columns and stone steps. Its lobby featured vaulted ceilings and marble floors that held firm under her heels. What a bank should look like, Candace thought, as she took her seat in the manager's office.

Hm. She never noticed a computer in here before.

A buxom brunette in a mauve suit marched in, the jut of her breasts preceding her into the office. "Mrs. Green, I'm Gina Lippman," she said, shaking Candace's hand and then swinging briskly behind her desk. Even before her rear reached her chair, Gina was tapping away on the computer.

"I was expecting—"

"Todd Fowler. I'm sorry, he's retired." Gina's fingers released a barrage of taps on the computer keys, finishing off with a final, dramatic tap. "Send," she announced. "There." The woman peeled her eyes from the screen and her fingers from the keyboard. "What can I do for you?"

Things do change, thought Candace. Even at First Mutual. Todd was a big chitchatter, trading local gossip and stories about the grandchildren. This Gina was all business. Today, that would work.

"I need you to trace activity in our accounts," said Candace, pulling a printout of a statement from her purse and pointing to the line. "Was money moved in or out of late?"

Gina looked over the statement, nodding with a relish that struck Candace as unseemly until she likened it to a hound before the hunt. This woman liked a task. Gina attacked her keyboard again. "Aha," she said, triumphant. "Looks like it was all but drained two weeks ago." *Tap, tap-a-tap tap.* "Then, in a matter of minutes, restored."

Curious. "Can you tell me where it went?"

Gina tapped at her keyboard again and shook her head. "I see here that a number of people are authorized for access to this particular fund. It's linked to accounts held by"—she peered at the screen—"Beth Aaron Congregation and Mosque of Central Georgia. And one called the Oversight Committee. It'll take me a while longer, but I can trace it if you like."

The central heating unit burped hot air at Candace's elbow. Still she pulled her shawl tighter against her sudden chill.

* * *

"I just got your message," said Candace, breathless. "Where are they?"

Alice nodded toward the entrance of the Children's Center, following her in. Jeannie Holbrush began her usual greeting, but Candace ignored her and hurried on inside, barreling through the starlit tunnel and brushing past the open arms of Jesus. The center was nearly empty, with a few harried parents rushing in to collect their children after a rough commute.

Candace found them in the toddler room. Tali was helping an aide stack a tower of puffy blocks and knock them down again. Jordan sat in a rocking chair in the corner, reading a picture book about dinosaurs. He looked so inconsequential in that chair—a five-year-old, after all, albeit with a face as old as Abraham's.

They had not yet spotted her. Candace took a moment to regain her breath and composure, touching her hair and wiping her palms on her skirt.

"Do you want to read it?" Alice held out a folded sheet of paper.

"It was on your desk when I came in. I hope you don't mind that I opened it. I thought it was one of the forms from career services—"

Candace snatched the letter from Alice and turned away. It was in Ginger's hand, which she'd always found loopy and uncommanding, not helped by her daughter-in-law's loose relationship with grammar and her penchant for pastel-colored pens. But today's message was penned in a sober black.

> *Dear Candace,*
>
> *I don't know how you learned about my past but now that you have I want to say sorry for not telling you myself. Someday I will explain my side to you. That is if you care to hear. For now I am going away for a short while. I am coming back. I just need a little time alone to get my head on straight. I asked Timothy to stay but he had Indonesia (the typhoon). Until he is back could you please please take care of my Jordan and Talitha. Please please tell them Mommy loves them and I will come for them soon. If you do this for me I will ask nothing from you ever again.*
>
> *Ginger*

"And there's this." Alice handed Candace another letter, this one sealed in an envelope. Ginger's handwriting on the outside labeled it for Timothy.

Candace gripped both letters to her chest. So Ginger would leave her family rather than confront her. And to think Candace had lost sleep over her own un-Christian treatment of her daughter-in-law. To think she had prayed on how and when to offer forgiveness. All while

Ginger plotted escape. *To get my head on straight.* Candace longed to knock that head right off.

Time enough. There would be time enough to cogitate on what to do with Ginger's head. Now there were her precious babies, her grandchildren. Candace looked through the doorway at the two of them, blissful in their ignorance of their mother's abandonment. She arranged her face in a smile.

"Jordan!" she called from the door. "Tali, darling. Get your things. We're going to Mamie's house."

CHAPTER FIFTEEN

Ginger

One of the hardest and bravest acts of her life, Ginger always thought, was escaping a lying, controlling, unpredictable, and possibly psychotic boyfriend, the one she left behind along with her old life in Miami. Turned out that was easy as pie. Easy as pie compared to leaving her family.

I'm not *leaving* leaving them, she reminded herself, again and again and again, so as not to throw up from panic. I'm coming back for them. I'm not *leaving* leaving.

Once she knew where she was headed, the next toughest decision, and by far the more anguishing, was whether or not to take the children. On the one hand, she could not breathe without them. It was one thing to flit off for a weekend retreat with pastors' wives. It was something else completely to vanish without a return date and without her little muffins by her side. No, no. She could never abandon her babies, never let them wonder for even one second where Mommy could be.

On the other hand: Amber Alert.

Not even a mother could just up and disappear with her own children, not in this day and age. Timothy might not raise an alarm for days, or for however long this current trip kept him away. But Candace saw her grandchildren every day. Not a single day could pass, not even a consecutive series of hours, probably, without her inquiring or checking in on their whereabouts.

She thought of simply telling Candace. But that would mean facing her.

Ginger wilted. No. Not an option. Not yet.

She would use Candace's involvement as an advantage. With Timothy away, Candace would fill in as their caretaker. The children would be in not merely good hands, but the most fiercely protective of hands. Grandma grizzly hands.

Yes. Jordan and Tali would be safe with Mamie. Not just safe. Happy. Content in their everyday routine, comfortable in Mamie and Poppy's house, fed, schooled, clothed, loved. They'd slept over there before; in fact, Candace had her guest room set up especially for such occasions. Timothy would return before they tired of the extended sleepover at Mamie's, and soon enough Ginger herself would come for them.

Yes. This was the best solution for the children. And, she admitted, for her.

Ginger needed to do this alone. Six years of marriage, almost as many of motherhood. Six years of denying her past. Of avoiding atonement in favor of assembling s'mores and squirting Purell on sticky hands. Her children always came first for her, and with them around she would be too preoccupied to properly repent her sins. In order to confront the past, she needed to retreat from the present.

But not for long. And certainly not forever. She wasn't *leaving* leaving them.

Ginger would take the hated Prius. She had not much choice otherwise, and Greenleaf always had an extra car Timothy could borrow when he returned. She would pack the children's bags for Mamie's. Candace possessed a key to their house and was certainly capable of locating toothbrushes and pajamas, but Ginger felt compelled to gather up the things they'd wake at night inconsolable without.

Here was Tali's blankie, pilled green fleece with yellow duckies. Here was Jordan's Stevie Stegosaurus. Tali's *Goodnight Moon* board book, the corners gnawed damp. Jordan's Spider-Man underpants, the butt scratched nearly to threads.

Ginger pressed Jordan's underpants to her cheek until it soaked through with her tears.

* * *

Kaycee got herself by Greyhound to Atlanta, where Ginger picked her up. Her friend stepped off the bus carrying only a paper shopping bag. As soon as she saw Ginger, she burst into tears.

"Oh, Kaycee," murmured Ginger, and for a moment her own troubles receded as she beheld her friend.

When Kaycee steadied enough to catch a breath, Ginger took her by the shoulders and held her away for a look. Kaycee's right jaw looked like an eggplant, all swollen and discolored. On the left side of her neck shone three marks in the distinct shape of fingers. And when Kaycee tried to smile, Ginger glimpsed only gum where once her left incisor had grown.

They looked mournfully at each other. For once, even Kaycee could summon no words. Ginger picked up the paper bag and they made their way to the car.

They drove mostly in companionable quiet, stopping at a 7-Eleven for a frosty Big Gulp, which Kaycee kept pressed against her jaw. Kaycee drifted in and out of sleep, and Ginger flipped from radio station to station with the volume turned low. In the vicinity of Jacksonville they caught the airwaves of WAYL, the Christian station she'd heard sometimes growing up.

"I know this song," said Kaycee, reaching over and turning up the dial. "Rebecca something."

"Rebecca St. James," said Ginger. Together they listened, and when the chorus hit they began to sing:

> *Go and sin no more*
> *He said I will not condemn you . . .*

"You're gonna be all right," Ginger said.
Kaycee flashed a gummy smile. "So are you."

* * *

Ceecee had upgraded.

The double-wide that stood in place of the old trailer could almost pass for a real house, what with its cement foundation and fresh beige siding. She had even bothered to plant a couple of shrubs alongside the front door, beside a proper mailbox on a proper post, not the old aluminum bucket on the steps that used to collect the bills and supermarket fliers.

"Baby!" Ginger's mother yanked the door open and threw wide her arms. She enveloped Ginger and then pulled back for a smooch on her cheek. "Skinny. So skinny! What happened to your face? You know men like a little flesh! Look at you—" Ceecee's hands moved down to Ginger's ribs, causing her to squirm like Jordan did when he was tickled. "My God. No meat at all. Like a starved rabbit. Oh—"

Ceecee spotted Kaycee, who hung back, a little shy, cowed by this leather-faced, flame-haired loudmouth. Ceecee put her hands on her hips, the inch-long fuchsia nails tapping, tapping. She looked at Ginger for an explanation.

"Mom, this is Kaycee," Ginger said. "I told you I was bringing a friend."

Ginger watched Ceecee process this information. Her mother was no bigot, but her fifty years had unfolded almost entirely within a can's throw from right here, leaving many things and many situations out of her personal experience. Television widened her world somewhat, but the shows Ceecee favored exposed her to caricaturish representations of those unknowns. Take black people. Of course she came across them on a daily basis, driving to work in a strip-mall beauty parlor or at the Winn-Dixie. But white folks dominated the trailer park (which, Ginger saw upon driving in, had upgraded its status to "Mobile Community"). And Ginger would bet that this would mark the very first time Ceecee had been asked to share her roof with a woman of color.

Ginger understood. After all, she had grown up here, too. Until she'd started stripping, she hadn't known any black girls, either.

Kaycee must have sensed that particular brand of hesitation in Ceecee, the one rooted in a mistrust based on nothing more than the color of her skin. Ginger wondered how that must feel, to have to employ that antenna when meeting strangers, to have to read into the subtext of their greetings. She hated that her own mother warranted this antenna. Just as she prepared to intervene for her friend's sake, Kaycee stepped forward.

"How do you do," said Kaycee, holding out her hand. Her lips turned upward in an awkward smile that struck Ginger as un-Kaycee-like, until she remembered the missing tooth. The swelling in her jaw had subsided somewhat, but she still looked beat.

And Ceecee knew from beat.

Ceecee paused only a moment before she took Kaycee's hand in both of hers. "Any friend of Ginger's is a friend of mine," she said firmly. "Now, you girls get inside. You must be exhausted. I picked up a bucket of fried chicken—"

That was one thing about Ceecee. No Mona Lisa smiles. No feathery baby-girl voice translating for a computer-like brain. She said what she meant, and she meant what she said.

* * *

There it was. The Doll House.

Precious name for a strip club hard by a strip mall hard by a strip of interstate, Ginger always thought. The painted exterior wall featured a coquettish girl with spots of red on her cheeks, like a doll. She wondered how many families had driven by and found themselves explaining to their distraught little daughters, no, sweetie, we can't go inside—it's not that kind of place.

Nothing about it had changed in the eight years since she'd last worked here, at least from the outside. Same tarred roof. Same blacked-out windows. She remembered the last time she'd pushed her way out of those red pleather-coated double doors into the sunlight, with Miami in her sights. Movin' on up, or so she'd thought then. Ha.

Even from inside the Prius, parked a good distance away, Ginger twitched her nose to rid it of the smell memory. The rug-deep skunk of beer. The tang of Aqua Net hair spray. The reek of copious cologne on the necks of unsavory men.

As she watched, the doors opened. A woman stepped out. She could tell it was a woman, even though she wore a loose sweatshirt with the hood pulled up. The woman shuffled toward the back of the building, checking over her shoulder. Ginger knew that move: That was to make sure none of the patrons followed. Then the woman leaned against the wall and pulled out a cigarette. The first of her shift, probably. And definitely not the last.

Ginger watched her smoke it down to a stub, flick it to the ground, and grind it out with her flip-flop. Off the stage, Ginger had never worn heels, either. Finally the woman pushed herself off the wall and headed back inside.

Repent You Sinner. Sinner Repent You.

Ginger got out of her car. She knew what she must do.

CHAPTER SIXTEEN

Ruthie

The arrival gate at Newark airport was chaotic, but I had no checked luggage and thus could avoid the choke point at the carousels. Knowing Dad would rather circle the airport ad infinitum than pay the parking fee, I trotted straight toward the exit.

"Ruthie! Oh, Ruuuthie!"

What the——? I rubbernecked around the place. And there, sure enough, was Dad, which meant that for the first time in his life he must have actually parked. I saw why. Beside him was her.

So it begins. I straightened my shoulders, Candace-style.

I approached and bussed Dad's cheek. "Hey, Daddy," I said. "You look great." He did. His hair was trimmed and he had color in his cheeks, which were freshly shaved. I sniffed. "Is that cologne?"

He beamed some more and then he drew his arm around the woman. Suddenly, he appeared almost shy.

"Ruthie," he said, "this is June. June, my younger daughter—Ruthie."

She was small. Candace-sized, I gauged. And pretty, in an AARP way. Her hair waved to her shoulders in the too-regular pattern of a perm. A pair of glasses with pink plastic frames hung from a chain around her neck. The puffy black jacket, the brown pants, the sensible boots—all her clothing items seemed well kept but not particularly well matched. I'm sorry if this isn't PC or whatever, but June looked like every other Korean lady in Hoogaboom.

She took my hand in both of hers and held it. "Wooty," she said, then tried again. "Woo-teee." She laughed and looked at my father. "That's gonna be a hard one."

"Sometimes we call her Toothy," he said.

"Not helpful, Dad," I said.

"Tooty," she tried, and grinned. "No, no, better. Tooty. Yes? Okay?"

Despite myself, I smiled back.

In the car they sat in the front and I in the back. I tried not to think about my mother sitting in June's seat, reminding Dad to take the Turnpike North exit and not the South.

June had selected a Korean restaurant in Hoogaboom, one of a dozen, none of which I'd ever been to. I'd tried Korean food a few times with Jerry in Manhattan, and I loved the barbecued short ribs and atomic-orange kimchi. But the local joints in my own hometown intimidated me. The waitstaff seemed to glower as we strolled past, as if daring anyone other than their countrymen to want bibimbap.

When we walked in with June, though, the servers shouted out greetings in Korean. *"Ahn nyeong ha se yo,"* replied June.

My father—my *father*—added his own truncated hello, which came out more like "Ahn-say-oh." A man who looked to be the manager came out to shake Dad's hand. Dad soaked it in, grinning and waving like a celebrity. Maybe he was. The white man who crossed over.

As soon as we sat—June and Dad on one side, me on the other—two servers covered our table with small dishes. June pointed them out: marinated spinach. Pickled radish. Vinegary cucumber. Bean sprouts in sesame oil. "Banchan," she said, waving her arm over the array.

"Side dishes," translated Dad, as he hoisted the silver chopsticks.

Another shocker. "When'd you pick that up?" I hissed, indicating the chopsticks, as June ordered from the waitress.

He shrugged as he wielded a sliver of kimchi into his mouth. "This old dog has some new tricks," he said.

"Ew."

"What?"

"Never mind."

A waitress tapped my knee. I moved it aside so she could twist open the gas valve under our table. She whipped a metal cover off the table to reveal a grill. Another waitress bustled out to spread marinated short ribs on the sizzling bars, and soon the smell of charring beef filled my mouth with drool.

"First, we eat," June announced. I didn't argue.

As I sucked my last rib bone dry, I looked up to see June watching me with approval. Must be universal, this maternal desire to stuff the young.

"Delicious," I said, a needless statement considering the picked-over cow carcass on my plate.

She nodded happily. "Next time," she said, "I make."

"June's a great cook," said Dad.

I took a deep breath. Okay, Viv, I thought. Here goes nothing.

"So," I said. "What's going on?"

"Well, Toothy," he said, glancing at June, who watched him expectantly. "I wanted to be the one to tell you. June and I are getting married."

"*What?*" I leaped up, knocking over my glass of barley tea. A flurry of waitresses descended to mop up the mess. June grabbed one of their dish towels and stood to wipe at my wet lap.

Dad looked dejected. "Of all the kids, I thought you'd understand."

"Understand? What's to understand? Mom died *six months ago*. You don't just—you don't just up and marry some stranger. No offense," I said to June, who sat back down.

Dad stiffened. "June is no stranger," he said, taking her hand. "We're in love."

"Love! Love—oh, God, Daddy. You loved Mom. You loved Mom for forty years."

"Mom's gone, Ruthie."

He said it so simply, so sadly, that I felt the air leave my lungs. I crumpled into my seat.

* * *

Outside the restaurant, as we waited for Dad to fetch the car from the meter, June turned to me and took my hands in hers. Her palms felt soft, her fingers like a child's. I wondered if she washed dishes wearing rubber gloves, like my mother, if this was a trick known among housewives of all nations.

"My husband, he die almost year ago," said June. "I love him all my life. We come together from Korea. We raise a three children, now all gone, California, other place. I miss him every day."

She blinked back her tears and continued. "Your father, he come and help me with estate, other thing. He so kind to Soong-sa many year. And now to me. I love him very much. Not same way I love my before husband. But very much."

She shook my hands a little for emphasis. "Old people, we get so lonely. We give each other, how you say—comfort. Not same as before marriage. For him or me. But love, all same."

We dropped June off at her house, a recently built brick and stucco structure that for being a two-family looked somewhat ostentatious, with its columns and gold-bordered windowpanes. Her dead husband, Soong-sa Kim, had designed it for their dotage—half to live in, the other half to rent, an entrepreneur's pension plan. A young family lived in the rental unit, or so I guessed from the overturned tricycle out front. Dad planned to move in here with her, they told me, as soon as he sold the house where I grew up.

In the car she said little, but before she got out, she turned back to me. "Good-bye, Tooty," she said. "I see you again."

I nodded. They didn't kiss. I was grateful.

"Call you later," Dad said, as she waved and scurried toward her house.

We drove on in silence toward home. Home. Even after I'd married, even now, I thought of it as home. Isn't that always the case? The clapboard split-level of my childhood wasn't much to look at. My luxury McMansion in Magnolia trumped it by every real estate marker: rooms, fixtures, number of cars that fit in the garage. But as we pulled into the stubby driveway, a little fist inside me unclenched, a grip that let go only when I came home.

Though Dad told me he had already contracted a real estate agent, no sign yet swung from a metal rod in our front yard, and inside, nothing had changed. Not only had he declined to start packing, Dad hadn't moved a thing from when Mom died. He had not emptied the canvas magazine rack of its *Good Housekeeping* back issues. I'd bet a dollar he hadn't even canceled the subscription. He had not removed the "World's Best Mom" mug from the mug tree on the counter, or the five mugs she'd bought for each of her kids in different colors that read, "Mom Likes <u>Me</u> Best." The musty spice rack, the KitchenAid mixer with the tines still crusted from her last baking endeavor, the shopping list in her handwriting stuck by magnet to the refrigerator. It read:

OJ
Tomato soup
Liverwurst

Mom didn't eat those things. Toward the end, she ate nothing at all. Judging by the weak hand, she wrote this list for Dad just before she died, to remind him of things to get for himself.

TP
Coffee
Soap

I pictured her lying in bed, feebly manipulating a pen and notepad, thinking of the things her husband would need to get by.

Detergent
Shampoo
Q-tips

I opened the fridge. "Dad," I called, "you got nothing to eat."

"It's okay," he called back from the den, where I could hear him flipping through the sports channels. "I eat at June's."

Oh. Of course. He had already moved in.

I went up to her room, Mom's room. The door was open. Here, everything had changed. The hospital bed was gone; the hospice service reclaimed it the very day of her death. That had pissed Dad off no end. "What, they can't leave things the way they are for even a night?" he had raged.

No, they could not. An hour after the men from the funeral home took Mom's body, the hospice workers arrived. Not Dolores and Kinesha, the hospice nurses we had come to treat like family, but two quietly efficient men who folded up the bed and removed the IV stand, the wastebasket, the metal nightstand crowded with medical supplies. Later my sister and I tossed the flowers and boxed up the cards and framed photos propped around her bed. I took with me a collage I had called upon my grade-school crafts skills to make for her, a cheerfully crappy mélange of cutout photos and pressed flowers and funny captions I had affixed to the wall at the foot of her bed. All that remained in the room was the leather chair to the side of where the bed had stood, where Father O'Riley had sat with her on that final day.

I sat down in that chair and remembered.

Her breath came shallow and ragged then. Dolores and Kinesha told us of the signs: a bluing of the fingertips, a rattle in the chest, prolonged periods of unconsciousness.

Father O came to administer her last rites, anointing her forehead and hands with oil. He lay his hands oh so gently on her, one on her arm, the other on her shoulder. He placed the slenderest sliver of a Eucharist wafer on her tongue.

"The body of Christ," he said to her, then to us: "The viaticum. A last meal to sustain her in the journey from life to death."

He asked us to pray. We bent our heads and said the Our Father, then the Hail Mary. He took her cold hand and kissed it. Then he blessed us and left.

Viv reached for an oversize Q-tip, dampened it with water, and dabbed at Mom's lips, just as the nurses had shown us.

We were all there, we siblings. But not Dad. He went to see a client that day.

"We think you should be here," Tom told him that morning in the kitchen. We had held bedside vigil all the previous night, the five of us, as Dad snored in his own bed down the hall. I made the coffee, as Paul caught a snooze on the Barcalounger and Michael checked e-mail on his handheld. Viv stayed by Mom's side, which I thought a good thing, as the following conversation would have made her hurl something hard.

"Why?" Dad asked. "Sunny-side down for me, Ruthie."

I flipped his egg. Tom sat down next to Dad. "Because," he said, "I think this is the day."

"For what?"

Michael and I glanced at each other.

Tom stayed calm. "Dad, we think Mom's going to—we think this is her last day."

"Nah," said Dad.

I put a plate before him. "Daddy," I said.

He cut into his yolk. I watched the golden ooze. "I don't buy it."

"The nurses say so," said Michael.

"What do they know?"

We watched him eat. "Look," Dad said finally. "You're all wrong. She's not going to die."

Oh, God. We looked at each other. It was worse than we thought.

"Dad—"

"I know she's sick," he snapped. "Okay? Don't condescend to me. I know. But she's not going to die today. And that's final."

He stood up and stormed out of the house. We heard his Caddy revving up outside.

Upstairs, I recounted the conversation to Viv, who as predicted threw a greeting card at the wall. "Mother of Christ," she said.

"Cut him a break," said Tom. "He's in denial."

We were silent for a while. "And that's *final*," said Michael.

We started to laugh. Paul stumbled in, rubbing his eyes. "I miss something?"

Just then, Mom inhaled. It was barely a sip of air, but something about it signaled us. We rushed around her, Viv and Tom on one side; Michael, Paul, and me on the other. Viv and I clutched each of her hands. The boys stroked her hair, her feet, her face.

"Mom," said Tom, and it came out as a whimper.

All at once we began to cry. We each spoke to our mother, the final words each of us wanted her to hear. I don't know what the others said. Our messages were private, insofar as they could be, with all of us wailing and crowding against each other.

This is what I said: "Don't worry about me, Mommy. I'm going to be okay. Don't worry. Don't worry about me."

To this day I don't know why I didn't spend those last minutes thanking her or telling her I loved her or that I hoped she wasn't in pain. I don't know why I felt my final words to my mother ought to reassure her of my own well-being. I don't know why this was what I felt my mother should know as she breathed her last breath.

It was not a great gasp, her last breath. Not even a sigh. We watched as the waxen skin above her clavicle rose and fell one last time.

Viv touched Mom's throat. She was long past a discernible pulse in her wrist, but Paul reached for it anyway. We waited.

She was gone.

* * *

"Ruthie, honey? We should get going."

Dad called from the bottom of the stairs. With everything going on at Greenleaf, Candace had granted me only a day trip back home, then sweetened the blow by paying for the ticket. Dad would drive me back to the airport. I looked around my mother's room. A tissue box gathered dust on a dresser. I reached for a piece and wiped away my tears.

From the car I took in the town I loved, the town I would always call home. If Magnolia was a glossy Hollywood romance, Hoogaboom was a gritty film-fest indie, a place of narrow streets and prewar buildings and bars with unironic Irish names. It seemed more, I don't know, authentic. Despite the near-total makeover of Main Street into Little Korea, enough remained of the past that I still had my bearings. There was Saint Ann's, with its stern stone facade. There was Mel's Bakery. There was Stew Kozlowski's funeral home, where my mother's body lay during its last hours aboveground.

As we turned the corner around Saint Ann's, Dad asked, "Getting to church?"

It was a question he asked me and his other kids every time we spoke, from the day we left his house for college. It wasn't really a question at all but a regular reminder to hit Sunday Mass.

And so there was no right answer but "Yup," which is what all of us said, though I knew for a fact that the various encumbrances of adulthood—work, unruly toddlers, Sunday morning hangovers—had prevented all of us from making regular appearances in a pew for years.

"Yup," I said.

I'd lied before about my weekly obligation as a Catholic, like the time when Dad caught me by cell phone mid-mimosa at Isabella's, our favorite Sunday brunch spot in Manhattan. It felt like less of a lie whenever I accompanied Jerry on his Great Church Search, but I knew attending Protestant services didn't count, not in my father's view.

Including, of course, Greenleaf. For the fact remained that in my family's eyes, my husband's congregation did not count as church.

Sometimes I thought back to what Viv asked when I first announced our move, if my husband's new job as a pastor at an evangelical church meant I would convert. But months into my life as a pastor's wife, conversion was no longer the question in my mind, if it ever was.

Never mind selecting a denomination. The question was whether or not I would find faith.

Every week, Greenleaf held an altar call, during which attendees new to the Word of Christ were encouraged to receive a special blessing at the front of the sanctuary. What followed was a rush of people toward the stage, their emotions ranging wildly from the exuberant to the subdued, the somber to the sobbing. The worship team kicked into some surging, heart-twisting tune, which of course had on the rest of us the effect of the theme song from the movie

Titanic, bullying us into reaching for our hankies. Pastor Aaron spoke patiently to each caller upon his altar, which is to say the stage, putting one hand on their shoulders and the other atop their heads. Many cried. Some fainted.

Jerry accepted altar calls without judgment as part of Greenleaf culture. As a born and bred Catholic, I viewed altar calls with the fascination and—I'll admit it—the condescension of a Westerner spying on tribal rituals in the Amazon, or of a liberal watching Fox News. It goes without saying that never once was I tempted to join in. But while my Northeasterner's disdain may have kept me from such blatant displays of spiritual experience, that's not to say I did not long for one.

How could I not? I saw with my own eyes the good Greenleaf did. Not just the diaper drives for single moms and the hospital visits to the lonely, but the sustenance and comfort of faith. I saw with my own eyes the faces of church members who unloaded a terrible grief during service and left refueled with hope. I saw alcoholics recovered and exhausted parents helped to cope and desperate people of all stripes changed by faith. I saw my husband reborn. I saw these things.

I wanted to believe, like Jerry did. I wanted it with all my heart. But I did not hear the call.

We passed Saint Ann's and veered toward the Turnpike.

"You know," said my father, "there was a stretch I didn't go."

So unlikely was the statement, it took me a moment to grasp his meaning. This was a man who, when I asked him to describe himself in one word for a third-grade project, answered "Catholic" in his next breath.

"You mean to church?" I asked, to be sure.

He nodded. "After your mother died. After the funeral, in fact. When they wouldn't let me say a few words. Remember that?"

How could I forget? We learned then that the Newark archdiocese forbade family members—or anyone at all outside of the clergy—to give the eulogy. The archbishop deemed laypeople unqualified to deliver an appropriate send-off for their loved ones from the pulpit. Too windy and emotional, apparently. When I told Jerry later, he muttered something dark about "the rules of Rome." Though he avoided criticizing Catholicism to me, I knew his reasons for never considering the church for himself had in part to do with sour and senseless decrees like this one.

Now that Dad mentioned it, I did recall him getting up in the middle of the funeral Mass, mumbling something about needing a smoke. Later I found him outside sitting on the steps watching the traffic. He got up as his wife's casket left Saint Ann's, hoisted high on her sons' shoulders, never to return. I guess he left feeling the same way.

"Why?" This was big news. I had to get to the bottom of it.

He sighed from somewhere deep. "I was just so mad," he said. "Not about the eulogy thing. Nah, I was pretty pissed off about that, too. But when I thought about it, I was really mad at God. For taking Edith away from me. You know? Why her? What kind of god would take her and not one of those Middle East dictators? Or that asshole Karl Rove?"

We shared a dry chuckle and then sat in silence for a while. The Manhattan skyline shimmered before us, from this distance flimsy as a cardboard cutout.

He continued. "It was June talked me back."

"She Catholic?"

He shook his head. "Goes to one of them Protestant Korean

ones. But she went through it with her husband, you remember. She said to me, 'You gotta believe.' "

"And what if you don't?" I was not in the habit of challenging my father, especially on matters of faith. On matters of faith, I was in the habit of shutting the hell up. And so I did not complete my thought, the one that weighed on me day and night: What if you don't believe in God?

Still, somehow, he seemed to know. He angled his face toward me to underscore his point.

"You gotta have faith, Ruthie," he said.

I slumped a little. He wouldn't understand, after all.

Then he surprised me. "You gotta have faith in something. In your family. In your marriage. In love or whatever the hippies say. Doesn't matter. You gotta have faith. Else you got nothing."

You gotta have faith. In something, or someone. He did understand. At that moment, I had faith in my father.

"Dad," I said. "I know you loved Mom. And I know you don't love her less just because you want to marry June."

He kept his eyes on the road. But I could see them grow wet. "I think of your mother every moment of every day," he said. "Everything I see, I think, 'Oh, Edith would like that.' Or, 'That would make Edith laugh.' " His Adam's apple bobbed as he swallowed several times, but his voice still broke. "I miss her so much."

"I know."

"You remember Kevin Lutz?" he said. "Old Lutzy from the hardware store? After his Winnie died, he just stopped living. Couldn't remember names. Didn't eat. Had to piss in a diaper. A year later, he's dead. Just willed himself to death, that's what his kids said."

"That's awful."

"Nobody wants to watch an old man die of a broken heart. It's not romantic, and it sure ain't pretty."

"Aren't we reason enough to live, Daddy?" I hated how plaintive I sounded, but I had to ask. "Your kids? Your grandkids?"

"Nothing takes the place of a wife, Ruthie. Not even you."

I found a few Burger King napkins in the glove compartment and handed him one. We wiped at our wet faces.

"I'm glad I came," I said.

"Me, too," he said. "The others . . ."

This time, he was the one with the plea in his voice. I knew he meant my siblings, and I knew just what to say.

"Let me take care of it."

CHAPTER SEVENTEEN

Candace

I f there was a single event the elders of Greenleaf uniformly despised, it was the Christmas Spectacular.

They called it that, after the famous Radio City show featuring the Rockettes, indicating exactly what they thought of its spiritual significance. Candace ignored the slight. She and the rest of the congregation referred to it simply as the Pageant. But she had to admit: It was indeed spectacular.

Candace watched from the belly of the sanctuary as Hugh Dolly commanded the skittering army of angels, barn animals, snowmen, bunnies, elves, shooting stars, snowflakes, magi, and a perfectly cast Santa through a dress rehearsal. The stage crew had their hands full, rigging flying angels from cables, ringers she'd hired from the Cirque du Soleil traveling troupe. Above them all hung this year's pièce de résistance, a North Star that Candace had had modeled after the chandelier in the Metropolitan Opera in New York City. She'd flown in gaffers from Hollywood to coordinate entrances and dramatic high points with lighting. There was a newly purchased snow machine.

Down on stage left, a makeup girl fussed over Giovanna Disantana, who would play the Virgin Mary this year. Candace had given Taylor—the little boy traumatized by that malignant storyteller at Talitha's birthday party—the role of the Little Drummer Boy, and he did her proud by holding his drumsticks still and listening to Hugh's instructions. The rest of the children, not so much. Hugh looked ready to explode.

Welcome to fatherhood, Candace thought.

Off to her right on the sanctuary floor sat Hugh's wife, Missy, nursing their infant girl. She looked blissful if still bovine, not at all like a woman who had any intention of returning from maternity leave. Candace supposed that was just as well. In those three months, Missy's replacement, Gee, had ascended from backup singer to superstar. Evergreen planned to build its next album around her. Some in the congregation compared her to Amy Grant crossed with Taylor Swift. Soon, Gee could draw an audience all on her own.

Suddenly Gee smacked off the makeup girl's hand and struck a pose. Candace followed the girl's gaze. Sure enough, three men had entered the sanctuary: Aaron, Elder John Swain, and Jerry Matters.

Watching the men, Candace thanked the Lord that the Global Interfaith Conference in London was over, though by all accounts it had gone off brilliantly. Google News alerts tallied more than three hundred mentions of Aaron or Greenleaf in publications, blogs, and TV reports around the world. Candace most appreciated a long feature in the *Guardian*, a British newspaper. It chronicled the deep bond between Aaron, Rabbi Bernstein, and Imam Chaudry, and what their relationship said about the movement toward religious tolerance in the United States. Exactly the kind of article they had expected in the *Atlanta Journal-Constitution*, which in the end ran only a photo and a caption about the local leaders' participation.

The three men headlined a panel discussion at the conference, but Aaron told her the most productive talks had taken place behind closed doors with religious leaders from other countries. Aaron added that Jerry Matters proved invaluable in those talks, offering well-formed opinions and a touch for diplomacy. Together the various groups ratified an agreement on how best to spin public response to world events toward peace and away from violence.

"It's huge," Aaron told her over the welcome-home dinner she'd prepared, for once eschewing upscale takeout in order to cook a four-course meal with prime rib and scalloped potatoes. "If it works, this could really impact world peace. It's happening. It's really happening."

"Praise the Lord," she had murmured.

Giovanna Disantana represented Greenleaf in a gala performance on closing night, with a solo performance of the song "Beautiful" by the Christian rock group Mercy Me. Candace thought she sounded pitchy and nervous in the video, but posted it anyway on the Greenleaf Web site. She edited out the end of the clip, when Gee ran off the stage and into the arms of Jerry Matters. It was hard to tell from the video if he reciprocated, but Gee's hug looked so fierce as to foment suspicion.

Across the sanctuary, Aaron caught sight of Candace and waved. The men approached. Candace couldn't resist a glance back at Gee on stage. The young woman followed the trio's movements with a hunger Candace thought obvious and unbecoming. After a few moments, Jerry looked up and met her gaze. She waved frenetically. He smiled and waved back, then turned to follow Aaron.

Candace ought to have taken care of this before the conference. It occurred to her that she might be too late.

Aaron roped his arm around Candace's shoulder for a brief hug. "How go the preparations?"

"Oh, you know," she said. "Act One is slow, Act Two is rocky, and Act Three is anticlimactic."

"Does it matter?" said Jerry. "We all know how the story ends."

Aaron guffawed. John Swain grinned and shook his head.

"It matters to me," said Candace.

Jerry bowed his head in apology. Aaron looked upon her fondly. "And that's why we leave the Pageant in your capable hands."

They turned to go. "Oh, John," Candace called.

The elder looked back.

"May we have a word?"

* * *

It must be said. Candace struggled with forgiveness.

When she scoured the Bible for guidance, she found the Gospel confusing on the matter. On the one hand, Matthew 5:44 advised:

But I say unto you, Love your enemies, bless them that curse you.

On the other, Matthew 18 told:

Then Peter came to him, and said, Lord, how oft shall my brother sin against me, and I forgive him? till seven times? Jesus saith unto him, I say not unto thee, Until seven times: but, Until seventy times seven.

In other words, to forgive was to run the risk of being taken advantage of. So should she turn the other cheek? Or demand an eye for an eye?

It did not help that forgiveness rubbed against her very grain, rode against her very nature. People should be held accountable. Her world ordered itself on this belief. Wrongs must be not just righted but paid for. Evil must be both eradicated and condemned.

Sometimes Candace imagined herself living in Jesus's time. She tried to picture herself joining the masses who gathered in the desert to hear Him speak, or inviting Him, dirty and strange, into her hearth. But she simply could not envision herself among the Marys and Elizabeths, hanging on His hem or washing His feet with her tears.

Instead she saw herself among the Apostles, a Peter, maybe, swinging a blade as he came for Jesus in the Garden of Gethsemane, fighting for His survival.

What is my purpose?

I know the answer, Candace realized.

I am a Crusader. I fight for the Word, and I guard its bearer. And if that means slaying Judas, then that is my lot.

And so she faced John the Elder.

They exited the sanctuary outdoors onto the campus grounds and stood at the edge of the man-made pond. Candace recalled that they had spoken three months ago to the day, just before the arrival of Jeremiah and Ruthie Matters. It was then John Swain had asked to assist the church in financial oversight. She recalled his very words: "I want to serve." It was then that John Swain set in motion his plan to undo Aaron Green. And it was then that she, Candace, failed to stop him.

And that, of course, pinpointed her greatest struggle: She could not forgive herself. As she gazed upon John's splintered face, she *saw* his intentions, *smelled* his hate. She *knew* of his history. How could she have opened the doors of the inner sanctum to this wolf?

She turned and faced the church. Greenleaf. The house of worship John and the other elders had conceived, and that she and Aaron had raised. "We're so blessed to be Christians, aren't we, John?"

One side of his face creased with a wary smile.

She untucked the Bible from its usual nest under her arm and beheld it in her hands. "We don't have to wonder. It's all right here. In the Good Book. All the answers. All the rules." She turned again to face him. "Ten Commandments to lead a moral life. Ten. Simple. Commandments."

He squinted but nodded.

"I know them by heart. Do you, John?"

When he shrugged, she held up a hand. "Don't worry. I won't bore you by reciting all of them. Just one."

He watched her, alert now.

"*Thou shalt not bear false witness against thy neighbor,*" said Candace.

After a pause, John spoke. "Okay. I'm not following."

"Someone recently moved two million dollars out of the Harmony fund and then back again."

He whistled. "What for?"

"To mislead a reporter and cast doubt on Aaron's mission."

They locked eyes. John clocked a good foot over Candace in height, but her size never made her feel small. The righteous shall rise.

"Accusing a public figure of fraud is slander," she continued.

"Doing so in a printed publication is defamation of character. But those are just the laws of the land. I care more about the laws of Our Father. And the ninth commandment makes them clear."

Comprehension and then disbelief lifted John's rough brow. "You think it's me. You're accusing me of slander." He croaked out a laugh. "Know what? You're something." He shook his head. "Okay. I'll bite. How do you suppose I pulled that off? I don't have that kind of access to our accounts."

"You used to, through the Oversight Committee."

"You dissolved the committee when you changed the bylaws."

"Yes. Which was why you volunteered to assist Jerry Matters."

"Why aren't you investigating him, then?"

"We did. Tosh traced the fund transfer in question to Jerry's office computer, entered under his access code."

"Well, then."

"It happened while he was with Aaron on prison ministry."

"So? He could have used his mobile."

"The county prison blocks Internet access."

"Maybe he came back."

"The prison log shows he was there from 10:08 in the morning to 12:52. The transfer occurred at 11:14." Candace paused before the final thrust. "We have security video showing you entering Jerry Matters's office at 11:08, and leaving at 11:32."

She waited for this to sink in. John stared at her, radiating an enmity so toxic she could almost see its fumes.

"This is rich. This is just rich." John took a few steps back. "Since you have all the answers, maybe you can tell me. Why would I want to do that? Remember I've been accused of worse. I was a financial planner acquitted of stealing from my clients. Remember that? So you tell me. Why would I play peekaboo with that kind of money? Why wouldn't I just take it and run?"

"That puzzled me," Candace said. "And then I realized: You want the church more than you want the cash. You hate us more than you love money. That article was leverage to drum us out of Greenleaf. That is, it would have been, if it had run."

A frog leaped from the edge of the pond into the water. She watched the concentric circles widen out, widen out. She waited for the satisfaction she anticipated from this encounter, but it never materialized. Instead she felt a rippling sadness.

She turned back to Elder John. "When it failed to run, you called the reporter Juan Diaz and learned of my involvement. You must have known then that this day would come."

He swayed like a ghost now, a transparent husk of the man she'd once compared favorably to Clint Eastwood. Like if she blew hard enough, this Pale Rider would just flutter away. It's over, she thought.

But not to him. Elder John stopped swaying and pointed a finger at Candace. "Everything I do," he rumbled, "I do for the church. You must realize this. Your time here is done. It's time for the Greens to leave Greenleaf."

Candace stared at his finger, aimed squarely at her chest. She lifted her eyes to his, and saw in them something wild, something changed. *He means to harm me,* she thought. *He means to do me harm.*

But I am a Crusader. I fight for the Word, and I guard its bearer. I am Aaron's protector.

This is my purpose. And this time, I shall not fail.

"No, John," she said. "It is you whose time is done. It is you who must leave Greenleaf. Leave now, leave forever, and your transgressions will be forgiven."

There. She'd said it. The word tasted like dust in her mouth, but she managed to spit it out. Forgiveness. She offered it to this grave sinner.

She noted only later that she had not offered to forgive him herself. God, she figured, could take care of that part.

CHAPTER EIGHTEEN

Ginger

"Hi," said Ginger to the bouncer at the door. "Can I talk to the manager?"

The man was standard-issue muscle: hulking shoulders straining a black button-down shirt, head shaved smooth and decorated with a snake tattoo. He checked out Ginger in her pink T-shirt and jeans, her ruddy hair in a ponytail, her face scrubbed clean. He lifted a studded eyebrow.

"Oh, yeah," he said. "He'll wanna talk to you, sweetheart. In the back."

Ginger gave him a smile and headed into the strip club. Only a handful of customers slumped in the velveteen booths. It was four o'clock, approaching happy hour, a time when she knew the girls would be straggling in and primping for their shifts.

This was what Ginger had come to think of as her Jason Bourne moment. After she gained access to an establishment of ill repute but before she had ventured too far in, she assessed the threat level. She noted the three exit signs glowing chemical green in the darkness. She checked out the customers for their size, number, and drunkenness. She picked out the potential ally: the bartender, as usual, a deceptively unobtrusive man who nevertheless had a handle on everybody in the place. The bartender met her eyes and quickly looked away. No stairs. No blinding strobe lights. Not too many chairs blocking the way to the left side exit door.

Good. If need be, she could make a quick escape.

A door on the back wall opened, and a young man with canola-oil skin stepped out. He made Ginger and beelined toward her.

"Well, hello," he said, his lips stretching into a smile that did not reach his eyes. He folded a stick of red gum into his mouth. "Looking for work?"

Ginger smiled back. "Not exactly," she said.

This was a key moment. In her experience, strip-club managers fell into three types. One: pool of sleaze. Two: calculating businessman. Three: good-hearted slob. This one looked to fall into type two.

In the space of a chew, his smile snapped away and he looked her up and down. "Don't know what you're selling, but there's only one thing we're buying in here."

"I'm not selling anything. Least of all me."

"What do you want, then?"

Ginger pulled round the canvas book bag she carried, drawing out a small, plastic bag, the kind Candace had used for goody bags at Tali's birthday party. These were pink, like her T-shirt. She held one open and offered it for inspection.

"I want to hand these out to the girls. That is, if they want them."

The manager squinted at her, then at the bags. He peered inside. Ginger helped by cataloging the contents. "Bath beads. Incense sticks. A satchel of jasmine. Chamomile tea. Just—things to help a girl relax. All legal." She tried a smile.

"What's this?" The manager pulled out a pink piece of paper cut in the shape of a heart. He read it, then lowered his lids at Ginger. "You a Jesus freak?"

She ignored the insult. "It's just a little message, and our Web site and hotline," she said. "If they want it."

He thrust the bag back toward her. "Jeb," he called toward the front door.

The hydrant-necked bouncer got up and lugged toward them. The bartender kept wiping glasses but watched them closely. Ginger needed a new tack, and fast.

"Look," she said, in her sweetest, calmest voice, a voice she felt would do Candace proud. "It's not a trap. I'm not here to wreck your business. If girls want to work here, that's their call. All I want is to give them a little care package. Everyone deserves a care package." Finally, this: "It was my life once, too."

The bouncer closed in. The manager kept his eyes on Ginger. "You got ten minutes," he said finally. "And no preaching. I need them in position in fifteen."

Ginger exhaled. Then she headed toward the dressing rooms.

* * *

God is love. Whoever lives in love lives in God, and God in him.—*1 John 4:16*
www.MagdalenaMinistries.org
866-IAMMARY

Ginger clutched the pink paper heart and stared at the words. She had typed and printed them out onto a sheet of candy-colored paper, painstakingly cutting each into hearts, her right middle finger blistering from the metal handle of Ceecee's heavy kitchen scissors.

Kaycee had designed their uniforms: pale pink baby tees, labeled only with the cryptic acronym MM over the heart. Magdalena Ministries. Ginger's ministry, named after Mary of Magdalene, patron saint of working girls.

The Web site was a work in progress, rudimentary in design. It featured a hot pink background and an image of the same heart Ginger handed out, with the verse from John 1. Tabs led to lists of resources like clinics and help lines, as well as a daily spiritual meditation and first-person stories by women who had found Jesus. She made it a point to refer to readers and contributors as "sisters," just as Lorraine Lawson had. To Ginger, the word felt like a hug.

The Web site design was the work of Melissa, the Indiana pastor's wife from the retreat. Ginger remembered Melissa mentioning having set up her church's site after taking a course online to learn how. Melissa also confided that she was the anonymous pastor's wife behind the lively and popular blog *IrreverentPW*.

Ginger telephoned her one night, and after catching Melissa up on all that had transpired—Candace's discovery of her past, her flight from Magnolia, Kaycee's own escape from her abusive husband—she explained her new mission.

Melissa listened, breaking in only with indignant humphs and grunts, especially at the part about Kaycee's assault.

"Let me help," Melissa said finally. "You tell me what I can do."

Ginger hesitated. Even now, even after having come this far, she struggled mightily with asking people for help. "I need someone to do our Web site," she blurted.

"I'm on it."

"I can't pay."

"Please. My whole life is a volunteer mission. Between this and chaperoning the Sunday school field trip to the butter factory—let's just say it'll be a joy."

"You have so much on your plate," Ginger apologized. "What about your family?"

"The kids are in school all day, and I can also work on it while they sleep. That's usually when the old biddies call Jimmy with some emergency. 'Pastor, I've got a clog in my toilet. Help me, Jesus!'"

It felt good to laugh.

Melissa continued. "And off my husband goes to do God's work. A superhero with a plunger." She paused. "Never mind my family. What about yours?"

For the first time, Ginger noticed a lanyard propped behind the phone cradle on Ceecee's kitchen counter. It was a homely thing, but what else could you expect from a lanyard? Ginger remembered making it in school for a long-ago Mother's Day. Ceecee had hung on to it all these years, she realized. Ginger didn't know why she'd find that so surprising; after all, she herself kept almost everything Jordan and Tali made, displaying finger paintings on the refrigerator and clay turtles on the family-room divider until boxing them carefully away. A tear formed on a lower lash.

"I miss them, Melissa," she said. "I miss them so much."

She heard the front door opening, and hastily swiped at her face. Hanging up, she turned to greet Kaycee and Ceecee.

Kaycee was supposed to be back in Memphis by now. She swore up, down, and sideways that she wasn't going back to Devonn. Instead she would stay with her cousin Neisha and enroll in an introductory theological class at the community college. She would join the church where Neisha and her aunt Shell were active, and try out various volunteering duties. "Baby steps," said Kaycee. Baby steps toward her calling. Baby steps toward becoming a pastor.

But days turned to weeks, and still Kaycee delayed her departure for the Greyhound station. When Ceecee told her of an opening for a hair washer at her salon, Kaycee rode to work with her the next day and applied.

"Don't know the first thing about white-people hair," Kaycee fretted.

"Round here, they come for the company, not to get all fancy," said Ceecee. "Just say 'mmm-hmm' and 'uh-huh' a lot while they yammer, and you'll do just fine."

Ginger spent her days working on her ministry, planning or conducting her evangelical missions to strip clubs, coordinating with Melissa on the Web site. Evenings were harder. She read her Bible, prayed on her past sins. She asked over and over for forgiveness. She tried to keep her mind free of intruding thoughts.

But she could not. Ginger missed her children too much. Her mind would travel to Magnolia, where early evenings were the busiest time, what with the feeding and the bathing and the nighttime prayers. Often her back ached from picking up toys and her head spun from coordinating the whole routine. Often she longed for the moment the children would quiet into sleep and she could collapse into her comfy chair with her Psalms. But then she'd tuck Tali in with her blankie and kneel down by the bed, nuzzling her nose and smooching that spongy cheek. Tali would blink at her with eyes that would soon flutter shut. Ginger would stay there until her knees complained, watching her baby sleep, her hand spanning the girl's rib cage as it rose and fell, rose and fell.

Her plan, once she arrived at Ceecee's, had been to make a plan, for which she figured she'd need a few days, maybe a week, of single-minded focus. A few days, maybe a week, of putting herself before her children. It would be better for them, too, she reasoned, to settle into the routine at Mamie's house. Better for Candace, of that she was sure, not to hear Ginger's voice for a spell.

Five days into Ginger's departure, when it became clear her absence was no idle threat, Candace ordered Timothy home. Ginger knew this because he called her from the Jakarta airport.

The call came at midnight, just after Kaycee and Ceecee had retired from their reality TV marathon. Ginger stumbled to the kitchen phone and picked it up.

"What's this?" he said. His voice sounded high and tinny on the phone line, like a child actor from an old movie. "Mom called and read me some letter you left?"

Of course. Ginger had half-expected it. In anticipation of the probable event that Candace would open a sealed envelope addressed to her son, Ginger had written a near copy of the note she wrote to Candace. Dry. Factual. Nothing about her love. Nothing about her pain.

"She says you've been gone almost a week?" He was turning his sentences up at the end, making them questions, as if he found all this so improbable that surely she would refute it.

"Five days," she said, her eyes on Ceecee's red plastic wall clock. And nine hours and twenty-three minutes.

"And that you left her with the kids?"

And forty-one seconds. Forty-two. Forty-three. "I needed some time on my own."

She heard what sounded like a stifled explosion of consonants.

"Now?" he said, in something like a wail. "While I'm mid-mission? I have to come back?"

I see, thought Ginger. I ask you to stay, and you go. She tells you to come back, and you're on the next flight.

"And we're just in the thick of things here, we got supply issues, no backup . . . *God*, Ginger—"

Her husband never, ever took the Lord's name in vain. He must be spitting mad.

"Is this because of the note thing?"

"The note thing," she repeated slowly. The note thing. So that's what this was to him.

"You know what I mean. Mom finding out. About your past."

"Yes. No. It's about—it's about all of it, Timothy. My past. And my life now. I have to figure some things out. I never did, and now I have to. *I have to.*"

He didn't respond right away. She pictured him leaning against a wall in an airport as travelers streamed past, but beyond that could fill in the picture no more. What does an airport in Indonesia look like? That's where Jakarta was, she was pretty sure. The people there . . . what did they speak? Eat? Wear? She wouldn't know. Her husband regularly touched ground in the remotest corners of the world, and she'd never even left this country.

"Can't you do that at home?" he asked finally. "With us?"

"The thing is," she said, "it wouldn't be us. You're never there. As soon as I go back, you'd leave again. Am I right?"

Despite everything, she asked this last with a remnant of hope. *No,* she wanted to hear. *No, I wouldn't leave again. I'd stay. Just like you asked.*

He didn't answer. She was right.

* * *

Divorce papers. Ginger had always figured they would be labeled as such, when she'd heard the term on daytime TV. *I'm going to serve him with divorce papers.* Or, *I got the divorce papers right here!* And here they were, just another legal form. "In the High Court of Justice," it read, "Principal Registry of the Family Division." There was a blank beside "PETITIONER," and another beside "RESPONDENT."

"Take these home, sugar," the secretary said, sliding them into a manila envelope. "Then call us when you're ready." She slipped in the law firm's business card.

Ginger pulled them out now and spread them on her mother's kitchen table. Kaycee was at a movie with a new friend from the salon. Ceecee was out on a date, her first in months. She'd met the man at the Winn-Dixie—"I'm the only dinosaur who meets men on line, not online"—and she was excited about him. "He's a mailman," Ceecee said, as she doused herself with J.Lo's Glow. "That means two things: He'll get a pension, and he still drives."

Ginger obtained the divorce papers for Kaycee. Or so she said. Even with that as a cover, Ginger pulled into and out of the parking lot of the law firm three times before she worked up the nerve to walk in. A yellow clapboard cabin on a busy street, the offices weren't exactly intimidating, and the secretary welcomed her with a smile. Still, Ginger couldn't get out of there fast enough. She grabbed the envelope and bolted.

Now she stared at the papers that could sever her from her life. The papers that would end her marriage to the only man she'd ever loved.

The only man she'd ever loved. The only man she *would* ever love. The only man who, from the moment they'd met, looked at her and saw only good. Who never once equated her with her former job. Who despite the awful things she had done, looked inside and saw her heart was pure. The man who'd introduced her to Christ. The man who'd raised her up. The man who'd *saved* her.

She closed her eyes and saw his face. That jaw, so sharp that a stroke along its edge might very well draw blood. The freckles spattered across his cheekbones. The odd hair that sprouted inexplicably from the middle of his forehead, which she plucked for him every few weeks. Eyes the color of the ocean, fixed forever on the horizon.

Oh, God. She loved him so.

Maybe hers was the love of Mary Magdalene for Jesus. The prostitute loved Him with her whole being, though she could never have Him for herself. Had Mary hurt this way?

People said love hurt. That was the title, in fact, of Ceecee and Kaycee's current favorite reality show, some screechy program about dating and being dumped. For the painted women on that show, the hurt played out in hair-pulling and broken objects. For Ginger, her love for her husband registered as a pain somewhere in her bones, a deep and quiet pain that nevertheless ate away at her soul.

"PETITIONER holds that the marriage be dissolved for the following reasons," said the form. Ginger thought of all the reasons that a marriage dissolved. Adultery. Addiction. Abuse. The one she often read about in relation to celebrity divorces: irreconcilable differences.

She could blame Timothy for none of those things. Neglect, maybe, but what pastor's wife could not complain of that? Communication problems, yes, but surely that was true for every married couple in America.

Abandonment. That was it. His. And now, also hers. Abandonment—but not without reason. Ginger had abandoned the life she had lived, or tried to live, for six years: that of a pastor's wife. The obedient daughter-in-law, the perfect mother, the upstanding wife. A pious pillar of society. It was a sham, all of it. And the lie had done her in.

No one in Magnolia knew the real Ginger. Not even Ginger. And it became ever more clear—not her husband, either.

"Come back," was what Timothy said to her. "Just come back."

His face glowed blue and choppy on the computer screen at the Internet café. Now that he'd returned to Magnolia, he was the one to set up her Skype visits with the children, after which he shooed them away for a private chat.

He looked whipped. And you thought *your* job was hard, thought Ginger. Now you know saving the world's got nothing on single parenting.

"I'm not ready," said Ginger.

"She's your mother-in-law," Timothy continued, yawning. "She's the grandmother of our children. She loves you. So what if she knows about your past? She'll forgive you."

"You don't understand," said Ginger.

"You're right," he sighed. "I don't." He rubbed at his face. She could see that his razor had missed the usual spot just under his chin. The back of his neck looked scruffy. "So tell me. Make me understand."

She told him then. He already knew of the Repent You Sinner cross; she'd told him of it the very night they met. She told him now of her epiphany at the pastors' wives retreat, of her need to repent her sins. She told him of her budding ministry. Of the little pink hearts and the Web site and walking into strip clubs around the region and handing naked women little goody bags of soap. Of getting up in the morning, alone and so, so lonely, until she remembered she had a mission, a purpose. A way to atone. Of feeling stronger day by day.

He listened. He listened, without interrupting.

"Ginge," he said when she finished. His voice and face—he reminded her of the night they met, the night she laid her history bare. "I never knew you carried all that around with you. And I'm sorry I haven't been around enough to, to—I'm sorry I haven't been around. For you."

"You don't think it's—stupid? The ministry, I mean."

"Stupid? I think it's brilliant."

Ginger's heart expanded. *Brilliant* was not a word anyone ever associated with her. She was about to tell him of the baby, their baby, their third child, growing so fast inside her now that she had to borrow her mother's stretchy-waisted pants. But he continued.

"And what's brilliant is you can do it from here. Right? There's no reason for you to stay at Ceecee's. The Mom thing—we'll talk to her together. You and I. As soon as you're back."

Ginger drew back a little. "But I told you I'm not ready."

"Honey," he said gently. "I gotta get back to the mission. I'm needed."

So that's what it was. *He doesn't care what I do so long as I leave him free to do his thing.* "Damn the mission," she whispered, letting a tear escape her lashes.

"What?"

"Damn the mission," she repeated, louder. "*I* need you. The children need you."

He looked stunned. "What are you saying?"

"I'm saying you have to choose."

"But it's my work. It's *God's* work."

Of course. Who was she? Who did she think she was, asking Timothy Green to choose her over God?

She reached toward the screen and touched his face. How she loved this face. "Good-bye, Timothy," she whispered. Then she clicked the "end call" icon, replacing the face she loved on the screen with the reflection of her own.

Fool, she told herself. You thought you were in a fairy tale. But this was the problem with fairy tales: There was no epilogue. Once the prince rescued Cinderella from her wretched life and married her, what happened then? Happily ever after didn't exist, not in marriage. Marriage was messy and painful and annoying and dull. Marriage was strange and funny and joyful and sweet. She'd take it all. She didn't need perfect. She just needed him there.

And it was time to admit he wasn't. Never was, never would be. Not in his heart.

Ginger got up and went to her car. Then she drove home to fill out those divorce papers.

CHAPTER NINETEEN

Ruthie

What's it like when the guy you married decides to marry God?

Viv asked me this months ago, when I revealed my husband's career change to my siblings in our childhood home. Since then the question popped into my brain at unnerving intervals, kind of like the expository captions in that old VH1 show *Pop Up Video*. I almost expected to hear that ridiculously addictive sound of a bubble popping.

Bloop. What's it like?

I knew the answer now. Nothing I could share with Viv, of course, or anyone from my old world. Or, for that matter, from my new world.

My work at Greenleaf mattered. I knew my purpose there. That I offered it on a volunteer basis made me feel surprisingly good, surprisingly free of the resentment that stalks most nine-to-fivers. It made me feel a mite closer to Jerry. I helped my husband's church, and therefore I helped him.

Which led me to the most painful reality of life as a pastor's wife.

Bloop. What's it like when the guy you married decides to marry God?

Bloop. It feels lonely as hell.

By the night Jerry returned from his jaunt in London, I was wiped out by all the drama that had taken place in his absence. I'd recapped some of it to him already by phone: the day trip to New Jersey, meeting June, and my father's intention to marry her. I told Jerry about Ginger's curious disappearance, which Candace attributed to an emergency visit to her mother, sans kids.

I could not tell Jerry about the snafu with the newspaper article and Juan Diaz. One reason was that Candace had sworn me to secrecy until she "sorted it all out." But it's true I felt an oily coating of guilt over the whole thing. About how close I came to making a really big mistake.

The point is I could barely scrape up the energy for dinner, let alone a Big Talk About Us. Besides, I hated to trample his excitement over the proceedings at the conference, at which it sounded like he'd played a real role in peace talks between the global religions.

We'd spread out on the couch with beer and pizza. I dusted off my best Regis Philbin. "And the contestant from New York wants world peace," I said, with a pageanty wave.

He looked at me strangely. "What's that supposed to mean?"

It wasn't like him not to take a joke. "You know. World peace. Like what they say on *Miss America*."

He grew quiet. I hate quiet. More than anything I hate quiet.

"Oh, come on," I said, shoulder-bumping him. "I meant it in a good way. Like, everyone wants world peace. And here you are, actually making it happen."

No response. I put on a sad-clown face. "I had no one to talk to but Candace for a week. My conversational skills have suffered. Have pity."

Tomorrow, I thought. We'll have the Talk tomorrow.

But tomorrow came and Jerry busted out of the house on some Greenleaf mission before I even finished my coffee. He'd taken to carpooling with Aaron instead of with me. "His schedule is my schedule," Jerry explained when I expressed disappointment. He had a point. That night he returned at nine. The next night, ten. Some nights he came home before dark but took a sandwich up to his office to plow through church financial records.

And so it went.

I was busy, too. Christmas approached, and with it what Candace and other staffers reverentially called the Pageant. When I first heard the plans at a committee meeting, I looked around the table in astonishment. They couldn't be serious. It sounded more like a holiday episode of *South Park* than an actual staging of the Nativity scene in an actual church.

If I understood correctly, the performance would somehow fuse the story of the birth of Christ with that of Santa Claus, with the fat bearded man assisting the denizens of Jerusalem and in the end kowtowing to the glory of the baby Jesus. Reindeer would join barnyard sheep, and elves would link arms with angels. For the finale, a rousing original number written by Hugh Dolly and starring Giovanna Disantana as the Virgin Mary.

I was speechless. I mean, have you ever heard of such a thing? Even for Greenleaf, it was way, way over the top. It's supposed to be the Greatest Story Ever Told. Why would you embellish it?

But Candace looked satisfied.

"You know my rule," she said to Hugh.

He nodded. "Bigger and better every year."

The Pageant committee meetings grew bigger, too, and more frequent. Asked by Candace to attend but having nothing whatsoever to add to the discussion, I instead scoped out church members, whoever fell into my line of vision that day.

One time it was Sandi Lillet-Smith, whose sunny smile and uniform of pastel T-shirts and capris read stay-at-home mom to me—until Candace let slip that, by night, Sandi sang in an eighties cover band at the bar in the Sheraton wearing a red sequin dress that showcased her silicone D cups.

Another time I checked out Brand Overtree, a recovering alcoholic once jailed for assaulting a fellow bar patron with a pool cue. He looked that part, in his tattered and gelled rocker getup, a scar hooking from his upper lip toward his cheekbone. But I knew that Brand volunteered regularly for our hospital ministry, visiting the ill twice a week, sitting bedside and holding the hands of the dying.

You can never tell about people by looking at them, is what Mom used to say. You just can never tell.

That day I watched Giovanna Disantana. She sat a few seats to my right with her spine unbent and her hands folded in her lap, a model participant. But when she raised her eyes, they looked irretrievably bored. Gee attended the meetings because of her starring role in the Pageant, a role I, and apparently only I, thought ill suited. I don't know. Despite her holier-than-everyone getup, something about her just reeked of naughty.

As if to make my point, she leaned forward. There, in the inch of space between the hem of her blouse and the back of her waistband, I saw it. Yep. A tramp stamp. I knew it. Virgin Mary, my untattooed ass.

The doors to the conference room opened and Aaron came in. As usual he sucked toward him the spotlight of our combined attention. And as usual he beamed back grace.

I sat up straighter because I knew that wherever Aaron went, so, too, went Jerry. Sure enough, he trailed his boss by a few steps, engrossed momentarily in his iPad. He didn't command quite the same kind of adulation, but it was clear to me that in our time here Jerry had picked up some of Aaron's magnetism. When he looked up and around at the room, even I could see that my husband—in his celadon green shirtsleeves, his hair waving to his shoulders, his blue, blue eyes—even I could see that my husband was a star.

Sitting as I did at the far end of the conference table, I knew a few people obscured me from his view. I waited for his eyes to scan the room and land on me, for that smile to change briefly from charming and public to intimate and soft. A smile just for me.

But before he saw me, he saw Gee.

I could not see her face. But I could see she had thrown back her shoulders. Then she tossed her hair.

I knew this move. Every girl who's survived high school knows this move. It's employed effectively by only the truly confident girls (say, Viv), and anyone else who tries it (say, me) looks like they're having a seizure.

My eyes flicked to Jerry's face. For no good reason, I held my breath.

His smile changed briefly from charming and public to intimate and soft. A smile just for me.

Only it was for her.

So here's something I'd like to know. When a woman catches

her man cheating, why is it that *she* wants to hide? With my next breath I angled myself so the pillowy bulk of postpartum Missy Dolly shielded me from my husband's view.

"Sounds like things are under control," I heard Aaron saying to the room. "You know what Candace says."

"Bigger and better," everyone said, laughing.

"We'll leave you to it," Aaron said. He leaned down to kiss his wife, then turned to go. I heard the door click shut, and I knew Jerry was gone.

I looked down at my hands, the knuckles white from their death grip on the armrests of the chair. *Good Lord in heaven. If you exist, please do not let me pass out.* Without thinking, I began to mumble. "Hail Mary, full of grace, the Lord is with thee—"

"Hmm?" said Missy, leaning toward me. "Did you say something?"

The meeting was breaking up. Gee stood up to go. When she turned to pick up her sweater from the back of the chair, I saw on her face a little smile.

"Nothing," I said to Missy. As I said it I realized, "I was just— praying."

Missy patted my arm. Candace sneered at her for gaining so much weight in her pregnancy, but I thought the music minister's wife was sweet. "Want me to pray with you?" she asked.

"No," I said automatically. Then, an apology: "I don't know how to do that yet."

"Honey, there's nothing to know," she said. Missy extended her hands out to me, palms up. She had such kind eyes. "Shall we give it a whirl?"

The other staff members and volunteers milled around gathering their things, trading church gossip, going over their various Pageant assignments. No one paid us any mind.

"Okay," I whispered. "Yes. Okay."

I put my hands in hers. She closed her eyes and bent her head. I did, too.

I didn't really pray. And I can't tell you Jesus appeared to me during those brief moments of holding a colleague's hands in a conference room. The unfamiliarity of the act, my self-consciousness, my sense of betrayal—those discomforts crowded out any chance at spiritual revelation. But for those moments, I can tell you the screaming inside my head stopped.

Tears burned the backs of my eyelids. I opened them to catch Candace, standing across the room, staring straight at me. Her gaze shifted to watch Gee exit the room, and then returned to me.

It's crazy, it's impossible, but I felt then that somehow she had seen everything, understood everything. I don't know. Maybe not so crazy. Candace Green was the closest thing I'd ever experienced to an omniscient presence.

"Amen," said Missy, opening her eyes. She squeezed my hands and let go.

I repeated the word carefully, like a foreign greeting.

"Amen."

* * *

The last time I prayed with people was at my mother's deathbed.

After she died, the five of us siblings stayed awhile by her side. We touched her hands, smoothed her hair away from her forehead, stroked the hills and valleys of her wasted cheeks.

Viv cradled her head. "Back of her neck's still warm," she murmured. And we wondered for how much longer.

At some point Michael said, "Shouldn't we say a prayer or something?"

We looked at each other and shrugged. Aside from saying grace at mealtime and mumbling the liturgy at Sunday Mass, Catholics aren't much for public prayer. Our repertoire pretty much comes down to our two go-to devotions: the Our Father and the Hail Mary.

"Our Father," Tom began.

"Wait," said Michael. He held out his hands.

Viv recoiled. "What're we—Protestants?"

Michael thrust one hand firmly at her, the other at Paul.

"Oh, all right," said Viv. "Just this once."

So my siblings and I joined hands, forming a ring around our mother. We said the Our Father and the Hail Mary in succession. Seeing as our hands were otherwise occupied, we hunched our shoulders to our cheeks to sop up our tears.

My sister and I don't touch much. I'm not sure why. We're not a touchy-feely family overall. But my brothers dispense with the bear hugs from time to time, while my sister and I don't so much as bump fists. I liked to think maybe it's because she and I were so close that we didn't need to express our affection that way. It would be like hugging yourself.

That day, though, I leaned my head on her shoulder, and she laid her cheek against my head. We stood that way for the longest time, still holding hands, still weeping for the mother we both had lost, the mother who would not return.

Afterward, Tom took charge. "Right," he said. "I'll call Stew Kozlowski."

"And Dad," I said.

Tom nodded. "Paul, go find him."

"I'm here," we heard from the doorway.

We turned. Dad stood there, still wearing his client-meeting blazer, his eyes on the body of his wife.

He looked a hundred years old. Not sad so much as tired—so very, very tired. When he finally started toward her he moved like Claymation, each bend and twitch and step a stop-motion frame. After what seemed like an hour, Tom took Dad's elbow and eased him into the leather chair.

My father then laid his hand on my mother's, never moving his eyes from her face. He traced the index finger of his other hand down her cheek.

"Edith," he whispered. "My Edith."

"Oh, Daddy," I said. We began to cry again.

But my father did not shed a tear. As if he watched his wife sleep and came only to bid her a tender good night.

Tom must have left the room to make the call, for within the hour Stew Kozlowski and his son Sean arrived. Dad rallied, as he always did when greeting old friends, standing up to accept Stew's embrace. I heard the twins sniffling out in the hallway as they bro-hugged Sean, their old school buddy. Stew nodded formally at my sister and me.

"I am so sorry for your loss," he said.

Stew Kozlowski had the kind of spotted pink skin you see on newborn farm animals, and his fluffy white-yellow hair furthered the effect. The irises of his eyes had almost no color, which normally would freak me out but on him seemed designed to minimize offense. His whole aspect conveyed calm and a sense that things would be handled. Usually he wore a suit. He instructed his staff—made up of his wife, two sons, daughter, and niece—to dress conservatively at all times. On that late spring day he wore a short-sleeved button-down shirt tucked neatly into slacks, as did his son.

When they had made their condolences, Stew asked us politely to give him and his son a little room. Reluctant to leave altogether, Viv and I backed against the wall. They worked swiftly and silently, communicating through glances and nods. Sean unfolded what could only be called a body bag, black and made of some shiny material rippled with fibers. Stew folded Mom's blankets back and spread on her a sheet he'd brought, tucking it neatly around her body as Sean unfurled the body bag along her side. Ever so carefully they slid her body in.

As if reading our thoughts, Stew said, "This is only to get her down the stairs. We have a stretcher waiting there."

They lifted her body then, each holding straps at the head and foot, and carried her out of the room, out of the house, onto the stretcher, into the waiting hearse. Stew returned to the door, shook Dad's hand, nodded at the rest of us. Then we watched the hearse drive away.

The next few days blew by in a maelstrom of phone calls, flower deliveries, and neighbors bearing casseroles and baked goods. Tom found Mom's address book and methodically called everyone in it. Paul and Michael took to Facebook and Twitter, generating another avalanche of condolences. Viv dealt with the florist and Carmelo's, the restaurant where we would hold the post-funeral luncheon. The repast, Stew Kozlowski called it.

I visited my mom.

Upon Dad's preference, it would be an old-fashioned, open-casket funeral, complete with a wake. None of us much liked the idea of embalming and displaying Mom's desiccated body, but neither did we have the heart to fight his wishes. Stew informed Viv and me that we could assist in the preparation of her body, if we so wished. "Some people find it comforting," he said, his eyes lowered in respect.

Viv shuddered. And so I went alone.

In Mom's room I collected some of her favorite items. A silk scarf with ponies galloping along the hem. Opal earrings Dad bought for her in Atlantic City. Her wedding band, which the hospice nurses removed for safekeeping when her fingers narrowed to the bone. In the bathroom I rifled through her makeup drawer for Revlon Dusty Pink nail polish and Desert Rose lipstick.

Maryann Kozlowski buzzed me in. She was a stout, busty lady with the kind of hair they call frosted, each strand dyed a different shade of blond. Unlike her husband, Stew, she forswore formality for squishy hugs. I liked her.

She led me to a viewing room. I worried about Mom lying all alone in some sterile embalming space, but no—that gruesome work had already been completed. Her body lay in a blonde-wood casket at the head of a square room with spongy carpeting, the room where we'd hold the wake. Funeral wreaths propped up on wire easels already lined the walls. The scent of roses and lilies mugged my nostrils. I followed Maryann toward the casket. Its lid stood open. And inside lay my mother.

Or, at least, a corpse in the shape of my mother. At that moment I understood the power of the open casket, a ritual I abhorred as crude and unnecessary, and it came as a surprise: Seeing the body affirms the death. Simple as that. Seeing her that way, something shut off inside my brain, the wishful-thinking switch, maybe. She was dead. I saw the body. I still didn't see the point of spending thousands of dollars gussying it up, but then again this version was certainly more presentable.

She looked better than she had in months. I read that embalming fluids contain color to give the appearance of life, but that wasn't the only thing. "We call it the restorative arts," said Maryann, gesturing at my mother's face. "It's my specialty."

"You're a genius," I said, and I meant it. The makeup job was phenomenal. Maryann explained that she had used a gadget popular with professional makeup artists to spray-paint my mother's skin with a coating of bronze pancake. Mom's cheeks looked plumper and were tinted a healthy pink. Painted eyebrows arched over matte-beige eyelids.

"You brought some things?" Maryann prodded.

I opened my bag and slowly accessorized my mother's corpse. It felt like dressing a fallen-down mannequin. The lipstick didn't go on quite right. Her upper lip pushed away like Play-Doh and remained there, caught in an eternal sneer.

"Here, let me," said Maryann, taking the tube and fixing Mom's mouth. "They don't call it an art for nothing. There. She looks beautiful."

We both leaned in and took one last look. Yes, she looked beautiful. She just didn't look like Mom.

* * *

As swiftly as it crossed my mind that Jerry was having an affair, I began to question my conclusion. What had I seen, really? A smile. I had seen my husband smile. A fractional upturn of the lips, a crinkling of the eyes. For, what? A second. Two, max. That's all. That's all I saw.

After the committee meeting, I claimed nausea and begged

excusal. Surrounded by Alice and Hugh and her other minions, Candace only nodded. But I could feel her X-ray gaze on my back as I rushed out. I made straight for the ladies' and threw up.

The drive home took forever and a day. Paradise Estates was only two miles from Greenleaf, but the church attracted such traffic even on a weekday that it clogged the only access road. Woozy and disoriented, I concentrated on not bending a fender. The car crawled while my brain careened between suspicion and explanation, doubt and faith.

London. What happened between Jerry and Gee in London? Was that where it began? I remembered reading somewhere that a gross percentage of adulterous affairs occurred on business trips. But on *church* business? Weren't holy men immune to that sort of thing? Immediately I thought: Hell, no. Ted Haggard. Jim Bakker. Jimmy Swaggart. Seemed like every time you turned around, some pious bastard with spray-on hair was weeping his regrets on worship cable.

And there, just off his shoulder, would stand the wife. The pastor's wife. Wronged, betrayed, cuckolded. And yet presenting an expression of forgiveness. If not forgiveness, then endurance. This too shall pass, her tragic smile said. This too shall pass.

Well, I couldn't be that woman. This too shall *not* pass, because I would not let it. For once in my life I had to act.

Jerry. I needed to talk to Jerry, of course. But the very thought convulsed my insides so violently that I belched out a dry heave. How would I even begin? How does a wife ask her husband if he's seeing someone else? Would he laugh at my idiocy? Scowl at my lack of trust? Lie and deny? Or—worst of all—confirm?

Upon this most terrible discovery, other women might blame

their husbands. Of course, right? He cheated; he lied. But I wasn't thinking that way. I just wanted to understand. If it turned out Jerry loved someone else, then my whole world made no sense at all.

And yet. And yet. Giovanna Disantana was something I was not: a believer.

My memory reel spun back to a month ago, when I glimpsed the two of them sitting close together in one of the Sunday school classrooms, bending their heads over a Bible. It spun again to a recent Sunday service as Gee performed on stage, her body practically shaking with devotion as she expressed her love for Jesus in song. I'd glanced at Jerry then, and saw his eyes closed in prayer, his face infused with shared emotion.

Was that what he wanted? Why *wouldn't* he want that? Someone to pray with and talk Scripture with. A fellow traveler on the path toward heaven.

The winter sun glared. Winter. Ha. In Georgia, it was just summer with an occasional call for a cardigan. So warm you could drive with your windows rolled down, blasting your radio, as the cars around me did. A fragment of song drifted past. I couldn't pull up the band or the title. But I caught a lyric: *You don't have to go home but you can't stay here.*

Home. Our house in Paradise—it was never my home. The word *home* evoked two things for me: my parents' house in Hoogaboom, and Jerry. The former would soon be sold, a loss my heart still denied. I never thought I'd lose Jerry, too.

Homeless. I was homeless. I couldn't even live out of the car, for Pete's sake; Greenleaf owned it, as it owned the house. As it owned my husband.

Idling at an intersection, I caught sight of something in the distance. A spire. A church spire, one I hadn't noticed before. In these parts no architecture seemed to date back further than thirty years, and without the Gothic clues I had trouble distinguishing a Catholic church from all the others. But, craning and twisting, I made out a municipal street sign pointing in its direction.

OUR LADY OF REFUGE, it read. Catholic, all right. I turned the wheel.

The church was open but empty. Unlike Greenleaf's, which bustled throughout the week, these pews probably creaked with bottoms only during services. I had counted on that. The dark and the cool and the trace of smoky incense—I had counted on that, as well.

I looked for her. And there she was, to the right of the altar, so close to her son. Our Lady of Refuge. The Virgin Mary. The *real* one.

My fingers reached for the brass bowl affixed to the wall at the side of the door, then dabbed the holy water on my forehead. My feet padded up the side aisle, and my knees found the velvet-covered pad in front of the statue of Mary. Four rows of ruby glass cups lined her feet, each encircling a tiny electric bulb, some flickering, others dark. Candles, or what stood for them in the age of fire safety. My thumb flipped the black button before one of the cups and lit up a votive. My hands folded together.

All this I performed without thought. My body moved as if programmed, merely following its prescribed path, a path of ritual shared by millions over the millennia. There is a relief in that. I had forgotten how deep.

The statue was formed of terra-cotta, grooved and rough, unpainted. It fit the style of this particular church, a modern structure with pale wood pews and abstract designs in its stained-glass windows. This Mary stood barefoot and plainly robed, one hand on her heart, the other cupped forward. Her eyes, unpainted like the rest of her, had no irises or pupils and so stared unseeing straight ahead.

In style she matched the Jesus crucified at the center of the altar. His terra-cotta body slumped from a wooden cross, his head lolling onto his chest, each rib delineated. Jesus on the cross. That's one image you never saw at Greenleaf. Evangelicals preferred not to think of the cross as an instrument of murder.

I turned back to Mary. His sacrifice was great, but hers? In her clay eyes I read unparalleled loss. Her only child, killed. That was not the order of things. My grief could not match hers. My pain could not match her son's.

Jesus suffered for us. Isn't that what the Bible says? He suffered for our sins. I could see that believing someone suffered more than you, *for* you, could in a weird way alleviate your own suffering. Misery loves company, I suppose, especially if the other party is worse off. Only it didn't work. Not for me. In my lifetime I'd never be nailed to a cross. But I hurt. And it didn't make me feel any better that a long time ago, someone else hurt more.

Jesus was good. I heard that all the time at Greenleaf. And I think he *was* good. Great, even. Following his teachings, emulating his ways—I got that. I saw the value in that. But in my pain and grief and confusion, I did not find solace in Jesus. Or, more important, in the celestial being he was said to represent.

Here's what it came down to. I did not believe I could sit there in that house of worship and pray away my problems. I did not believe an all-powerful source could right wrongs, correct evil, and make things better for me. I did not believe a universal father watched over me or controlled my destiny.

Here's what it came down to. I did not believe in God.

I had tiptoed around this realization for years. And yet I clung to religion and its bosom of tradition and belonging. I still longed for those things. Sitting there in that Catholic church before Christ on the cross, I yearned to hear a priest mumble the Latin prayer over the Eucharist, words heard around the world and over the centuries. I ached to share the faith of the believers. Of my mother. Of my husband.

I wanted to. But I did not.

This, then, was my truth. The first step, at long last, toward finding me.

* * *

I would have to quit Greenleaf.

Whatever would fall out between me and Jerry, I had no business representing an evangelical Christian church when I myself did not believe in God. You might think publicists have no moral code on this matter. You might think we shill for any paying client, be they Mother Teresa or Saddam Hussein. But in order to be effective, you want to take work pushing products you endorse or at least don't oppose.

I would quit Greenleaf. I would find Jerry and I would learn the truth. Then I would figure out what came next.

I found Candace in the sanctuary, where a lighting check for the Pageant was in full swing. She stood in her usual spot, murmuring into her headset, nodding at something Alice showed her on her iPad.

"Candace," I said. "I'd like to talk to you. In private."

Candace held up a hand. I still marveled at how a flick of those Lilliputian appendages could command grown-ups like dogs. Come, stay, wait. Like everyone else, I obeyed.

The stage manager, a tree trunk of a guy named Hank, stepped to center stage and motioned the control room. A voice boomed from the speakers.

"North Star, ready to test."

As we watched, the stage sank into black. A single twinkle emerged from far above, then another, then another. Suddenly light exploded from the rafters. I gasped. A giant spiked globe descended, spitting shards of light. It reminded me of something, and then I remembered: the Met. Jerry had taken me to a performance of *Madama Butterfly* at the Metropolitan Opera in New York City two years before, and I recalled staring with amazement at the magnificent chandelier that hovered above us. This North Star was its exact replica.

There was silence. Then applause.

The lights came up and Hank stepped out of the wings to throw a thumbs-up to Candace. She nodded, looking pleased.

"Moving on," boomed the voice. "Testing lighting and markers for Pastor Aaron."

The lights went down again and a single spotlight beamed on the stage, just under the North Star. Into it stepped Aaron Green.

The senior pastor had shed his suit jacket and rolled up his sleeves. It impressed me that he carved out time in his packed schedule for a mere rehearsal, but then again, what Candace requested, Candace received. Aaron lifted and held his arms straight out to either side in what I had come to recognize as his signature gesture. He struck this pose at the end of every sermon. It was both beseeching and welcoming. Come, it said. Behold the glory of God.

That was when I heard the pop. Then, another.

Loud and staccato, like the Fourth of July firecrackers Dad used to sneak from the Pennsylvania border down to the Jersey shore, where they were illegal. *Pop,* then *pop*. A festive sound, a thrilling sound. Not a scary one.

Then Aaron fell.

He fell straight back, with his arms still outstretched on either side of him, his body rigid, as if a mattress would cushion his fall. What I'm saying is it looked like a gag.

Until the shouting began.

"Lights! Lights!"

Tosh Takai sprinted out of the wings and toward Aaron. But somehow Candace got to him first. In a fluid move I would later recall with wonder, she hurdled chairs and high-jumped onto the stage, so by the time center stage flooded with light, she was diving to Aaron's side.

Beside me, Alice slid whimpering to the floor, cowering behind her iPad. I left her there and raced up after Candace, scaling the stage steps and skidding toward her.

Tosh spoke urgently into a cell phone, instructing emergency crews to our location.

Aaron lay with both arms still extended. Like Jesus on the cross tipped backward. His eyes were closed. With his left hand he gripped Candace's hands. Or maybe she gripped his.

And then I saw the blood. The crisp white fabric of Aaron's shirt on the left side of his chest soaked through with a startling crimson.

"We gotta stop the bleeding," said someone. Maybe Hank.

I yanked off my fleece vest and pressed it to Aaron's chest. I hoped to hell it was clean.

Candace looked at me then with wild eyes. Wild, wet eyes.

That was the first and only time I saw Candace Green cry.

CHAPTER TWENTY

Candace

"Here's a nice one," said Candace. "*Globe and Mail*. Canada." She touched her iPad screen. Initially she refused to give up her clipping service, a small company outside Boston she'd employed for a decade to collect newspaper articles from around the world mentioning Aaron and Greenleaf. But Aaron convinced her the church's green initiative took precedence. "One company might lose our business," he said, "but without trees, we'll all lose our lives."

So now she read the news on this tablet-sized computer, encased prettily in a lime-green leather sheath Aaron had ordered specially for her. And Candace had to admit she'd come to adore the little thing. It tucked so neatly right into her Fendi, and propped up handily on their café table at home while she sipped her morning tea. Not to mention its technological wizardry. The Google app she had set up delivered every mention of Greenleaf instantly to her in-box. Far cry from the weekly LexisNexis printout the clipping service in Boston used to FedEx. A tree a week, saved. You're welcome.

She scrolled down the page using her middle finger, skimming past the familiar headline and lede. " 'Megachurch pastor . . . Magnolia, an affluent suburb,' blah, blah—oh, here we go. 'Green, 54, was internationally lauded for his efforts to improve interfaith relations. His tight friendship with a rabbi and imam landed the three in countless media profiles and on national TV talk shows. Despite his high profile, Green's public message remained focused. "The Buddhists say there are many paths to the top of the mountain," he once told Christiane Amanpour of ABC. "Let's say world peace awaits us at the peak, along with God. My path there is to heal the rift between the religions."' Strong quote." Candace nodded in approval. "Smart but humble. I'm glad they used that one."

The VIP rooms at Grace Memorial Hospital looked more like hotel suites, with laminate floors that resembled real oak, soft lighting, and moss-green upholstery. Anthony snored with abandon, sprawled on the microsuede couch. His size-fourteen feet splayed across Sophie's lap, no doubt limiting her own attempts to snooze sitting up.

Candace stood to stretch her legs. She walked to the picture window, its blinds open to the night sky. So quiet, so still out there. So peaceful. The elementary school down the street . . . she recognized its brick facade. Greenleaf had once loaned the school some set props for a play. Martin Luther King Jr., it was called, though of course every other school in Georgia was named for its hero. Deservedly so. Good man, that Martin Luther King Jr. Also a pastor. Also shot.

A nurse bustled in. Ana, this one was called, a Filipina in pink scrubs and pigtails. Could she possibly be of age? And how old did a nurse have to be, anyway?

"Just checking his vitals," said Ana in a low voice, so as not to wake Anthony and Sophie. *Vai-talls,* she said, her tongue clicking on the *t.* She had an unfamiliar accent, one that enunciated the consonants rather than swallowing them, as was customary around here. Candace didn't know many Filipinos. Some had migrated to Georgia of late, but they tended to stick to their Catholicism.

Ana checked the various machines, jotting on a clipboard as she went. She seemed unalarmed. That was good. Unalarmed was good.

"Now," said Ana, returning the clipboard to its slot at the foot of the bed and crossing the room to Candace. Her white Crocs squeaked on the laminate. Hideous shoes. But Candace supposed there was little need for style among medical staff. "I go off my shift soon. Do you have any questions for me? Concerns? Can I get you some more tea?"

Candace tipped her head in gratitude at the nurse's kindness. "Thank you," she said. "We're fine for now."

Together they turned to look at the inert form of Pastor Aaron Green. A tube fed him oxygen through his nostrils. Various wires connected to tabs stuck to his chest, the better to monitor his heart. A light blue hospital gown covered one shoulder. A mound of gauze covered the other.

Candace never asked people to pray with her. When she held out her hands to a church member and said, "Pray with me," it came out—and was taken—more like an order. Unlike some Christians, she would never march up to a stranger, least of all a presumed Catholic, and ask her to share a prayer. That kind of request would introduce the possibility of rejection, and Candace did not place herself willingly in positions of vulnerability.

But God must have intervened. For when she turned back to

Ana, the nurse reached for Candace's hands. Without a word the two women dipped their heads.

"Have faith," the nurse said.

* * *

"I know you don't think so right now," said the doctor, "but your husband is a very lucky man."

A single bullet had ripped through Aaron's chest, shaving the top of his heart. "About like this," said the doctor after the surgery, holding his two palms together to show just how close the bullet had come to puncturing Aaron's artery and the organ itself. Another piece of great luck, Candace would note later, upon calmer reflection: Ruthie told Candace she had heard two shots. The other must have gone wide. The police would later find a hole in a wooden stage prop, and the bullet, spent, nearby.

"The entry and exit wounds were clean," the doctor continued. "Of course any penetrating chest trauma will result in tissue damage. But the gravest initial danger is blood loss. Up to forty percent— just over two liters—usually results in death. Your husband lost about half that. I'd say stanching the wound so quickly probably saved his life."

It was her, Candace thought, dimly recalling Ruthie ripping off some article of clothing and pressing it to Aaron's chest.

Ramani, his name tag read. S. Ramani, M.D. He looked so young, but then she thought that of everyone these days. Plus, medical scrubs seemed to act as some sort of magical age defier. Someone could make a fortune marketing them that way to the civilian population. If only they weren't so ugly. Whatever happened to those starchy white lab coats that bespoke authority? Creases crisscrossed

Dr. Ramani's pale green scrubs, like he'd taken them out of the dryer long after they'd cooled, not immediately, as he ought. Or maybe he'd just slept in them. They looked enough like pajamas. And residents pulled endless shifts, she knew.

A resident. Ramani was a resident. A resident, operating on Pastor Aaron Green. Chief surgical resident, but still. Confident and clearly competent, but still. A calamity she would not have faced had not the chief of surgery, Ross Monroe, whose wife, Linda, she knew from the children's museum board, been away on vacation.

"Call him!" Candace had screamed when she learned of this scheduling travesty.

"He's in Hawaii," the hospital president apologized, his face drained of color. Charles Brubaker, his card said. She didn't know him. An overcooked spaghetti noodle of a man. "We have our best surgeons on it. Mr. Green is in very good hands."

"Pastor," said Candace, breathing hard.

"Sorry?"

"Pastor," she repeated, louder, like he was deaf or foreign. "That's Pastor Green to you."

She felt a hand on her arm and, looking, saw it was Ruthie's.

"Please," said the noodle man. "Use my office. It's quieter than the waiting bay."

Ruthie led her there. "Sit," she ordered Candace, then rooted around in a Fendi bag Candace recognized as her own.

"Here," said Ruthie. She peeled open a blister pack of Imitrex, holding Candace's palm steady as she helped her guide it into her mouth. Candace took the plastic cup of water from Ruthie and drained it.

Ruthie dug around some more in Candace's bag. She pulled out Candace's phone and began scrolling and tapping. "Anthony," she

said into the phone. "It's Ruthie Matters, from Greenleaf. I know—
I'm on your mother's phone. Listen. You need to get to Grace Memorial. No. It's your father. He's been shot. Alive, he's alive. In surgery
now. How soon? Okay, good. We're in the president's office."

Funny. Over the past months, she'd grown quite fond of Ruthie.
But in her capacity as mentor, boss, and teacher, Candace had remained fixed on her initial assessment of the younger woman as un-
focused and in need of direction. Funny to hear Ruthie operate so
calmly and efficiently now.

What was it again about the measure of a man? The search engine in her brain hunted down the quote. "The ultimate measure of
a man is not where he stands in moments of comfort and convenience,
but where he stands at times of challenge and controversy." Martin
Luther King Jr. To her surprise, Ruthie was measuring up.

Ruthie was saying something. " 'On my way,' " she read from
Candace's phone. "Timothy. I texted him before. He's just dropped
the kids at the Children's Center."

The mention of the children punctured Candace's torpor. "The
Children's Center," she repeated, and her voice sounded to her own
ears like it belonged to another, the way it did when she heard herself on TV or radio. "The Children's Center closes at six."

Ruthie tapped Candace's phone against her jaw as she worked
out this new problem. "I'll pick them up at closing time and take
them to their house," she said. "You'll want Timothy here with you."

"I don't want them to know," said Candace. "They're dealing
with enough already."

Ruthie nodded. She began to dial again. "Ginger," she said into
the phone.

Now, this should be interesting. Candace knew her estranged
daughter-in-law had not returned any of Ruthie's messages in a month,

ever since she deserted Magnolia for God knows what new or old life-style. Candace herself had not spoken with Ginger, instead communicating by text and e-mail, and then only in regard to the children.

"It's Ruthie Matters," she said, businesslike but urgent. Her face betrayed no emotion. "Please call as soon as you get this. Pastor Aaron is in the hospital. Candace and Timothy are with him. Your children need you."

She sounds like me, Candace realized. I have taught her well.

"There," said Ruthie. She tucked the phone back into Candace's purse and got up. "Now let me go shake someone down for an update."

As Ruthie passed, Candace reached out and took her hand. Aside from the occasional shared prayer, she rarely touched her staff, disliking their resulting presumption of familiarity. Ruthie's hand felt dry and strong.

"Thank you," whispered Candace.

Ruthie looked a little surprised. Candace tried to remember if she had ever said those two words to her before. She tried to remember if she'd meant it.

A profusion of curls ringed the younger woman's face, and with the office light behind her they glowed like a fluorescent halo. Candace remembered something. "What did you want to tell me? Back in the sanctuary. Before. You said you wanted to discuss something."

Ruthie shook her head. The halo bobbled. "Not now," she said. "Let's focus on what matters most. And that's Pastor Aaron."

* * *

She recognized the man and the woman.

Not for any particularly distinguishing characteristics: both in their thirties, white, properly if blandly dressed. She remembered scanning them as they entered the sanctuary for Sunday service two weeks ago, noting their unfamiliarity and their lack of Bibles. Prospects, she'd determined, memorizing their faces. She never failed to pinpoint prospects, a trick that in turn never failed to amaze her husband. It proved immensely useful in recruiting new church members. Imagine a newcomer's delight when the senior pastor's wife knew them before they knew her. Reeled them right in.

Those few seconds of memory skittered away in the video bank of her brain, and up came another clip: the same man browsing in the bookstore a week later; the woman reading the electronic bulletin board in the lobby.

They sat across from Candace at a table in the hospital cafeteria. It was late, and night-shift staff lined up at the cashiers with their coffee and PowerBars. Her own hands wrapped around a paper cup of Earl Grey tea. She wished for the cashmere cardigan she'd left in Aaron's room upstairs.

"I'm Michael Ratzinger, and this is Leslie Fadiman," the man sitting before her said. He unfolded a black leather ID case and slid it across the table toward her. The woman did the same. FBI, it said.

Where were their navy nylon jackets with the yellow stenciling? On TV the FBI agents always wore those jackets. These two—not a couple, like she'd presumed—these two wore civilian clothes, blending into the surroundings, just as they had when they infiltrated her church.

"I've seen you," Candace said softly. "At Greenleaf."

They glanced at each other and looked back at her. They had not expected that. They must have thought it easy enough to blend into a megachurch community of thousands.

"Yes," said Ratzinger. He seemed to be the lead partner. He

appeared slightly older than the woman, who despite her reticence seemed to miss nothing. "Our investigation began a few weeks ago."

"Investigation," repeated Candace. She felt off her game, uncharacteristically cotton headed. But it had been a long night. A long day into night.

Ratzinger began. "Are you familiar with Five Loaves?"

"Mark 6," Candace said blankly, automatically. "*And when he had taken the five loaves and the two fishes, he looked up to heaven, and blessed, and brake the loaves, and gave them to his disciples to set before them; and the two fishes he divided among them all. And they did all eat, and were filled.*"

Candace caught Leslie Fadiman bulging her eyes at her, like she was some freak-show exhibit, some Bible savant. She glared back, and the agent lowered her gaze.

Ratzinger nodded. "That would be the reference," he said. "Five Loaves, Incorporated. It's an investment firm—or purported to be. Clientele made up of churches. Invested in gold mines in Nigeria, telecom companies in China. Tech in Russia. Twenty percent returns, according to the Web site. Of course the whole thing was a sham."

Candace felt cold. Yet she could not lift the cup of hot tea to her lips.

"A very successful sham," continued Ratzinger. "Collected almost twelve million dollars in assets over the past five years. All from churches along the Eastern seaboard. Including Greenleaf."

Candace was already shaking her head. "No," she said. "All our funds are in cash. They always have been. For maximum liquidity to supply capital during our growth. In fact we've only just hired a financial manager in order to set up an investment plan."

Ratzinger produced a document and spun it around on the

table. He pointed to a line. "For one day a few weeks ago, Greenleaf was a leading shareholder. We're not clear on why yet, but the money came in and went right back out."

There it was. Two million dollars, from Greenleaf.

Finally the woman agent spoke. "We got word a local newspaper planned to publish a piece on financial improprieties at Greenleaf," said Fadiman. "That was when we moved the investigation. Probably around the time you saw us on your premises."

"From where?"

"Excuse me?"

"You said you moved the investigation," said Candace. "From where?"

"Five Loaves," said Ratzinger, "was based in Maryland. Or should we say a PO box in Baltimore."

Baltimore. Candace knew before Ratzinger spoke the name.

"We traced the PO box to John Swain," he said. "Head elder of Greenleaf Church."

She knew, too, before Fadiman said it.

"Magnolia police have John Swain in custody," said the agent. "He's going to be charged with the attempted murder of your husband. And he'll face federal charges for fraud."

A pain knifed through her jaw. Candace loosened the grit of her teeth.

"How?" Breathe, she ordered herself. Breathe. She tried again. "How did you catch him?"

"We have your security chief to thank," said Ratzinger. "It appears he spotted movement in the balcony."

In the fog that still hung over the incident, Candace recalled Tosh sprinting off into the wings, where a utility staircase led to the balcony.

"The suspect got away, but your man got us security video that identified Swain," said Ratzinger.

"Officers apprehended him on I-85 near Greenville," said Fadiman.

"With a Remington 7400 in the trunk," said Ratzinger. "A long-range hunting rifle."

"Forensics matched the bullet," said Fadiman.

Candace heard all this. She heard it. She swallowed to ensure she spoke in an even tone, one that would not betray her consuming fury. "Why," she asked, "if you knew all this before—if you knew it was him—why did you let it happen?"

At this, Ratzinger lowered his eyes. He flattened his palms on the table. "My partner and I, we specialize in financial forensics. Fraud. We had no reason to believe the suspect would attempt violence."

"What we're trying to determine, Mrs. Green," said Fadiman, "is motive. By all accounts, John Swain and your husband were cordial, even friendly. As far as we could tell, the pastor had no knowledge of Swain's fraud. So, what happened?"

Ratzinger leaned forward. "Was there an incident that could have provoked John Swain to shoot your husband?"

Oh, God in heaven. Candace's anger evaporated as she realized: It was all her fault.

* * *

What is my purpose?

   My purpose is to love and serve Jesus Christ.

   My purpose is to love and serve my family, my church, my community.

But above all, the reason I, Candace Green, was placed here on God's earth was to love and serve my husband.

You are my purpose, Aaron. You. My purpose is to give you comfort and sustenance. To help you spread the Good Word. To raise your descendants. To protect you from evil.

And I have failed.

I failed to keep our family together. I failed to forgive those who trespassed against us. I failed to keep you safe from harm.

I failed you.

She cried now. She cried with violence, howling, her face red and twisted and ugly, she was sure, but she didn't care. Alone, finally alone, in the hospital room with her husband, Candace disgorged her grief and her guilt. She cried aloud, her face buried at his side, with no one but Jesus as witness.

No, she heard.

Candace raised her ruined face from Aaron's bed. She grabbed his hand with both of hers.

"Darling," she said. "My love. What? What did you say?"

He did not wake.

Yet she heard the voice again.

You did not fail me. You saved me.

CHAPTER TWENTY-ONE

Ginger

The call came during group. The women were gathered in the basement rec room of a church a mile from her mother's, a boxy structure Ginger didn't recall from growing up. New Hope Church. OPEN TO ALL, it said on the sign outside, and somehow the accompanying rainbow flag had given her the boost of courage she needed to go in. Maybe the gays would not judge.

The pastor was a woman, Melora Jimenez, maybe forty. In her past life Ginger had known girls who went with girls, but not full-on lesbians with the buzz cut and side-to-side gorilla walk. Ginger almost wilted at the sight of the D-Y-K-E tattooed on the knuckles of Melora's extended hand. Timidly she explained her mission. To her surprise, Melora clapped with glee and immediately offered free use of the basement. Free was free. She took it.

This first event was a meet-and-greet. Ginger sent out an e-blast the week prior to all the women in the area whose names she had collected from the Magdalena Ministries Web site. A surprising number responded, and she expected maybe a dozen to show up.

From there she would set up monthly gatherings, she figured, for women to come and relax and talk. They'd start and finish with prayer, Ginger decided after consulting Melora, but they wouldn't talk Scripture until they all felt comfortable.

Melora turned out to be a tremendous asset. The pastor took charge of logistics unasked, setting out tables and chairs, donating soda and leftover bake-sale cookies. "I prayed for this," she confided one day, after Ginger thanked her for the hundredth time. "That New Hope would find a community to serve, a community in need. A few days later—boom—you walk in the door. How about that? You know?" Melora's jaw hinged open like Jordan's nutcracker doll and unleashed what Ginger thought was called a hearty laugh. Full of heart. Like she meant it. "Crazy, or what? Prayer. It works."

Ginger scheduled the meeting for Monday, a day many of the women took off to recover from the toll of the weekend. She hovered by the church door, pulling at her pink MM T-shirt and peering up and down the street.

"Stop fidgeting," said Kaycee, who came to help. "They'll come."

"*You* stop fidgeting," said Ginger. "Oh, look!"

The first car arrived, a rut-tutting little VW bug. Then another car, then another. Ginger stepped back inside the vestibule for a moment to collect herself, shake off her nerves. She said a quick prayer.

"Lord, give me strength to help my fellow traveler," she prayed. This had become her mantra, a daily, sometimes hourly mumbling. The key word was *help*. If she could not be strong for herself, maybe she could for another girl.

Woman, she corrected herself. Woman. In their line of work, no female worker was ever referred to as anything but "girl," no matter her age. Ginger had never thought much of it until recently, when, upon a strip-club visit, the bouncer got on his walkie-talkie and referred to her as "a girl." Huh, she'd thought then. Girl. Here she was, a mom, almost thirty. It didn't sit right. You never called a grown man a boy. But then, most grown men didn't have to remove their clothing for money.

Melora dug up sticky name tags from the church supply closet. As the women came in, Ginger penned their names in with a red Sharpie. Jenny. Cindy. Kim. Aubrey. Meimei. Sienna. When a charcoal-rooted blonde first offered "Bambam," Ginger hesitated.

"It's okay if you don't want to say your real name," she said to the woman. "But let's leave our stage names on stage."

Wow, Ginger thought. That there sounded very nearly like Candace.

The woman looked put out. She stretched her toothpaste-green gum between her top and bottom teeth. "Sarah," she said finally.

The women were a colorful mix, but then dancers usually were. A manager once explained to her that strip clubs had to account for the range of men's tastes. Kim, a muscular blonde with last night's mascara still raccooning her eyes. Jenny, whose spray-on tan peeked out of baggy gray sweats tucked into stained pink Uggs. Meimei wore a tiny tank top stretched over her tiny torso, revealing a tattoo of some sort of reptile, possibly a dragon, crawling across her belly.

The one commonality: bust size. Apparently, the tastes of men who frequent strip clubs never ranged to small breasts. Ginger could tell at a glance whose were real. The trick was the bra. Real boobs answered to gravity and required girdling; fake ones saluted the sky all on their own. She counted three women, including herself, with straps lumping at the middle of their backs.

Her phone vibrated while she chatted with Sienna, a plumpish dancer no older than nineteen whose frequent smile betrayed not a smidgen of self-consciousness about her Bugs Bunny teeth.

Ginger checked her phone, expecting a cancellation or last-minute request for directions.

CANDACE GREEN, read the panel.

How long would it be before that name stopped clenching her gut?

The children, Ginger thought, her insides squeezing again. She hit the Talk button, but only in time for the bleak buzz of the dial tone. She punched through to voice mail. When she heard Ruthie announce herself, Ginger exhaled.

But she sounded different. Her friend sounded professional, like when you call the bank and get those customer-service recordings. Not at all like Ruthie's previous unanswered messages, friendly and inquiring, then worried. Not at all like her friend.

A friend she'd abandoned, Ginger reminded herself. A friend she'd left behind, along with the rest of her life in Magnolia. Maybe Ruthie had moved on. Maybe friendship, like milk, had a shelf life.

Something about a hospital. Something about Aaron and Candace. Something about her children.

"Oh, God," she breathed. She pressed the Replay button. Then, again.

When she was certain she understood, Ginger's head snapped around the room until she located Melora and Kaycee.

"Something's happened," she told them. "It's my family. I have to go." Her eyes explained more than she could, then and there.

"Jesus Lord!" cried Kaycee, always the Nervous Nellie, hands flying to her throat.

Melora, however, simply nodded. "Go," she said, thick hands flapping forward in a shooing motion. "We got this."

As Ginger collected her purse and ran out the door, she heard the pastor bellowing, "All right, ladies! Whaddaya say we join hands for a welcome prayer?"

She got in her car and began to drive.

* * *

By nightfall she reached the iron gates of Paradise Estates, draped with pine garlands accented by enormous red felt bows. Horatio waved at her from the security booth, a tiny Christmas tree at his elbow. The faux-antique streetlamps competed with holiday-bedecked houses to light her way. Management decreed that homeowners use only white exterior lights. In fact its rules on holiday decorations took up a full three pages of the development bylaws, cowing Ginger in previous years into hanging only a Candace-approved wreath. The compound looked like a calendar photo, a far cry from Ceecee's trailer-park neighborhood, which featured lit-up plastic crèches and motor-operated reindeer and those gigantic air-filled Santas. For her money, Ginger preferred the Santas.

It was almost eight, bedtime for Jordan, a little past that for Tali, although who knew what kind of schedule they followed under Timothy. Ginger felt tears pushing up once again at the thought of seeing them. The whole ride she had cried on and off, veering psychotically from tears to laughter at a sudden memory of Jordan squirting milk through his nostrils or Tali farting in the bathtub.

Her babies. She was going to see her babies.

And Timothy. She would see Timothy.

What would she say? She tried but failed to come up with anything at all. She tried but failed to imagine their meeting. She could not see beyond the past.

Ginger parked the car across the street from her house. It appeared dark, but there was a Prius in the driveway.

The front door was unlocked. "Hello?" Ginger called.

Blue lights flickered in the otherwise dark family room. TV. Ginger stepped toward the light, farther inside, until she stood at the room's threshold, blinking to adjust her eyes.

Jordan sat upright on the couch in his Spider-Man pajamas, eyes locked on the TV screen. Beside him sat Ruthie, and on Ruthie's other side, Talitha, fast asleep. The chenille throw, a housewarming gift from Candace, stretched across all their laps.

But no Timothy, she realized, with equal parts relief and regret. If Ruthie was here, he must be at the hospital. With Candace and the rest.

"Mommy?"

Jordan had caught sight of her. He stood like a startled meerkat in those nature shows he liked so much.

Ginger's legs failed her. She fell to her knees.

Jordan stayed frozen.

Ruthie looked at Jordan, then at Ginger, then back at Jordan. When he still didn't move, she leaned forward and gave him a little push.

She may as well have flung him, for Jordan leaped forward and charged into Ginger, torso trembling and arms flinging around her neck, the force of him almost rocking her flat. She could not tell who cried harder. His *Mommy, Mommy* competed with her *baby, baby* until the chorus woke Tali up.

Tali rubbed her eyes and whimpered. Holding Jordan with one arm, Ginger reached the other toward her waking daughter.

But Tali clung instead to Ruthie. She began to wail. "Mamie," she sobbed. "I want Mamie."

Ginger felt punched. A ragged "unngh" escaped her.

Ruthie rubbed Tali's back and looked at Ginger. Her eyes told Ginger how pathetic she must look, how forlorn. The prodigal mother, rejected by her child.

No, Ginger thought. No. This is not how it's going down. I won't let it.

On her knees Ginger dragged over to where they sat, no mean feat with Jordan wrapped around her like a long-limbed koala. She placed her hands on either side of her daughter's scowling face and wrenched it toward her until they were nose-to-nose.

"It's Mommy," whispered Ginger, then kissed her baby's lips, plump and sleep-sweet. "Mommy's here."

Tali struggled to twist free. Ginger held her head firm while her thumbs stroked her child's velvet cheeks. Tali's eyebrows propped in diagonal lines sloping to a point in the middle of her forehead, a cartoon portrait of fear.

Without warning, the eyebrows released. "Mommy," said Tali. "I do pee pee on a potty."

Ginger breathed out a sob. "Oh, yeah?" she said, laughing, crying, hugging her children close. "Oh, yeah?"

If she held them tight enough, maybe she could absorb them whole. Maybe she could.

* * *

Ruthie filled her in. Ginger sat on one end of the couch, cradling a now-sleeping Tali in her arms, like the baby she so recently was. Jordan pressed his nose into his mother's ribs, breathing her: Yes, she's real. Ruthie sat on the other end to give them space.

So as not to tip off the children, still shielded from the awful news, Ruthie spoke in medical jargon that, truth be told, even Ginger had a tough time following. Ruthie spoke in that voice, the same one from the voice mail, the one Ginger had heard her use a few times before on the phone for church publicity business. Official. Conveying information, not intimacy.

"Now that you're here with the children," Ruthie said, "Timothy is staying the night at the hospital. He says he'll drop back in the morning, depending on Aaron's status."

Ginger only nodded. Ruthie's tone did not invite confession, nor did Ginger offer it. Ruthie did not ask, for instance, if Ginger had heard from Timothy since the shooting. The answer was no. It was okay; she hadn't expected to. She was not bitter. Things were clear now. Now, finally, after everything, she understood.

Ministry came first for Timothy, and family second. But even before his wife and children came his parents. It would be all about his father for the foreseeable future, as it should. As it should.

Ginger had a purpose here. She had come for the children. She would never, ever leave them again.

They slept in a dog pile on her bed. Not my bed, she thought. Not for much longer. She lay awake, listening to the breathing of her children, a hand on each. Even in sleep Jordan clung to her like a gangly burr. Tali sprawled horizontally, one chubby arm thrown dramatically across her forehead, a habitual sleeping position Timothy once dubbed "woe-is-me." Ginger smiled, remembering.

Dawn. Maybe. Hard to tell through the blackout curtains Timothy insisted on to help him sleep. Ginger preferred the kind of gauzy window coverings that filtered the light and puffed in the breeze. The kind that didn't make her guess night from day.

She felt sadness, but not regret. She was sad to be leaving this life. She was sad to have missed a month of her children's lives. But she did not regret what she had done. She did not regret escaping this place to find her own path to redemption, to learn her purpose, to learn she was someone. More than a pastor's wife, more than a former stripper, certainly more than a reluctant porn star. Someone, and with something to give.

Ever so carefully she untangled herself from her children's limbs and tiptoed downstairs. The place looked shockingly neat despite her absence. Not Ginger clean, but not Timothy dirty, either. At first she suspected Candace, but upon closer inspection she saw her husband's hand.

Dishes lined the counter, but they were washed, dried, and stacked—just not put away. It would be like Timothy to ignore the cabinets. Inside the fridge, a spoon stuck out of a half-eaten container of YoBaby and a jelly jar was missing its lid. But the shelves were stocked with low-fat milk and strawberries and Babybel cheese, the food her children favored. Likewise, the laundry was divided into three piles, clean though unfolded. She picked up Tali's favorite green tights and sniffed. Not just Tide, but Bounce. Her husband had learned the purpose of a dryer sheet.

No decorations, she thought. By this time of year, the rooms in her house usually swarmed with lighted garlands and knitted stockings and her personal favorite, a Nativity scene she had built entirely out of Legos.

But wait a minute. What was that, on the side table? Timothy had indeed pulled out the Lego crèche. Jordan must have asked, for Ginger didn't believe Timothy would even remember its existence. Somehow he'd found it, though, unearthed it from the storage containers in the back of the garage.

A piece of doodle paper taped to the window caught her eye.

OVER HERE, SANTA, it said across the top in aqua crayon, in Timothy's blocky handwriting. The house lacked a fireplace, which upset Jordan terribly when he learned earlier this year of Santa's usual home-invasion entry point. She hadn't yet figured out a solution. It seemed Timothy had.

Something else was different. But what?

She took a slow turn around the family room and realized: me. I am looking at me. Everywhere. Snapshots of Ginger were taped to walls and doors and table edges, down low, eye level for little people. She didn't even remember these. Timothy must have taken them with his phone, saved them in a digital album she never knew existed. He must have printed them out for the children and taped them up all over, so they could see her face every day. So they would not forget.

Ginger sprawled in the grass, laughing. Ginger in Hawaii, gazing out to sea. Ginger tickling Jordan, Ginger crooning to Tali. Private moments, recorded by her husband.

Her husband had kept photographs of her. It blew her away.

She felt a little faint, and leaned against a chair, her Bible chair. Its pillowy depths beckoned, and she sank into it, accepting its welcome. She pulled her knees up to her chin and hugged them to her chest, looking out the window to their exactingly apportioned backyard, twenty square feet of Kentucky blue clipped to 2.3 inches, as the development bylaws dictated. The Fanta-orange dawn spotlighted hundreds, thousands of dewdrops on the blades. The yellow plastic swing swayed a little.

In her haste she had not stopped to fetch her Bible from Ceecee's house, but Ginger found she didn't need it. The verse, from Proverbs 3, came to her as if whispered in her ear. She closed her eyes and recited aloud:

"Happy is the one who findeth wisdom,
and the one that getteth understanding:
for the merchandise of it is better than of silver,
the gain thereof than fine gold."

"And have you?"

Ginger kept her eyes shut. Timothy. That voice. She'd know it anywhere. Like a wind in the glades, always moving away from her. The voice of the only man she'd ever loved.

When she opened her eyes he knelt before her, his hands on her bare feet. They had sat like this before, she remembered, a night he left on yet another mission. He looked up at her now, not as he had then, with impatience, but with—she didn't know it; she couldn't name it.

Could it be—surrender?

"Have you found wisdom and understanding?" he asked.

He smelled of a long night with scant toothpaste. She longed to pat down the paintbrush hair. The morning light shifted and reflected a sheen in his eyes. A tear? Ginger had seen this glint before, when Timothy railed against the injustice in the world. But never for her. He never cried for her.

"Because maybe then you can share some with me," he said. "Maybe you can tell me how to keep from losing you."

The tear balanced on his lower lash, a diver on a cliff edge, until it tumbled quite suddenly onto her foot. It splattered there, warmer and wetter than she'd expected.

"And thou shalt never wash my feet," she whispered.

Tenderly, so tenderly, Timothy rubbed his tears into her foot with his thumb. *"If I wash thee not,"* he replied, as Jesus had to Peter, *"thou hast no part with me."*

She loosened her arms and unwrapped them from her knees, sliding her legs into what her children called crisscross, applesauce. Taking her husband's hands, she placed them on the slope of her belly.

Yes, she had been shown a new path. She would take this path. But maybe she was not meant to walk it alone.

A surge of something powerful and warm coursed through her, a feeling not unlike a shot of vodka, back in the day. Joy, she decided. This was joy. Joy in learning she, of all people, a sinner, a Mary Magdalene, might deserve love after all.

Happy is the one who finds wisdom and understanding. Her profit is better than gold.

CHAPTER TWENTY-TWO

Ruthie

The problem with modern hospitals is that they try to be something they're not. Used to be a hospital was a place you went when you got sick or injured, and the doctors and nurses there did their best with the equipment at hand to make you better. Not today. Oh, no. Today they're all about the customer service. The patient experience. The gourmet coffee and the tasteful decor and the piped-in Kenny G. The problem is that no one who goes to a hospital wants to hang out there. They want to get the hell home. Why pretend otherwise?

The third-floor lounge area of Grace Memorial, a section reserved for VIPs, emulated an airport business-class lounge: forgiving lighting and smooth sofas, baskets of Danish and bananas on a granite counter, flat-screen TV tuned silently to CNN. As I entered, I caught a glimpse of Aaron's face on the screen, a promo shot I myself had e-mailed the producer earlier.

I'd spent the day fielding calls from news outlets around the world, but CNN got there first, breaking into regular programming to cover what for them was a local story with international significance—and, let's face it, how many of those did they get, based as they were in Atlanta? The anchor Carmen Wong herself arrived in the careening news van, broadcasting live from outside Greenleaf, its entrance blocked off by local police and FBI.

Once Anthony and Sophie arrived at the hospital, I left Candace in their care and dashed back to the church to deal with the media frenzy. I later drove to the hospital one more time to check in on Candace and help settle Aaron in his room after surgery. Then I raced back to pick up Jordan and Tali from the Children's Center and get them home. My only downtime so far today was the sweet hour I flopped with the kids on the couch in front of Nick Jr. After I handed them off to Ginger, I returned to Greenleaf to plow through my voice- and e-mail in-boxes.

It was close to three a.m. when I returned to Grace. If I so much as tripped, I would fall facedown on the floor and stay there.

"Over here," said Jerry.

He slumped on one of the slippery sofas, tapping at the iPad propped on his lap. The careful congeniality of the VIP waiting room somehow did not extend to comfortable seating. He finished tapping, rubbed his eyes, and looked up.

I had not seen him all day. Although I called and texted him immediately after the shooting, I could not reach him and had not heard back. At some point I remembered he was spending the afternoon at the county penitentiary, which required cell phones be left at the gates. Jerry cherished the prison ministry, and with Aaron committed to the Christmas pageant lighting check, he must have gone alone. He arrived at the hospital hours after the shooting.

I had not seen him all day—not since the morning meeting. The one where I had seen him, but he had not seen me.

"Coffee?" I called, heading to the concessions counter.

"No more for me," he said, a yawn garbling his words. "No, what the hey—I'll take another."

I assembled his coffee—milk, no sugar—and a Lipton, black, for me. I bought time sweeping used stir straws into the bin. When not a single granule of sugar remained on the counter for me to tidy, I carried over our hot drinks. Jerry stared blankly at the TV screen.

"Any news?" I asked. "I don't mean on CNN."

"I dropped by a half hour ago to see if Candace needed anything," he said. He yawned again. "She's alone with him, but she didn't want me to stay. She said she's fine."

"What about Aaron?" We spoke in a hush, though no one else occupied the lounge.

"No change." He sat up straighter, remembering. "Weren't you watching the grandkids?"

"Ginger came back," I said.

He nodded slowly as he processed this. "How'd she seem?"

I shrugged. "Good. Actually, really good. Different, somehow. Less, I don't know . . . twittery."

"Twittery."

"Yeah. You know. Nervous. She always looked that way to me. Anxious—and kind of sad. Now she's—she seemed kind of like a whole different person, now that I think about it. She might even have gained a little weight."

"Did she tell you why she left?"

I looked away as I said, "I think she was unhappy."

"Enough to leave her kids?"

He said this mildly enough. It angered me anyway. I looked squarely back at him as I said, "There comes a point when a marriage becomes untenable."

Already this was the longest conversation we'd had in weeks. His words challenged me, though his tone remained benign. "Maybe," he said. "But would you leave, just like that?"

Ginger wasn't the only person who had changed recently. Jerry had transformed in our time here. Not so much in appearance but in the way he held himself. Like a swaying reed that grows roots and sprouts into a tree. I heard it in the deepened timbre of his voice, in the pause before he spoke. If Ginger had gained weight, Jerry had grown weighty. He had become a serious man.

The question may or may not have been rhetorical. The "you" may or may not have been universal. Our conversations, when we had them, tended this way now. General news. Bland observations. Murmured responses, committing to neither agreement nor dissent.

Not this time. This time, it was personal. I'd make it so.

"No," I said, my voice a hair too loud. "I would not leave like that."

Jerry put aside his computer. We sat on two sofas at right angles, our knees close enough to touch. But they did not.

I shut my eyes to dispel my fear. Then I realized I was not afraid. I was ready. I was ready to say what I had to, come what may. I opened my eyes and saw clearly the way.

"All this time, I've been beating myself up because I don't have faith," I said. "I realized today that I do. I do have faith. I have faith in us. I have faith in our future, our happiness. I left my family and everything I know for it. It's the one thing I never questioned. Until now." Here goes with the world's oldest question. I took a breath. "Are you having an affair?"

In the pause before he answered—not hesitation, exactly, but a measured consideration—I watched all the possible endings to our story flash by, each one dependent on his answer. "No," he said finally.

It was something less than a vehement denial. More like an unsure answer to a pop-quiz question. "What's going on?" I demanded. And, as if it was necessary, "With Giovanna, I mean." I waited, still acutely aware of the scythe balanced over our marriage.

When he spoke again, he faltered. The serious man fell away, and I saw again a mortal, a man who made mistakes. The scythe wobbled. "Nothing is 'going on'—not in the way you mean," he said. "In London . . ."

He stopped. So did my breathing. I ordered myself to continue. "I want to know."

"She came to my room. She—said she wanted to pray."

The blade loomed closer. I saw its razor edge.

"We've prayed together before," he added, a bit defensively. "We're friends. I didn't think it was strange."

"A girl came to your hotel room, and you didn't think it was strange."

"I know. I know. I should have thought. But I had to be at a panel in ten minutes and she just showed up at the door."

When I could wait no more I asked, "And then?"

He had trouble forming the words. "When she came in, she immediately started to cry. Kind of—hysterical. And before I knew it she just kind of was hugging me. And then . . ."

He halted again, his eyes begging for a reprieve. Save yourself, they said. Save us. Make me stop. But I could not comply.

So he continued. "She kissed me." He looked heavenward, beseeching, then dropped his head into his open hand. He stared at the floor as he amended his confession. "We kissed."

My family had a shorthand for dire information. We'd copped it from the daytime dramas Mom used to like, a three-note announcement—*dun dun DUUHN*—during which the camera locked on the shocked hero's or heroine's face as he or she took in the news. When we kids employed it—"I got suspended/fired/dumped . . . dun dun DUUHN"—it served to leaven the situation, to make whatever it was seem a little bit silly and not so very bad. Well, that's what I heard in my head when Jerry told me he had kissed another woman. *Dun dun DUUHN.* Soon I'd throw the back of my hand against my forehead and faint dead away. And me without my smelling salts.

Looking back, I realize these ridiculous musings were a defense mechanism, a trick pulled by my brain to ease my panicking heart. Faced with the loss of someone I loved, *another* someone I loved, my brain simply did what my family always did in these situations: It ribbed me. C'mon, I told myself in their stead. Is this the worst thing that's happened in the world today? Buck up, kiddo. You'll live.

I suppose it worked, because when my focus returned, I found I still sat there, I still drew breath. I had not fainted, not even in jest.

Jerry's eyes met mine. His were filled with such pain, I almost couldn't bear it. Almost.

"Why didn't you tell me this before?"

"I'm sorry. I—there just never seemed to be the right time. There's no excuse. I'm sorry."

I had never before imagined my husband kissing anyone other than me. Now it was all I could see. My voice sounded strange to me. Squeaky. Like in an old cartoon. "What happened then?"

"And then," he said, "and then, I pulled away. I told her that I couldn't do this. I couldn't do this because I'm a married man."

"And what if you weren't?"

He paused. "What do you mean?"

"What if you weren't a married man? Is she someone you could love?"

"What do you mean by that? I am married. To you."

"Yes. But I'm not a Christian." I said the next with as much tenderness, as much love as I felt. "Do you want to be with someone who believes in God?"

Judging by the look on his face, I wager Jerry—even Jerry, given to intellectual rumination on every aspect of faith—even my husband had not considered this. He sat back slowly against the unforgiving couch.

Did a man of God need a woman of God to be happy?

I reached out then and touched his hand. We looked at where our skin joined, our first touch since we'd begun this apocalyptic day. "Because I can't do it, Jerry," I said. "I can't do it anymore. You've become your mission. You're Pastor Jerry. It's church first, life second. And that's not what I signed up for. I can respect it, but I can't do it."

He closed his eyes against what came next.

"I'm not Candace. And I won't become Ginger. I guess what I'm saying is I can't be a pastor's wife."

Don't cry, damn it. Don't—too late.

I read somewhere that grief is the price we pay for love. Without love, we'd suffer no loss, I suppose. But even as I opened this door to the end of my marriage, I understood my grief was a fair price. Loving someone as I did my husband meant wanting more than anything his happiness. *Go,* the priest says at the close of Mass. *Be with God.* I would say the same, and mean it.

Jerry reached for me, pulling me toward him as my tears swelled to sobs and I shook bawling, in his lap. He stroked my back now, the way my mother had when I awoke as a child from the frets. Stroke, pat. Stroke, pat.

"Okay," he said, over and over. "Okay." Stroke, pat. Stroke, pat.

At long last I lifted my face from his chest. "Okay what?"

"We'll figure it out," he said.

We, he said. He said *we*.

Ruthie

The magnolia is not what it seems. The plant originated before the time of bees, and so instead evolved to invite pollination by beetles. Thus, the thick, hard petals—which it turns out aren't called petals at all but tepals—tough enough not to bruise under a fat beetle's tread. Its leaves, too, are like leather, its outer face shiny-smooth and underside downy. The flower blooms voluptuous and showy, framed by those malachite leaves and propped by a steely root. The magnolia blossom looks as delicate as an orchid, yet it's as tough as old boots.

The magnolia have finally bloomed. They waited till late May this year, explained the botany professor on the Channel Four news, because of a quirk in the weather system, a cold snap that arrived late in the spring. So much for those global warming alarmists, yukked the anchor, to which the botanist snapped that global warming was but one symptom of the larger trend of climate change, and yes, indeed, it was very real. The anchor swallowed mid-yuk. Awkward.

"TV anchors should never go off script," I said.

"There should be a law," said Jerry agreeably from behind his newspaper.

"Hair that good is an indicator of below-average intelligence, is what I say. Is there more toast?"

Jerry put down the paper and got up. "I'll make. Cinnamon sugar?"

"Thanks, babe. Oh, and tea?"

"The doctor said about the caffeine."

"Decaf, then. With two lumps. Please."

I heaved my legs up onto the couch and puffed some cushions up for my back. I'd chosen the Thai silk for their gem tones, but Jerry was right; they did scratch a little. Still, they contrasted gorgeously with the carved mahogany and crushed velvet pieces I'd spent the past months excavating from antique shops far and wide. In my decor selections, I was like a newly graduated Catholic schoolgirl on a boozy bender. Released from the bland newness of Paradise Estates, I flung myself at curios and color.

A breeze floated in, carrying the perfume of magnolia. When we first toured this house, I fell hard for the floor-to-ceiling windows that opened onto the wraparound porch. This neighborhood of Magnolia resembled old Savannah in architecture, with its intricate ironwork fences and wisteria climbing the Italianate columns. There was even a square with a fountain.

"Special delivery." I heard the call through the open windows, though it came from the front door.

"Here, let me take that," I heard Jerry say. Then children's laughter.

I pretended to snooze. Soon enough I heard furiously,

unsuccessfully, stifled giggling. A tap-dancing elephant is stealthier than a mouth-breathing toddler. Without opening my eyes, I shot an arm out and grabbed.

Talitha shrieked.

"Never disturb a sleeping whale!" I hollered. I reached my other arm out and collared Jordan, too.

"Stegosaurus versus humpback!" he roared.

"Gentle, gentle!" warned Ginger.

The baby began to cry.

Ginger laughed and shushed. She bounced up and down on the balls of her feet to jog the baby out of her grump, and then resumed the side-to-side swaying that seems to afflict all mothers of newborns. Joy was in one of those front carriers, her chopstick arms and legs poking out of the holes, her hairless head completely invisible. BabyBjörns, they were called. I was learning these things.

"Did you hear that?" I said, pushing myself upright. "Your son called me a humpback."

"That's not polite, Jordan," said Ginger, trying for serious.

"It's also not accurate," called Jerry from the kitchen. "As you can see, the hump is in the front."

Tali put her mouth against my belly, as she did every time she saw me. "Hewwo," she called. "Anybody home?" She turned to lay her ear on the spot.

"Any answer?" I whispered.

She looked up and nodded, eyes wide. "He say he want a cookie."

"*He*, huh?" said Jerry from the doorway to the kitchen. We exchanged a look; we didn't know the gender yet. "Does Tali want a cookie, too?"

Tali nodded vigorously.

"C'mon," said Jerry, herding her and Jordan into the kitchen. "Let's dig into the ones your mom made before Aunt Ruthie eats them all."

I motioned for Ginger to sit. She shook her head, continuing to stand and sway, her hands rubbing the soles of Joy's feet. The baby had on tiny little socks printed with the pattern of a shoe, which of course was beside the point, until you realized the only point was cuteness.

"Where's Timothy today?"

"Filming," said Ginger.

"I just saw his latest. Powerful stuff."

"I know, right?"

"Sales?"

"Oh, my gosh. Last I checked, close to a million."

I whistled. "He's found his calling."

"Praise the Lord," she said, nodding for emphasis. "And right here at home."

Timothy still ran Faith Corps. But in her conditions for reconciliation, Ginger had demanded he drop the travel duties. He'd agreed. Of course, it hadn't been that easy. Every time he'd tried to extricate himself, some problem or issue arose that required Timothy's boots on some far-away ground. His successors weren't getting it.

Frustrated, he'd decided to create a video explaining Faith Corps to current and future aid workers. One of the workers posted it online, and the video went viral. Here was a sun-browned pastor in a torn T-shirt and punk-rocker hair, delivering an impassioned plea to young Christians to put down their venti lattes and iPhones and go help the desperate of the world.

"Don't just pray," he commanded, pointing a finger at the camera. "Act."

Something about the combination proved combustible. When the video hit the Most Viewed list on YouTube, something clicked for Timothy. He had always felt destined for revolutionary evangelism, Ginger told me, had always known that technology would prove its path. He called his new movement evangelical activism. In short order he set up a Web site, turned a storage room at Newleaf into a production studio, and set to work filming sermons for a new generation. They sold for $1.99 on iTunes.

All this pleased Ginger, though soon she complained that Timothy spent almost as much time on his new mission as he had overseas. After a few months of arguing, he agreed to set up a childcare center at Newleaf to keep Tali within his easy reach. As Ginger's pregnancy progressed, Timothy took over Jordan's school drop-off and pick-up, too. In between meetings, taping, and editing, Timothy loped by to hang with the kids, springing them for ice cream or a romp around the park. Then he'd come home in time for dinner. Within a year he'd gone from absent dad to superdad. Miracles did happen.

That left Ginger with time for the new baby—and to pursue her own mission. Bit by bit she unspooled to me the mysteries of her disappearance last year.

I listened to her confessions of a lurid past, the lies of omission about that past to her in-laws, the heart-in-mouth fear of being discovered and losing everything. I'd always sensed a sadness in my friend, but I'd never suspected the depths. While the separation from her children had gashed her heart, she'd needed the time alone to regain herself. In doing so, she'd discovered she had a calling of her own: to minister to the ladies of the night.

Well, not entirely her own. Ginger spent a lot of time on the phone and online coordinating with her partners: a friend named

Kaycee, who rented a room from Ginger's mom; a lesbian pastor named Melora, who ran their Florida chapter; and a pastor's wife in Indiana named Melissa, who managed the Web site. (I had Ginger go over all this time and again so I could get it straight. And besides, I loved the story.) The four women tended to their flock, the working girls of America. And Ginger and Timothy tended to their own little flock of Jordan, Talitha, and Joy.

Their baby arrived just as the first magnolia buds burst open. I was there in Ginger's house when her water broke, but then I was usually there, or she here. I had lobbied hard for Ginger and Timothy to follow us to our new neighborhood. With the money from Timothy's video sermons, they could afford to escape Paradise Estates, which had been, in any case, another of Ginger's conditions. She fell in love as I did with the old-fashioned homes and the wisteria, and the fountain in the square clinched the deal.

Jerry liked Timothy, once he got to know him. They circled their brand-new backyard grills like cowboys admiring unbroken steeds, all wary eyes and gleaming ambition. They swore they would master the art this summer. We'll see. Ginger and I predict a season-long diet of we-meant-to-blacken-it chicken.

Speaking of which, I was getting hungry.

"Iced tea for our guest," said Jerry. "Cinnamon toast for the humpfront whale." He laid a tray on the coffee table. "Kids are on the porch swing with cookies. So if it's okay, I'm going to go do a little work."

"Enjoy it while you can," Ginger called, as he creaked up the stairs to his study. "The countdown to slavehood has begun."

"Bring it on," he called back.

"How's it going?" asked Ginger, nodding in the direction he went.

"Oof," I said, sitting up to scarf my toast. "Great. Really great."

It was true. Things were great, really great. That dramatic night at Grace Memorial began a new phase for us, and not just because Giovanna exited the picture.

Which wasn't to say she went quietly. In the days after that night in the hospital VIP lounge, Jerry talked about his relationship with Gee. It twisted me up to call it that, but that's what it was, even without a physical element—a relationship. It had begun innocently enough, when she joined the worship team and began attending church leadership meetings. She sought him out at prayer meetings, sat next to him at committees. Men are slow to pick up on these things, but even Jerry soon figured out that everywhere he went, there'd be Gee. He didn't mind. He found her lively and sunny, and, yes, a part of him gravitated toward her unabashed faith.

I didn't ask if he was attracted to her. I didn't ask if he fantasized about her. I didn't want to know if he saw her face when he kissed mine. It took everything I had to ask, "Did you ever think about leaving me?"

He did not answer the question, exactly. But he looked me square in the eyes when he said, "I could never do that. I *would* never do that."

I knew it was true. And that was enough.

He explained what happened following the kiss in the London hotel. He said that within seconds, his brain overcame his jangled senses to sound a very loud danger alarm. His body acted as if on automatic pilot by launching into emergency protocol.

First he ushered her out of his room and down the hallway so fast they both gasped for breath. When they reached the bustling lobby, he quietly assured her he would forget this ever happened, and they would continue to be friends. This in the belief that his rejection would mortify Giovanna.

The opposite was true. Their kiss galvanized Gee, who believed it marked the start, not the end, of a relationship. The only obstacle in its path was me. Our departure from Greenleaf and Paradise Estates shielded me from most of her *Fatal Attraction* behavior, but when she began phoning our new house, I called in the big guns.

Telling Candace confirmed my sense that she had suspected all along. As soon as I began, she winced in something like self-recrimination. A face you make when the doctor tells you the lump you knew you should have gotten checked out ages ago has in the meantime turned malignant. She said nothing as I told her everything. When I finished, she gave me a tissue and a smile.

"Let me," she said, "take care of it."

Candace invited Gee in for a private conference in her office. Oh, how I would have loved to be a fly on the wall as she smacked some sense into the young singer. Then, just to be sure, Candace dangled a recording contract in Nashville, under the condition she never contact Jerry or me again. Gee left the next day. We haven't heard from her since.

With Giovanna vanquished, Jerry and I could focus on each other. Sometimes you need to press Pause on life in order to save a marriage. We spent the next few months as goofy honeymooners, wandering around the open-air antique markets hand in hand, sharing ice-cream cones and dippy smiles. Of course, this sweet calm would be upended soon enough by the storm of impending parenthood. It made us savor the time all the more.

Ginger gave me a poke with her toe. "Wipe that icky grin off your face. I wasn't talking about Jerry. How's the Harmony Center going?"

"I knew that. Uh, they just hit the three million mark. Blueprints approved. So they're talking about breaking ground this fall."

"Wow. Oh, I saw that profile of Jerry in the paper."

I choked on my toast. After all this time, I couldn't hear mention of the *Atlanta Journal-Constitution* without a little blockage in my throat. After Jerry confessed about Gee, I felt it was only fair to tell him about Juan Diaz. About the night at the bar. About my temptation. And, finally, about his betrayal. In the wake of the shooting, Juan was investigated by the FBI for his involvement with Elder John Swain. Though in the end they didn't charge Juan with anything, Catherine Oppelheimer, the publisher of the *AJC*, was furious at the negative attention and the public connection with a heinous crime. She fired Juan herself.

Ginger shook her head. She knew about the whole Juan Diaz debacle, too, just as she knew about Giovanna. She'd unveiled her secrets to me; I couldn't very well hold back. "Oh, forget about him already," she said. "Plus it was a nice piece. Really flattering. Great photo."

I pulled the paper from the pile under the coffee table. The front-page article was written by an earnest young woman named Kimber Lee Chen, and headlined INTERFAITH LEADER: "WE NEED PEACE NOW." It ran beside a close-up of Jerry looking thoughtfully into the middle distance. It began:

> Jeremiah Matters was born for this job, though no one knew it but him. The son of New York financier Ernest H. Matters enjoyed a rarefied childhood of live-in help and ski trips to Switzerland. At Columbia University he studied political science and later

obtained master's degrees in both business and theology.

Compelled to join the family business, he proved a rising star at his father's firm—until he could no longer ignore a greater calling.

He left Wall Street to join the Magnolia mega-church Greenleaf, swiftly becoming Pastor Aaron Green's right-hand man.

Then, in December, Green was shot while re-hearsing for the church's Christmas pageant. John Swain, church founder and former head elder, was found guilty of attempted murder and fraud, and received a life sentence (see p. 8 for more on Swain's appeals trial).

After Green's shooting, his wife, Candace Green, chose Matters to take over his mentor's beloved project, his interfaith ministry. Under agreement with cofounders Rabbi Joshua Bernstein of Beth Aaron Congregation and Imam Amin Chaudry of Mosque of Central Georgia, Green appointed Mat-ters the director of the Harmony Center for Inter-faith Peace, to open in the coming year.

"There is simply no one better equipped— morally, spiritually, strategically—to run a 21st-century institute promoting peace between the religions," said Candace Green.

I chuckled. "Figures the first quote in a profile of Jerry is from Candace."

This time it was Ginger's turn to cringe, as she always did when the topic turned to Candace. Ginger refused to explain the whys and wherefores of her disappearance to her mother-in-law, or to reveal her ministry. She remained convinced Candace would always view her with a jaundiced eye, tainted forever by the discovery of Ginger's past. And so Ginger's vanishing act the year prior continued to baffle

Candace. And then, upon return, to move away from Paradise Estates! As Candace saw it, Ginger had abandoned her son and grandchildren, then swooped back without so much as a thank-you-ma'am to whisk them away. The arrival of Anthony and Sophie in the gated development appeased Candace somewhat, but I knew losing regular access to her adored grandchildren devastated her. Even the arrival of Joy could not pave over the past.

Candace, for her part, had yet to tell Ginger what she had done in Miami. When I discovered it (through extremely nosy and persistent questioning), I couldn't believe my former boss kept it a secret.

"Are you kidding?" I shouted. I long ago dispensed with propriety around Candace, or, more accurately, she gave up on expecting it from me. "You battled a porn king to save your daughter-in-law from ill repute! You're like some—some superhero grandma! *Why* won't you tell her?"

Candace looked a little pleased, I thought, at the image of herself in a cape. But she forbade me to say a word.

"In due time," was all she would say. "In due time."

I pleaded the case on both ends. If Ginger would only explain her odyssey to Candace as she had to me. If Candace would only tell Ginger of the lengths she had gone to retrieve her past mistakes from the clutches of a profiteer. Each had within their power the ability to disabuse the other of their misconceptions. Forgiveness awaited, I was sure—though it was obstructed, for now, by pride. In due time, I hoped. In due time.

But listen to me—the Christian deserter, preaching forgiveness.

My own journey in faith did not end that night at Grace Memorial, when Jerry and I resolved to start anew.

We waited a few weeks before we tendered our resignations, given the state of things at Greenleaf. Candace took our joint meeting with gravity but in the end wished us well. It took not a day for her to summon us back to her office. She had different roles for us, she said. If we wanted.

Then she pulled out the blueprint for Harmony Center.

The article had it right. Jerry was born for the job. All his studies and his talent and his passion and his dogma—everything aligned with the mission of leading an organization dedicated to peace among religious groups. The center was still defining how it would set about obtaining that objective, but already the international community of religious leaders welcomed Jerry as a pragmatist well schooled in the art of diplomacy. His easy yet serious manner befitted the role of emissary. I took to calling him Ambassador. I think he secretly liked it.

As for me, I thanked Candace for her offer to make me the center's publicity officer. I would help out, pro bono, I promised.

But I realized my calling was not in telling other people's stories. It was in telling mine.

Our new house, which was actually an old house—1920, the real estate agent said—had a writing nook. A writing nook! Imagine such a thing. When we first saw it listed in the property information, I laughed it off as fancy talk for an alcove off the dining room. But when I saw it, my breath caught a little.

The builder had installed a desk right into the wall, a notched slab of chestnut that upon a tug of a latch folded out into a desk. It fit snugly into a corner next to a window that opened onto our flower-tangled garden. Adjacent to the desk were empty bookshelves built into the wall, calling, just begging for residents. A Tiffany-style lamp glowed overhead.

"It's perfect," I whispered.

Jerry smiled. "Does it bring out the writer in you?"

"I think it very well might."

And so I began to write this story. I say "began" because, for such sedentary work, it turns out writing is a labor-intensive endeavor—and I soon had another form of labor on my mind.

Jerry and I were expecting our first child, gender unknown (except maybe to Talitha), in a couple of months. If it was a girl, we planned to name her Edith, after my mother. If it was a boy, Aaron. After our friend Aaron Green.

The latter was no posthumous tribute. Aaron Green, the baby's would-be namesake, was not dead. Far from it. The doctors said he ought to be at "one hundred percent capacity" in about a year's time.

Still, the injury took a great deal out of him. The week following the shooting, he suffered a heart attack. Candace insisted this was God's good work, as the profusion of monitors attached to him in the hospital bed instantly alerted the staff, and "only the good Lord knows how it would have ended" had he already been discharged. He moved from the hospital to rehab and finally home, where he began work on the latest installment in the Serve Your Faith series, this one a pensive rumination on life. With his hours of daily physical therapy, we all could hope for his triumphal return to the pulpit by the next Christmas pageant.

So Candace liked to say. Privately, Aaron told Jerry he's perfectly content watching her soar in his place.

For Candace had filled the void. The Sunday following Aaron's shooting, Candace Green herself appeared on center stage at Greenleaf.

The sanctuary was standing room only with church members and well-wishers and members of the media. Jerry and I took our places in our usual row. The lights went down, the crowd hushed, and then the spotlight found her, the worship team flanking her in shadow.

She could not seem to help but look down at the very spot her husband had been gunned down. For a moment, she appeared lost for words.

We held our collective breath.

Then she opened her arms.

She opened them the way her husband had, every Sunday, for so many years. She opened them wide to embrace the church. She opened them to the love and the hope and the faith of the people. She opened them to her new role, a role she no longer denied: leader of Greenleaf Church.

The crowd roared. None of us, not a one of us, held back our tears.

Finally, finally, she lowered her arms and spoke. She spoke in that signature butterfly voice, its soft flutter disguising power to equal an eagle's wings. She quoted from Isaiah:

> *"Fear thou not; for I am with thee: be not dismayed; for I am thy God: I will strengthen thee; yea, I will help thee; yea, I will uphold thee with the right hand of my righteousness."*

She held up her right hand, cupped. And for the moment it seemed that tiny little vessel could indeed carry us all.

"Friends," she said, her voice fraying. I remembered then she had not left the hospital since the day of the shooting, which meant she had not really slept at all.

"My soul," she continued, "is weary with sorrow. Let us be strengthened by the Word."

She raised her right hand higher, toward the sky. The worship team burst into its opening number. Beholding that remarkable woman offer tribute amid the rainbow of raised voices, I felt my spirit stir.

* * *

The wedding of Frank Connelly and June Kim took place on a toasty October afternoon in the Hoogaboom Town Hall. Mayor Stew Kozlowski conducted the proceedings in an office on the second floor, not nearly enough room for our sprawling, squirmy clans, which spilled down the stairs and into the registrar's office.

June's two sons and daughter flew in with their respective families. One son, Albert, had married an Asian woman, producing two black-eyed moppets. The other, Jason, had married a blue-eyed California girl, and the beauty of their three children was, to me, an irrefutable argument in favor of the mixing of the races. June's daughter, Grace, brought her Hispanic boyfriend. The group photo we took on the Town Hall steps made for a veritable diversity poster.

Afterward we trooped toward our cars to head to Jade Palace, a Chinese banquet-style restaurant.

"Why Chinese?" I asked Vivian, who'd made the arrangements.

"Because Dad needs his MSG," she replied. "Why not?"

"I don't know."

"What, they're Korean so they gotta eat kimchi? Geez, Tooty," said Paul. Once they'd heard it, there was no stopping my family from adopting June's mispronunciation of my nickname. "That's so racist."

"Shut up, clown face."

It was good to see my siblings.

"Gimme my kid," I said to Michael.

"No way," he said, nuzzling the baby's head. "You wanna ride with your uncle Mikey, don'tcha?"

"We're just gonna make a quick stop," I said, prying Edy from his arms.

Tom nodded, patting Jerry on the back. "Tell her we said hello."

The Madonna Cemetery held a prominent place in our town, but then it kind of had to, with its wrought-iron gates opening right onto Main Street. Growing up, the east enclave was a favorite partying spot, until the grounds crew grew sick of picking up our crushed Budweiser cans and convinced management to acquire some German shepherds. The managers were good-humored enough, though, to decorate its street-side fences with scarecrows and witches every October. Not even a Catholic cemetery can deny Halloween.

Mom's plot lay at the foot of a ginkgo tree, its fan-shaped leaves just yawning toward yellow. The ground squished from a recent shower. Jerry maneuvered so as not to wake Edy, snoozing in a sling strapped to his chest. The smooth granite of the tombstone shone, its top edge rough-hewn and curved.

We'd had a tough time picking the epitaph. Those suggested by the cemetery were all religious in nature.

"*Returned to Jesus*," read Viv from the list supplied by the cemetery. "That sounds like a postal error."

"What about *I told you I was sick*?" said Paul.

"You're such a hack," said Michael. "You read that online."

"*The best is yet to come*," said Paul. "She liked Sinatra."

"Not that much," Tom said.

"Anyway, it's bull," snorted Vivian. "We all know she would've preferred here to heaven."

Paul tried again. *"That's all, folks?"*

"Mel Blanc's tombstone," said Michael. "C'mon, you plagiarist. We can at least be original."

"I don't know," mused Tom. "I don't think originality is what Mom would want to shoot for in an epitaph."

We fell into thought.

"In loving memory of," I said softly.

They considered.

"Yeah, that's nice," Viv admitted.

Tom wrote it down, adding Mom's full name and years of birth and death. He slid the sheet across to the cemetery administrator, a man with a Trump-esque comb-over you had to see to believe.

"So we'll put the name of the deceased on the left," said Comb-over. "And her spouse to the right."

We all stared at him. Mom and Dad had purchased the plot a decade ago, when the Madonna offered local residents discounts on what its sales staff called pre-need planning. They had even purchased the stone. It hadn't occurred to us, but, of course—they would share it in death.

"The spouse," repeated Tom. "He's not dead."

"Yet," muttered Vivian.

Comb-over blinked at us. "Right," he said. "In these cases we engrave the spouse's name and birth date, but leave the other date open." The date of death, he meant. Why didn't he just say it? The death business was full of euphemisms, we were learning. He looked around at us. "It saves on the engraving costs to do it all at once."

And so there was Dad's name, next to Mom's, the hyphen next to his birth year dangling like an unfinished sentence.

But not forever. He would be buried here, as planned. That's what Dad told me, though I had not asked, the morning of the wedding as I helped him with his tie. June had her own prepaid plot in another cemetery—her late husband, Soong-sa, was also a plan-ahead type—and she intended to inter her ashes next to his. They would return to their original spouses when they left this world. Frank and June were each other's—for now. Till death do us part.

"Never forget," Dad said, his chin strained high to let me straighten the knot. "I still love your mother. I always will."

Crouching now before my mother's grave, I laid a bouquet of her favorite marguerite daisies under her name. Edith R. Connelly. The "R" stood for Ruth. She was my namesake, as she was my daughter's.

"Hi, Mom," I said. "I brought someone to meet you."

Jerry knelt beside me, the wet earth soaking his suit pants at the knees. He angled his chest so that Edy, asleep in the sling, faced the grave. The baby yawned.

After a time, I helped Jerry up and brushed the wet grass from his pants. Edy cracked one eye open and looked at me. It looked for all the world like a wink.

See, Mom? I'm not alone. Just like you said.

I am not alone. I'll always have love.

ACKNOWLEDGMENTS

This novel began with a press release. My editor Jan Simpson dropped by my office at *Time* magazine and handed me a piece of paper. "It's a convention of pastors' wives," she said.

"A what of what?" I said.

"Exactly," she said.

Raised Catholic, I pictured a pastor's wife—insofar as I pictured one at all—as the smiling woman behind the man behind the pulpit. In the weeks and months that followed, I learned the pastor's wife is way more complex. She's strong. Passionate. Devout. Sometimes angry, often put upon—and, to me, fascinating. The article published in 2007. But the women I interviewed kept bothering me (by which I mean I kept bothering them). I wondered: What's it *like* when the man you married is married to God?

What happened next is not typical in the birth of a novel. I pitched it first as a TV drama series. Complications ensued. Suffice it to say the whole thing ended in disaster—heart-ripped-out-of-chest-by-alien disaster. (I'll tell you sometime over many cups of tea, or please visit www.lisacullen.com.) At that point I had quit my job as a staff writer at *Time*. My book agent shook me hard. "You have the characters and the storylines and two years of reporting," she said. "Just write it as a novel, already."

My first thanks go to my agent, Theresa Park. Theresa represents Famous Authors who sneeze out bestsellers with attached movie deals. I am her charity client. Yet she read every word of my pinched efforts as they evolved into something resembling a manuscript. She gave me blunt, hard notes, the kind that made my face sting but invariably improved the work. *Pastors' Wives* exists because Theresa said it could.

I prevailed upon many pastors' wives in researching this book. *Just Between Us*, the magazine for pastors' wives, allowed me to attend its retreat, and the Global Pastors' Wives Network its gatherings. The women tolerated my nosy questions and shared with me their moving stories. Heavily pregnant with my second child, I had my belly blessed by nearly every woman I met. Books by pastors' wives including Carol Kent and Lorna Dobson provided insight. Pastors' wives are terrific bloggers, and among those I followed I most enjoyed my candid conversations with Amy Lynn Andrews, who now preaches technical how-tos at BloggingWithAmy.com.

I reserve particular admiration for Becky Hunter, the gracious wife of Joel Hunter, senior pastor of Northland Church near Orlando, Florida. A doting mother and grandmother, she labors in support of her husband and church, has authored two books, and at the time also led the Global Pastors' Wives Network. Becky let me trail her as she performed her many duties, offering thoughts, observations, and advice. "Be kind to your husband on purpose," she likes to say. I try, Becky! I try.

Time magazine employed me for many years, affording me remarkable experiences around the world that will fuel my imagination for a lifetime. I admired most everyone I worked with there, but it was Jan Simpson who greenlighted some of my weirdest and most memorable assignments. They led to not just this book but also my first, about the strange new ways Americans celebrate death. She's like my Rumpelstiltskin without the demand for my firstborn. (Likewise, my husband's aunt Rita Valenti played a supporting role in both books; her home outside Atlanta inspired me to set the story there.)

I'm not sure which was the chicken and which the egg: this book, or my desperate need to understand faith. Believers and nonbelievers alike discussed their views with me. My colleague David Van Biema shared with me his expert contacts. My bookshelf grew crowded with versions of the Bible (the King James, the New American Standard, the Good News), the Catechism of the Catholic Church, the writings of St. Augustine and C. S. Lewis. Mine is an ongoing education.

Feedback is a dreadful necessity for a first-time novelist. I dipped my toe in at an online workshop at Mediabistro led by the author Erika Mailman, subjecting classmates including Helen Mitternight and Liz Pink-Bell to my earliest outlines. Friends who offered pointers on everything from characters to story arc include my sister Emy Seeley (Petit Bateau *is* for underwear), the writer Rebekah Sanderlin (who provided the joke about the casserole and the anecdote about the knee-highs), my manager A.B. Fischer, my TV agent David Park, the screenwriter Joseph Gangemi, the novelist Laura Zigman, the writer Susan Kim, and, of course, Becky Hunter (meerkat!). Thank you all; I'm fortunate to know you.

Denise Roy, my editor at Penguin, is a calm and thoughtful guide whose notes are unfailingly wise. She believed enough in the manuscript to take a chance on a tricky subject matter, even after she met me and I regaled her with a disgusting story involving my baby, an airplane, and a diaper. Kathleen Napolitano, copy editor Kym Surridge, and the art, sales, and marketing departments put time and effort toward my book. I received immeasurable encouragement and support from the Park Literary staff: Rachel Bressler, Peter Knapp, Abigail Koons, and Emily Sweet. The remarkably effective publicity firm Litfuse, led by Amy Lathrop and Audra Jennings, shared with us their wisdom. Brian Van Nieuwenhoven designed my website, and Matt Dine snapped my author photo, for which Laura de León made me pretty.

Just before I began this book, both of my parents died—my mother of cancer, my father of a broken heart. For Thomas J. Reilly, a former priest from Philly, and Hiroe Takeuchi Reilly, a Japanese convert (and his reason for leaving the priesthood), perhaps the only thing stronger than their shared Catholic faith was their love. They taught me all they knew about both. And just in case I forget, I have my siblings George Reilly, Emy Seeley, and Ken Reilly to remind me.

Through the drama of these past few years, I relied on my husband, Christopher Cullen, to keep calm and carry us on. He listened. He opined. He fixed stuff. And he made me laugh. Our daughters, Mika and Kana, are pretty good at that, too.

See, Mom? I am not alone. I'll always have love.